CW01149372

A Slice of Sky

Book 1 in the Last Call Series

✳✳

Nancy Moser

Mustard Seed Press
Overland Park, KS

A Slice of Sky

ISBN 13: 978-1-961907-69-0

Published by:
Mustard Seed Press
Overland Park, KS

Copyright © 2024 by Nancy Moser. All rights reserved.

This book, or parts thereof, may not be reproduced, stored in a retrieval system, or transmitted in any form or by any means, electronic, mechanical, photocopying, recording, or otherwise, without the written permission of the publisher.

This story is a work of fiction. Any resemblances to actual people, places, or events are purely coincidental.

All Scripture quotations are taken from The Holy Bible, Contemporary English Version.

Front cover design by Mustard Seed Press

The Books of Nancy Moser

www.nancymoser.com

Contemporary Books

A Slice of Sky (Book 1 of the Last Call Series)
If Not for This
An Undiscovered Life
Eyes of Our Heart
The Invitation (Book 1 Mustard Seed)
The Quest (Book 2 Mustard Seed)
The Temptation (Book 3 Mustard Seed)
Crossroads
The Seat Beside Me (Book 1 Steadfast)
A Steadfast Surrender (Book 2 Steadfast)
The Ultimatum (Book 3 Steadfast)
The Sister Circle (Book 1 Sister Circle)
Round the Corner (Book 2 Sister Circle)
An Undivided Heart (Book 3 Sister Circle)
A Place to Belong (Book 4 Sister Circle)
Senior Sisters (Book 5 Sister Circle)
The Sister Circle Handbook (Book 6 Sister Circle)
Time Lottery (Book 1 Time Lottery)
Second Time Around (Book 2 Time Lottery)
John 3:16
The Good Nearby
Solemnly Swear
Save Me, God! I Fell in the Carpool (Inspirational humor)
100 Verses of Encouragement — Books 1&2 (illustrated gift books)
Maybe Later (picture book)
I Feel Amazing: the ABCs of Emotion (picture book)

Historical Books

Where Time Will Take Me (Book 1 Past Times)
Where Life Will Lead Me (Book 2 Past Times)
Pin's Promise (novella prequel to Pattern Artist)
The Pattern Artist (Book 1 Pattern Artist)
The Fashion Designer (Book 2 Pattern Artist)
The Shop Keepers (Book 3 Pattern Artist)
Love of the Summerfields (Book 1 Manor House)
Bride of the Summerfields (Book 2 Manor House)
Rise of the Summerfields (Book 3 Manor House)
Mozart's Sister (biographical novel of Nannerl Mozart)
Just Jane (biographical novel of Jane Austen)
Washington's Lady (bio-novel of Martha Washington)
How Do I Love Thee? (bio-novel of Elizabeth Barrett Browning)
Masquerade (Book 1 Gilded Age)
An Unlikely Suitor (Book 2 Gilded Age)
A Bridal Quilt (Gilded Age novella)
The Journey of Josephine Cain
A Basket Brigade Christmas (novella collection)
When I Saw His Face (Regency novella)

Dedication

To New Mexico

The grandeur of your scenery was instrumental
in sparking the initial idea for the Last Call series.
And then you showed me a full rainbow
to confirm the idea was a good one.
You truly are the Land of Enchantment!

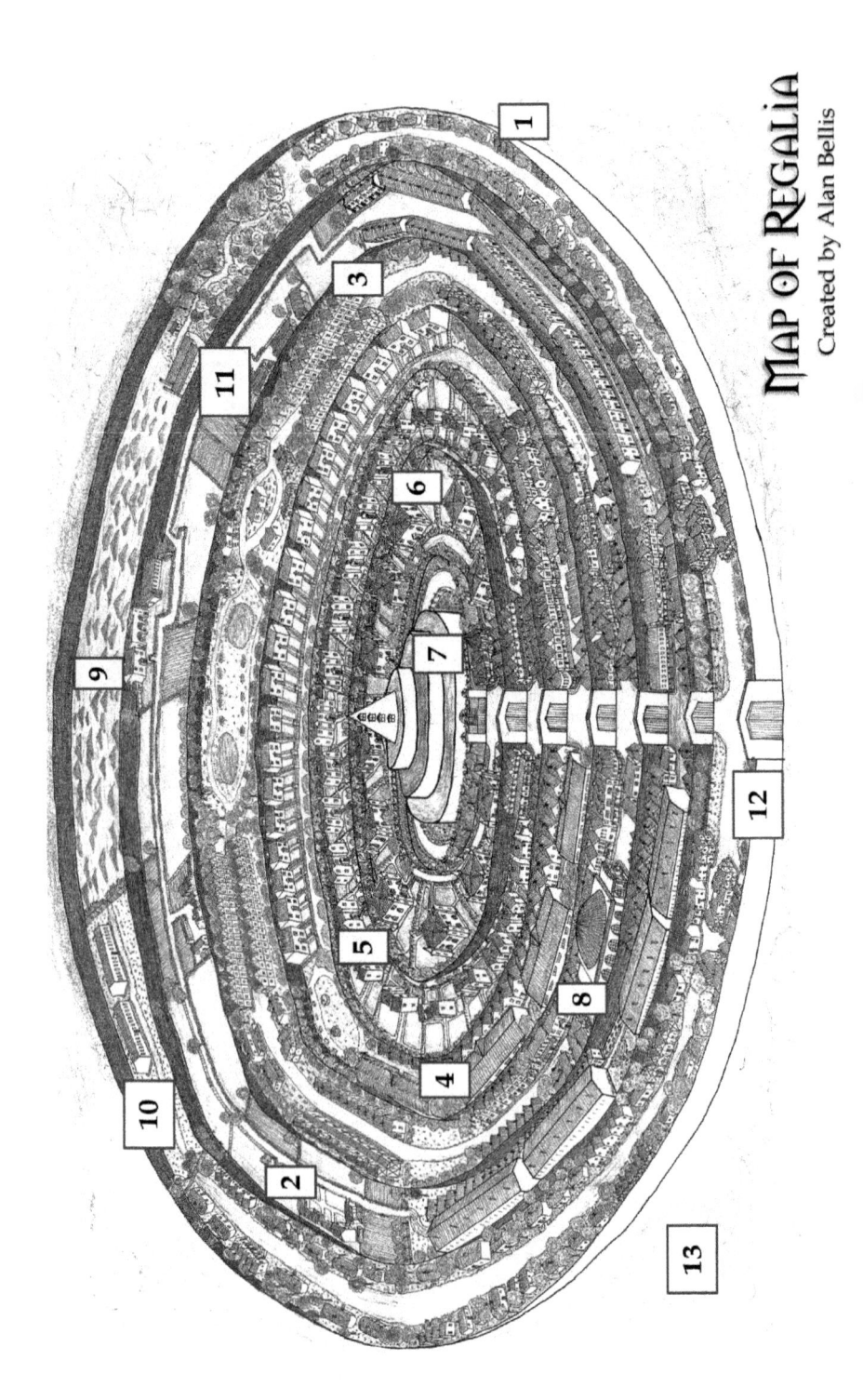

Map of Regalia

Created by Alan Bellis

Legend for the Map of Regalia

- [1] Server Ring
- [2] Implementor Ring
- [3] Favored Ring
- [4] Creatives Ring
- [5] Patron Ring
- [6] Council Estate Ring
- [7] Council Tower Ring
- [8] Dome of the Reveal
- [9] The Pile
- [10] Debt Camp
- [11] The Farm
- [12] Desert Gate
- [13] Swirling Desert

The Rings of Regalia

- **The Council Ring** is the innermost Ring where the Council of Worthiness rules Regalia.
- **The Council Mansion Ring** is where the eleven Council members have their estates.
- **The Patron Ring** consists of twenty influencers whose job is to dramatically present new fashion to the Favored.
- **The Creatives Ring** is where the fashion is designed—the more outlandish the better.
- **The Favored Ring** is where the consumers live. They vote on their favorite fashion, it's produced, they buy it, and show it off in a constant stream of parties.
- **The Implementor Ring** focuses on four specialized factories creating clothing, headdresses, shoes, and jewelry to be sold to the Favored.
- **The Server Ring** is the largest, outermost Ring that houses the Servs of Regalia; those who serve everyone else in the other Rings.

Chapter One

Cashlin

The Land of Regalia

I stand in front of the full-length mirror in my dressing room and let my Dressing-Servs adjust the finishing touches on my latest Reveal costume. I'm used to having people flutter around me, touching and tucking, pinning and prodding, making sure the clothing I've selected looks its best.

Honestly, I made my latest choice reluctantly, and if it would have been possible to choose *none* of the three offerings that had been designed for me, I would have done so. I realized too late the quality is lacking. If I want to hold onto my position as the Premier Patron in Regalia, I need amazing above-and-beyond clothes. Unfortunately, today I'm stuck with what I have on. It's always a challenge to keep the top position. There are too many ambitious Patrons nipping at my vine-covered heels.

Yet what my costume lacks, I'll make up for through the production I've put together for its Reveal. I know how to make an entrance memorable. As the top Patron, I get to choose which of the twenty Patrons — ten women and ten men — goes first. I always choose the first spot. When I wow the audience of the Favored, I set the competitive bar high. Too high for most of my colleagues to beat.

I study my reflection. My fern green chiffon dress has tendrils flowing from the waist, hem, and sleeves. I wear a corset of gold brocade that makes my tiny waist look its best. The platform boots make me massively tall and are entwined with vines. A choker of gold and copper leaves winds around my neck three times. But as good as my outfit looks, I'm not sure those in the Favored Ring will vote it into the top ten because of one thing.

The headdress.

It consists of stylized cobra heads. They are attached to a headband, their fangs, ready to strike. When I first saw it, I'd been impressed by the drama and novelty of it. But today I'm not so sure. A crown of snakes? What was I thinking?

Marli, my Personal Serv, holds the bizarre headpiece in front of me as the final addition to my costume. "Are you ready for it?"

"As I'll ever be."

She sets the headband in place, and I adjust it in front of my ears in a way that feels balanced. Then Marli and the other Servs begin arranging my copper hair around it. My family calls me a redhead, but I prefer to call my hair "burnished copper." In Regalia, words matter.

How odd that the hair that was the bane of my childhood—with all its tangles and flyaway curls—is now the highlight of my brand. None of the other Patrons have hair like mine.

Lucky them?

A Makeup Serv adds finishing touches to the elaborate eye makeup that ignores the position of my natural brows and creates new ones that curve diagonally toward my hairline. Green, copper, and brown eye shadow create the perfect setting for stick-on sparkles. I look radiant.

"There," Marli finally says. "You look ssssscintilating. Absolutely sssssstunning."

Very funny. My look is what it is, yet as I hear the murmurs of the restless audience in the Dome of the Reveal, I know I will make it *more*. Make *me* more.

The door opens and my brother, Amar, strides in—Amar never simply walks into a room, he conquers it. "It's show time," he says. "Turn around so I can do a final check."

As my Creative Director Amar is instrumental in guiding three Creatives to propose options of clothing, shoes, head coverings, and accessories for me to choose from each quarter. The final choice is mine. The Patron who earns the most votes from the Favored moves up among the twenty, which earns us prestige, better housing, and other perks. Only the top ten looks go into production to be sold in the Favored Ring. Our lives as Patrons are glamorous but stressful, as our quarterly Reveals create never-ending contests.

And yet, I love it. I love wearing fanciful costumes, I love being number one, and I love the adulation and attention it brings. I love being the best.

Amar adjusts one of the snake heads. "You're good to go. Follow me."

Marli gives me a smile and a nod for luck, and I follow my brother out to the wings of the Reveal stage. I commissioned the music myself and have approved every note. I also created the choreography and designed the set. The Favored have no idea how much time and planning goes into each Reveal. I leave nothing to chance. As a haunting melody of strings and woodwinds begins to play, I walk behind the backdrop to my center entry-point. I close my eyes and take a deep

breath, willing myself to perform on demand. *I am Cashlin, Premier Patron of Regalia. The world is mine for the taking* –

I recognize the phrase in the music that signals my entrance. With my heart pounding I step onto an elaborate set. With sweeping arm movements I am a snake, slithering through a dark forest. I veer behind one tree, then slide behind another, teasing my audience with glimpses of my beauty. The audience quiets; mesmerized.

I finally twirl into full view, my body bent, my arms undulating gracefully. Seductively.

The Favored go wild. Their cheers spur me on, and I continue my choreography, finding inspiration in the mystical mood.

On cue two costumed men appear out of the woods, one with the stylized markings of a deer, the other, an owl. They swirl around me, teasing me with their scripted dance.

The owl winks at me. It's Quan, a dancer I've worked with many times.

As the music rises to a climax Quan takes my hand and spins me under his arm, not once, but twice before releasing me at the edge of the stage.

I extend my arms to either side, letting the tendrils on my sleeves wave in the breeze of the applause. I lift my chin, basking in the attention. I am dazzling.

"Spin!" someone yells.

Their wish is my command. I love the feel of the fabric floating around me. I hear the sound of a dozen camera shutters.

I notice some of the Favored wearing my past outfits. Two women hold up a sign: *We love you, Cashlin! We wear you!* I blow them a kiss. I know one of them by name. Kiya is a loyal supporter.

I walk along the edge of the stage, twirling and preening, making sure everyone sees what I offer them. As I head back to the center, Quan and the other dancer run up to me and lift me onto their shoulders. I am more than a little surprised. This was *not* scripted but the audience roars. I hold out my arms, reveling in their approval. *This* is what I live for.

The exit music begins to play. The other dancer steps aside as Quan takes hold of my waist and guides me gracefully to the ground. He holds me close. Too close.

Then he kisses me hard on the mouth.

I hear camera shutters catching the moment.

The crowd hoots and cries out.

I push him back. Hard.

I am mortified. Innocent flirting is one thing but Quan kissing me in public?

On the outside I put on a brave face. But inside . . . I know what he's done is dangerous.

He kisses my hand and spins me under his arm, then keeps hold of my hand as he raises his other arm, accepting the applause as if we are a couple. I have no choice but to do the same.

I'm seething. I know he enjoys attention as much as I do, but for him to be so reckless is unacceptable.

He pulls my hand around his arm and we walk offstage. I catch a glimpse of the next Patron getting ready to go on. LaBelle is dressed in shiny black, with feathers splayed across her head like a cap.

"I never took you for a rebel, Cashlin," she calls out.

"We both are," Quan says.

I don't answer. Instead of lingering to check out the competition as I usually would, I make a beeline for my dressing room.

Unfortunately, Quan follows me inside. As soon as the door closes, I turn on him. "Excuse me? You can't be in here."

"It appears I can."

"Says who?" What's got into him? "Why did you kiss me in front of all Regalia?"

"You prefer kissing in private? Fine." He puts his hand behind my waist and tries to pull me close, but I shove him back.

"What are you doing?"

His dark eyebrows dip in the middle. "That's the thanks I get for making people remember your Reveal. You know that kiss will bring extra attention when the Reveal Revelations are published tomorrow."

"The wrong kind of attention. I won't be surprised if we're brought before the Council of Worthiness. It was irresponsible—against the law. There *will* be consequences. Did you ever think about that?"

He makes himself at home by sitting in my makeup chair and spinning around like a child enjoying the ride. "What are they going to do to you, their star? You were born a Patron. They can't take that away from you. As a Serv I'm already at the bottom."

They can't take away my Patron status, but could they demote me? I stop the chair and make him look at me. "You're an Entertainment Serv. They might assign you to a tougher Serv position. One that involves manual labor."

"Being a dancer involves plenty of labor. I work hard—"

"As hard as those working in the fields?"

He hesitates for just a moment. "I'm strong."

Since we're getting nowhere, I try another approach. "You are one of the best dancers I know. Why risk it all for a meaningless kiss?"

He shoves past me to stand. "Don't you dare say you didn't enjoy it."

I'd been too shocked to enjoy it. I would never enjoy it, not from him. "I did *not* enjoy it."

"You're the one who flirted with me during our rehearsals."

Had I? I shove the thought away. "The kiss is a complication I don't need, Quan. Don't you remember what happens next year?"

He gives me a questioning look.

"Next year I have to marry whomever they assign me to marry."

"Which is totally idiotic."

"Yes, it is. But it's the law, and you kissing me . . ." Surely, he can see the danger in his actions.

"Laws have nothing to do with your anger, Patron. You're mad because I did something beyond your control."

I'm stunned by his words. "You don't know me well enough to say—"

He takes a step toward me, but I hold my ground.

"I believe I do," he says. "We've worked together for many hours on many Reveals. I know how controlling you are."

It's a negative word for a worthy trait. "Just because we work together does not mean you know me. And there's nothing wrong with wanting everything to be perfectly orchestrated and planned. That's how I got to the top, and that's how I'll stay here."

He rolls his eyes. "Despite what the Council says, romance shouldn't be orchestrated and planned."

Romance? With Quan? Romance is nearly unheard of for Patrons. The mating process is clinical: during our twenty-third year, the Council assigns each of the twenty Patrons a marriage partner chosen from the twenty Creative Directors. The couples are to have two children to replace themselves when they retire. Such arrangements are necessary to keep the lineage pure and keep the economy of Regalia stable.

Since I didn't answer him, Quan runs a finger up my arm. "As I said, romance shouldn't be planned—though it could be."

I slap his hand away and look at his face. He actually thinks he has a chance.

I'm so used to showing my outfits in glamourous and seductive ways that I fear I've been careless and played the part too well in rehearsals. I've played with fire.

I need to bring our relationship back to business. "Beyond everything we've just discussed I'm afraid news of the kiss will distract from my Reveal."

He gives me a slow onceover. "Any news of that outfit will benefit from a distraction." He lifts one of the tendrils, letting it float back into place. Then he touches a snakehead on my headdress. "Really, Cashlin? Snakes? It's not your best look."

I know that. I don't need him telling me—

Amar storms in. "What in the name of Regalia was that all that about?" he asks.

"It was a mistake," I tell him.

"That's a matter of opinion," Quan says.

Amar grabs the front of his shirt and gets in his face. "If you ever do anything like that again, I'll send you into the Swirling Desert myself."

"I'd like to see you try."

Amar drags him to the door and shoves him out. Then he points at me. "*Never* use him again, do you understand?"

"I agree." I'm more shaken than I let on. I'm used to things going smoothly. I'm a planner. I don't do well with improvisation—on stage or off.

We hear applause and look toward the door. "You need to get backstage and see what your competition is wearing," my brother says. "And let them see you. Hiding back here implies guilt and shame."

The guilt and shame are real. There's no denying it.

He opens the door for me, but I shake my head. "I don't want to go out there. I'll read about the other Reveals in the paper tomorrow."

"I'm pretty sure you'll read about more than that," Amar says.

Marli appears in the open doorway and looks from me to my brother and back again. "Would you like me to come back?"

"No," I say. "Come in. Amar was just leaving." I look directly at him. "And I'm not."

He raises his hands in surrender. "Fine. Do it your way. But don't come running to me when it blows up in your face."

My brother leaves. Marli comes inside and closes the door.

"Are you all right?" she asks.

I feel tears of frustration threaten. "No, I'm not."

She touches my shoulder. "I can't believe Quan did that. It's careless. It's foolish."

I nod, still incredulous. "I had no idea what he was up to. I've used him multiple times and never had any problems."

"I would guess this is his last time?" she asks.

"The very last." I look at the door and consider making an appearance like Amar told me to do, but I just can't. The only thing preventing me from cowering in a corner in complete humiliation is my anger. "I can't believe this is happening."

Marli hesitates then says, "May I speak freely?"

"Always. I prefer it."

"Quan kissed you like you were . . . familiar."

I'm appalled. "We are not familiar! At all. I would never . . ."

"I know you wouldn't. But Quan is pushy, and being pushy has consequences. People like him do what they want without thinking about how it affects others."

I start to rub the space between my eyes but stop when I feel jewels pasted there. "I'm done for the day. Get me out of this."

As Marli removes the headdress my hair pulls away with it, as if the snakes are hesitant to let it go.

She unlaces the corset, and I'm free to breathe deeply. She helps me take off the dress, hands me a robe, and I sit so she can help with the shoes. Then she secures my hair back and begins to remove my makeup.

"I'm not sure what to do next," I say. "Amar thinks it might get dicey."

Marli stops with her palm full of face jewels. "It could. The truth is, you can do more for Quan than he can — and will — ever do for you. He's an Entertainment Serv. His entire assignment is to perform wherever he's asked to perform. To *serve* as an entertainer. You're the star. The Patron Ring is Rings away from the Serv Ring."

She's right. "Regalia has very strict rules about fraternization between Rings, much less, romance. I will marry a Creative Director. End of discussion."

"When do you find out who you're matched with?"

"I already know."

"Who is it?"

"Rowan, the Director for Patron twelve."

"Isn't there usually a big announcement? I must have missed it."

"There will be. I know it's him because we're the only two who will be twenty-three next year."

Marli scoffs. "So, he's your husband by default?"

"And vice versa."

"How well do you know him? Is he nice? Good looking?"

"Nice enough, I guess. I don't know him that well." I think of Rowan's looks and can only say, "He's not bad looking."

"Such a recommendation."

I shrug. "It is what it is. We are who we are. We will marry and he will become *my* Design Director until our children are of age and take over for us."

Marli empties the face jewels into a bowl. "Who would have thought being a Serv had any advantages? At least w*e* can marry for love."

She *is* lucky that way. "It's hard to believe I'm going to be the mother of two by the time I'm twenty-six."

Marli gives me a mock salute. "As ordered by the Council. Yes, ma'am! Yes, sir! One family, made to order!"

It sounds as absurd as it is.
The entire day is absurd.
I am absurd.
I need to go home.

**

I sit in my parlor, trying to mentally and emotionally sort through the drama of my day. Any answers that begin to form immediately throw themselves back into my rushing mind-stream to be drowned.

I lean my head back and glance out the window at the row of Patron houses that rim the curved street. As the Premier Patron I live in the house at the midpoint of the Patron Ring, halfway around from the Road that bisects the walled Rings of Regalia. I have the most luxurious home, with those ranked Two and Three living in slightly lesser homes on either side of mine. The Patrons who are ranked four and beyond live on either side of the Ring that culminates in my house. Their homes are smaller and less elaborate than mine. From there to the Road are retirement homes for past Patron couples, along with a few shops and cafes. Each Ring is self-contained and other than occasionally visiting the Creatives and the Favored Rings, this Ring is my entire world.

As a child I never lived in the worst homes—though none are bad, by any means. But my parents had never risen higher than number four. After my first Reveal I was in the sixth position and each Reveal since I steadily moved up until reaching the Premier position two quarters ago.

I look around the wood-paneled parlor, its furniture upholstered in jewel-tone velvets and brocades. The fireplace burns brightly, with oil sconces of crystal and gold above the mantel. It's too ornate for my taste but I don't have a say in the decorating. Everything is Council-approved.

Someone once asked if I minded the potential move four times a year, and I'd said no. We Patrons don't own any of the furnishings or décor in the houses, so moving is fairly simple. And since the same twenty families have inhabited the street for hundreds of years, we are never in any space that's too unfamiliar.

I hear a knock on the door and hope it isn't Amar. I don't need another lecture.

My butler Dom answers it.

Unfortunately, I hear my mother's voice. She's far worse than Amar.

She sweeps into the parlor, her orange and red caftan flowing around her like a warning flag.

My thoughts scatter to the floor, unneeded. Mother will supply thoughts enough for both of us.

She places herself between me and the window and stares down at me. "Well? Must we add a lack of manners to your list of blunders?"

I stand and give her a requisite hug. "Hello, Mother."

She barely touches me, then sits in the other chair. When she takes a cleansing breath, I prepare myself for her assault—which comes immediately.

"I only have one question for you."

"Only one?"

"Don't get smart with me."

"Sorry."

"I merely ask this: Cashlin, what were you thinking?"

Mother doesn't *merely* ask anything. "The kiss was not my doing."

"Whether that's true or not, there will be hell to pay."

"Quan surprised me."

Mother shakes her head. "That's not what I heard."

My stomach tightens. "What *did* you hear?"

"He's telling anyone who will listen that it was planned, that you two are—as they say—an item."

I pop out of my chair. "That's a lie!"

Mother presses her hands down. "Be that as it may . . ."

"No! Not *be that as it may*. Anyone who knows Quan knows he's an opportunist, a publicity hound, a womanizer, and . . ." I take a fresh breath. "And a lot of lesser names I won't repeat in your company."

"Then why did you hire him?"

It's a good question with a simple answer. "Because he's a good dancer."

She shrugs. "The kiss *will* be reported in the Reveal Revelations tomorrow—if everyone doesn't know about it already."

I feel wrung out and return to my chair. I'm sick to my stomach. "What should I do?"

"First off, you need to talk to Rowan, for I'm sure he's heard all the titter-tatter."

Of course. Why haven't I thought about Rowan? My soon-to-be fiancé will not be pleased.

"The point to remember is that Quan has little to lose and much to gain by the attention, and you . . ." She shrugs.

Marli had said something similar. "I have nothing to gain and everything to lose."

"Your late father and I worked tirelessly to make you the best Patron you could be. For you to throw away everything we taught you is an insult to us and to our family legacy."

"*I* did nothing wrong. Don't you understand that?"

She waves the question away with a hand. "Unfortunately, it doesn't matter."

I'm afraid she's right.

"My second question to you is simpler. Snakes, Cashlin? Really?"

Since there's no defending my Reveal, I stare outside and let my mother decimate what is left of my life.

Chapter Two

Cashlin

I stir from a fitful sleep when Marli opens the curtains in my bedroom, letting the daylight flood in. The smell of coffee and bacon does the rest. Although I could have slept longer, I cannot resist the aroma of my two favorite foods.

I open my eyes. "Morning, Marli."

"Morning, miss. I have a tray for you."

As much as I enjoy the aroma, I'm not sure my nervous stomach can handle food. "I think I'll pass this morning."

She nods, then shakes her head. "Scrambled eggs should be settling. You need to eat, miss."

She's probably right. After Mother's visit the evening before, I'd only asked for a bowl of soup for dinner.

I sit up in bed and smooth the covers to make way for it. She sets the bed tray over my lap.

But something is missing. "Where's the paper?"

Her eyes look furtively away. "Oh."

As my sleepy brain begins to function, I realize what might be going on. Today's paper will focus on the Reveal. And Quan.

Quan and me.

"I need to see the paper, Marli. No matter what it says."

She looks forlorn but leaves to get it.

I haven't slept well, worrying about the paper. I heard an ancient adage that any publicity is good publicity, but that isn't true in Regalia. Not with the Council of Worthiness at the helm. And not when my success or failure is dependent on the fickle Favored buying my clothes—which they may or may not do if they have reason to turn against me.

All because of Quan.

And—if I am totally honest—because of me. I'd flirted with him and the other dancer, not out of genuine interest, but with an eye toward getting a good performance out of them. Apparently, it worked too well on Quan's part. I was naïve not to anticipate such actions going astray.

Marli returns with the newest copy of the Reveal Revelations. She doesn't linger as she usually does by busying herself with wardrobe tasks, but quietly steps out. Obviously, the news is *really* bad.

In today's paper all the Reveals are reviewed. Unfortunately, since I am the Premier Patron, mine is first.

A picture of Quan kissing me spreads across the front page accompanied by the headline: "Unlawful Tryst Slithers on Reveal Stage."

Once more, I regret the snakes.

I read the article:

> During her Reveal, Patron Cashlin turned heads with a sizzling kiss at centerstage. Her partner was Quan, an Entertainment Serv who's appeared in more than one of the Patron's productions. This reporter has to wonder how long this illicit tryst has been going on. It won't be the first time we've witnessed a multi-Ring relationship, but we have never seen it so blatantly revealed by someone who has reached star status. The big question I have for Cashlin applies to the kiss as well as her fashion choice. "What were you thinking?"

I feel sick. There is no way I will win the Reveal. After this fiasco I'll be lucky to be number twenty.

And what about Rowan? Will he stand by me?

Why should he? We barely know each other and the engagement hasn't been announced. Why would he defend me?

Do I need defending? Perhaps it will blow over.

There's a soft knock on my bedroom door and Marli returns, carrying a letter. "This was just delivered, miss." She holds it out to me at arm's length as if wanting to keep her distance.

I take it and immediately see black wax on the flap. In our world of bright colors who would use black wax? I study it closer and am appalled to see it's the seal of the Council of Worthiness.

I drop the letter on the bed, shaking my head. "No, no, no . . ."

"Do you want me to send for someone?" Marli asks.

I immediately think of Mother yet I'm not sure I want her to know about more bad news—for it has to be bad news. The eleven people on the Council are the governing body of Regalia—its dictators. As with everyone in Regalia, they are born into their position. There is no voting them in—or out. There is no argument against their decrees. What they say will be. Long ago they'd created our society and all the Directives that keep it running smoothly—or smoothly according to their judgment.

They are not to be messed with.

I'm overwhelmed with fear about what the letter might say. I need support. I have no choice but to tell Marli, "Please fetch Mother for me."

"Yes, miss."

I quickly get dressed. I repeatedly glance at the letter on the bed. I feel like it's watching me, like it's a physical being just waiting to pounce and condemn me.

As I brush my hair, I look out the bedroom window, waiting to see Marli and Mother. I second-guess sending for her. I know exactly what she'll do. She will berate me about the paper's scathing report and will share multiple I-told-you-sos with an attitude vacillating between concern and glee. Then, when we read the Council's letter together, she'll take their side and lecture me for angering the powers that be.

I have enough words of contempt for both of us. Enough fear too.

Yet, how could I have known Quan would go too far? Entertainment Servs are supposed to follow directions, which in his case meant following the choreography — my choreography, which did not, and will never include two dancers hoisting me onto their shoulders and letting me slide down his body to the floor, to culminate in a kiss.

The gall. The effrontery. The arrogance.

Movement outside catches my attention. Marli walks back to the house. Her head is down as she returns home. Surely Mother hasn't said no.

I grab the letter and leave my room to meet Marli halfway. "Well?" I say as I descend the stairs.

She closes the front door carefully as if she doesn't want to make a sound.

I reach her in the foyer. "Where is she? When is she coming?"

Marli's face is stricken. "She's at home, miss. She *not* coming."

That's *not* possible. "What did she say?" Marli looks past me, and I see Dom standing nearby. "Go ahead. Dom can hear."

Marli takes a deep breath. "She says she's sorry, but she can't risk being seen supporting you."

"But I'm her daughter."

"I know. But she's adamant."

Adamantly against me. "Anything else?"

"She wishes you good luck."

I put a hand on the stair post to steady myself. If my own mother shuns me there is no hope that anyone else will risk siding with me.

My legs feel weak, and I sink onto the stairs. "What am I going to do?"

Dom steps forward. "Excuse me, miss, but what did the letter say?"

With a start I realize I never opened it. I am just about to break the seal when there's a knock on the door. Mother?

I nod at Dom.

He opens the door to a gray-haired man. He wears a black caftan, signifying he works for the Council.

This can't be good.

"May I help you?" Dom asks.

"My name is Nerwhether. I've been appointed as the defense solicitor for Citizen Cashlin. Is she in?"

I have a solicitor? I need a solicitor?

I stand. "I am Cashlin."

He nods once. "Very good to meet you. May I come in so we can get started?"

I hold the letter between us. "You're ahead of me. I just received the letter. I haven't opened it."

"Oh dear," Nerwhether says. "I apologize for the breech in protocol. You should have received the declaration last evening. This is very unfortunate. Very." He seems to collect himself. "Shall we go somewhere to discuss it?"

Declaration? Not merely a letter, but a declaration?

I lead him into the parlor and oddly find myself glad to see him. I definitely need guidance.

We sit in the two chairs facing the fireplace.

He nods toward the letter. "Open it."

My stomach tightens as I break the seal. I read aloud, "'The Patron Cashlin is called to appear before the Council of Worthiness to face the charges against her: the crime of Illegal Immoral Relational Public Display Between Rings.'" The date is two days from now. "Charges? As in a . . . ?"

"A trial."

I look at the note again. "'Illegal immoral relational public display between Rings'?"

"The kiss between you and a Serv. The affection you showed each other during the Reveal," Nerwhether says. He flicks a hand in the air. "When you've worked with the Council as long as I have, you get used to their insipid, ponderous, and loquacious choice of words."

I stare at him, unsure what *loquacious* means.

He explains. "They like the sound of their own voices. They're wordy."

That, I understand.

He crosses his legs, and I notice his black shoes look newly shined, as if dust wouldn't dare settle on them. He takes out a pad of paper and a pencil. "Tell me what happened."

I've mentally relived it a hundred times. "During my Reveal one of the dancers—Quan—started to act like we have a relationship—which we don't. He took liberties beyond what I was comfortable with, beyond what *I* had scripted."

"When did the dance go astray?"

"When he and the other dancer suddenly lifted me onto their shoulders."

"That wasn't choreographed?" Nerwhether asks.

"It was not. Rather than make a scene in the middle of my Reveal I smiled and pretended it was a part of the plan, but then Quan took hold of my waist and slid my body down to the floor against his."

"Hmm."

"Then he pulled me close and kissed me." I thought of something else. "As we left the stage he drew my hand around his arm, as if we were a couple."

Nerwhether writes everything down. "So there is nothing between you?"

"Nothing. I am due to be engaged to a Creative Director next year."

"Name?"

"Rowan."

"What does Rowan think of the situation?"

Since it's embarrassing that I haven't heard from him—or contacted him, a lie escapes. "I sent a note, but he hasn't responded."

"You haven't spoken?"

"We have not. The Reveal just happened yesterday. The paper came out this morning. We haven't had a chance."

"Hmm."

"Is that bad?" I ask.

"It's not good. And being called before the Council is always bad."

"But *I* didn't do anything. Quan kissed *me*."

"Who has the power?"

"Excuse me?"

"You are a Patron. He's an Entertainment Serv. He does what you tell him to."

I sit forward in my chair. "I never told him to kiss me. I wouldn't do that."

"Who can speak to your honor?"

My honor? I've never thought about my honor. Not once. "You need someone to speak as a witness?"

"Yes. On your behalf."

Mother is out. Rowan is probably out. And none of the other Patrons will want to get involved. "Marli, my Personal Serv was with me afterward. She saw my reaction. And my brother, Amar." Though Amar often seems more against me than for me.

Nerwhether writes this down. "Those two can vouch for your character?"

"They can." I thought of someone else. "Patron LaBelle was backstage, ready for her Reveal. She saw me yank my hand away from Quan's arm as we exited the stage."

"Good..."

"And there's the other dancer, Goff. Quan might have confided in him about his plans to kiss me."

"*His* plan. So, you were surprised?"

Haven't I made that clear? "Fully and totally." I sit back, feeling done-in by the conversation. "I know the Council's rules on fraternization. I would never, ever break them." I add, "I have too much to lose."

"Yes, yes," Nerwhether says. "The logic of that is in your favor."

At least something is.

He turns the page on his notepad. "How long has Quan been your dancer?"

"This is his third Reveal for me."

"You gave him no encouragement?"

Ahh. The sticky point.

His gray eyebrows rise. "You have something to tell me?"

I wish I didn't. "I did not give him encouragement. But when we rehearsed the Reveal, I was friendly to him — to Goff too. I've found being friendly is the best way to assure good results. There's nothing at all romantic about our association. It's professional. My status as the Premier Patron is at stake."

Nerwhether nods. "And your future marriage."

He states it so plainly. "I would never risk that either."

He looks skeptical. "People have been known to throw caution to the wind for the sake of ... passion."

Passion? I shake my head vehemently. "I have passion for my work — which I take very seriously. I have no time for any other connotations of the word."

"Hmm. As to your upcoming engagement? Are you passionate about Rowan?"

I'm weary of talking about Rowan. "I hope to be passionate about him." In truth, we've barely spent any time alone. I know him from various marketing and social gatherings when I saw him with *his* Patron. And I've heard chatterings about him from my brother. That's it.

He closes his notepad. "I think I have enough to defend you."

It's my turn to be skeptical. "Do you think I'll win?"

He stands. "That depends on what Quan says in his own defense."

"So, he's being tried too?"

"Of course."

I wonder what he'll say. He'll be in trouble for the inappropriateness of the kiss, but will he blame me for it? Will Quan claim I had the power?

I walk my solicitor to the door. "I'm supposed to start the three-day marketing tour tomorrow. Can't the trial be delayed?"

Nerwhether looks over his glasses. "Surely you jest."

The thought of having to be out in public at all suddenly fills me with dread. "Since I'll be missing one day, maybe it would be best if I skipped the other two days too." Usually I'm confident about facing the press and the Favored. But not this time.

He pauses with his hand on the door. "If you don't go, you won't have *any* chance of winning the Reveal, correct?"

"Slim to none. Though with the publicity about the kiss, I —"

"The kiss and the trial."

Ah, yes. The trial. Everyone will know about that too. "I have no idea what kind of reception I'll get from the Favored. They can be fickle. And judgmental."

He runs his fingers around the doorknob. "Their reception *is* unknown. Yet presenting a confident face is beneficial. People need to see you're unworried about the trial. Act blameless. The Favored have been on your side for the past few Reveals, so help them stay on your side."

Feeling any level of assurance seems a thing of the past, but he's right. "I'll do my best."

He opens the door and smiles. "As will I."

I close the door behind him and lean against it. Despite its support I sink to the floor.

Marli and Dom suddenly appear and help me to my feet again. They lead me to a chair.

"I'll get some water," Marli says.

I hate feeling so helpless. "I'm fine," I say, even though I'm not.

Their faces are drawn with concern. Their quick response indicates they were standing nearby, which means they heard the entire conversation.

"What can we do to help?" Dom asks.

Unfortunately, nothing.

My mind spirals, and a realization that I need witnesses hits me, clearing the fog. "I need you to contact my brother. And Rowan. Tell them I need to see them as soon as possible."

"I'll go right now," Marli says.

She leaves me with Dom, standing close like a concerned father.

"I'll be all right." I stand, pretending it's true. "I'll be in my room." I manage the stairs and find my stone-cold breakfast waiting for me. The lingering smell of bacon disgusts me, so I put the tray in the hall.

I move a chair close to the window and peer out, watching for Marli to return. Or Amar. Or Rowan. Surely one of the men will come. Surely one of the men in my life will know how to make things right.

With a start I realize that very soon I might not have this lovely view out this lovely window. Very soon I might live in another, smaller home. Very soon I might be demoted from the first to the last.

It all feels very, very hopeless.

**

I must have dozed because I'm awakened by a knock on the bedroom door.

I bolt out of my chair. "Yes. Come in."

Amar sweeps in, taking over the room — a talent he's learned from our mother. He sits in the chair beside me.

"Thanks for coming. I welcome your support."

He grimaces as if I've said something nasty. "I'm not sure you have it."

"What?"

He shrugs. "You let a stupid thing happen, sister."

"I didn't *let* it happen, it happened *to* me."

"Same difference."

Actually, no . . .

He runs his hands up and down the arms of the chair. "Marli says you've been called before the Council and a solicitor came by?"

"A Council-appointed solicitor."

"Did he sound optimistic?"

Had he? "I'm not sure."

"That doesn't sound good. What's the penalty for . . . what you did?"

"I don't know."

"It would have been a logical question to ask him."

"I'm sorry. I was a little rattled." Amar has no compassion whatsoever. "You're the one who's a stickler for rules. Why don't *you* know?"

"I know what I need to know to do what I have to do." He checks his manicure. "Surely they won't take away your Patron status."

"Can they do that?"

"The Council can do whatever they want to do. And if they demote you, will they demote me?"

How like my brother to worry about himself.

He continues. "They can't demote me. I mean, *I* didn't lead Quan on."

I am appalled. "Neither did I. We worked together. I was polite. I was friendly. End of story."

"Obviously it isn't."

"My solicitor is going to call you as a character witness."

He scoffs. "Don't drag me into this."

"But you're my brother. You're my Creative Director."

"This is your problem, sister. Leave me out of it."

Why had I ever thought he would make things better?

I've had enough of him. I go to the bedroom door and open it. "I should have known better than to turn to you for help and encouragement."

He stands. "If you can't handle the truth . . ." He walks through the doorway but stops. "Are you going to brave the marketing tour tomorrow?"

"What do you care?"

"I guess I don't."

I really want him there. I want someone there. "Will you be there, by my side?"

He laughs. "Not if you offer me a thousand tokens." He chucks me under my chin. "Good luck, sister."

I slam the door behind him.

Almost immediately I hear Marli's gentle knock. "Miss?"

I open the door.

"Are you all right?" she asks.

I shake my head. "When is Rowan coming?"

"I'm afraid he isn't. He says he has other commitments." She draws in a breath. "I'm so sorry, miss. You must be terribly frightened."

"I am." Her compassion allows my tears to flow. I return to my chair. "It's such a mess. I'm going to lose everything."

"No, you won't."

I'm not sure if I like her unsupported optimism more than Amar's full-on pessimism. "But I probably will. My Reveal isn't the best, and now with the scandal . . ." I look at my lovely room. "I doubt I'll be here for the next Reveal."

Marli stands by the chair vacated by Amar. "You're still the Premier Patron. People love you."

I scoff. "The Favored are unpredictable."

She doesn't argue. Yet when she looks down, then back at me, her face has changed. There is a lightness to it.

"There *is* someone who always loves you and will always be there for you."

"I appreciate that, Marli."

She shakes her head and lowers her voice. "I'm talking about... the Keeper."

I shush her. "Stop. You mustn't speak of him. If a simple kiss sends me to trial, I can only imagine the kind of punishment there'd be for spouting anything about a deity. It's expressly forbidden. I won't risk my life by speaking of it." I take a breath. "No more, Marli. Please."

She nods but seems pensive.

"What's wrong?" I ask.

"I understand the truth of what you say and yet . . . being one of the Devoted is something I *am* willing to risk my life for."

She talks crazy. "Nothing is worth that."

"I disagree." Marli's face softens. She looks completely content. "Devotion to the Keeper is worth everything we are and everything we have."

I stand to give her a signal that our discussion is over. "Thank you for all you did today, Marli."

"I will send my prayers to the Keeper on your behalf."

"You don't have to do that." Don't do that.

"I want to, miss. I care what happens to you. Be strong and courageous in front of the Council."

She's so calm and certain.

While I'm confused. The man who is supposed to be committed to be my husband wants nothing to do with me. My brother thinks only of himself. And my Personal Serv wants to talk about a mystical godlike creature that can get us both punished.

"Can I get you anything?" Marli asks.

"Not at the moment."

I shut the door.

I am completely alone.

And utterly doomed.

Chapter Three

Cashlin

Instead of walking to the Dome of the Reveal for the first day of our marketing tour, I arrange for a carriage for Marli and me. I usually walk because it lets me saunter through the Favored Ring where I can chat with the customers. Making myself accessible is always advantageous.

But today is different because I'm afraid of how they'll receive me. The last thing I want is to walk among them and have them shun me or say disparaging things. I need the protection a carriage will provide. A closed carriage.

Marli and I stand inside my front door to wait. We watch other Patrons leave their homes, walking toward the Road. I begin to wonder if I've made a bad choice separating myself.

Marli interrupts my doubts. "I do like the caftan you've chosen today, miss," she says. "You have an eye for choosing the most flattering patterns."

"Thank you." I love how the flowing fabric makes me feel free and unencumbered. It's a good contrast to my confined, worried state.

"You get to wear so many lovely clothes," Marli says.

"*Some* lovely clothes. I'm not looking forward to changing into my snake outfit for the Q&A session."

"I know it's not your favorite," she says. "But it's creative and seems well made."

Well made? It was like telling someone their shoes looked sturdy. "But…?" I want to know more.

She meets my eyes. "But where would the Favored wear a snake headdress?"

"At their parties. You know Regalia's motto: 'Always something new.' Their job is to revel in our Reveals—the more outlandish, the better."

She shakes her head. "I've always wondered… other than partying, what else do they do with their time?"

I look out the door's window as I try to scrape together an answer. "I honestly don't know." Should I know? "They come to the Reveal every quarter, vote for their favorites, the top ten get produced, and the Favored buy them. It's their job to show them off."

"To each other."

It does sound a bit inane, but I feel my defenses kick in. "That's how it works. That's how it's always been."

"Not always," Marli says.

Is she talking about the Before Time? Such discussions are forbidden. All history has been lost and the Council has ordered us to let it stay lost. There is nothing to be gained from digging up ancient news — ancient bad news. "You know the Council's mantra: 'What was, was. What is, is.' We have to accept that. Embrace it for our own good."

"Mmm." Marli polishes the doorknob with her apron. "Can I ask you a sensitive question?"

Actually no, but I say, "I suppose."

"If the Favored spend their time partying and don't work, how do they earn money to buy the clothes?"

I'm confused at the question only because I assume everyone knows the answer. "The Council pays them to buy the clothes."

"So they don't have to work?" Marli asks.

I feel defensive. "They do not." I'm done with this conversation. "What is, is and we shall embrace it. Imperfect though it may be, without the system, without the Favored wearing the clothes we Patrons have chosen from our Creatives, which are then manufactured by the Implementors, and sold in the shops, there would be no Regalia. You wouldn't want that, would you?"

It's not like me to put people on the spot, but Marli's attitude has to be bring to a halt before she gets in trouble.

She nods and manages a smile. "I'm sorry to bring up such a serious subject. I'm fully aware that without the Cycle of Regalia I would not be able to live in this lovely house, serving you."

Cycle of Regalia. I've never heard the term, but let it go. "And there you have the truth of it."

"I didn't mean to upset you, miss. It's just that I know there's more to life than parties and clothes."

"Parties and clothes *give* us our lives. We are nothing without them."

She lowers her voice, and I can barely hear her. "That's not true."

Surely, she's not going to bring up the Keeper again? "What did you say?"

She meets my eyes with a look of courage tainted by trepidation. "Parties and clothes don't give our lives meaning. There's so much more."

"If there is, I don't want to hear about it." I take a step away from her. "I have enough on my mind without you forcing me to delve into subjects beyond the realm of my responsibilities and control. I suggest you keep your rebellious opinions to yourself."

Her eyes grow wide, but she nods. "Yes, miss. Sorry."

I hear a carriage approach. I hope our ride to the interview is accomplished in silence.

Once we get in the carriage she says, "I do wish you the best of luck today, miss."

I'm not sure I believe in luck. Actually, after our discussion I'm not sure what I believe in.

**

We ride in the covered carriage toward the Dome of the Reveal in the Favored Ring. Marli *is* silent, which is a relief. Yet our earlier discussions plague me.

Who is she to question the way things work in Regalia? Who is she to imply that there's more to life than what we already have?

We approach the Road that connects all seven Rings—from the centermost Council Ring, to the outermost Serv Ring, with the deadly Swirling Desert beyond. Each walled Ring has its own guarded gate, strong evidence of how serious Regalia is about keeping everyone in their proper place.

I watch as two Servs dressed in their brown tunics and pants enter the Patron Ring, no doubt going to work for one of my colleagues. It strikes me as odd that the citizens who pass through the most gates are the Servs. They live in the largest outer Ring and constantly have to travel the Road through the Imp Ring, the Favored Ring, the Creatives Ring, my Ring, the Ring of Council mansions, and finally the innermost Council Tower Ring. They have full access to serve us all.

Which means they know a lot about how the people in the other Rings live, while we of the inner Rings know very little about their lives. I've traveled outward to the Creatives Ring to choose my Reveal costumes, and of course the Favored Ring to present, but have never entered either the Imp or Serv Ring. I've never even thought about going there.

Why not?

The realization of my willful ignorance makes me uneasy. Why am I having such thoughts? They make me feel as though the balance of my life is at risk. I push them away. I don't need to think like this right now.

If ever.

My name is noted by the guards and our carriage is allowed through the gate leading to the Favored Ring. A few days ago, I'd come to the Dome of the Reveal with thoughtful, hopeful confidence. Today is a different story. Our three-day marketing tour always begins with a question-and-answer session. I didn't sleep well last night, imagining how it might go. Imagining the trial tomorrow. Imagining the potential lifelong repercussions of one stupid kiss.

I haven't eaten much either—which is probably a good thing. My entire body is on high alert, anticipating assaults from all sides.

The streets are lined with the Favored watching me pass. I wave but they don't smile, and look at me skeptically. I pass some fellow Patrons walking and talking with the Favored and the shop owners. Laughing. Making good impressions. It's what I've done many times.

Until this time.

I am torn between acting as though nothing is wrong and hiding away. Yet, there is no good impression made by cowering in a closed carriage. But it's too late now.

Or is it?

I thump on the roof of the carriage and call out, "Stop. We want out, please."

Within seconds, we stop, and the driver opens the door for us, extending a hand to help us out.

"Would you like me to wait for you, miss?"

"No, thank you. I won't need you further." I *hope* I won't need him.

I paste on my best smile and step away from the carriage as Marli walks behind. I focus on a young woman who wears one of my past winning costumes. "Don't you look nice," I say.

She gives me a little curtsy. "Thank you, Patron Cashlin. I always like your clothes the best."

"I appreciate that."

A woman who looks to be her mother steps up beside her. "Come now, girl. We need to move on." She looks at me with glaring eyes. "*You* need to move on."

I shudder. "There's no need to be rude."

She steps in front of her daughter, pushing her behind as if protecting her. "I'll be as rude as I need to be to keep her away from the likes of you."

I'm taken aback. "The likes of me? She *likes* me. She's wearing one of my outfits."

"Not anymore." The woman waves at the girl. "Go change, child. I won't have you wearing this floozy's clothes ever again."

"But Mama . . ."

"Go!"

I look around the street. All eyes are on me. I smile and try to make light of it. "Well then." I approach another group, but they hurry away like I'm poison.

Then people start yelling. "Floozy!"

"You're guilty!"

"Get away from us!"

"Exile! Exile!"

I freeze. I'm living a nightmare.

More people gather and someone throws an apple at me, hitting my ear.

Then I see a flash of color as Amar bursts through the crowd, "Go on! Off with the lot of you!" He puts an arm around my shoulders and leads me through the crowds toward the Dome as Marli runs behind.

He doesn't speak until we're safely inside. "What do you think you're doing, walking alone like that?"

"I've never had problems before."

"You've never been brought before the Council before." He makes a beeline to my dressing room and closes the door behind me and Marli.

"I never thought they'd react like that. It was just a kiss."

Amar points at me. "You *are* dense. It isn't about a stupid kiss, sister. It's about crossing Rings, being intimate with a Serv." He glances at Marli. "Sorry, but it's the truth."

She doesn't respond.

Amar begins pacing in front of the door. "Today is going to be a blood bath. They're going to devour you."

"Thanks for the boost of confidence, brother."

He stops and points beyond the door. "What makes you think the Favored in the Q&A are going to be kind and understanding? You saw what they think of you."

I had. It was terrifying.

I feel like crying but know it won't do any good. "No one is going to listen to anything I have to say. They've already convicted me."

"It's not fair, miss," Marli says.

"No, it's not!" I turn to Amar. "So what am I supposed to do?"

He shrugs. "I have no idea."

Panic sets in as I imagine harsh questions hurled at me. Angy voices. Jeers. Panic. Pain. "I can't face them, Amar. I have to get out of here. I just want to go home." I turn toward the door.

Amar puts his hands on my shoulders, pushing me back. "If you don't show up, they're going to think you're to blame; think you're guilty."

"They already think I'm guilty!"

Amar rubs his chin, thinking. "I . . . I guess I can tell them you're not feeling well."

"That's certainly true." I want to throw up.

"They'll see it as the ploy that it is, but it's all we've got."

That is also true. "Thank you, brother. I appreciate it."

He opens the door and points at me. "You owe me."

As our plan is set in motion my heart beats wildly. Have I made the right decision to leave? "I can't believe I'm being put on trial — twice," I say aloud.

"They're not being fair," Marli says. "Let's get you home."

A good idea, but the logistics overwhelm. "How can I go out among the Favored who might not be in the Dome? How can I make it past the store owners? They're all vicious."

Marli looks around the dressing room. She rifles through a rack of my mother's old costumes, then pulls one out. "This," she says. It's a navy velvet dress with a black cape my mother revealed years ago. "Today the Favored are wearing outfits from the past. You'll look like one of them." She glances at my copper hair. "Except for that."

My mane of glory is a problem. "Maybe if you pull it back?"

She points at the chair. "Sit."

Marli pulls my hair into a nondescript low ponytail like the Servs and Imps wear, and slicks it down, which changes the color from copper to brown. She attaches the costume's tall top hat. I change from my caftan into the blue dress, and tie on the cape.

"Here." Marli hands me the blue heels that originally belonged with the outfit.

Once they're on, I stand before her. "Well?"

"You look like one of the Favored. It's good. It will work."

It has to.

Marli cracks the door of my dressing room and peers out. I hear voices, but I also hear music playing from the stage. The event is about to begin. She closes the door. "Let's wait a minute."

The anticipation about what *might* happen nearly does me in.

Then Marli touches my arm and peers upward. "Keeper? Keep us safe from all evil."

That would be good.

She looks out the door a second time, then opens it. "Let's go."

It takes all my self-control not to run. I walk beside her, but she slows and whispers, "I have to walk behind you."

Which means I have to lead. I don't want to lead. I want to be led to safety, preferably hiding in the shadow of someone far braver than me.

There are fewer people on the street, mostly shop owners chatting in the doorways. Instinctively, I want to put my head down, but I force myself to show interest in their display windows like a Favored who has all the time in the world.

Two women look at me suspiciously. I nod at them, and even manage, "Good day, ladies."

They stop talking but resume after I pass. I swear I hear them say, *Is that Cashlin?*

I quicken my pace. The gate looms ahead, my portal to safety.

We stop in line with four others. One of the guards looks skeptical when I give my name.

"You don't look like yerself, Patron. And shouldn't you be at the event?"

I put a hand to my midsection. "I'm not feeling well."

Marli puts her hand on my arm. "I need to get her home."

He puts our name on the list and waves us through the gate. I let myself breathe.

Finally, we are home. I lean against the door, out of breath and totally devoid of courage.

"We made it," Marli says.

Dom walks into the foyer. He takes note of the costume. "Miss? Are you all right?"

Words fail me. I am full to the brim with emotions and can only shake my head. "Upstairs. Please."

With an arm around my waist Marli helps me conquer the stairs. I sit on the bed, wishing for nothing more than to slide under its covers.

She helps me off with the shoes. I pull the tie of the cape, but only make the knot tighter.

"Here, let me," she says.

I'm used to this dear woman helping me get dressed, but at the moment I feel like a useless child as she rids me of the costume. She brings me my night dress and pulls back the covers of the bed.

I fall onto the pillows with a moan, relishing the way they mold around my head and shoulders, keeping me safe from the world. So much for being the Premier anything.

Dom appears at the door. "Can I get you some tea?" he asks. "Something to eat?"

"Nothing," I say.

"I don't understand what happened," he says. "Was the interview called off?"

I don't have the energy to explain. "Marli will fill you in."

They leave me alone but I hear Marli's soft voice telling Dom about the end of my career.

**

I swim through the luscious sea of sleep and drift upward, bursting through the watery edge into full wakefulness. I draw in a deep breath.

Marli rushes to my bedside.

"How are you feeling?" she asks.

I push myself to sitting and she adjusts the pillows behind me. "How can every muscle hurt like I've run a marathon?"

"Tension will do that," she says.

I notice it's still day. "How long did I sleep?"

"A couple hours."

We both turn toward the sounds of loud footsteps in the hall. Amar bursts into the room and marches toward the bed. He brushes Marli aside and whips off the covers. "Get up!"

I cringe and pull a pillow to my chest.

Marli brings me a robe.

"Out, you!"

She looks at me for direction, but I nod. I would love for her to stay, but I hate having her witness my brother's anger.

I tie the robe around my waist and stroll to the chairs, trying to capture a calm I do not feel. "Have a seat," I tell him.

"You sit. You sleep, while I clean up your mess—and it is a mess, Cashlin. A disgusting, humiliating, stinking mess."

My heart drops. I pour myself a glass of water, my shaking hand letting droplets spill. "Would you like—?"

He sweeps his hand across the glasses and pitcher. Water sprays everywhere, and glass shatters. He stands in front of me, his chest heaving. "They annihilated you at the interviews."

"I wasn't even there."

"It didn't matter. They started asking questions about your absence. Someone saw me in the wings and called me forward to answer for you. No one believed you were sick. You put me in a horrible position."

I can't believe my ears. "You're the one who suggested playing sick."

He flips my words away. "They called you a coward—and worse."

I start to scoff—yet *coward* was appropriate. I draw my knees to my chest, balancing my heels on the edge of the chair. "I might as well quit right now. After the trial, they'll want nothing to do with me."

"No go on that. A Patron *can't* quit, stupid," Amar says. "And what about me? We're a team. You lose, I lose."

I glance back at the bed, longing for oblivion.

"Actually, you might not have to think about marketing much longer," Amar says.

"How so?"

He shrugs. "If they find you guilty at the trial . . ."

From bad to worse. "Will they really do that? Surely if it's my word against Quan's, my words will hold more credence."

36

"From what I've heard, it all depends on the mood of the Council. I can easily imagine them declaring you guilty as charged." He pulls a finger across his neck.

"Don't be so dramatic. It's one kiss."

He shrugs. "It's way more than that, sister. They'll *have* to make an example of you."

"How? What will they do to me?"

He paces in front of the window. "I don't know. Nobody knows. There is no precedent that I know of."

"Maybe they'll take away my Premier position."

"Maybe."

That would be bad, but doable. "What's the worst they can do to me?"

He looks at me as if I'm stupid. "Exile, of course. Exile into the Swirling Desert—which is basically death."

I'm stunned. "Death? They'd sentence me to death?" His shrug enrages me. I pop out of my chair and grab his upper arms. "You're my brother! Do something!"

Amar easily pries my hands away and takes hold of my wrists, squeezing them to the point of pain. "Watch yourself, sister."

I yank my hands free, weary of his bullying. "Or what? I'm already facing exile so why should I be afraid of you?"

He smooths his tunic where I've mussed it. "By the way, I'm testifying tomorrow."

"Thank you! I appreciate—"

He stops my words with a hand. "I'm not going to lie for you, Cashlin. I'm going to tell the truth."

"That's fine. I have nothing to hide."

His eyebrows rise. "You flirted with him, sister. You led Quan on."

"I did no such..." His expression is hard and devoid of compassion. "I don't know what to say to you."

"Yeah. Well. Join the club." He walks toward the door.

"Amar, please do what you can to help me."

He calmly turns around and smiles. "Honestly, sister, I think you're beyond help." He walks out.

I stand there, frozen.

People always say things can't get any worse.

But I know they can.

I climb back in bed and pull the covers over my head.

I feel very alone.

I might as well get used to it.

Chapter Four

Helsa

After working at the factory all day, I flip through the latest edition of Reveal Revelations. I love reading about the fancy fashions, the new dresses and garments that the Favored choose from. Fashion that Nana and I help sew as Implementers.

I turn the page and see the glaring words "Is Cashlin, guilty?" I read disturbing news: my favorite Patron, Cashlin, is getting bad press about a kiss. With a Serv. That's a big no-no.

"A Serv kissed Cashlin onstage," I say aloud.

"Who kissed her?" Nana asks.

"Her dancer."

Nana stirs a pot of soup nearby. "That's risky. Everyone knows it's against the law to have a romantic relationship between Rings — especially a Patron with a Serv. I think it's archaic, but no one cares about my opinion."

I'm heartbroken for Cashlin. Though nobody knows this, I want to *be* Cashlin. I want to be gorgeous, have thick red hair, wear amazing clothes, have my picture in the newspaper, and have thousands idolize me. I want to *win* something. But I doubt if more than a few dozen people even know my name.

"What else does it say?" Nana asks.

I go back to the bad news. "She's been called to trial before the Council of Worthiness." I shake my head. "I hate the Council. Can't they leave people alone?"

"No, actually they can't."

"Will they send Cashlin and her dancer to exile like they did Papa?"

Nana tastes the soup and adds a few grains of salt. "I stopped trying to understand the whims of the Council a long time ago."

I wish I hadn't brought it up because talk of Papa makes both of us sad. "Papa didn't deserve to die."

"No, he didn't. My son was an honorable, courageous man, speaking truth."

I toss the newspaper aside, suddenly disgusted with a paper I usually absorb word for word. "I don't know why I read this thing. None of this news has anything to do with us."

"Actually, it has everything to do with us. We Implementors make the clothes for the top ten winners. Without that, *we* don't work. We don't eat."

"That's not what I meant."

Nana's voice softens. "I know what you meant. Soup's ready."

She serves two bowls and we sit at a table meant for four. I rip off a hunk of bread and hand her the loaf.

"I can't believe we have Mama's funeral tomorrow," I say.

"I know. It's difficult."

A funeral makes her death real. If I didn't have to go to the funeral I might be able to pretend Mama will be home any minute, that the three of us still work side by side at the factory. It doesn't help that I've never been to an actual funeral. The unknown element adds nerves to my grief. "With Mama's death I'm an orphan," I say.

"Yes, you are."

"I assumed I'd be an orphan someday, but to have it happen when I'm only nineteen seems unfair. Especially after losing Papa only three months ago."

"It's extremely unfair." Nana eats a spoonful of soup. "I wish your mother had been stronger. It's heartbreaking to witness someone grieving herself to death."

I share the heartbreak but feel something more. "I'm mad at her."

I expect Nana to argue with me, to defend her son's wife, but she only says, "Me too."

I'm shocked. "You're mad too?"

"I am. When bad things happen everyone has a choice to deal *with* it or be done in *by* it. Unfortunately, your mama chose the latter. She didn't think about you and me being left behind. Dying was a selfish thing to do."

I agree, yet her words are so harsh.

"I'm not wrong, am I?" she asks me.

I shake my head. "I miss her."

"Me too."

**

On the awful day of the funeral, I check my brown hair in a mirror, then adjust the black arm band on my gray tunic—the only concession to grief the Council allows us Imps—one we can only wear for a week. Not that it gets us anything other than one day off from work and the kind words of people who see us.

That hardly feels like enough compensation for losing Mama. And Papa.

I notice the time and find myself nearly calling out to Mama to hurry up, we'll be late.

She's most certainly *late* now.

The weight of my reality seeps into my pores making my entire body feel heavy.

Nana is putting on her shoes when someone knocks on the door. I open it to Lieb, my best childhood friend. The lilac blossom he holds is in stark contrast to his brown tunic. He holds it out, awkwardly. "Sorry about your mama."

I take it from him, draw in the sweet scent, and tell him to come in. "See what Lieb brought us, Nana?"

"You're a kind boy. Thank you." She pours water in a glass. "Put it here."

I do, willing the pretty bloom to last. Nana and I need some beauty in our drab lives.

Lieb lifts up the hem of his tunic to reveal his "scraps." Years ago, he made a vest out of scraps from the factories and keeps adding to it. "See here? I found this flowered scrap and it reminds me of your mama, so I sewed it on."

"It's pretty," I say. "She'd like it."

"I know." He pulls his requisite brown tunic over the forbidden colors and pats the spot of the newest scrap.

"We should go," Nana says.

Lieb is the last one out. He too wears an arm band, an honorary member of the family since the Council only allows four mourners per Imp death. All other Imps are needed at the factories. Unfortunately, it's just us three.

We walk to the Road. The black armbands get us past the guards, allowing us passage to the Serv Ring, to the Pile where Mama's ashes will be scattered.

We walk through narrow streets among small dwellings on their last legs, to the Pile, halfway around. There aren't many Servs around, as most travel to the inner Rings during the day to serve. But when we pass Lieb's house, his mother is outside and nods once before retreating inside.

"Mama's sorry for you," Lieb says. "But she says *your* Mama was weak and should've tried harder to be happy again." He looks at me sideways in that childlike way he has. "Are you happy again, Sa-Sa?"

"Not yet." I hate what his mother said about mine—even though it's true—because it's *her* saying it. Lieb's mother wears bitterness like armor. She's mad at her husband for leaving her and mad at the world for giving her a son who's a 'blithering fool'—her words, not mine. No one who's ever gotten to know Lieb for more than three minutes would ever call him that. If speaking the truth makes him blithering, so be it. He's less of a fool than most, because Lieb has a heart that celebrates purity like a sunbeam celebrates air.

Lieb puts a hand on the back of my neck, squeezing once. He has always been my rock, even though we live in different Rings. His position as a Messenger Serv allows our paths to cross. I miss our time learning to read and solve arithmetic in the combined Serv-Imp Kid Camp. It feels like yesterday even though those childhood days are nearly seven years past. We've both been working since the age of thirteen and share a bond that is the core of our nature. Like the lilac stem, Lieb and I are leaves and blossoms, two parts of a greater whole. He understands me better than I understand myself.

Papa understood me too. He knew me to be stubborn, analytical, and never quite accepting of what is. He had a calm way about him and was trying to teach me to pause, consider consequences, and pick my battles. It's been hard to deal with life without his steady guidance.

Mama also looked to Papa for direction and wisdom. It's not surprising she faltered, withered, and died after he was exiled. Because she'd been so upset at the mere thought of his death, Papa forbid all of us from going to the actual exile, which meant he'd been sucked into the Swirling Desert alone.

I should've been there for him.

I glance at Lieb, walking so tall and strong beside me. We're the same age in body, but he's younger in mind. Yet he's wise in his own way. Will he be able to stop me from making bad choices like Papa had? Like the time I'd pretended to be sick, so I didn't have to work. Papa reminded me that the Enforcer-Servs would check on me, and if they thought I was lying I'd get a demerit. Ten demerits means exile. Though sometimes it only takes one. And a few times I've heard people hanging on with eleven. One or eleven, we are all subject to the Council of Worthiness.

That time, I'd heeded Papa's warning and had gone to work. But will I remember his other lessons or will I slip up and have to deal with the consequences?

"Your forehead is scrunchy," Lieb says, mimicking my expression. "You're thinking hard about something."

"I'm thinking about Papa. I depended on him. Without him here to help me . . . without Mama here . . ."

"I'm here. I'll help."

I know Lieb will try, but we are very different. He's intuitive where I'm factual. He's impulsive where I tend to be more cautious and careful. And he is never forceful like Papa could be — and sometimes needed to be — with me.

The Serv village ends and a single narrow path continues. Oddly, the path winds through a forest. A wilderness. I hesitate because it looks scary. "Are you sure this is the way?"

"I've never been here," Lieb says, as he peers into the dense trees. "Do boogeymen live in there?"

"Don't be frightened," Nana says. "I've been here too many times. This is the way to the Pile."

We have to walk single file and Nana goes first, a tiny woman being the bravest of us all.

Lieb holds a low branch upward so I can pass under it. "This is a dreadful path, in dreadful woods, leading to a dreadful death. It fits, doesn't it?" he says.

Whether it 'fits' or not, it's appropriate. It's dark, unknown, and creepy, like a forest would be in a bad dream.

I shiver as the temperature drops dramatically. The sun's rays only reach us in ever-moving splotches of light, like fireflies trying to flit through a maze.

The Imp Ring has green areas too, but they're allocated to farming. This uncultivated land seems wasted. Regalia isn't that big. Every area should serve a purpose. What purpose is there in downed branches and tangled briars?

"Ouch!" I say, as a thorn scratches the side of my head. My point is made.

The path goes on a short distance ending as dramatically as it began. Stretched out before us are low mounds of dirt like huge ant hills. To the side are a few low buildings. It's as barren as I expected the Pile to be.

"This is it?" I whisper.

"This is it," Nana says. "Here are the ashes of Imps and Servs, all strewn together. Gray and brown in life becomes gray and brown in death."

So, the mounds aren't dirt, they are piles of . . . I shudder.

"That makes me sad," Lieb says.

"I'm almost glad we couldn't have a funeral for Papa," I say, though I don't really mean it. Having the Swirling Desert sweep him away—being here, then not here—was beyond cruel. It was vicious.

A Comfort-Serv with black hair and a pointy beard walks toward us. Instead of the usual brown tunic and pants of the Servs, he wears a brown caftan. He stands with his hands in front of him, holding a corked bottle. He looks solemn—and rather bored. With no greeting he instructs us to get in a line facing him. I have no idea what to expect. What will he say about Mama? He hadn't known her, nor had he visited us to gather the highpoints of her life—or provide comfort.

I don't know what to expect, but I don't expect there to be nothing.

His gaze skims my face and he hands me the bottle. "Spread the ashes there," he points to his right.

I am stunned to realize Mama's ashes are in the bottle. I'd heard that was how things worked, but to have him simply hand me this nondescript container . . .

I hold it out to Nana. "Do you want—?"

She shakes her head vigorously.

It's up to me.

I step forward, remove the bottle's stopper, and pour the ashes of my mother onto the Pile. A breeze intervenes and carries some further away, which is oddly more comforting than seeing her ashes fully dumped with the rest.

Nana begins to cry. I step beside her, and Lieb draws us both close.

"Ashes to ashes, dust to dust," the man says.

I wait for more.

But he turns and starts to walk away.

"Wait!" I say.

He pauses to look over his shoulder. "Yes?"

"Is that's all you're going to say?"

"It is all that's prescribed."

I let go of Nana and take a step toward him. "You're presiding over my mother's funeral when you know nothing about her."

"That is not a requisite for saying the words."

"Six words. Meaningless words." My breathing turns heavy, and I feel my face grow hot and red. "What was my mother's name?"

The Serv blinks. "That is not a—"

"Not a requisite either?"

I'm glad he doesn't nod.

"Her name was Fet," I say. My anger spits out the words: "Say her name!"

I watch him battle with my request, yet as his eyes scan mine and Lieb's beside me, he must think it wise to give in. "Fet."

I point at him. "Remember it."

He nods briefly and turns to walk away a second time.

But I'm not through with him. "I . . ." What I'm about to suggest is forbidden. "There was no prayer."

The Serv's eyes grow large, and he looks to his right, then his left. He takes a step toward me. "You know such talk is forbidden."

I do. Which is why my stomach flips. Yet I can't let it go. "The Council has canceled the Keeper, but I have not." I look back at my family. "We have not."

Nana's eyes look panicked. We haven't forgotten about the Keeper, but we only call to him when we're alone. Is she really afraid of this nothing-man turning us in?

Lieb moves beside me, takes my arm, and whispers, "Sa-Sa. Don't be upset."

I shake his touch away. "If not now, when? Mama is dead!"

"Helsa, please . . ." Nana says.

I ignore them and glare at the man. "You call yourself a Comfort Serv? I find no comfort in your pitiful words, in your reluctant mention of Mama's name, and your quick dismissal of us as if we're nothing."

His jaw tightens as he steps toward me. I nearly step back but hold my ground. Lieb stays by my side.

The man points a finger at me. "Watch yourself, Helsa, for now I know *your* name." He touches the finger to his head. "And I will not forget."

With that, he walks away from us.

My heart beats in my throat. My legs turn weak and wobbly.

Lieb takes my arm forcefully. "We need to get away. Now, Sa-Sa."

Nana's fear has silenced her tears and we quickly retreat through the dark forest toward the village.

What have I done?

**

Mourning is hard work.

We return from the funeral and thank Lieb for coming with us.

But after that, I fall into a chair, totally spent.

Nana sits at the table and begins to write a note. How does she have the energy?

"What are you doing?" I ask.

"It's Donda's birthday tomorrow. I want to send her a note."

I shake my head. Nana is always writing encouraging notes to her friends in need, even when *she's* the one in need. I often find her writing in the middle of the night when she'll tell me she had a dream about someone and just had to get up and write them a note.

I close my eyes and let the weariness seep through my body. I don't dream much, which is probably best.

"I'm glad that's over," I say.

"As am I." Nana has dark circles under her eyes.

"Leave the note be. You should go to bed," I tell her.

She sets the note aside. "We need to have a serious talk." She moves to her rocking chair — her domain.

I know what's coming.

With effort I push myself upright. "I know I should be sorry about what I said to that non-comforting Serv, but I'm not. He was awful at his job."

"He was no worse than most."

Being in her sixties, Nana has experience with death. "I can't believe he's always so blunt," I say.

"Believe it." She waves a hand in front of her face, swiping the subject aside. "You've put us in danger, Helsa."

Danger? "For insisting he say Mama's name?"

She shakes her head. "For talking about prayer. For saying the Keeper's name."

As soon as I'd said it, I'd felt a twinge, wanting to take it back. It was impulsive—which isn't like me at all. But now I feel defensive. "If we can't say 'Keeper' at a—"

Nana shushes me, wanting me to lower my voice.

I do as she asks. "Papa talked about the Keeper all the time."

"And it got him exiled."

"But the lack of any special words at the funeral really got to me. If we can't mention him at a funeral, then tell me what—or who—are we supposed to turn to in times of trouble? You're the one who always wants us to pray."

Nana sighs. "I used to be braver, but since my son's death . . . you ask who we turn to? I think it's safest to turn to our assigned work and let our emotions and our faith stay within the confines of our home. We can't make them public, child. We just can't."

She's probably right. The danger of what I said suddenly washes over me and I feel a sudden twinge of fear in my gut. I sit on the floor at Nana's feet and take her hands in mine. "They're not going to come for me, are they?"

Although her knuckles are swollen from all the handwork we do, her grip is strong. "It all depends on that Comfort Serv. He has every right to turn you in. Turn us in."

I remember his dark eyes, his aggressive step toward me, and his pointing finger.

"You know what you need to do, Helsa."

"Hide?"

"The opposite."

I shake my head. "I'm not going to apologize to him. I never want to go to that awful place again."

She sighs.

A sigh I know well. Sentences are written with Nana's sighs.

"Do you really think I need to do that?"

"I do."

"But the man didn't give his name. He'll be hard to find."

"You remember the buildings near the mounds? You try there."

"And say what to him?"

"Start by apologizing for being rude."

I thought of something. "I could blame it on my grief."

Nana shrugs. Then she says, "What else will you apologize for?"

"For mentioning . . ." I point upward.

This time Nana nods. "Be humble and contrite."

"Will that keep me from getting punished?"

"There's no guarantee."

I lean my head against Nana's leg. She strokes my hair and whispers softly, "Dear Keeper, protect this child from all harm."

Please.

Chapter Five

Helsa

On the day after Mama's funeral, our mourning is declared over. So saith Council Law. Do they actually expect us to extinguish our flame of grief as easily as lowering the wick of an oil lamp?

Mama never recovered from Papa's death and now Nana and I have two deaths to mourn. Yet we're expected to be at work, on time, or risk multiple demerits.

As we walk toward the factories with the other Imps, many offer condolences. Three months ago, Papa walked with us, chatting with Mama and our friends, making everyone laugh. Making everyone better by making us feel like there was some purpose amid the boredom of our lives.

I remember his special words to me: *You have a unique purpose, Helsa. You will do great things one day.*

Great things. As an orphaned factory worker in Regalia.

The first time he said it I'd laughed—which was not the right reaction. He'd stopped walking, put his hands on my shoulders, and stared into my eyes. "Don't laugh, daughter. A father knows these things." He'd pressed a fist to his heart. "I *know* these things."

"How do you know, Papa?"

With a quick glance around he'd simply tapped two fingers to his heart—a silent gesture the Devoted share to acknowledge the Keeper, without the risk of saying his name out loud.

Where is the Keeper now? Why had he let Papa and Mama die? Forget doing great things, how am I going to survive without them?

I hear Nana sigh deeply and put an arm around her shoulders. She smiles up at me wistfully. Her eyes are sad but determined. She's the strongest woman I've ever met, yet I doubt I'll ever be like her. I think you either have courage and strength or you don't.

I don't.

The crowd splits into four groups, each headed to their assigned factory: shoes, headwear, clothing, and jewelry. Once inside, we go to our tables, where the day's sewing is waiting; bright islands of colored leathers, fabrics, and trims in the sea of gray workers.

Nana and I thread the supply of needles we'll need to hand sew the details on some custom pieces. Nearby, workers use treadle sewing machines, and beyond them, are the weavers and the cutters. As soon as the Favored vote on the top ten designs from the Reveal, all the factories will be pressured to sew hundreds of new outfits to sell to the Favored. For now, in the downtime, we make personal items for Patrons.

I spot our boss at the far end of the room as he makes his rounds. Instinctively, I tense up. Lately, Master Bru has been extra hard on me, nagging me, showing no compassion for either Papa or Mama's death. I can only guess how he'll deal with Nana and me being gone yesterday. Forget demerits, no one likes to be on Bru the Brute's bad side.

I quickly pick up a cuff and continue the embroidery along its edge.

I hear his heavy footfalls come close. I feel the air vibrate as if even *it* wants to escape. Not surprisingly, he stops by my table. He doesn't just stop, he looms.

"You're flushed, Helsa."

I hate feeling the heat in my face. I don't want him to know his effect on me. "Am I?"

"I heard you caused trouble at the Pile yesterday."

I stifle a gasp. He'd heard? "Dealing with the loss of my mother is stressful, sir." I don't dare mention Papa's death, as he'd been disgraced by exile.

Bru runs the back of his hand along the side of my head, making me flinch. "I expect you to work harder than anyone else to make up for the day you missed."

As if I had a choice? "That won't be a problem."

"It better not be." With a final squeeze of my shoulder Bru walks away to torment someone else.

He gives me the creeps.

His comments about my run-in with the Comfort-Serv freaks me out. If *he* heard, how many others know about it? Has anyone on the Council heard?

Am I in trouble?

I catch Nana's eye.

"People know," she says.

"Seems so."

"Remember what you talked about doing last night?"

"Apologizing? I'm not sure that will help."

"I'm not sure you have a choice."

I have no idea how to go about it. Beyond the huge fact that I'm at work and can't just leave, once I get to the Pile how do I find the right man? I assume the Comforts live in the buildings I'd seen, but beyond that . . . I don't know how many there are. Will I be looking for my pointy-beard Comfort in a group of ten or a hundred?

And when will I go? We have thirty minutes for lunch. The Pile is in another Ring, which means going through a guard gate. And then there's that creepy forest.

Plus, what will I say when I find him? Will an apology do any good? Will it prevent the Council from hearing about it?

Or is it already too late?

Nana suddenly taps her fingers against her table to get my attention.

Yes?

She holds up a finger. Then in a blink I watch her face go from calm to distressed. She lets out a mournful cry and slips off her chair to the floor.

I run to her, taking her into my arms. "Nana, are you —?"

She winks at me. "When I'm through go make things right." Then she goes back to awful carrying on, clearly a woman overcome with grief.

Bru runs over. "Solana! Stop it! Get a hold of yourself!"

Nana shakes her head. "I need to go home. My heart is broken. I can't work today. I just can't."

Bru hisses at her. "You have to work, Imp."

Nana clings to me, a pitiful grieving woman. "Take me home, Helsa. I need to go home!"

Understandably, we have an audience. People are clustered around. No one is working.

Bru sees what I see and makes his choice, "Fine. Go. But you're responsible for the consequences."

Nana nods and I help her up. "Can I . . . ?"

He huffs. "Get her outta here."

"Yes, sir."

Bru points at me. "I need you back fast, understand, Helsa?"

"I understand."

When Nana and I get through the exit I hear Bru's voice ring out. "Back to work!"

We hurry away from the factory, my arm supporting her. She staggers like her legs are jelly.

But when we're beyond their sight, Nana stands up straight. Strong. "Go now," she says. "Find the man."

"You'll be all right?"

"Of course. I'll go home." She squeezes my hand. "Fix it, child. I can't lose you too."

I kiss her cheek and run toward the Pile.

**

I hope the black armband will help me through the guard gate leading to the Serv Ring.

"Back again?" the guard asks.

"I miss my mother."

"So, you want to visit her dust in the Pile?"

It's not hard to let tears well up in my eyes.

"Nah, nah . . . don't get blubbery on me, Imp. I'll write you down. Move on with ya."

I feel out of place walking alone through the Serv Ring, a dab of gray in all its brownness. But no one bothers me. Is it because of the black armband, or the fact there's no reason to fear a female Imp?

The forest is threatening but I hurry through it, feeling way too much like a child afraid of the boogeyman. I'm relieved when I'm safely through its cold darkness.

I pass the spot where I'd scattered Mama's ashes, but don't linger. There's no time to waste in a bittersweet moment.

I turn back to the low buildings near the forest. One has ominous smoke curling out of its chimney.

I don't want to think about it.

I feel an uneasy stirring in my belly. Up until now my life has been ordinary and expected. Protected. Now it seems anything but.

A Comfort-Serv comes out of one of the buildings. He spots me and stops.

I stop.

He goes back inside.

For reinforcements?

I brace myself for trouble. Are Enforcer Servs nearby?

Three Servs come outside. Luckily, one of them has a familiar pointy beard. He walks toward me.

I don't know whether to walk toward him or stand my ground.

Since time is ticking, I approach him. Somehow, I manage a smile.

"Morning, Serv," I say.

He stops six feet away. His dark eyes study me. I spread my hands to let him see I'm no threat to him.

"Why are you here?" he asks.

My heart beats in my throat, making my voice stutter. "I . . . I want to apologize for being rude at my mother's funeral." I hurry on with my excuses. "It was my first funeral. I didn't know what to expect, and I guess I wanted more, but I didn't know you couldn't give more and—"

He raises a hand to stop my words. Then he looks around—even behind himself. He steps closer. "You can't say what you said, Helsa. It's too bold."

Two thoughts flash by. He remembers my name, and he isn't mad. His words are those of an advisor not an adversary.

I need to make sure he's talking about what I think he's talking about. "You mean . . . mentioning the Keeper?"

His face twitches and he nods. "I agree with you, but…"

I take a half-step toward him and lower my voice. "You believe?"

He nods, though his eyes flit nervously. "So grows the seed."

"The seed?"

He cocks his head as though my ignorance surprises him. "You have much to learn."

"I'm sure I do." Which begs the question, "How can I learn more? Can you — ?"

He shakes his head vehemently. "It's not going well here."

"Are you alone in what you . . .?"

He holds up three fingers. Three Comforts believe?

Four Comforts come out of the building, spurring the man to say, "You need to go."

Gladly. "Why did you tell on me?" I ask.

"I didn't."

"Then who? Others know. The boss in my factory knows what I said."

"*I* didn't tell him." His eyes flit toward the buildings. "Someone must have overheard."

He clearly has someone in mind.

"You *must* go."

I turn to leave, then ask, "What's your name?"

"Teel."

Two Comforts walk toward us. "Where can I go to learn?"

He whispers one word before turning away: "Oria."

What was that?

Who was that?

I hurry away.

When I'm halfway through the forest, I notice movement to my right. It doesn't sound like an animal, it sounds . . . bigger. I glance in its direction and see a tall, bald man among the trees. He stops moving and stares at me. There's something menacing about him, as if I've caught him doing something he shouldn't.

Since there's no reason that any person would willingly spend time in this place, I run away.

**

I know Bru has been watching for me because as soon as I reach my worktable, he's in my face.

"You were gone too long."

"Sorry. It took a while for Nana to calm down."

"I'm docking your pay."

It's a small price to pay.

Throughout the rest of the day a single word repeats itself in my mind: Oria.

**

After work I find Nana eagerly waiting for me at home. "Did you find him?"

"I did. I have a lot to tell you."

We sit at the table where I cut the bread and cheese while Nana slices apples. We thank the Keeper and eat our meal as I tell her about Teel and the three believers.

"I had no idea his kind believed," Nana says. "It gives me hope there are others—in all the Rings."

I can't imagine. "The Serv Ring, for certain, and maybe the Creatives Ring, but the Patrons, Favored, and Council?" I shake my head. "Their only devotion is to themselves. I can't imagine them believing."

"Don't count them out, Helsa. I don't think the Keeper will be denied."

That sounds kind of scary.

"The Devoted need more followers from all the Rings," she says.

The idea is way too daunting. "There's no way for us to find the Devoted in other Rings without exposing ourselves to danger. And where would we start looking?" I ask. "And why should we look? It's not our job."

She points a piece of bread at me. "It's everyone's job, Helsa. There are many like your father who boldly share their faith." She nods toward our neighbor's house. "Thom and Tamar, right next to us. Many a time we've heard people singing at their house."

"Which puts them in danger—and us too for being their friends. Right?"

"Yes. Probably." Nana sets the bread down. "I'm ashamed of how timid we are. We may call ourselves Devoted, but we aren't as bold as we should be."

I don't like her talking like this. "Papa was bold and look where it got him. We *know* the consequences of calling attention to ourselves. We're lucky the Council didn't exile all four of us."

Nana nods, resigned. I fear I've been too harsh. I hate seeing her discouraged and think of something to draw her out of it. "Teel said something to me I don't understand: So grows the seed."

"What does that mean?"

I shrug. "He wouldn't say. I asked him where I could learn more about the Keeper. He gave me a name: Oria."

"What's—who's that?" Nana asks.

I take a bite of an apple. "I have no idea."

"We need to ask around—discreetly," Nana says.

I'd thought about a first step. "We can ask Lieb. As a Messenger Serv he knows the names of almost everybody and has access to all the Rings."

Nana nods. "We've forgotten the most important *ask*," She points skyward.

Why do I always think about the Keeper last?

We hold hands across the table and ask the one who knows everything about the person, place, or thing called Oria, about which we know nothing.

Chapter Six

Helsa

Nana is wisely back at work. But even if we're both where we're supposed to be, my mind is elsewhere—which is a problem. First, it makes me work too slow, and secondly when I speed up to make my quota the quality of my embroidery suffers. My last stitch isn't straight, and the thread is twisted. I pull it out and try again.

I'm so focused on fixing my mistake that I don't see Bru until he stands beside me. He's too close, letting his arm brush against mine. He smells stale, like something that should be tossed in the dump heap.

He picks up the cuff I'm working on, then tosses it on the table. "Do it over."

"That's what I was doing."

"You talking back to me, girl?"

I inwardly sigh. Weariness and grief have made me reckless. "No."

"No, what?"

No, you disgusting man? "No, sir."

He points a beefy finger in my face, moving close enough that the foulness of his breath is added to his other stench. "Your problem, Helsa, is that you don't appreciate favors. I'm nothing but nice to you, letting you take your nana home yesterday."

"And I appreciate it, sir."

He leans even closer and lowers his voice. "What do I get for my trouble?"

I know what he wants. Everyone knows what Bru is capable of.

His lips brush my ear, making me pull back. "I'm not done with you, Helsa. I'll never be done with you."

Unsuccessfully, I try to suppress a shudder. I don't want him to know how scared I really am.

But he does know. And he'll use it against me.

**

I meet Lieb for lunch by the communal water pump. We try to meet every day, but there's little constancy to it. If his message deliveries take him to the other Rings, I eat alone.

I'm glad to see him. We share cheese and jerky.

"Have you ever heard of Oria?" I ask.

He shakes his head. "Is that a person?"

"Maybe. But it might be a place. Or a thing."

His blond eyebrows dip. "I don't understand."

I wish I did. "I think Oria is a person because the Comfort-Serv said the word after I told him I wanted to learn more about . . ." I look around to make sure no one is walking nearby. "You know."

"The Keeper."

I shush him. He says his name too often and too easily.

Lieb leans close. "I want to learn more too. When my mama was real sick I called out to the Keeper. I think she's better now because of him. At least I think it's because of him."

A nasty woman lived. Which leads to a question: "Why did *my* parents die?" My wonderful parents. It doesn't make sense.

Lieb shakes his head back and forth, getting agitated. "I don't know, Sa-Sa. Don't ask me such things."

I touch his arm to calm him. "You're not expected to know. No one knows."

His pale eyes light up. "Maybe Oria knows."

"Exactly. Or maybe there are answers *at* Oria, or . . ." I sigh deeply. "Did you know there are a few Comfort Servs who follow him?"

He shakes his head. "And we follow him too."

"In private. But Nana says that might not be enough."

"Some of my Messenger friends shove me around if I say his name."

I hate the thought of people hurting Lieb. "Then maybe you should save your talk of him for when *we're* alone together, all right?"

He nods and tears some jerky with his teeth.

I put a hand to my gut, feeling an unfamiliar stirring inside. "Deep down I think knowing more about him might be important—maybe it isn't yet, but it could be."

Lieb's blue eyes soften. "If it's important we should definitely find Oria."

"So, you'll do a little digging?"

"Of course I will, Sa-Sa. Anything for you."

I can imagine Lieb asking all sorts of questions to all sorts of people. I touch his arm. "If this Oria has anything to do with what we think it has to do with, then you need to be careful in your asking."

He nods more than once, yet somehow, I'm still nervous.

**

When Nana and I approach our house after work, I see a crowd gathered. Behind them I spot the brown helmets of three Enforcers.

My stomach tightens and I hold back. Did Teel turn me in? Did someone hear Lieb and I talking during lunch? Are they here to take me away?

But then I see that the Enforcers aren't gathered at our door, but at the neighbors'. They go inside.

"What's going on?" I ask someone in the crowd.

"Thom and Tamar are being arrested."

Our middle-aged neighbors are good people. "For what?"

He lowers his voice. "Unlawful Piety." He leans closer. "Having people over to talk about... you know."

Another woman leans toward me. "They were singing too."

Nana and I had just talked about their singing.

The man points toward the door. "Here they come."

The Enforcers come out of the house, leading the husband and wife, hands tied in front.

"Move!" the Enforcers yell at the crowd.

"Clear a path!"

The couple is led away. I expect people to call out in support, but every voice is silent. Fearfully silent. Then instead of words they all bow their heads and tap their fingers to their hearts.

Nana catches up with me. She's winded. "Why have they been arrested?"

"Unlawful Piety."

"Oh dear."

"Will they be exiled?" I ask.

"Depends on the mood of the Council." Nana takes my arm. "We should get inside."

I hurry in, close the door, and stand with my back against it. "Someone must have turned them in."

Nana puts a hand to her chest. "Which means they could turn us in."

I hope not. "We don't sing. We don't have people over."

Nana shrugs. "The Council Directives clearly state there shall be no worship of any deity. Your papa paid with his life for breaking that rule."

"Maybe *we* shouldn't even talk about him anymore."

Nana bites her lip. "It certainly would be safer."

"Exactly. So let's—"

"But we need him now more than ever."

We sit at the table. None of this made sense. So what if people believed in some... whatever the Keeper was. "I don't understand why it hurts Regalia if we believe in something beyond the Council."

"Because there *is* nothing beyond the Council. And remember one of their mottos is 'Always Something New'. The Keeper is old. Very old. From the Before Time."

"Which doesn't mean he's real."

"Which doesn't mean he's not." Nana takes a cleansing breath then squeezes my hand. "I know what to do." She bows her head and begins to pray.

I suppose it can't hurt.

**

My sleep is cut short when Nana shakes me awake. "What? What's wrong?"

She puts a finger to her lips and sits on the side of my narrow bed — fully clothed. "We need to get into Thom and Tamar's house."

"Why?"

"To rescue their Relic."

I'd heard about Relics from the Before Time but had never seen one. "What is it exactly?"

"A piece of paper. Tamar let me read it."

"What did it say?"

Nana waves my question away. "We need to sneak into their house and find it, to keep it safe."

"Now?"

"We can't go when it's light."

I push back the covers and get dressed. "Do you know where it is?"

"I know where it *was*. Let's go."

We peek out the window. The street is empty and dark. The moon casts odd shadows that make me want to stay inside.

But this is a time to tap into Nana's courage — or perhaps her stupidity — for we're about to retrieve something that can get us arrested. Or worse.

We go outside but keep close to our house as we hurry to their door. We slip inside. Their curtains are open, allowing us some much-appreciated light.

Nana makes a beeline for a bench at the table. "Help me."

I help her turn it over. It looks normal.

Nana runs her hand along the rough wood, then backtracks. "Knife," she whispers. I find a knife in the kitchen. Nana pries off a thin piece of wood held in place with two tiny nails. Inside the space is a small piece of paper, folded in half.

"Thank the Keeper it's still here," Nana says. Then she holds up a finger and freezes.

I freeze too because I hear a noise outside.

Then nothing. A dog barks in the distance. We both exhale.

Nana hands me the Relic and pushes the wood cover-piece back in place. I help her turn the bench over and put the knife back where I'd found it. After a quick check outside, we're home.

My heart pulses wildly and I'm out of breath from fear more than exertion. "We did it."

"We did." She holds out her hand, wanting the Relic.

Although I haven't read one word, I'm reluctant to give it up. I've never held anything that is precious enough to be hidden away. But I hand it over.

Nana holds it reverently. She unfolds it and reads: "'I am the Keeper of my sheep. I know them and they know me.'"

I'm disappointed. "That's it?"

"It's a lot." Nana refolds the Relic. "We can't discuss it now." She looks around the room. "Where should we hide it?"

I know the perfect place. I move my bed away from the wall and pry up a plank of the wood floor. "Here. Give it to me."

Nana peers at the hole. "What do you have in there?"

I haven't looked in a long time. "Just kid stuff." I set the Relic inside, put the board back, then scoot my bed to its place. "I won't let anything happen to it. I promise."

Nana cups my cheek with her hand. "I believe you. Sleep now."

It's a nice thought but I know it's impossible.

Chapter Seven

Cashlin

Marli and I have one task this morning: choose something for me to wear to my trial.

We look through the rows of colorful caftans in my closet. "How am I supposed to dress to show that I deserve to be the Premier Patron but also imply I respect the rules of Regalia?"

"You can't be too flamboyant," Marli says. "Perhaps a pattern with more subdued colors? Your navy and royal-blue caftan?"

It seems like a good choice. I depend on Marli to know my wardrobe better than I do.

She chooses navy boots—vetoing my choice of the royal blue, saying they are too flashy.

My hair is a problem. To look my best it needs to hang free in curls or waves. Yet both styles make me look *too* pretty. Sensual. And pulled tightly back is trying too hard to look serious. We settle on a loose, low bun. My makeup is tastefully—minimally—applied.

I stand before the mirror. "Do I look trustworthy? Innocent?" I amend my words. "Innocent of any crime?"

"Definitely," Marli says.

I'm not so certain but I've run out of time. When I take a step toward the door, I notice Marli hesitates. "What?"

"I'd like . . . oh dear. I'm nervous about asking this, but—"

"Just ask."

"Can I pray for you?"

I am not enthused. She knows my view of the whole Keeper situation. Why does she keep pressing? "I'm already being tried before the Council. I don't want to risk a charge of Unlawful Piety too."

She sighs. "I understand."

Her face is heavy with disappointment. She, who's done so much for me, who is testifying for me.

"I suppose," I say. "If you think it will help."

"It will," Marli says. "I know it will."

When she bows her head I do the same.

She implores the Keeper to watch over me, protect me from all evil, and grant me great mercy and favor.

As she talks I can't help but be mesmerized by her words of hope and trust. I don't understand why such encouraging words would be against the law. And for her to reveal her faith, knowing the consequences astounds me. But it also does something else: her courage gives me courage.

A knock on my bedroom door stops her prayer.

"The carriage is here, miss." Dom says from the other side of the door.

"Thank you. We'll be right down." I suddenly wish Marli had been more discreet. "I hope Dom didn't hear your words."

Marli smiles. "There's no need to fear Dom."

Oh. Really? "I do thank you for the comforting words, Marli. I may not believe the same as you, but I'll take whatever help I can get."

"You may not believe in the Keeper, but he believes in you."

I find her words rather unnerving. The thought of some deity knowing about me...

"You look confused," she says.

"I guess I am. Why would the Keeper believe in me—in someone who has no intention of ever believing in them?

She cocks her head, thinking. "I don't really know. Love, I guess? Unconditional love?"

I have never experienced such a thing. It's rather unfathomable.

But it is also a mystery for another day.

**

We ride in the carriage toward my trial in the Council Tower.

As we wait at the guard gate to enter the next Ring, I realize we are both entering new territory. No one ever enters the Council Rings for a good reason. Like me, they only come when they're summoned.

I hear the driver talk to the guard and hear the word "trial." He lets us through, but I see him peering at me with a stern face, as if I'm already condemned.

The gate closes behind us, and we are immediately shocked by the change in atmosphere.

"It's so quiet," Marli whispers.

So quiet I hear birds singing.

On our right are shops, but on the left is a tree-lined street lining a row of large mansions with lush grounds covered with flowers and greenery.

Marli points out the carriage window. "They're twice as big as your house."

"At least. This must be where the Council members live," I say. I'd like to take a tour of the entire Ring but I'm sure the Council wouldn't appreciate curious tourists.

The carriage moves on, yet the last gate is different from all the others. Its doors aren't a solid barrier like the gates we know. This one is created from iron, designed with swirls and curves, almost a piece of art. It's not so much a keep-out gate as an appreciate-where-you're-going gate. We *know* this gate will lead to somewhere important.

Like a trial where my life is on the line.

Through the gate we see the massive Council Tower. I've caught glimpses of the top of it from my Ring, but it's more impressive in person. It's a circular building of white stucco. The first story is the widest, while the subsequent two stories are smaller, culminating in a spire at the top. It's cold and hard. Domineering and menacing. **I shiver at the power it exudes.**

"There aren't any windows except at the very top," Marli says.

I lean forward to see. The view from the spire must be magnificent. Yet how odd **not to have any windows on the other levels.** "It's like once you're inside, you're trapped." My throat tightens. "This does not give me confidence."

"And where are the people?" Marli asks.

As we turn onto the street that rings the Tower we don't see any pedestrians at all. I only spot one other carriage. We drive to the left, around the building. Where is the entrance?

Then I see a break in the Tower's whiteness. The carriage turns into an opening that takes us downward into a space below ground. Below the building. **But it isn't dark. There is light everywhere, a strange intense glowing.**

"I've never seen lights like these," I say.

"There's no flame," Marli says.

"How can there be no flame?"

"It's magical," Marli adds.

I see it another way. "It's mean."

"Mean?"

"If these kind of lights are available, why don't the rest of us have them?"

There's no time to discuss the issue as the carriage stops and we step out. Passengers exit other carriages. It seems appropriate that all of this is done underground. We, who are accused of marring the perfection of Regalia society, are brought to trial out of sight. It reinforces the seriousness of the charges against me; a warning that such imperfect acts are not allowed and will not be tolerated.

I'm done for.

An Enforcer Serv approaches. He wears a breastplate and helmet over his brown uniform. "Citizen Cashlin?"

I notice he doesn't say Patron. "That's me," I say, then gesture toward Marli. "This woman is testifying on my behalf."

He nods. "Follow me."

We are led inside the Tower and follow a corridor that is populated with a succession of doors. The Enforcer opens one marked *Nine*, and we enter a plain room with a small table and four chairs.

Nerwhether sits facing us. I'd longed to see a friendly face, but knowing he is all I have is not encouraging. I hadn't chosen him. He'd been appointed to me. There is a difference.

The Enforcer leaves us, closing the door.

"Sit, ladies."

We do as we are told. I sit to Nerwhether's right. "What now?" I ask. I'm used to directing people to implement *my* plans, so asking for direction is foreign.

"Now, we wait to be summoned." He checks a list in front of him. "As the door indicates, we are number nine on the docket."

"Out of how many?" I ask.

"Twelve."

"That can't be good." I'm used to going first.

"It's not. The members of the Council of Worthiness tend to get cranky at the end of the day. So nine is iffy. At least we're not last."

It's not even a small comfort at a time I long for comfort. Yet even though I don't like his answer, I have to ask, "What are my chances?"

He hesitates. "I dislike giving numbers. Let's just say I will do my best, and both of you must do yours."

Marli nods. I'm not sure what our "best" entails.

"Let me run through how this will go," he says.

Good. I want as few surprises as possible.

"The Council decided that you and Quan will be tried together."

"Together? We're not the same. We're not equals. I assumed he'd be questioned, but I never imagined . . . I don't really know what I imagined."

"They have charged both of you with the same crime."

"That's absurd. *I* didn't do anything wrong. It's all on him."

"That's what I have to bring out in the trial. May I continue?"

I would like to argue the point more, but nod.

"Both parties will be led in with their solicitors." He looks at Marli. "Witnesses will wait in the hall outside the Council Chamber so as not to be influenced by testimony."

"Is my brother here? And LaBelle?"

"They are."

I feel relief, even though I'm not sure Amar's testimony will help me.

"Is there anything we *shouldn't* say?" Marli asks.

Nerwhether seems pleased with her question. "Don't embellish. Answer simply. Tell the truth. Above all, please don't imply or say that there was *any* personal relationship between Quan and Cashlin."

"There wasn't," Marli says. But she looks troubled.

I know she doesn't want to hurt my case, but will she accidentally say something that doesn't help?

He looks at his watch. "If you'll excuse me, I have another client whose case comes up before yours."

The fact I'm not his only client on this particular day adds to my worry.

He motions to Marli. "Come with me. I'll take you to the witness waiting area."

I feel a surge of panic. I'm going to be left alone? I feel like a needy child and want to beg her to stay.

But I have no say in the matter, and she leaves with Nerwhether.

The silence of the room closes around me, pressing in like invisible hands. I feel extremely small, an ant in an enormous anthill. I pull the sleeves of my caftan over my hands and cross my arms.

I'm not used to being alone. Even in my bedroom the Servs are close by. A driver takes me where I need to go. And once I leave the carriage in the Favored Ring, my fans surround me. At all times, help is but a moment away.

Except now. My only friend in the entire building has been led away. My solicitor is busy defending someone else. If I scream, Enforcer Servs will rush in because it's their job to keep me contained and controlled.

I look at the ceiling, remembering the comfort of Marli's words this morning. I feel an inner nudge, fight it for a moment, then say in a whisper, "Keeper? I'm alone and scared. If you're real, I really could use your help. I feel so discouraged—"

Suddenly the door opens and an Enforcer Serv walks in.

I stand up. "Is it time?"

He looks confused. "You're not Citizen Gleis."

"No, I'm not."

He looks down at the paper in his hand. "I have a message for room nine. Gleis."

"This is room nine. Cashlin."

His blonde eyebrows rise. "As in *the* Cashlin, the Patron?"

"That's me."

For a moment he looks pleased, but his smile fades. "If you're not Gleis, then where is he?"

"I certainly don't know."

He looks at the number on the door, then at his note. He holds the paper closer. "Wait. I can't believe this . . . it says room two, not nine. How could I get that wrong?" He tries to scratch his head, but the helmet gets in the way. "Sorry for the intrusion, Citizen Cashlin." He turns toward the door, then does a doubletake. "It isn't my place, but I need to ask: are you all right? When I came in you seemed —"

"Scared to death?"

"Quite the opposite. You seemed oddly calm."

Me, calm? I'd been asking the Keeper for encouragement when he opened the door . . . "I was *trying* to feel calm."

He nods. "It's a noble goal. But it's normal to feel scared — and *most* are. I mean, who wouldn't be?"

"Most are . . . except?"

He glances at the open door and lowers his voice. "Except for the ones being tried for 'Unlawful Piety.' I don't know what it is with those people — actually, I can guess but . . ." He seems to study my expression to see which side I'm on. "Those who are the Devoted are always peaceful about their trials. Calm. Like you."

I'm not sure I want this Enforcer to think I'm one of *them*. "You simply caught me in a calm moment."

"Good. Keep it up. By the way, I'm Xian. It was nice to meet you, Patron Cashlin."

"You too."

He hesitates as he opens the door. "I'm almost glad I got the wrong room."

So am I.

His face grows serious. "I wish you the best of luck."

"Thank you."

With a nod he leaves.

What just happened?

Actually, the evidence was clear. Not only had the Keeper calmed me, but he'd also sent encouragement. And Xian telling me about the calm attitude of those who were called the Devoted? Had I been like one of them by calling out to him — this one time?

I shake my head. I know nothing about the Keeper, which means he has no reason to listen to my pleas for help. I'm sure he has better things to do and is certainly busy taking care of his own. I hear daily stories of members of the Devoted being arrested and exiled for speaking in public or meeting secretly.

Enough of this train of thought. I have enough trouble in my life. I certainly don't need to purposely bring more upon myself by having anything to do with *him*.

And meeting Xian is simply a nice coincidence, nothing arranged by some superior being.

And yet . . . I feel the need to acknowledge the Keeper one last time, just in case. I look upward and keep it short, "Thank you."

Then I quickly look away lest he mistake my one-time interest with devotion.

Chapter Eight

Cashlin

My time has come. I'm both ready and panicked; brave yet terrified.

I follow Nerwhether into the Chamber of the Council of Worthiness. It's surprisingly small. There are eleven chairs for the Council placed in two rows across the front. A single chair sits alone to their left. The chairs are flanked by two Enforcer Servs, standing at attention. One of them is Xian. Our eyes meet for the briefest instant. I'm glad he's here. Though not a friend, I sense he isn't a foe.

There are two tables facing the Council, each with two chairs. I have to pass in front of Quan and his solicitor to reach my place. He smiles smugly. My nerves rattle. I'd like to reach out and slap him. All of this is his fault.

As soon as we reach our seats, Xian calls out, "All rise!"

Quan and his solicitor stand as a side door opens and the Council enters, all wearing black caftans. Five women and six men. I know little about them—I couldn't list them by name. I've never wasted two moments of my life thinking about them.

Until now, when our paths unfortunately cross.

One Council member sits in the middle seat of the upper row. He has silver hair, eyeglasses perched on the tip of his nose, and has a commanding aura about him. Is he the main judge? Should I smile at him? It doesn't seem appropriate, which unnerves me even more. I'm used to my smile and charm having power. Today they are moot incidentals, as worthless as glitter on sand.

After the noise of movement fades, he confirms his authority by speaking. "Good afternoon, citizens."

We return the greeting.

He looks at some papers, then removes his glasses and looks directly at Quan. "Citizen Quan. I'd say it's nice to see you again, but in truth we are weary of having you in our presence. What's this make? Four times?"

"Five," he says. His solicitor nudges him, and he adds, "Your honor."

Quan has been on trial five times? I had no idea.

The judge waves his hand. "Well then, Solicitor Corton. Let's get on with it."

Quan's solicitor calls him to the single chair and begins his questioning. "Thank you for coming today, Citizen Quan."

As if either of us have a choice?

"Let's dive into the issue at hand. Did you kiss Citizen Cashlin during a Reveal?"

Quan's smugness is gone and he wears a mask of contrition. "I must confess, I did." He looks in my direction. "At her request."

I'm not surprised by his lie, but it stirs anger in me.

"Please explain."

"Cashlin choreographs every detail of her Reveals. She instructed me to kiss her at that particular point in the choreography."

I'm fuming inside. Nerwhether touches my arm to keep me from bursting out of my chair. I feel completely helpless. I might as well be wearing an actual muzzle.

"Can you explain why she pushed you away?"

He grins. "She was acting, playing hard to get. She said it would add drama. She's a good actor."

He's the good actor. I can't believe what I'm hearing.

"So, you were only following her directions?"

"Exactly."

"Did you have a previous romantic relationship with Citizen Cashlin?"

"I must admit . . . yes. Again, at her request."

This is too much. I can't stand for the lies to grow beyond the kiss. "That's a lie!" I call out.

The judge points at me. "Quiet! You'll get your turn."

I feel the walls closing in. My heart is going to burst out of my chest. I'm going to faint and have to remind myself to breathe.

"When did this relationship begin?"

"Two Reveals previous, when Cashlin first chose me as one of her dancers." He sighs dramatically. "Again, I must confess it was difficult not to succumb to her advances during our many rehearsals."

"But eventually, you did?"

"I did."

I grab Nerwhether's arm and squeeze it. He stills my hand.

"Did Citizen Cashlin promise you any type of compensation in exchange for your . . . affection?"

He puts on a forlorn face. "I liked my job. I wanted to keep my job."

"So, she threatened you with dismissal if you didn't . . . ?"

"Yes."

I'm ready to explode—or throw a chair at him.

"Are you aware that it's unlawful to have an intimate relationship with a citizen from another Ring?"

He hangs his head and nods. "I do."

"Since the Reveal have you had any additional contact with Citizen Cashlin?"

He nods again. "She sent me a note, wanting us to get together."

Note? What is he talking about?

"Do you have that note with you?"

"I don't. I destroyed it."

How convenient.

"No further questions." Corton turns to Nerwhether and nods.

Good. Now it's our turn.

Nerwhether moves between our table and Quan, yet to the side enough so I can see the cretin.

"Citizen Quan, how many private liaisons did you and Citizen Cashlin enjoy?"

His grin reveals the Quan I know. "Dozens."

"Where did these alleged trysts take place?"

He hesitates. "At her house. At my house."

"I see. And where do you live?"

"In the Serv Ring, of course."

Nerwhether retrieves two papers from the table. "Here is a list I had transcribed from the Server gate of all who came and went for the past two years. Your name is listed."

"Of course it is. I live there."

"And here is a list of all those who passed through the Patron gate."

Quan squirms in his chair.

Ha! Gotcha!

Nerwhether peruses the list. "Actually, your name *is* on the list. Ten times."

Quan looks relieved.

"Before today how many times have you been in this Council Chambers, Citizen Quan?"

He lets out a breath. "Five."

"Indeed. And here I see five notations of your name going into the Patron Ring on your way to the Council Ring and five notations leaving. Ten notations. Period. Yet you say you had dozens of liaisons with Citizen Cashlin in the Patron Ring?"

Quan's mouth moves before words come out. "While I was going through I stopped at her house."

"Hmm," Nerwhether says. "I see." He strolls to the left, then returns to his place. "I find another thing extremely odd: Citizen Cashlin's name never appears on the list passing into the Serv Ring."

Silence.

Nerwhether continues. "Actually, her name never appears on a list passing through the Implementor Ring *or* the Serv Ring—meaning she has never visited any of the two outer rings. Ever."

More silence.

"How do you explain that, Citizen Quan?"

Quan blinks too much. He pushes himself straighter in the chair. "I was mistaken. I *wanted* to meet with her at my house in the Serv Ring, but she acted snobby about it and said she wouldn't demean herself by going there. So, we only met at her house. Those times I'm on the list."

"I see." Nerwhether gets another piece of paper. "Here is a statement from the House Servs that have worked for Citizen Cashlin for the past two years. None of them have ever seen you there, plus they state that there have been *no* Entertainment Servs in her home. Ever. Which includes you, Citizen Quan."

"That's easy to explain," he says. "She has money. She paid them to say that."

"I see." Nerwhether takes a moment, then says, "I'm done with this witness." He returns to his seat beside me.

Quan also returns to his seat, looking a little less cocky.

"Do you have another witness, Solicitor Corton?" the judge asks.

"I do. Citizen Goff."

The other dancer from the Reveal takes the witness chair. He looks petrified.

So much so that the judge says, "Don't be nervous. Just tell the truth."

Yes. Please do.

Corton begins the questioning. "You had rehearsals with Citizen Quan and Citizen Cashlin for this last Reveal?"

"Yeah . . . yes. Your honor."

Corton smiles. "I am not 'your honor'. Only he is." He points at the judge.

"Oh. Okay. Sorry."

"Was Citizen Cashlin attracted to your fellow dancer?"

Goff hesitates. He looks at Quan. "Sort of. Maybe. She was nice to both of us."

"So, you had a relationship with her too?"

His eyes grow large. "No! No. Nothing like that. She was friendly. Professional. She's good at what she does."

"She's good at seducing those beneath her?"

Goff sits up straighter in the chair. "I didn't say that."

"Has she ever made advances toward you?"

He shakes his head adamantly. "No. Never."

"So, she was only inappropriate with Citizen Quan?"

"Yes. I mean no."

I feel sorry for him.

"Were *you* aware of the choreographed kiss?"

He looks uneasy. "Quan said to be ready, something was going to happen."

"Which it did."

"Which it did. So when he motioned me to pick her up on our shoulders, I did."

"You followed Citizen Quan's instructions, while he in turn, followed Citizen Cashlin's instructions."

"I don't know about that but—"

"I'm done here."

The judge says, "Solicitor Nerwhether? Do you have any questions for this witness?"

"A few, your honor." He approaches Goff. "Other than the kiss on stage, did you ever witness any intimate contact between Citizens Quan and Cashlin?"

"None."

"Did you have knowledge of any extracurricular intimate contact between them?"

"None." He glances at Quan. "Not until after the kiss when Quan started talking like they were . . . you know."

"Lovers?"

"Yeah. That."

"This was before Citizen Quan learned he was in trouble?"

He hesitates, as if remembering. "And after."

"Did you ever hear Citizen Cashlin give any instructions about a kiss—and the rest of the choreography that went with it?"

"No, I didn't."

"Thank you. I appreciate your honesty, Citizen Goff."

Goff is visibly relieved and quickly leaves the courtroom. I worry that the witness experience will be just as hard on Marli, Amar, and LaBelle.

"Any more witnesses, Solicitor Corton?

"Just one. We call Citizen Rowan."

I gasp. I haven't spoken with Rowan since the kiss. What can he have to say against me?

When he sits in the witness chair, he doesn't even look at me. Which isn't good.

"What is your relationship with Citizen Cashlin?" Corton asks.

"We are engaged to be engaged."

"Why aren't you fully engaged?"

He shrugs. "No reason. At least none before all . . . this."

"But since all . . . this?"

Rowan looks at his lap, then at Corton. "I wasn't happy when I heard about the kiss, read about it in the paper, and heard all the hoopla. Then, when I found out about the charges here . . ." He shakes his head.

"Are you rethinking your engagement?"

"Of course. It's the smart thing to do. I mean if Cashlin is convicted of anything, then . . . that changes everything."

So much for any inkling of love between us.

"I understand how betrayed you must feel," Corton says sympathetically. "Do you believe Citizen Cashlin and Quan are guilty?"

He glances at the judge, then away. "I . . . I don't know. That's up to the Council to decide."

"Thank you, Citizen Rowan."

The judge looks at Nerwhether. "Questions for the witness?"

Nerwhether stands. Had he known Rowan would be called?

"None, your honor."

I'm relieved. I don't need to hear Rowan cross-examined about how little he thinks of me. He walks out of the courtroom without even glancing at me.

Coward.

"Solicitor Corton?" the judge says.

"I rest my case."

I'm shocked. That's all he has? Amar implied he was being called as a witness—maybe for the other side. And we wanted to call LaBelle and Marli.

"Your turn, Solicitor Nerwhether," the judge says.

He stands. "I call Citizen Cashlin to the stand."

Despite my innocence, my stomach rolls. My legs feel weak and wobbly as I walk the short distance from here to there.

Nerwhether stands before me and offers a supportive smile. "At any time did you have an intimate relationship with Citizen Quan?"

"I did not. Ever. Never."

"Did you choreograph a kiss into your Reveal?"

"I did not. I was totally taken by surprise. And I didn't like it one bit. That's why I pushed him away."

"Was that an act?"

"It was an instantaneous, horrified reaction."

"What did Citizen Quan do after you were off stage?"

"He followed me into my dressing room and tried to kiss me again. I threw him out." I didn't want to mention Amar.

"Were you aware of the law against intimate relationships between the Rings?"

"Of course. I wouldn't do such a thing. I was—I still am—nearly engaged."

Nerwhether cringes the slightest bit at my last statement. I shouldn't have brought Rowan up again.

He runs with it. "Before seeing him here today, have you had any contact with Rowan since the incident?"

"I have not. I sent a note to him, asking him to come see me. I longed for his support."

"Sadly, it's obvious he is unwilling to support you."

"Sadly so."

"Do you still love him?"

Love? We'd never spoken about love. It was not a requirement of our marriage. "I would still marry him, yes." I have no other options.

Nerwhether quickly moves on. "Have you ever been to the outer two Rings?"

"Never."

"Have you ever hosted Citizen Quan at your home?"

"Never."

"Thank you." He returns to his seat.

I feel relief at being halfway through my questioning. But the worst is yet to come.

"Solicitor Corton?" the judge says.

He stands in front of his table, so I have a view of Quan when I look at him. "Who is in charge of the details of your Reveals?"

"I am."

"You choose the music, choose the dancers. Create the choreography."

"I do."

"You are currently the Premier Patron, are you not?"

"I am."

"Which means you're good at your job."

"I try my best."

"Are you a good actor, Citizen Cashlin?"

I guess where he's going with the question. "I am a good performer. A good marketer of the goods designed for me." I glance at the Council. "I take my duties very seriously—for the good of Regalia."

"Is it in your power to force anyone to break the law?"

It's an odd question. "I wouldn't even thinking of doing that. Nor would I break it myself." I look at the judge. "I did *not* break it."

"You didn't answer my question. Is it in your power to force anyone to break the law?"

I wasn't sure how to answer. "I use whatever power my position holds to do my job to the best of my ability. In Regalia everyone has their assigned function—which I think works well. As such I have never used my position to try to influence anyone to break a law. If they do so, it's their own choice."

He blinks at me, as though he's uncertain whether I've helped or hurt his cause. "Thank you, Citizen Cashlin." He sits down.

I look at Nerwhether. He's smiling.

"Hey," Quan says loudly. "Question her more."

Corton shakes his head. "We have no more questions, your honor."

"Very well," the judge says. "You may step down."

Have my answers been convincing?

Nerwhether begins to stand to call the next witness, but there's a stir among the Council members. After conferring with the Councils on either side of him, the judge asks, "Solicitor Nerwhether. We see three more witnesses on your list. What facts are they going to support?"

"They will testify as to Citizen Cashlin's state of mind after the kiss and the negative publicity. They will also testify as to her unimpeachable character."

"Will they offer any new evidence?"

He looks at me. I have no idea what he'd planned for their questioning. "No, your honor."

"Then for the sake of expediency, we shall end this hearing. You may all withdraw. We will call you in when we have a verdict."

I follow Nerwhether into the corridor where we walk to the left, while Quan and Corton walk to the right. Xian and the other Enforcer also exit and guard the courtroom door. We exchange a glance. He winks at me.

Why does a single wink from a near stranger give me confidence?

Nerwhether and I sit on a bench.

"Do they often cut the hearing short like that?" I ask quietly.

"Occasionally. When they feel they've heard enough."

"Does it bode well for me?"

"Most definitely. They believe what you said and don't need corroboration." He touches my arm. "I wouldn't worry."

I appreciate his encouragement but find it hard to be fully confident.

I glance to my right and see Quan arguing with his solicitor. From what I'd heard *he* had reason to worry.

"I'm glad Marli and the others didn't have to go through this."

"I'm sure they appreciate it too," Nerwhether says.

I take multiple deep breaths, trying to calm my racing heart. Eleven people of power—whom I don't know and who don't know me—are deciding my fate. And yet . . . I can't imagine the trial going any better. Quan's lies were blatant and refuted by facts. His cocky attitude was grating to me — and hopefully to the Council. I'd told the truth. There was little more I could do.

I finally find a steady rhythm to my breathing. Surely everything will be all —

There's a faint knock and Xian and the other Enforcer open the door.

"It's time," Nerwhether says.

"So quickly?"

"It happens. Follow me."

We return to our seats in the courtroom. The Council sits solemnly before us.

"Will the defendants stand."

We stand with our solicitors. A glance shows me that Quan is cocky no more.

"We, the Council of Worthiness, as to the charge of 'Illegal, Immoral Relational Public Display between Rings' have determined that Citizen Cashlin is not guilty."

I squeal and hug Nerwhether, who quickly shushes me.

"As to the other defendant who faces the same charges, we have determined that Citizen Quan is guilty."

"What?" Quan shouts. "You can't do that!"

The judge ignores him. "Because you have appeared before this Council five times — and been found guilty in each case — we sentence you to exile in the Swirling Desert."

Quan collapses onto his chair. I gasp, unbelieving.

"Isn't that rather harsh, your honor?" Corton asks.

"He has acquired twelve demerits. Exile is our only choice. It will be carried out in three days' time. What was, was. What is, is." With that the judge and the rest of the Council file out.

Quan is crying. I feel bad for him. "A sentence of death, for kissing me?" I say to Nerwhether.

"His other offenses were also serious. He just can't seem to stop himself from pushing the boundaries of our laws." He ushers me to the chamber door.

As I pass Quan, I hesitate. He looks up at me, his face stricken. "I'm so sorry it turned out this way," I say.

He scowls with utter hatred in his eyes. "I bet you are."

I leave the courtroom, shaken. I'm not used to having people hate me.

"Cashlin!"

Marli runs toward me. "They said I don't have to testify."

"You don't. I'm glad you don't."

Amar and LaBelle join us.

"What's the verdict?" Amar asks. "What's going to happen to you?"

"Nothing. They declared me innocent. I *am* innocent."

"I'm glad," LaBelle says. "I saw how upset you were after the Reveal."

"Thanks," I say. "And thank you for being willing to testify."

"We didn't have a choice," Amar says.

Marli looks troubled. "If you've been found innocent, why do you seem upset?"

"They sentenced Quan to exile."

Everyone gasps and shakes their heads.

"Death," LaBelle says. "That's harsh."

"I'll be glad to see him go," Amar says. "At least you won't have to worry about the likes of him again."

I don't want to talk about it. I look at Nerwhether. "Can we go home now?"

"You may." He points at Xian, who is closing the courtroom doors. "Please escort these people to a carriage."

"Of course, Solicitor." To us he says, "This way."

Xian walks beside me. "Congratulations."

"Thank you."

"Your solicitor is good. Having the records from the gates was brilliant."

"Yes, it was."

"I'm sorry about the dancer."

"Me too. The judgment seems cruel."

"Not really."

"You know about his other offenses?"

"I've been in court every time."

"Can you tell me what they are?"

He looks around to see who's close. The others walk behind us and are busy talking. "I suppose it doesn't matter now. He's been here for stealing, not paying his taxes, assault, and one other I can't think of."

"It makes me feel better that his sentence was for an accumulation of crimes, not just this one."

"I don't agree with the law you were charged with at all." He lowers his voice. "I think people should be able to choose who they want to have a relationship with, no matter what Ring they're from." He pauses, then adds, "Don't you?"

He obviously isn't talking about us, yet the way he says it makes it seem personal.

"I do. I agree with you. All in all, arranged relationships don't work well."

"As with your almost-fiancé?"

I nod. "I never imagined that he'd turn on me."

"It's good you know the truth about him before you marry." We reach the doors leading outside. "You deserve better." He steps forward and raises a hand, calling a carriage.

When it arrives, he opens the door and helps all four of us inside. Before he shuts the door, he says, "I wish you the best, Citizen Cashlin. May we meet again."

The door closes and the carriage moves on.

"*May* we meet again?" Amar asks. "What does that mean? He's a Serv. Don't get yourself in trouble again, sister."

"He was very forward," LaBelle says. "Have you known him long?"

"I met him today." I look out the window to hide the happiness I feel. "He encouraged me when I needed encouragement." I want to mention that the Keeper had sent him but I'm wise enough not to share.

"Tell us everything that happened in the trial," Amar says.

That I can talk about.

**

I sit in the dark of my bedroom and look out at the quiet night. It's hard to reconcile my awakening this morning as being in the same day as me sitting here tonight. I started the day a prisoner of fear and worry, and end it a free, exonerated woman.

There are still many unknowns in my future. Rowan, for one. But oddly, his betrayal makes my decision *not* to marry him easier. Yet I have no idea whom I will marry. It might be fodder for another scandal, yet since we weren't officially engaged I refuse to think about it. I refuse to let Rowan ruin my victory and the elation I feel after surviving the trial.

And *not* being exiled.

Poor Quan. Yet too quickly I push thoughts of him aside. He caused all of this. I'm not implying he's getting what he deserves — for I don't wish exile on anyone — but he did make a string of bad decisions. The Council had no choice.

I stretch my arms overhead, enjoying the pull of my muscles. To fully celebrate I decide on a long bath that will lead to a long, restful, and worry-free sleep.

As if anticipating my needs Marli knocks and enters.

"Ah," I say as I stand. "I was thinking of a bath."

"It's a good idea to wash off the day in preparation for the parade tomorrow. I'll fill it for you."

Reality hits me like a slap. While I've been consumed with the trial and wallowing in my victory, the world has continued its scheduled course. Tomorrow is the final day of marketing—the most important day that involves a parade through the Favored Ring followed by the all-important vote.

"You forgot, didn't you?" Marli says.

"I did. Completely."

"It's understandable."

Understandable but unacceptable. Marketing is a huge part of my job. It determines my status and my identity.

Marli heads to the bathroom and turns on the water. Then she sets out fresh night clothes.

"I'll finish filling it," I say.

"Are you sure? I'll stay . . ."

"No, go on. I'm good."

She sprinkles lavender bath salts in the water and leaves me alone.

I stand in front of the tub, a bit concerned that I'd completely forgotten about tomorrow. It's not like me. I'm usually in control and am always detail-oriented. This mental celebration of my victory will mean nothing if I lose tomorrow.

Suddenly I wonder what kind of reception I'll get with the other Patrons and the Favored. Will they boo and harass me, not caring that I'd been tried on a bogus charge? Or will they welcome me back as victorious?

I need to look victorious.

The new thought takes hold, and I shut off the bath water and head to my closet. The thought of the snake costume disgusts me. If I want to look victorious my snake outfit is anything but. I know, with a certainty that surprises me, that I have to wear something completely different.

But such a thing isn't done. What's worn in the Reveal is always carried through the full three days of marketing.

Of which I've already missed two.

Yet what can they do to me? Automatically assign me to last place? If I wear the snake costume last place is a certainty.

My thoughts spin into new territory. Perhaps my trial victory has emboldened me beyond my usual confidence. I'm always self-assured and daring in my Reveals, but this time more is at stake. I need to bend the boundaries of what's been done before.

It's a matter of survival. I have to take the chance.

Frantically, I look through my previous costumes. I don't want to wear something that's already won but want to give an outfit a second chance.

Just as *I* am getting a second chance.

Then it comes to me. I know the outfit I want to wear—my first offering. It had earned the eleventh spot out of twenty. As only the top ten are produced, no one in all of Regalia has it in their closet.

I retrieve its headdress from a shelf—a gold halo crown. I stand in front of the mirror and place it on my head. It's definitely the crown of a victor. I get out the dress that goes with it: a purple velvet dress with a circle skirt, along with purple patent leather heels with satin bows at the back of the heel. There is one other accessory: intricate gold bands that cover my arms from wrist to elbow.

It's flashy. It's in your face. It will show any naysayers that I am not slinking back to join the marketing tour—pun intended. The Council of Worthiness didn't break me—and neither can they.

I place my purple wonder on the ottoman.

With a deep breath and a sigh, I end the day feeling triumphant once again.

This will work.

It has to.

Chapter Nine

Cashlin

The day of the parade starts in the Dome. I'm excited to present my new ensemble to the other Patrons, to the Favored, to the reporters who will share the highlights of the day, and to everyone who cares or doesn't care. Whether the results are good or bad, I am determined to do it my way.

Of course, when Marli brings in breakfast, she is the first to see my outfit, all set out to take with me. "You wore this a long time ago, yes?"

"It was my first Reveal."

She runs her fingers along the intricate detail of the halo crown. "It's impressive. But why are you bringing it out now?"

"I'm wearing it today. Instead of the snake outfit."

Her head jerks back. "Can you do that?"

"I'm not asking." I polish one of the arm bands with the edge of my caftan. "I'm already two days behind, plus being behind for the bad publicity Quan created, and the drama of going before the Council, so if I'm going to lose, I'm going to lose wearing clothes I love."

"But *because* of all your troubles, can you afford to do something so…rebellious?"

I feel deflated. She has a point. And yet . . . "I don't think I can afford not to."

Her eyes take in all the elements. "How do you plan to get these clothes to the Dome without anyone seeing?"

Every Patron's outfit is kept in the Dome, where we get dressed. "I need you to place it in luggage of some sort."

"I'll figure something out. I'll get these packed right away."

I'm glad she'll be there to support me if and when the Favored turn against me. I'm guessing there's a 70/30 chance they'll eat me alive.

**

In my dressing room Marli unpacks the crown. "Last time you wore this, you wore your hair down and extremely curly, correct?"

"I did. I wanted them to be wowed by my dramatic copper mane against the purple fabric. This time I want them to see the clothes differently." I have a vague image in my head, one that will elicit an emotional reaction rather than something tangible. "I'm not sure how to explain it."

Marli thinks for a moment. "Perhaps if we minimize your hair the crown will steal the show? After all, it *is* a crown."

She's pegged it. "Befitting a victorious Cashlin."

"Exactly."

I sit in the makeup chair. Usually, I have additional help getting dressed, but today, I only want Marli. "Along those lines I'd like normal makeup. No jewels, no dramatic eyeshadows. Just make me look my best—as me. I want to show off more of Cashlin the strong, confident woman, and less of Cashlin, the flashy Patron."

"Understood."

As she applies my makeup, Amar walks in.

He immediately sees the purple dress hanging nearby. "What is this doing here?"

"It's what I'm wearing today."

His head shakes back and forth. "You revealed the snake outfit so today you wear the snake outfit."

"Why?" I love seeing him confused.

"Because. It's what you presented to the Favored."

"In a Reveal where a law was broken and my reputation was tarnished. I don't want people to remember that moment. I want to show them something better."

"You'll get in more trouble, sister. Is that what you want?"

I scoff. "Of course not. But get in trouble with whom? I've already been before the Council—and won. As far as I know, there is no law against presenting a different outfit. Do you know of one?"

Amar stands with his hands on his hips, shaking his head. Then he flips a hand at me. "I don't know of any law, but that doesn't mean we should tempt fate."

"*I'm* willing to risk it."

He claps his hands together. "Then I wash my hands of you. It's your funeral, Cashlin."

Hopefully not.

When he leaves, I feel rattled. I've talked the strong talk, but . . .

"You made the right decision," Marli says.

"Did I?" My churning stomach says otherwise.

She puts a comforting hand on my shoulder. "I wouldn't expect anything less of Cashlin, the Premier Patron of Regalia."

Hmm. Time will tell.

**

Someone knocks on the door. "Parade in five, Patron Cashlin."

"Thank you."

It's showtime.

I stand before Marli. "How do I look?"

"Stunning. The Favored will love it. And you in it."

The butterflies in my stomach flutter mercilessly. What if people rise up against me? What if the press berates me? What if there *is* a law against doing what I'm doing?

It's too late now. "Wish me luck."

My friend points upward. "If it's all right with you, I'll pray that everything goes well."

I'm about to tell her that I'd appreciate it but come to my senses. "Silently, do what you will, Marli, but I forbid you to do it out loud. I'm already running perilously close to the edge of the law."

She looks stricken, as if I've stabbed her in the heart.

I try to soften my tone and make her understand. "I won't turn you in for being one of the Devoted, but I have to protect myself from any hint of misconduct that I *know* is against the law. And if Amar saw or heard you? He'd turn you in like this." I snap my fingers for emphasis. Then I think of something to lessen the harshness of my words. "I can't lose you, Marli. I need you. I count on you. As my helper and as my friend. Do you understand?"

Marli nods. "I do. I wouldn't want to get you in trouble."

"Or *you* in trouble." I take a deep breath and say again, "Wish me luck."

She doesn't say anything. Surely, she believes in luck?

I can't think about that now. I have the Favored to face. I leave the dressing room and walk toward the Dome exit where the other Patrons gather for the parade.

The comments begin at once. "That's not new. You've worn that before."

"The snakes slither away, Cashlin?"

"You can't change your outfit at the last minute."

"Did the Council approve that outfit?"

I expected a few negative reactions, but they are relentless.

Once the comments stop, the looks linger as I walk past them with my head held high, taking my Premier spot, first in line.

LaBelle, who is Patron number two, grins at me. "Well look at you. It's much better than the snakes."

"Thank you. And thank you for offering to testify on my behalf yesterday."

"Of course." LaBelle smooths the feathers of her headdress. "When is Quan exiled?"

"In two days."

"Are you going?"

I haven't thought about it, and I can't think about it. Not right now. The doors open. The bright daylight makes me squint, and I hear the crowd before I see them.

I walk outside, wearing a regal expression worthy of the crown I wear. I raise my hands, letting the sunlight glint off my gold armbands. I am a queen, walking past my loyal subjects.

There are gasps and chattering. For or against?

Within seconds, their applause and cheers tell me I'm forgiven. They love me.

I want to turn back to the Patrons who've given me a hard time, but I keep my attention on my fans. The butterflies leave me, and I walk with genuine confidence.

Premier Patron Cashlin is back.

**

The parade through the Favored Ring culminates back in the Dome. As the musicians play a victory march, all twenty Patrons line up on the edge of the stage as the Favored fill the auditorium. I will never tire of the excitement of this moment.

And in this case, the relief that all is well.

When they've settled, the host parts us Patrons in the middle and claims center stage. "Favored of Regalia! Welcome to the Vote!"

Suddenly, dozens of Servs appear at the ends of each audience row, handing out vote cards. The voting is simple: choose one Patron whose clothing you would most like to wear.

I look across the stage at my competition. LaBelle's is elegant and there are a few others that are contenders. Plus a few outfits that are worse than my snake costume.

Good or bad, better or best, I have done all I can to hold onto my Premier position. Now it's up to the Favored.

It's physically painful standing there for minute upon minute. My shoes are cute but uncomfortable, and the weight of the halo crown is giving me a headache—all for the sake of fashion. Drawing on my extensive experience, I don't let my pain show and wave at various people in the audience when they call my name. I'm glad there aren't any hecklers—at least that I've heard.

As we wait for the voting to finish, LaBelle keeps smiling, but says to me, "They've obviously forgiven you."

"Apparently they have."

"Changing your outfit was a good play."

"You think?"

"Of course. The Favored always like the brightest bauble. Today that's you, dear."

That's me. I haven't purposely chosen a bright purple velvet—the dress already existed in my closet—but the fact that the richness of the velvet and the flash of the patent leather shoes is to my advantage.

The host wheels a large box to centerstage. Then he claps his hands. "Time is up! Please place your votes in the boxes as they are passed."

Voting boxes pass down the rows and the Servs bring the votes to the front of the stage, emptying them into the large box. Once all votes are deposited, it's wheeled backstage to be counted.

This is always the most awkward part, just standing there on display during the long minutes of the count.

The musicians play lively music, which makes the Favored move and dance in an undulating mass of revelers. It's what they do best.

A tall woman located at my end of the stage waves to get my attention. I recognize her from other interactions. She calls out, "Love the shoes, Cashlin!"

"Thank you!" It's Kiya. She's very exuberant and a strong supporter. She always wears my costumes—including today. We met a quarter ago when she boldly approached me in the Favored Ring and introduced herself. I've always thought we could be friends—if such friendships were allowed.

Kiya blows me a kiss.

I wink at her, then carefully sway to the music, concentrating on keeping my crown from toppling.

For the first time I spot a few Favored giving me a less-than-approving stare. I try not to let them bother me.

But they do. Public opinion is as erratic as a new puppy—and has the same attention span.

Finally, the host walks to the center again. He holds an envelope.

The crowd silences.

"The people have spoken. In the number twenty spot is . . ."

Shockingly, the current number nine's name is called. I'm not the only Patron who is stunned.

She bravely waves a hand, but I can tell she's on the verge of tears. Her outfit is beautiful. I don't understand.

Numbers nineteen through eleven are called in quick succession. They file off the stage to make room for the winners. Their costumes will not be produced or sold. Some of them will have to move into different homes, a humiliating downgrade.

"Let's applaud your top ten!" the host says.

The crowd cheers us on as photographers take pictures.

I'm in shock at making it this far. I'd wanted them to accept me back—which they have—but I never thought they'd put me in the top ten.

"Number ten..."

With each number my nerves tighten. How can I go from persona non grata to redeemed so quickly?

With five left, LaBelle takes my hand. She's nervous too.

Number five, number four...

"Number three... LaBelle."

She lets go and steps forward. She's moved down one spot.

The eight that have already been called take a step back and the host beckons Patron Jennika and me toward centerstage.

We hold hands—though we don't know each other very well. During the last Reveal she'd been number twelve, so her current position is a huge win for her. Win or lose.

Win or lose? I might win?

And then I hear her name listed as number two.

When she hugs me, I nearly lose my crown. The crowd noise is insane.

The host takes my hand and raises it as the victor. "May the glory be yours!"

It's surreal. Yesterday I was on trial. Today I retain my Premier Patron position for another quarter. I have a fleeting thought of Marli, praying to the Keeper for my success.

Who's to say it helped?

Innumerable pictures are taken of the top ten. I usually revel in the attention, but this time it's almost embarrassing.

It seems like forever before he leads us offstage. But instead of my fellow Patrons congratulating me, or even heading to their dressing rooms, they stand around in small groups, talking among themselves. Some give me sidelong glances. Their attitude hasn't softened toward me, in fact, it's worse. The Favored forgave me, but my peers have not.

LaBelle comes over. "Congratulations, Cashlin."

I almost say, 'You too' before I remember that she's fallen from two to three. "Thanks." I tell her.

Which is where the praise ends and the sniping begins:

"You never would have won wearing your snake monstrosity."

"Did you plan on being gone the last two days so you could make your big play today?"

"Did you even *go* before the Council or was that all a publicity stunt?"

"Maybe we should all dig up our old outfits."

I can't believe what I'm hearing. These are *my* people. How can they turn on me like this after the Favored have chosen? My heart beats faster and I find it hard to breathe.

"You don't deserve to be number —"

Amar sweeps through the Patrons to my side. "My, my, you're a jealous bunch. Have you no compassion for your sister who's been through hell after being falsely accused? And you should be rejoicing — and feel relief—that the Favored have forgiven her." He sweeps a pointed finger from left to right, taking them all in. "Is this the way you want to be treated when your time of crisis comes? For I guarantee, it *will* come."

There are a few shrugs and assorted grumbles. Only LaBelle and Jennika offer approving smiles.

Amar ushers me toward my dressing room.

Once inside I thank him. "I appreciate you diffusing the situation."

"I couldn't very well let them strip your bones bare." He shuts the door. "Though they had every right to do so."

"What are you talking about? I was cleared by the Council." I point toward the auditorium. "I won the vote in there."

He looks at his reflection in the mirror, running a hand through his longish hair. "You were lucky. It could have gone either way."

I cross my arms. "Tell me this: would I have won the vote wearing my snake outfit?"

He opens his mouth as though he wants to say a lot, but only says, "No."

"See? I had to do something drastic or get tossed into the bottom ten. I've worked too hard to—"

"*You've* worked hard? Haven't I had something to do with it?"

Not really. "Yes, but . . . who encouraged me to go with the snakes?"

"You didn't have to say yes."

"You didn't give me any good alternatives. As my Creative Director—"

He gets in my face like he'd done as a child. "So, it's my fault?"

He doesn't deserve all the blame—but a lot of it.

He points toward the door. "If I hadn't saved you out there . . ."

I press my hands downward, appeasing him. "I know. And I thank you for it."

He huffs. "Maybe it's good you're going to be married soon, so your husband will have to deal with you." He cocks his head and touches his lips with a finger. "Oh. Right. Your fiancé testified against you."

Don't remind me. "I am *not* marrying Rowan."

"He obviously doesn't *want* to marry you either. Yet you don't have much choice. The only other Creative Director who's a contender for marriage is promised to someone else."

He's right. Changing the details of arranged marriages is never easy, and often impossible. I've heard my parents talk of one such time, but it was decades ago.

Yet the idea of marrying Rowan makes me wish I could stay single.

"Ta ta, sister."

After he leaves it takes a moment for the air in the room to stop vibrating.

There's a soft knock on the door and Marli opens it tentatively. "Is it safe to come in?"

"I welcome a friendly face."

Marli looks worried. "I couldn't help but hear your brother."

"Yes. Well. Amar has never been an encourager." I stretch out my arms. "Can you help me out of this, please?"

We don't talk as she helps me undress.

I won the vote. Then why do I feel like I lost?

**

Marli leaves to find our carriage, leaving me alone in the dressing room.

I sit in the makeup chair, staring at my reflection. "This is not the face of a winner." I press the wrinkle between my eyebrows. Up until the last Reveal I hadn't a care in the world. I shouldn't have any worry lines.

I force myself to smile.

It isn't convincing.

There's a knock on the door and I expect Marli to come in.

Another knock means it isn't her.

"Come in," I say.

I'm surprised to see Dronna—the Patron who'd come in nineteenth.

"Can I talk with you a minute, Cashlin?"

"Of course." I'm curious because we haven't exchanged a hundred words between us. "Please sit."

The woman is four years older than me, married, and has the requisite boy and girl. I've never paid much attention to her offerings, and she is regularly in the bottom five. Obviously, being a Patron doesn't come easy for her.

Dronna's busy hands keep each other company. Why is she nervous?

"How can I help you today?" I ask.

After a deep breath, she says, "Firstly, I want to apologize for the nasty reaction you got from the Patrons. As your brother said, we're a jealous bunch. You didn't deserve that. In fact, I want to congratulate you."

"That's nice of you. I know I shocked people."

She smiles. "That, you did. But what a wise move it was to use an old outfit. I never would've thought of it."

"The idea sprang out of pure desperation."

"Speaking of . . ." She traces the arm of her chair. "I'm not very good at this and wanted to ask—I shouldn't ask, but I wanted to ask…"

"Go ahead."

"Can you give me pointers on how to make the Favored vote for me?" She immediately waves her hands. "Never mind. We're competitors. You won't want to help—"

"Of course, I'll help you—as much as I can." I'm impressed she has the guts to ask.

We spend the next ten minutes talking through her Reveal outfit—which lacks any wow-factor. I hadn't seen her actual Reveal as I'd been dealing with Quan, but she volunteered that there hadn't been any choreography or a set, and only generic music. I try to give her ideas about what she could have done, but I also know a hard truth: some people are creative and some aren't.

"Above all," I say as we're wrapping up, "act confident even if you don't feel that way."

When Dronna leaves she shakes my hand exuberantly, overly thankful.

Thankful. With a start I realize I haven't shown any gratitude for my victories. I've focused on the negative instead of the positive. Miraculously, I am still the Premier Patron. Miraculously, I can stay in my home—the best home in the Patron Ring.

I could say it's all because of me—it *was* my idea to dress in an old costume, but in my gut, I know there's more to it than me, myself, and I. I know it could've gone either way. That it worked out well is a good part miracle, and *that* is not in my job description.

Plus, I know there was a miracle involved in me being cleared of all charges by the Council.

I could get witchy and be mad that I had to go through any of it, but I see a fact that can't be denied: I would never have won with the snake outfit, and I would never have worn the purple outfit if I hadn't felt out of it because of the missed marketing days, which were caused by me being on trial, and—

I take a breath and let the dominoes of the last few days topple over.

Anything I did was reactive because of situations beyond myself. Was that because of Quan? Nerwhether? Or anyone else?

They had a part in it, but someone else started all this, set up the dominoes and pushed the first one over.

Beyond all rationalization and past beliefs, that someone has to be the Keeper. If not for him, I would be packing boxes to move.

He deserves my thanks.

I bow my head like I've seen Marli do.

But then I stop myself. I've told her multiple times she needs to keep her prayers to herself because it's too risky.

It's hypocritical for me to say any of my own.

The dressing room door opens and a Serv peeks in. "Sorry. I was going to clean. I thought you were done in here."

I stand. "I am. The room is yours."

**

Mother is waiting for me at home.

She walks toward me with open arms. "Dear girl, you remain triumphant!"

I awkwardly accept her embrace—a gift rarely given. "No thanks to your support," I say.

She pulls back, as if incredulous. "Don't be rude, daughter."

I move away from her and sit by the fireplace. "You said the kiss ruined the family legacy."

"It *was* a nasty affair—and the Council agreed with me. They took you to trial."

Mother always has a way of making me think a cloudy day is my fault. "When I received the summons from the Council, I sent for you, yet you refused to come. In my darkest hour you abandoned me."

She sits in the other chair and presses her fingers against her forehead in a gesture of embellished despair I've seen a hundred times. "Surely you know that the entire situation was quite overwhelming for me."

"Yes, it was. For me." I stand and peer down at her. "You left me to handle it alone. It's pitiful when both my mother and my brother leave me to deal with the biggest crisis of my life."

She stares at me mutely for a long moment and I notice she has some makeup that needs to be blended on her left cheek. I don't fix it or point it out.

She shudders the slightest bit and smiles as if transitioning from one mood to the next. "But look at you! You've been exonerated by the Council of Worthiness, *and* you've held onto your Premier position."

I sigh inwardly. She isn't going to admit she's done anything wrong. The most frightening thing is that she truly believes she hasn't.

"What is your cook making for dinner?" she asks. "I'm going to join you and help celebrate."

Joy.

Chapter Ten

Cashlin

The day after a victorious vote is usually a day of resting on my laurels. I've done my job.

There is no rest for the top ten Creative Directors—including Amar—who are taking our creations to the Implementors to produce. I don't want to think about the creator of the snake outfit who is probably wondering what happened to their design—after all, I *had* chosen it. Instead, I like thinking about the creator of the purple outfit who is enjoying a surprise celebration.

I want to celebrate too, but I can't. Because tomorrow Quan will die.

I sit in my dining room and nibble on eggs and toast. I've mentally flipped a dozen times trying to decide whether I should go to his exile or not. There was no *should* to it. It's probably wiser to stay away. After all, Quan caused my problems with the Council. To go might imply we are close—a notion which Nerwhether worked hard to dispel. And do I really want to see anyone exiled into the Swirling Desert? I'm not sure I really want to witness any phenomenon that means certain death.

I should've asked Nerwhether for advice. Yet even if I get a hold of him, he's most certainly moved on to his next case. He doesn't owe me anything beyond what he's already done.

I can ask Marli about the exile process, but I don't want her to know about my newest state of turmoil, and I don't want her to share her faith-based views. The issue is complicated enough without adding the Keeper to the matter.

I think of Mother. I'd had enough of her views last night at dinner. And Rowan? I'd rather ask a rock.

I need someone neutral.

The image of Xian comes to mind.

Which is odd. I met him by chance. Yet in our few minutes of interaction, I sensed he was an honorable man. Kind. Sympathetic. All traits that I need at this moment.

I push my chair back from the table.

Dom immediately enters the room. "Is there something you need, miss?"

"Actually, there is. I need to get a message to an Enforcer Serv who works in the Council Tower."

His eyebrows show his surprise. "I . . . I'm not sure how to do that, miss."

Neither do I. "Could you send a Messenger Serv? I really need to see him right away. It's important."

"I'll do my best. Do you have a note for him?"

"A note. I'll be right back." I run upstairs to my desk, my mind juggling words that might bring Xian to my home. But when I begin to write, most of the words scatter to the floor, leaving me with but a few: *Xian. I need your help. Please come soon. Patron Cashlin.* I read it over, remembering that the guards at the gates will also read it, as it is his ticket through the Rings. It will do.

It has to.

**

As soon as Dom leaves to hire a messenger, I realize I don't even know if Xian is working today. Perhaps he is home in the Serv Ring. Perhaps he will never get the message.

Then what?

I try to get my mind off the situation by reading a book in my private garden, but the words on the page never fully enter my mind and are read and reread a dozen times.

I give up, closing the book and my eyes.

I must have dozed for I awaken to Dom standing beside me. "I have a return message, miss."

I eagerly read it: *I will come within the hour.* "When he arrives, bring him out here immediately."

"Yes, miss."

My heart beats wildly. Xian is coming.

**

I hear the door to the garden open.

I hear Xian thank Dom.

I stand to greet him. He holds his helmet in the crook of his elbow. "You came," I say.

"Of course, Patron."

I don't want my position to be a part of the conversation, yet I don't want to make him uncomfortable by asking him to call me Cashlin. "I know our meeting was under stressful circumstances, and you coming here is above and beyond your duties, but . . ." I feel the pressure of tears and press a hand to my forehead as the tension of the morning threatens to overflow. "I'm very glad you came. I really need to talk to someone."

His left eyebrow rises. "I'm honored you thought of me."

The whole situation seems presumptuous and is probably unprecedented. My legs feel shaky, so I sit down and offer him the chair nearby.

He sits and sets his helmet on his knee. But then he changes his mind and sets it next to his chair, out of sight. He clasps his hands in his lap as if he's sincerely ready to listen. "I'm here, Patron Cashlin. Why are you upset?"

"Quan's exile." I hope those two words are enough and he won't make me explain the myriad of emotions that plague me.

He nods once. "That's understandable."

"I mean, he was exiled, and I was . . . not."

"With good reason. Quan was a repeat offender. You shouldn't feel guilty for being exonerated."

I'm impressed by his insight. "You're quite perceptive."

He shrugs. "All day, every day, I stand in the Council Chambers and hear arguments and verdicts. Some I agree with, and some I don't. You never should have been called to trial. At least that's my take on it—not that my opinion matters."

"It matters to me, Xian. You helped make the day bearable."

He smiles. "I'm glad I could help then—and hopefully can help now." He shifts in his chair. "Are you going to attend the exile?"

I feel a wave of relief at his question. "I don't know. I mean he . . . the Council . . ."

"It's complicated."

"Completely and utterly."

He sits back and thoughtfully takes in the expansive garden. "It's really beautiful here."

"Thank you. It's my peaceful place." What about the exile?

"And with your latest win you get to keep it for another quarter."

"I do." The exile?

"Congratulations are in order. From what I read you're a brave woman to risk wearing something from a previous Reveal."

"Brave, no. Was it a risk? Yes. I'm relieved it turned out well." Why is he talking about all this?

He watches a bird land on the edge of a bird bath. "Will there be repercussions if you don't go to the exile?"

Finally. Back to the issue at hand. "That's what I have to figure out. I don't think the Council will care—"

"Not with the Council. Repercussions with the public, with the Favored, and even beyond them, with the citizens of the other Rings."

Other Rings? "I honestly have never thought about what they might think." I realize how snobbish this sounds. "Forgive me, but I haven't."

"They are well aware of everything that happens in your life, Patron, even if you're completely unaware of theirs."

I take offense. "That's rude, Xian."

He shrugs—a bold gesture. Most people seek to flatter me. He seems to have no such need.

"It is rude," he says. "But I assume you summoned me here for truthful advice. Useful advice."

"Absolutely. I don't want us to talk as Patron and Enforcer but... as ..." I want to use the word *friends* but wonder if that's going too far.

Xian says the word for me. "As friends?"

"Yes, friends. Yet there's that whole fraternization between Rings rule."

"We're just talking. Surely talking is allowed."

I nod once. "Surely. We're just talking." But I know it's more than that. Xian and I are sharing deep thoughts and ideas. Such interaction is new to me. But I like it.

He leans forward, resting his forearms on his thighs. "Returning to the subject of your knowledge of other Rings . . . as someone who has access to all the Rings, I know that the Cycle of Regalia affects every person in the land."

"My assistant used that cycle phrase."

"It's common in the outer Rings."

"You make me feel terribly out of touch."

"Perhaps in that sense you are." He stands and touches the leaves of an enormous purple rhododendron. "Your daily focus is on your next Reveal, while the daily focus in the outer Rings is survival."

I try to press down my offense, knowing it's my problem, not his. "But their survival depends on the success of the Reveals. We provide work for hundreds of people."

"That, you do. But maybe you . . ." He hesitates.

"Go on. As my friend . . . maybe I . . . ?"

"Maybe you need to consider there's more to life than fancy clothes."

It's uncanny. "Once again, you parrot what Marli said."

"If I'm repeating what you've already heard from a Serv, perhaps it's something you should embrace, or at least consider?"

I stand. His bluntness is welcome yet a little hard to take. He's turned the tables on me. I thought I would be in charge, but he's veered this conversation to another vein. An open vein. "I didn't foresee us having this sort of discussion."

He smiles slightly. "That doesn't mean it isn't good."

I'm not sure about that. "I am glad you're here, but I didn't ask you to dissect Regalian society. I want your opinion about whether or not I should go to Quan's exile."

He bows once, then plucks a purple bloom and hands it to me. "I apologize. Peace?"

I take the flower, which is *my* flower, yet has somehow gained a more important designation. "Yes. Peace. But I do need your specific guidance."

We return to our chairs. "I believe you should go."

I appreciate his direct answer. "Why?"

"Because of everything we just talked about. If you want to make an impact beyond your current Patron position, it would be wise to learn about the whole of Regalia, all its people. It would be advantageous to let them see you visiting their Rings, dealing with a punishment that hangs over each one of them."

I'm taken aback. "They fear exile?"

"Every day . . ." He looks to the ground. He seems hesitant to say more.

"Explain please."

"You may not like my words."

I can't turn back now. "Say them anyway."

He takes a new breath. "Here's the truth of it. The Servs and the Imps—who are the backbone of Regalia's cycle—are in the thick of harsh realities every moment of their lives." He sweeps an arm to encompass the garden and my house. "They have no idyllic buffer like this to keep them safe from demerits and doom. They're subjected to the whims of those in charge who hand out demerits for minor infractions of unpredictable rules."

"I didn't know. I'm sorry for that."

"I apologize for being blunt—so many times during this conversation. Perhaps it's the consequence of my job. An Enforcer doesn't deal in subtleties. But I must ask you this: up until your trial, how many demerits are on your record?"

"Well . . . none. None that I know of."

"I have four."

As an Enforcer I assumed he had none. "For what?"

He counts on his fingers. "Being late to work, bumping into a Favored woman as she passed in front of me at a gate, asking too many questions of a supervisor in the Tower, and returning spoiled meat to a store, demanding fresh."

"Those seem like minor offenses—if they are offenses at all."

"They are offenses that added together can send me to death, to exile."

"That's absurd. I had no idea."

He leans forward, his voice gentler. "I know. But I think attending Quan's exile can show that you are different from other Patrons. You have a heart and think beyond yourself. You have compassion — even for Quan, the source of your troubles."

Optics. That's something I understand. "Then I'll go."

"Very good," he says. "I truly think it's the right choice. It's tomorrow?"

"At noon."

He picks up his helmet and sets it in his lap. "I have a suggestion. Why don't you write a formal request to have an Enforcer Serv go with you? Request me, specifically. I could be your guide through foreign territory."

I know I'll feel safe with him. "I'd like that very much. I'll write the request now." I ring for Dom and ask him to bring me paper and pen. He quickly returns, I write the note, and hand it to Xian.

He stands. "I'll turn this into my superiors and will be here at eleven as your Enforcer guard."

"What type of carriage should I order?"

"None."

"Then how — ?"

"We need to walk."

I balk. "The only time Patrons walk is for marketing purposes."

"Understood," Xian says. "Yet for reputation purposes wouldn't it be more appropriate to walk?"

"To appear humble?"

"To *be* humble." He puts a hand to his mouth and suddenly draws in a breath. "But wait . . . I'm having second thoughts. The Servs aren't used to seeing Patrons. They may accept you or they may behave badly by taking their frustrations out on you."

I'd experienced the malice of the Favored *and* my fellow Patrons. How would Servs react to me coming to see one of their own exiled?

"Forgive me, Patron. I've made you doubt."

"Yes, you have."

"That was wrong of me." He thumps a fist on his armored chest. "I am an Enforcer. Tomorrow I will act as your protector. My job is to take away your fear, not add to it."

I can't discard my fears so quickly. "Do you still think I should go?"

His nod has conviction in it. "I do."

"Then we have a deal." I extend my hand to shake his.

He looks confused. "Us shaking hands . . . it's not . . . done."

"It should be." I persist and our hands wrap together as we seal the plan. Touching him... touching another person... I realize how seldom I do such a thing. I also realize how good it feels.

I see him out but am startled when I spot Nerwhether walking up my front path. I want to yank Xian back inside and tell him to hide.

But it's too late. The men see each other and pause. Then Xian bows his head in deference. "Solicitor Nerwhether."

"Enforcer."

Xian walks past him and away.

Though my stomach is turning over on itself, I force a smile. "Solicitor. What brings you out on this fine day?"

"You."

Has the Council of Worthiness changed their minds about my fate? He points inside. "Shall we?"

I lead him into the parlor. "Can I get you some refreshment?"

"No. Thank you." He sits and opens a briefcase. He removes a letter. "I'm here to give you this."

I see the black wax seal of the Council. My heart sinks. My hands shake as I open it.

It's short and I read it once, then twice. "The Council admonishes me for wearing a past outfit. What does this really mean?"

"It means you got their attention again—for all the wrong reasons. It was reckless."

"I knew it was a risk, but I simply couldn't wear my atrocious snake outfit. It would have landed me at the bottom of the vote."

"Aren't you the one who chose it?"

"It was a mistake—a mistake I chose to rectify by wearing something I already had in my closet." I try to spin it. "And it worked, didn't it? My costume was voted number one."

"Which is the only reason you're not being brought before the Council a second time." He leans back in the chair and sighs. "What isn't written in the letter—but what I've heard around the Tower—is that it's your attitude that bothers them the most. You seem determined to test the system in order to get your own way."

I feel defensive. "I had nothing to do with Quan's kiss—that's on him. The Council even said as much. But the purple dress? Yes, they're right. I ignored the rules and did what I wanted."

"It's got to stop, Citizen Cashlin. Most citizens of Regalia go out of their way not to let the Council know they even exist—it's the prudent way to live. I guarantee that next time they won't stop with a letter. You do *not* want to appear before the Council again."

I shudder at the thought of it. "I most certainly do not."

He pushes against his knees and stands. "I'll be on my way then. Promise me you'll be on your best behavior from now on."

"Yes, Solicitor."

When he reaches the door, he pauses. "Why was an Enforcer Serv in your home?"

My mind goes blank. Then I come up with a lie. "He and my cook are friends. They had a family matter to discuss."

"Hmm." He opens the door. "Hopefully we'll never see each other again, Citizen Cashlin."

Hopefully.

Chapter Eleven

Solana

When Helsa and I return home from work we notice people gathered at the door of our neighbors' house—our arrested neighbors.

I send Helsa ahead to see what's going on. I quicken my pace—which is far slower at the end of a workday than it is at the beginning. Though only sixty, I often feel ninety.

I see anxious words being exchanged by members of the crowd, and more than one woman is crying.

Oh dear.

Helsa runs back to me. "They've been exiled!"

My heart sinks. I'd feared this might happen. I'd warned both Thom and Tamar about exile as their faith gatherings grew larger and bolder. And how could they not know that singing would spark dangerous attention? But they'd only smiled and said, "We have nothing to fear, Solana. Come join us."

Although I am one of the Devoted, I prefer my interaction with the Keeper to be private. Losing my son to exile because of his public faith scared me more than a little. Call me a coward if you must. I feel no need to risk myself or Helsa by doing otherwise.

I reach the group and suffer with the others, my heart aching with pain, sorrow, and panic. We all know *of* people who've been exiled, but few of us—beyond me—know anyone personally.

The group grows larger. Suddenly, I fear its size will draw unwanted attention. I take Helsa's arm. "Inside. Now."

"But—"

"Now."

We go into our house and I bolt the door.

"Why did we have to leave?" Helsa asks. "Those are our friends. Isn't it good we're coming together to—?"

I raise my hand, stopping her words. "Getting people riled up will do no one any good. It's best to lay low right now. Thom and Tamar already brought too much attention to our street."

Helsa shakes her head and points outside. "They're going to be killed. Why shouldn't we get riled up about it?"

Is she that short-sighted? "Because of your father. Our family already has a target on our back."

She lowers her arm. "Maybe if people would've protested Papa's death, the Council wouldn't have sentenced Thom and Tamar to the same fate."

I take up residence in my rocker. The cushioned seat gives me relief from a day's worth of sitting on a hard stool. "What good does it do to make a fuss? The Council won't change, they won't suddenly approve the Keeper. Think about it, Helsa: now there are two houses — right next to each other — that have exiled residents. Who's next?" I rock up and back trying to calm myself. "Their exile makes me afraid. Very afraid."

Helsa pulls a chair close. "Don't be scared. You and I are careful."

We *were* careful. "We have one of the Relics now."

"Then . . . maybe we should get rid of it."

I shake my head vehemently. "That, I can't do. Relics aren't ours to dispose of. They've been passed on since the Before Time and are cherished. Since we have one in our possession, we *must* protect it."

The voices outside grow louder and Helsa looks toward the door. "You made us come inside to avoid danger. But since the Relic puts us in danger, maybe we could pass it to someone else."

I stop rocking. "Let me think on that a while."

Without realizing I'm doing it, I massage the joints of my fingers.

Helsa puts her hand on my knee. "I'll make dinner tonight. You rest. Would you like chamomile tea for your aches?"

She's such a good girl. "That would be lovely. Can you also fetch my liniment, please?"

Helsa brings me the salve but does one better. "Let me do it for you."

She sits beside me and massages the joints of my hands.

"That feels wonderful, child. Hand-sewing all day makes my fingers crampy. I—"

"Shhh. Just rest."

I lean my head back, close my eyes, and thank the Keeper for my granddaughter.

**

Go to the exile.

I jerk awake and find I'm in my rocker. Helsa is in the kitchen nearby, slicing bread. I must have dozed off.

Go to the exile.

I blink as the same four words repeat themselves.

The exile is the last place I want to go. I hadn't seen my son die, and certainly have no desire to see Thom and Tamar meet the same fate.

I rub my eyes, for I haven't just heard the words, I've mentally seen someone saying them.

"Nana?" Helsa stares at me. "Is something wrong? You look . . . confused."

I sit forward, trying to clear my head. "I must have fallen asleep."

"I'm glad you did. But supper is ready."

I move to the table to eat, feeling my walking muscles complain. We hold hands and give thanks.

Then unbidden, I say, "I'm going to the exile tomorrow."

Helsa drops her slice of apple. "Why would you do that?"

I shrug. "I just had a dream where I saw the Patron Cashlin saying, 'Go to the exile.'"

"Why would *she* want you to go?"

That part isn't clear at all. "She was called before the Council. Maybe she's exiled too?"

"She wasn't. You heard that."

I'd heard that. "Whether she's there or not, I have to go."

"What about work? You already missed a day for Mama's funeral, plus when you pretended you were sick. Another day and Bru might fire you."

The thought of that possibility comes. And goes. If I'm sacked? So be it.

I repeat my decision with more conviction. "I'm going to the exile."

"Nana, are you—?"

"Yes," I say. "I'm sure."

I'm lying.

Chapter Twelve

Cashlin

Déjà vu. Once again Marli and I pore over the clothing in my massive closet, trying to find something for me to wear.

"What does one wear to an exile?" I ask facetiously — though I truly need an answer.

"You want to be seen, but not stand out?"

"Something like that."

"I'm not sure that's possible, miss. Patrons aren't subtle people. Even your day-to-day clothing is splashed with bright colors. The Servs only wear brown."

I can't help but notice her plain brown dress and white apron. "Which means no matter what I wear, I'll stand out."

"I'm afraid you will."

I turn in a slow circle, trying to think of a solution. "I need something that is respectful." Then I spot the sleeve of a caftan that has a brown and gold print. I get it out. "The print is smaller than most, and the colors are a bit more subdued?"

"I agree," Marli says.

I put it on. The belt is embellished with metallic gold. "This will never do."

Marli retrieves a wide brown sash. "If you wrap it around your waist a few times . . ."

I do just that, tucking the end underneath. "I like it. It's simple." I look at myself and laugh. "I'm not used to simple."

"You look lovely no matter what you wear." She opens my large cabinet of jewelry. "You usually wear three chunky necklaces with this caftan."

"Not today. Today I won't wear any jewelry. And my hair will be tied back with no makeup." I comb my fingers through my waves and secure it with a band. "There."

Marli raises her finger then gets out some brown shoes. "Flats. You're going to be walking a lot."

I put them on and look at myself in the mirror. "I hardly recognize myself."

"But you're still you," Marli says. "It's a good choice."

Xian will arrive any minute. It is the best I can do.

**

Before we leave the Patron Ring, I pause at the edge of the Road and ask Xian, "Can you brief me about how this will go? Although my brother lives in the Creatives Ring and the Choosing is carried out there, and I'm very familiar with the Favored Ring, I am completely unfamiliar with the two outer Rings."

He doesn't seem surprised. "I'll display my permission paper and speak to the guards. I suggest acting confident, as if you know what you're doing."

"I'm not and I don't."

He smiles. "That's why I'm here. *I* am confident and *I* know what I'm doing because I go through the gates twice a day. The guards know me."

"Yesterday you said it's rare for a Patron to visit."

"I don't remember it ever happening." He acknowledged my clothing. "You chose wisely."

I look down, running my hands along the subtle fabric, "For the first time I don't want to be flashy and show off."

"Yet you still look beautiful." He stammers. "I apologize. I shouldn't—"

"It's all right. Thanks for the compliment."

"Shall we go?" he asks.

There's no turning back now.

**

As expected, I feel at ease walking with Xian through the Creatives Ring. But the line at the next gate is long.

"Sorry for the wait," Xian says.

Most of the people in line are Servs. Even in my toned-down clothes, I feel conspicuous. They seem to avoid eye contact—which is fine with me. A few whisper behind their hands.

Xian must sense my unease. "It'll be all right. Hopefully the wait won't be long."

It can't be helped. I try to think positively and focus on familiar territory. "I always enjoy the mood here in this Ring."

"Mood?"

"Creativity." I take a deep breath. "Can you feel it?"

He shakes his head, but points toward one of the studios. "I like the painted murals on the buildings. I assume that studio designs jewelry."

"Correct. And there are studios for headdresses, clothing, and shoes with living quarters beyond. My brother has a very nice home here. And Rowan lives here too."

"Actually, my mother works here."

I scoff. "So, my long explanation was unneeded?"

He smiles. "I wasn't going to stop you."

"What's her job?"

"She's an assistant for a designer."

"She must be creative too."

"She is—unlike me. I'm not a creative sort. And the competition for the Choosing? That's a lot of pressure."

"Constant pressure for them—and us," I say. "Pressure on the Creatives to get us to choose their pieces, then pressure on we Patrons, wanting the Favored to choose our completed outfits. They choose between twenty outfits—that's a lot of options."

Xian shakes his head. "That's too subjective for me. I much prefer things being black and white."

I see a flaw in his thinking. "Like laws?"

"Yes."

I hold up a finger. "But you implied that laws are often subjective, that Servs fear they will get demerits on the whim of those in authority."

He pauses a moment, then offers a small bow. "I stand partially corrected, though I stand by my preference for the absolute versus the unpredictable."

"I wouldn't mind a few more absolutes," I say. "I never could have predicted my trial—or the results. Or the reaction of the Favored to my purple outfit. The uncertainty unnerves me."

"Then you understand."

It's finally our turn to pass into the Favored Ring. Xian deals with the guards, and I nod when they look in my direction, trying to play the part of someone with authority who expects their compliance. It works well and we are allowed to pass through that gate, and through the next gate leading to the Implementor Ring.

New territory.

I am immediately struck by its grayness, not just because its people wear gray tunics and pants, but because the windowless factories in our view are gray stucco. Even the gravel in the streets is gray.

"Have you ever visited a factory where your looks are made?"

"I have not."

"You should. There are looms and sewing machines. Workers of leather and embroidery, jewelers, and every other kind of artisan. They do it all. For you."

"Not for me," I say. "For the Favored."

He cocks his head. "Round and round we go . . ."

An older woman dressed in gray walks toward the line. Her eyes meet mine and she does a double-take.

I've been recognized.

The woman comes closer. She is small, a good six inches shorter than me. She reminds me of my grandmother, with soft facial features that imply compassion and wisdom.

I miss my grandmother.

"Hello," I say.

She blinks as if my words pull her out of a daze.

"Move along, Imp," Xian says.

The woman looks at my clothes. "I sewed the embroidery on the caftan you're wearing."

I'm unsure what to say but touch the embroidery at the neckline. "Then I thank you for it. You did a fine job. And I love the feel of the fabric."

She nods. We make eye contact. "You look pretty in it."

"Thanks to you."

Xian shoos her away. "I said, move along, Imp."

The woman heads toward the back of the queue but I call after her, "Keep up the good work."

She nods.

I immediately regret my words. "That's a horribly trite thing to say. Even condescending?"

"I wouldn't worry about it," Xian says. "It's probably the first compliment she's heard in a long, long time—perhaps the only compliment."

I'm taken aback. "I live for compliments."

"It comes with your position."

"But I seek them out."

"As I said . . ."

Suddenly, everything feels off kilter. This woman who has genuine skill and creates beautiful things, rarely receives praise for it, while I—who possess no skill and create nothing—receive the adulation of hundreds.

"You seem troubled," Xian says.

"I'm just . . ." It's a new thought that I'm not comfortable sharing. "I've never thought much about the people who produce the clothes I promote, much less meet them."

"And they've never met anyone like you either."

I notice something else. "There are more people coming out of the Server Ring than going into it." There's a steady stream of people dressed in brown.

"That's because we *serve* the other Rings. We sleep in our Ring but spend as little time there as possible. It's pretty bleak."

"Do you have other family besides your mother?"

"I live with my parents and two siblings. They all work in other Rings."

"I'm sure they're proud of you for working in the Council Ring."

"They are. As I said, my mother works with one of the Creatives, and my brother and sister clean the houses of other Creatives." He looks away.

"And your father?"

"He works in the Debt Camp."

"What's that?"

His expression implies it's something I should know. "When Imps or Servs can't pay their rent or taxes they're sent there."

I'm taken aback. "They have to pay rent and taxes?"

Xian looks shocked at my question. "Don't you?"

"No. My rent is free, I pay no taxes, and I receive a stipend for incidentals..."

"That would be nice."

I feel guilty for the perks of my position.

"The Imps and Servs aren't so lucky. They earn a wage and have to pay taxes from it. If they can't pay, they're locked away at the Debt Camp."

"It doesn't sound like a camp."

"It's not. It's a prison."

"How long do they have to stay there?"

"Until the debt is paid."

That doesn't make sense. "If they're locked away, how can they earn money to pay the debt?"

He touches the tip of his nose. "It's definitely a flawed system." We move forward in the line. "Do you have family?"

"I do. My mother is still living. My parents retired from the positions my brother and I now possess."

"He's your Creative Director."

"He is—until I marry another Director. Or he marries a Patron."

"That sounds a bit... incestuous?"

I've never thought of it that way. "It really isn't. There are twenty families with two children each. Their positions are determined by the vacancies that need to be filled."

"So, one Creative marries one Patron."

"Exactly."

"That's assuming each family has one boy and one girl."

"Correct. It's worked out surprisingly well—most of the time."

105

"What happens when a family has two boys or two girls?"

"Arrangements are made to demote the excess child to another Ring."

"Excess child?"

Oh. My. "That's a bad choice of words."

"The spare child who has no mate?"

I sigh deeply, not liking the thread of this conversation. I can't logically explain the oddities of being a Patron. Or of living in Regalia for that matter.

Luckily, it's our turn to move through the last gate to the Serv Ring, which I've heard is the most populous Ring of Regalia.

All that was gray is now shades of brown and tan. The buildings on either side of a large dirt clearing aren't studios or factories, but tiny attached buildings, backing to the tall boundary walls of the Ring. Most are in disrepair. The streets are a mixture of dirt and sand. Some of it gets in my shoes, but I don't dare stop to empty them out.

How can anyone be happy in this bleak place?

As inconspicuous as I am dressed, I stand out amid the sea of neutrals. People look at me with suspicion. I can't blame them. I do *not* belong. I suppress the urge to run home.

Xian points toward the outer wall in the center of the clearing. "There." He nods at a massive double gate that is taller than any gate we've passed through. It's fortified with iron bands. "Beyond that is the Swirling Desert."

So the gate's mass is designed for a reason; to keep the death and destruction of the Desert at bay. I shiver at the thought of what swirls so close. Too close.

A crowd has already gathered. I look around for anyone I recognize, any of Quan's fellow dancers, but I don't see anyone. For that reason, I'm glad I came. No one should face death without friends nearby.

Am I his friend?

"Shall we join the crowd?" Xian asks.

He walks first, carving a path for me. People part, but don't look pleased by my presence. I am a beacon of brown and gold extravagance amid their woven and wrinkled essentials. I'm embarrassed by the distinction.

Xian takes me to the front of the throng. I spot the Imp woman who'd made my clothes standing on the other side of the Road. She's staring at me. I nod at her, but then she gets flustered and quickly looks away. I find her reaction unnerving.

As we settle in a spot, the people behind us complain they can't see. Xian flashes them a look and they stop complaining.

"What now?" I whisper.

"The condemned will be brought forward." He does a double take and says, "There. Here they come."

They? I never considered that I would see more than one exile. Enforcers lead four people to form a line in front of the huge gate: a tall brute of a man, a middle-aged couple, and Quan. He sees me, scowls, and spits in my direction.

Instinctively, I recoil.

He isn't done. He shouts, "You deserve to be here too, Cashlin!" He points a finger at me. "She is guilty too!"

Many in the crowd look in my direction. I tense up, ready to run.

Xian leans toward me. "He can't hurt you anymore."

I hold onto the truth of his words. I lift my chin and stand my ground, pretending to be brave and strong.

The big man is pushed toward the crowd a few steps.

An Enforcer raises his hands to quiet the crowd. "You, who are condemned to die may speak."

The man scans his audience, his face tight with anger. "I did what I did and I ain't sorry fer it. I'd do it again." He looks at the Enforcer. "Do whatcha gotta do. Let's get this over with. The rest of you can go to hell."

The Enforcer takes his arm and turns him toward the gates. He motions for the great gates to be opened.

As they are rolled to the side everyone gasps at the sight of swirling sand being blown horizontally, a barrage of windborne grit and powder, an imposing, frightening wall of death. Oddly, the wind doesn't blow sand through the gates at all. It whirls past, as if it's fully a separate entity. An entry into a separate world.

The moment seems surreal. Though I am obviously aware that the Swirling Desert surrounds all of Regalia, I've merely thought of it as a natural barrier, something to know about but not dwell on, like the ground beneath my feet or the sky above. Here in the Rings, we are safe. The Desert doesn't affect us. We live our lives.

Until times like now, when the Swirling Desert's ominous power is close enough to touch. Close enough to kill.

The Enforcer pushes the man toward it. "Go meet your fate."

The man's bravado is gone, his body is tense. He doesn't move.

"Go, I say! Or we'll throw you in."

The man hesitates, then walks forward, pausing at the edge of Regalia. He takes a deep breath and steps for —

He is immediately sucked away in a roaring black cloud of sand. His scream is quickly silenced.

There is a communal gasp at the implication, at the reality of his death.

I look at Quan. He's stepped back. His hands are by his face. He keeps shaking his head *no*.

I find my own head shaking. This kind of execution is horrible. Hideous. Appalling.

But the process moves on.

The Enforcer has the couple step forward.

Their demeanor surprises me. They don't cower or stand erect in tight anger, lower their heads in shame, or embrace each other, seeking comfort. They look back at the crowd, their faces glowing with utter peace.

"How can they look so at ease?" I ask Xian.

"It's like I told you about when they come to trial. They're always so calm."

A woman to my right says, "They're at peace because they're Devoted. They have faith in the . . . you know."

"The Keeper?" I whisper.

She nods, but suddenly looks uneasy. She's suspicious of me.

I think of Marli and Dom. Are they at risk of exile for believing? There has to be more to it than that.

"What did the couple do to deserve this?" I ask.

With a glance left, then right she says, "They had meetings, and shared Relics."

"Relics of what?"

She raises a hand to fend off further questions and steps away.

My attention is drawn back to the doomed couple. The Enforcer has told them to speak.

They smile at each other, hold hands, and raise their arms to the sky. "Death will never win!" says the man.

"We are free!" says the woman.

"All glory to the Keeper!" says the man.

"We willingly hand over our lives . . ."

As they continue their praises Quan shakes his head and smiles a mocking smile. I'm shocked at his arrogance. I don't understand the full meaning of their words, but for him to scoff when he's on the edge of death is disturbing.

The Enforcer raises his hands. "Enough. Go meet your fate."

With a nod the couple turns and walks arm in arm toward the swirling sand. But then . . . just as they reach the sand's edge, the sand blows upward and parts, creating a path for them to enter unscathed.

The Enforcer steps back. The crowd gasps.

Without hesitation the couple walk onto the path singing praises as they go.

"How did that—?" I ask.

Suddenly, Quan bolts for the path, but as he steps onto it, the sand sweeps down and sucks him into a dark cloud like the one that took the first victim.

"Why didn't he wait?" Xian asks.

I don't understand the question. "With the sand parted, creating a path . . . he took a chance."

"Parted? What are you talking about?"

I point toward the gates which are now being closed.

"Parted for the couple. They walked in peacefully."

"I'm not sure I'd call it peaceful to be swept up in a cloud—though it wasn't a dark cloud like the one that took the other two."

"There was no cloud at all," I insist. "The sea of sand parted."

He looks at me skeptically.

"Quan must have seen it," I say. "He ran forward to take advantage of the clear path."

"I thought it odd he ran straight into it, but the sands sucked him up the same as the first man."

I look around for the woman I'd talked to.

"Who are you looking for?"

"The woman who was standing next to me. Surely, she saw what I saw." I look around but can't find her. "She's left with the crowd."

"Which is what we must do. Come, Patron."

**

I don't remember much about our walk home through the Rings. As though reacting to the death of four people, the skies grieve with clouds of gray.

When we reach the Patron Ring, Xian asks, "You've been quiet. Are you all right?"

I nod, though I'm not all right at all.

"Are you glad you went?"

I muster up the energy to respond. "Yes."

He cocks his head as though unsure what to make of my short answer. "You have now seen what ninety percent of Regalia has never seen."

Actually, what ninety-*nine* percent of Regalia hasn't seen—not even Xian.

As we turn up my street, I stop him. "I can make it the rest of the way. Thank You for your protection. And your companionship. I've learned a lot today and couldn't have done it without you."

He offers a short bow. "You're very welcome. I am always at your beck and call."

With that, he turns back to the Road, and I continue home in a daze.

Dom meets me at the door. "You've returned. Shall I ring for Marli?"

"No, thank you. I think I'll spend some time in the garden."

"Would you like refreshment?"

"Not right now."

I walk into the garden and bypass my usual chair. I wander through the flower beds, strolling along the path—

The path. At the exile I *had* seen a path appear amid the swirling sand. Quan saw it too. No one can convince me it didn't happen.

Between beds of lilies and daisies I feel the weight of my experience press in on me. I fall to my knees and lift my face to the cloudy sky.

"What exactly did I see? I need to know."

I watch as two clouds part, creating a slice in the sky. The sun breaks through with a shaft of light—lighting on me.

I raise my hand to shield my eyes. Then I hear a voice.

"Don't look away. Look at me."

Me? I scan the garden. "Who's there?"

Out of a bed of lilies walks a bearded man. "I am the Keeper you seek."

Keeper? *The* Keeper? I scramble to my feet, terrified. "I'm not seeking you."

"But I am seeking *you*, Oria."

Logic takes over. "My name isn't Oria. You have the wrong person."

"I have the right person. You may not be called Oria now, but you will be."

"I don't understand."

"The name Cashlin has suited you for a time, as it means *vain*. But one day soon you shall be called Oria—one who is humble in spirit and manner."

I scoff. "That's *not* me at all."

"That's not you, yet." He walks toward me, an unassuming man in a tan caftan. His countenance is gentle, fully at peace. I'd seen such peace before . . .

"Are you responsible for the sand parting?" I ask.

He smiles. "I am. Were you surprised?"

"Of course. It was amazing. Miraculous."

"I enjoy making miracles."

I'm taken aback by the simple statement. He says he is the Keeper, and he knows things that no one else—

"I saw it and Quan saw it."

"He did. Yet it was not meant for him but only for those devoted to me."

"Then why did I see it? I'm not one of them, not one of the Devoted."

He smiles a patient smile. "You weren't, but you are now. Are you not?"

I press my fingers against my forehead. "I don't understand what happened then or what's happening now."

"You don't have to fully understand to believe. Do you believe what you saw was real?"

"I do."

"Do you believe I am real?" He extends a hand toward mine. "Go on. Touch me."

Tentatively I touch his fingers. Then he takes my hand in both of his. "There now. I ask you again. Do you believe I am real?"

His hands are warm, his touch comforting. "I do, but . . ." It's more than just the feel of skin against skin, there's something else exchanged between us. "I feel peace and calm and delight and —"

He laughs a genuine laugh. "Delight. I do enjoy that word. Delight and what else?"

A whirlwind of emotions dances through me. What I want to say seems presumptuous.

"Go ahead," he says. "Say the word."

"Love?"

He cups a hand behind my head. I look directly into his eyes and see beyond the brown or blue or hazel, into something limitless.

"*I* am love."

It's an absurd statement, and yet . . . I believe him. He exudes a warmth and joy and peace that is full of goodness and light.

I have no choice. I begin to cry. "I feel it."

He sweeps a tear away with his thumb. "I have always loved you and will always love you."

I nod, somehow knowing it's true. He takes me in his arms, and I cling to him in total surrender.

I don't know how long we stand there, but I know I never want to let go.

But then he pulls gently away from me.

I want to protest, but somehow know it's necessary.

"I have a job for you to do," he says.

I nod vigorously. "Yes, yes. Whatever you want."

He smiles. "You are to go into all Regalia and tell people about me."

My *yes* is prompted by the memory of the exiled couple. "I will, but . . . speaking about you is against the law."

"The laws of men are often fickle and misguided. I am the law." The details of my life interrupt the dome of faith he's woven around me. "I'm a Patron but—"

"Yes, you are a Patron. I chose you because you have the traits that are needed to influence others."

"But I'm a Patron of fashion, getting people to buy what I'm selling."

"Consider your product changed. Be *my* Patron. Influence people to buy what *I'm* selling."

"Which is?"

"Love and life everlasting."

I'd felt the love, but the other? "What is life everlasting?"

He raises a finger. "I will explain that to you when you are ready."

I'm actually relieved. My mind is already full to overflowing, but not just my mind, my heart, and even my soul. I think of the task he's given me. "How can I share when I know nothing about you?"

"Because I know everything about you, I will show you who I am, one step at a time. Open your eyes to see and your ears to hear." He seems to sense how overwhelmed I feel. "Trust me to show you what you need to know, when you need to know it."

"I do. I think I really do." I feel a deep stirring, wanting to absorb everything he wants to teach me. "What next?"

"You will receive a note from a stranger, wanting to meet. Say yes."

"All right. But what about my duties? I just won the Reveal. Am I still Cashlin or Oria?"

"You can present yourself as Cashlin—for now. It's not yet time for your new name to be disclosed."

"How will I know when it's time?"

He smiles. "I promise, you'll know."

I believe him. I believe everything he says. "Back to the Reveal . . . there are responsibilities I need to fulfill."

"Fulfill them. I will guide you in the way you should go." He puts his hand on my shoulder. "Do you trust me, Oria?"

"I do."

"Then we have our beginning."

"Of what?"

"Of my last call."

"Last call to what?"

"You shall see." He turns to walk back into the garden.

112

"Don't leave!"

He looks over his shoulder at me. "I will never leave or abandon you." He smiles and touches the leaf of a tree. "I do love gardens."

I watch him go, embraced by the garden he loves.

Then I panic, wanting him back. I run through the garden looking for him.

But he's gone.

I will never leave or abandon you.

I fall to my knees and let my body finish its downward motion, resting my forehead on my hands. "I am yours, Keeper. I am yours."

**

I remember little about the rest of the day. There was *him* and then there wasn't.

Yet as I muddle through dinner and get ready for bed, I still feel his presence, am warmed by his smile, and find strength and comfort in the memory of his embrace.

I see Dom and Marli giving me strange looks. I'd love to tell them everything but feel a need to privately wallow in the Keeper's visit, letting it percolate into every pore of my being like water seeps into willing soil.

Marli helps me into bed. "Are you sure you're all right, miss?"

"I am. Don't worry about me."

"But when I found you in the garden . . ."

I lay back on the pillows and smile. "I promise you, I'm fine. I'm better than I've ever been in my life."

Her eyebrows rise. "May I ask what happened?"

I'm not ready to talk about it. "Just know it's a very good thing."

The best thing that has ever happened to me.

Chapter Thirteen

Solana

I'm not sure what rouses me in the middle of the night, only that suddenly I'm wide awake, and sitting up in bed. It takes me a moment to make the transition from my dreams to reality.

I try to remember what I'd been dreaming about, but the images and thoughts dissipate like morning dew. I get under the covers again, knowing I need sleep. Witnessing Thom and Tamar's exile brought back sad memories of my son's fate. Plus, today I know I'll face the wrath of Bru.

I let my head hit the pillow, but it nearly bounces off when I sit up again as I hear a clear mental message: *Listen to me.*

All right. I guess I'm not supposed to sleep. The Keeper has obviously awakened me for a reason.

These nocturnal messages have happened before, and usually lead to me praying on behalf of someone I know. So, this time, I bow my head and open my mind to his guidance.

I immediately think of Cashlin.

I'm surprised—yet not surprised—because his previous directive to go to the exile caused me to cross paths with her. We'd only had a short verbal interaction, and one across-the-crowd moment of eye contact. But there was something meaningful about both.

And so, I close my eyes and purposely think about her. She is a stunning young woman. Even with her hair pulled back and wearing a conservative caftan, she stood out in the crowd. She could have been wearing our bland uniform and I would still stare at her beauty. But also stare at her for an element beyond that, some intangible essence that makes me think she's someone special. She obviously is, because she is the Premier Patron, but it's more than that. Deeper than that. It's like she—

Write her a note.

I started. A note? From an Imp to a Patron? It isn't done.

But the direction doesn't fade away.

Knowing that I won't get any more sleep until I follow through, I wrap a shawl around my shoulders and tiptoe out to the main room, being careful not to awaken Helsa who sleeps in the bedroom we used to share. I light a candle and gather paper and pencil.

I sit at the table, ready to write.

I have no idea what to say. I look upward and whisper, "Now what?"

The answer to my question doesn't come to me in words, but in images. I see myself sitting with Cashlin in a garden. A house is close by—one I've never been to. In a moment of clarity, I know it's her home.

Her home?

The idea of me going to a Patron's home is ridiculous. Yet the Keeper must know what he's doing.

And so, I begin to write: *Patron Cashlin. I am the woman you met on the way to the exile, the one who embroidered your caftan. I request a meeting with you at your convenience.*

I read the words through. They sound respectful. But then I'm faced with a harsh reality: why would she ever agree to meet with me? She must receive notes from her Favored fans all the time. What will make my request stand out?

Mention the parting sands.

Parting sands? What does that mean?

My mind goes blank except for those words.

So, I write them down: *I am urged to mention the parting sands? I don't know what that means, but hopefully you do.* I wait to see if I am inclined to write more.

Nothing else comes to me so I sign my name: *Solana, from the Implementor Ring.*

I read over the note one more time. At the worst she will think a crazed person is sending her a note and she will throw it in the rubbish bin. At the best . . .

What's best? I don't really *want* to meet with her. I have no clue as to what I will say—or why we would meet in the first place.

But it isn't for me to understand. If my son was here, he would tell me to carry on in faith.

So I do. I fold the note and seal it with some wax from the candle. I am just about to write Cashlin's name on the front when Helsa comes out of her bedroom.

"What are you doing at this hour, Nana?"

I'm glad I haven't written Cashlin's name yet. "Just writing a note."

"Can't it wait until morning?"

"I'm done now." I stand and blow out the candle. "Back to bed for the both of us."

As I try to get back to sleep, I panic. How will I get the note to Cashlin?

The answer immediately comes to me.

Lieb.

The problem solved, I go to sleep.

**

I want to personally give the note to Lieb to deliver, so I get up early. I'm at the door when Helsa comes out of her room.

"Where are you going?" she asks.

"I have a special errand."

"You can't be late to work, Nana. You're in enough trouble with Bru."

I can only imagine. "I won't be late. I promise."

I hurry toward the Serv Ring. After coming up with Lieb as the answer to my delivery problem, I realize he and Helsa see each other for lunch only occasionally. I can't risk him not showing up. And I don't want to give it to him in front of Helsa. For some reason I feel the need to keep this correspondence a secret.

My mourning band is my ticket through the Serv gate. I rush toward Lieb's house, hoping he's still at home. I don't want to leave it with his mother.

All these logistical thoughts reinforce an unexplained urgency that I don't understand.

Luckily, I spot Lieb coming out of his house. He rightfully looks surprised to see me. "Nana. What are you doing here?"

My heart pounds in my chest from the journey, but also from the importance of my mission. "I have a note that needs delivering." I hand it to him. "It requires special handling."

He looks at both sides of the note. "There's no name on it."

"I know." I look around, feeling suddenly nervous. "It's for the Patron Cashlin."

He cocks his head. "Why are you writing to her?"

"It's a long story. Will you trust me?"

"Of course. Completely." He slips it into his messenger pouch.

"Can you deliver it first thing today?"

His eyebrows rise. "I always start with the Council Ring."

"Can you detour and deliver this one first? Before all the others?"

He pulls on his ear, a habit since childhood. "I suppose. If it's really that important."

Relief sweeps my nerves away. "It is. Thank you so much."

"Will you tell me what it's about?"

"Someday." Maybe.

I hurry back to my Ring. To work.

Chapter Fourteen

Cashlin

With the dawn of a new day, I am relieved — and thrilled — that what happened in my garden yesterday didn't vanish from my mind during the night.

It happened. Somehow, some way, I was visited by the Keeper. He talked to me and made me feel full and satisfied. But also exhilarated, as though something amazing was going to happen — more amazing.

I don't wait for Marli to come into my room but get dressed on my own. The buttons feel foreign to my fingers. Of course, most people have to dress themselves. It was a silly realization.

I head toward the garden, and surprise both Marli and Dom who are chatting in the dining room.

Marli is clearly flustered. "I'm sorry, miss. I lost track of time."

"You didn't. I'm up early. I'm just headed to the garden for a little air."

"Will you be wanting breakfast out there?" Dom asks.

"Not right now." I need time alone without the distraction of food or drink.

Then I remember something. "I'm expecting a note to be delivered. Please make sure I see it immediately, and make the messenger wait so I can have him deliver a reply."

"A note from whom, miss?" Dom asks.

Hmm. "I don't know."

I can tell he's confused, but he simply says, "As you wish."

I leave them to sort out the oddity of the morning and enter the garden. I stop a few steps in as my mind's eye sees what I saw yesterday.

Him.

Talking to me.

Holding me close.

Choosing me.

I press a hand against my racing heart. It feels good to be chosen, but I'm not sure how I can do what he's asked. How can I publicly tell people about him? It's dangerous. Plus, I'm not equipped for such a thing. It seems as impossible as me telling people how the Swirling Desert swirls. It's knowledge . . . beyond.

Which is, somehow, the point.

I walk deeper into the garden, to the place where he first stood. I touch the lilies nearby. I take a deep breath, trying to drink in the air he breathed.

Then it hits me anew: he breathed air. I felt his touch. I heard his words and saw the gentle love in his eyes.

He was real.

I want him back with a desire that makes my heart swell and ache with needful longing.

I raise my face to the cloudless sky. "Please, dear Keeper. I'm scared of the job you gave me to do because I know so little about you. I want to know everything. But how—?"

I remember the note that's coming. Knowledge is coming. With a few deep breaths I let that calm me.

**

While waiting for the note I wander through the house and garden, feeling a kinship with wind: there's a power behind me, creating me, moving me, but I have no control as to whether I blow left or right, turn back upon myself, or dissipate into nothingness.

Marli is worried about me. She doesn't say so directly, but she watches me as I say I'm going for a walk only to return a few minutes later—lest I miss the note.

There's a false alarm when a messenger comes with an invitation to join LaBelle and some other Patrons for dinner. I decline immediately, citing that I'm not feeling well.

That seems to be my excuse of choice lately.

Yet in some ways, it's true. Every muscle in my body is on high alert, ready to jump or dart or flee or twirl around six times and stand on my head. I have no idea what the note will say or what I will be asked to do. The Keeper said the note would be an invitation. To where? To what? By whom? Round and round the questions swirl, and where they stop . . .

As I aimlessly walk through my house for the fifth time I notice a painting of a lush garden in the foyer. "Is this new?" I ask Dom as he passes.

"No, miss. It's always been here."

Hmm. I feel guilty for not noticing this beautiful piece of art. I've lived here for three Reveals. I have nothing to do with the furnishings, but to not even notice the details? To not appreciate them?

I don't like feeling guilty, so I let my mind rally back to thoughts that I shouldn't *have* to notice because I'm busy and have important decisions to make, Reveals to orchestrate, and Favored to please.

It isn't my job to notice.

"Are you all right, miss?" Dom asks.

I stand in front of a vase of flowers on a table. I don't remember moving from the painting to here. "Are these from my garden?"

"Of course, miss," Dom says. "Would you like different blooms brought in?"

"No, no." I don't want him to think these aren't good enough. "These are lovely."

I startle when there's a knock on the door. Dom turns to answer, and I have trouble restraining myself from rushing after him.

Calm, Cashlin, calm . . .

Dom opens the door to a young man. "A note for Patron Cashlin."

"I'll take it."

He smiles and turns to leave, but I step forward and say, "Stay a moment, in case I have a reply."

"Yes, miss."

"Dom, ask him in to wait."

The man looks barely twenty, with a tousle of blonde hair and fair skin. He's skinny and taller than Dom. His eyes scan the foyer and the parlor, in awe. I see the hint of something colorful under his brown tunic.

I assume—and hope—that this is the note the Keeper spoke about. I rush upstairs to my room to read it in solitude. I stand near the window for its light. The note reads:

> *Patron Cashlin. I am the woman you met on the way to the exile who embroidered your caftan. I request a meeting with you at your convenience.*
>
> *I am urged to mention the parting sands? I don't know what that means, but hopefully you do.*
>
> *Solana, from the Implementor Ring*

The woman? The old woman I spoke with? Why would she want to meet with me? I would never have met her if I hadn't been at—

The implication of our meeting becomes clear. For whatever reason, we were supposed to meet.

That's a big enough revelation, but then the logistics of the meeting come to mind.

An Imp and a Patron. Meeting. Alone. Where can such a thing happen?

I quickly discard the idea of me going to her. I've had enough of being stared at as an oddity in the outer Rings. Meeting in a public area is also out. Since the content of our meeting has to do with the Keeper, privacy is essential.

"Here," I tell the room. "We have to meet here."

I sit at my desk and quickly pen a note, asking her to come this evening, according to her schedule. I will arrange passage for her at the guard gates.

I read it through one more time, stamp it with my wax seal, and am about to address it, when I decide to leave the outside blank. The messenger knows who sent the note. I will trust him to take mine back to the sender.

I bring it downstairs. He's looking at the painting I'd only just noticed.

"This is pretty," he says.

"Yes, it is. Thank you." I hand him the note. "Will you please return this to the sender?"

"Of course, miss." He puts it into his messenger bag. "But it will have to be after I deliver the rest of my messages. Solana's working all day anyway."

I'm disappointed but say, "Of course."

I see Dom hand him a coin. As soon as he leaves, I tell Dom. "I'm expecting a visitor this evening."

"Very good, miss. Would you like me to arrange refreshments?"

"That would be nice. And I also need to arrange passage for her at all gates between the Imp Ring and here."

His eyebrows rise. "I'll take care of that for you, miss. What's the name of our visitor?"

"Solana."

And so, I wait.

Chapter Fifteen

Helsa

I spot Nana slipping into the factory to sit at her worktable. She's totally out of breath and her face is red.

What errands took her out so early?

She looks at me and I answer her unasked question. "Bru's been here already."

"What did you tell him?"

"I said you weren't feeling completely well, but you *were* coming in."

"And his reaction?"

"He said he doesn't like to be tested." I point at her station. "I threaded some needles for you." She needs to get to work. Immediately.

"Thank you." She wipes her palms on her pants and takes up our newest assignment: embroidered hems for the skirts on Patron number four's look.

Her forehead furrows. I can tell she's overwhelmed — with good cause. We've just received the instructions for the winning outfits of the top ten. Instead of sewing a personal outfit for a Patron, we're now ordered to work at our fastest speed to create multiples of each outfit in many sizes. The Favored are waiting.

She looks over the embroidery instructions, but to speed things up I go through it with her.

Of course, Bru chooses that moment to come by.

"Get back in your station," he barks.

"I'm just showing Nana how—"

He glares at me. "If she was here when she was supposed to be here, she would know what to do."

Nana keeps sewing. "I apologize. I'll work my hardest to catch up."

Suddenly, he takes her arm and lifts her to her feet. "You know what? Yer done."

Done?

"Sacked. Get outta here."

What?

I'm stunned. This can't be happening. I stand to defend her. "Master Bru, please . . . I'll work extra hard until she catches up. She just needs time—"

"Time's up." Bru drags her toward the door. Drags my grandmother as if she's a rag doll.

I run after them. "No! Don't do this! Please!"

Nana is shoved onto the ground outside and Bru blocks my attempt to go to her.

She looks up at me with pleading eyes but shakes her head. "No, Helsa. Don't. It's all right."

"It's not all right!"

Bru closes the door between us and glares at me. "Think carefully before you act, girl."

Everyone is looking at us. My pride wars against common sense. Everyone hates Bru, for no one is safe from his whims and anger. Most want revenge as much as I do.

But if things get worse, would they come to my defense—and risk their jobs?

Bru cracks his knuckles menacingly. "What'll it be, girl?"

I want to scream, charge at him, pound him, scratch his eyes out.

Instead, I turn on my heel and return to my worktable. There are whispers from other workers as I pass: *It'll be okay . . . you did the right thing . . . stay strong.*

I don't feel strong. I feel like a coward. My heart beats double-time in my chest. I pick up the piece I'd been sewing but my hands tremble.

I hope Nana's all right.

**

On the way home that night, people fall in beside me. I appreciate their kind words of concern.

Lieb shows up. "Hey, Sa-Sa. How was your day?"

Where do I begin?

He looks around. "Where's Nana?"

"She got sacked for being gone yesterday at the exile, for being sick, and this morning she was late—and she won't tell me where she was."

"I know. She came to my house and gave me a note to deliver."

I stop walking. "Why would she do that?"

"Because that's my job."

Lieb can be very literal. "Why did she write a note?"

"I dunno."

"Who did you bring the note to?"

He scrunches up his face. "I'm not supposed to tell."

Really? "You can tell me. I'm family."

But he shakes his head and begins to walk. "Nana got sacked? Is she okay?"

"I don't know yet. Bru wouldn't let me go to her."

Just then a man wearing the breastplate and helmet of an Enforcer Serv steps beside me. I've seen him around the Imp Ring. One time he carted off a coworker for drunkenness.

My nerves stand at attention. "Yes?" I ask.

"You're related to Solana? You live with her?"

"I am."

"I went to her house, but she didn't answer. So, I'll give you the message. You have two days to remove her from your home."

"What are you talking about?"

He nudges the edge of his helmet to sit straight, then sighs with impatience. "Council Commandment number nine states if you don't work you don't sleep. She's no longer allowed to stay in Imp housing."

"*I* still work. I can pay the rent for both of us."

He looks to the skies overhead as if his next words are written there. "In order to live in Imp housing, those aged thirteen and over must work."

"She was *at* work. She'll go back *to* work." My mind is ready to explode. "I've also heard of people getting illness exemptions."

"That doesn't apply here. Solana isn't certified ill and there is no injury."

My mind races trying to find a way to fight this. But I can tell that logic won't win out. I'm done with this man. "Is there anything else?"

He hands me a piece of paper. "This is her notice. She will be moved in two days."

"Moved where?"

"To Debt Camp."

"She doesn't owe anything."

"She will."

That's true. "So, she's being punished for debt she might owe in the future?"

"I don't make the rules, I just enforce 'em."

I've heard of the Debt Camp but don't know anyone who's been sent there. Word is they are awful places of hard labor. Once in, there's no way to leave until the person's debt is paid. It's basically a life sentence.

Nana will never survive.

"And be forewarned," the Enforcer says. "After Solana leaves, and because of the death of your parents, you will be moved to smaller quarters."

"I also have to move in two days?"

"The Council is finding you another dwelling. You'll be kept informed."

"Lucky me," I say under my breath.

He grabs my arm and squeezes hard. "Watch yourself, Imp." He pushes me back as he lets go.

The Enforcer leaves us standing in the middle of the street. Everyone other than Lieb has backed away, creating space between us.

I know what I would've done three months ago. I would have run home and told Papa about it.

Now there is no Papa. No Mama. And soon there will be no Nana. My family has been taken from me.

I will be alone.

Lieb and I rush home. We burst through the door, out of breath.

Nana looks up from scrubbing the wood floor—which is usually *my* job. "What's wrong?" she asks.

"You're being sent to Debt Camp!"

Lieb helps Nana to her feet. She wipes her hands on an apron. "Where did you hear that?"

"An Enforcer told me and gave me this." I hand her the notice.

She reads it and her head shakes back and forth.

"He said he came here, but you weren't home."

"I was home, but I didn't want to answer. He pounded on the door."

"What are you going to do?" I ask.

"I don't understand," Nana says. "I *can* work. I was planning to ask Bru for my job back." She shudders. "I am *not* going to Debt Camp."

She sounds so certain. "Good. Because if they take you away, *I* have to move to a smaller place."

Nana looks shocked. "I never dreamed..." She rubs a hand against her forehead. "This is my fault because I went to the exile."

Not just that. "And because you left work that day, pretending you were sick—"

"To cover for you going to the Pile to apologize."

Good point. "But you were late this morning," I add. "You gave Lieb a note? What are you doing Nana?"

Nana flashes Lieb a look.

His eyes are wide. "You did. You gave me a note."

Nana closes her eyes and opens them. "And told you not to tell her—or anyone."

He looks dejected. "I didn't say who it was to."

"I expected more of you, Lieb."

"It was just Sa-Sa."

"I know, but you need to keep secrets better."

Lieb presses a hand against his chest. "Secrets make me feel heavy inside. I don't like secrets." Then his face brightens, and he reaches into his bag. "But I have a return note for you."

Nana grabs it eagerly, reads it, then unties her apron. "I need to go."

"Go where?" I ask.

"I can't say." She points a finger at Lieb. "And neither will you."

He nods emphatically.

Nana is out the door before we can discuss it further.

"What's all that about?" I ask him.

Lieb makes a locked lips motion. "I need to get home." He opens the door and hurries out.

"But wait," I say to the back of the door as he closes it behind him. "Tell me what's going on."

I am left alone.

At least the floor is clean. Thanks Nana.

Chapter Sixteen

Solana

I rush out of the house, knowing I've left Helsa with questions. I don't have time to answer them—not that I even know what to say. For *I* don't know exactly where I'm going. Or why. Or what will happen when I get there.

It's unnerving. I'm a woman of black and whites, not these hazy shades of gray.

Speaking of gray . . . I'm still wearing my Imp grays that are smudged with dirt from washing the floor. It can't be helped. I touch a hand to my hair. It would have been nice to run a comb through it. Whatever. I am what I am. I'm not meeting Cashlin to impress her.

Why *am* I meeting Cashlin?

There's only one reason: because the Keeper told me to.

As I approach the gate leading to the inner Rings, I walk by people I know but only offer a wave. They give me forlorn looks. They've heard about my firing. I'm always astounded by how fast news travels in our Ring. One reason is because ours is a Ring of repetition. When anything happens that breaks the routine of our factory work the news spreads— good or bad doesn't matter.

I get in line at the guard gate leading to the Favored Ring. I've never been to their Ring before. Imps don't belong among the Favored. It's not as if they're better than us, but . . . their lives are certainly better. Their only job is to wear pretty fashion—that we help create—and shop and party. It's hard to fathom such a carefree life.

When it's my turn to speak to the guard I keep my voice low. I don't know how legal it is to visit a Patron, but I don't want it getting around. "Solana to visit the Patron Ring?"

"What's your business there?"

I can be partially honest. "I was summoned by Patron Cashlin."

He checks the list and must find our names because he waves me through.

The Favored Ring undulates with people dressed in gaudy costumes. It makes me self-conscious about my drab gray uniform, yet they take little notice of me. In truth, I wouldn't want to dress up like they do every day. It must be exhausting to be *on* all the time.

I move up the Road and go through the gate to the Creatives Ring. I'm stunned by its brightness. As gray as the Imp Ring is, the Creatives

Ring is full of color. I'm not sure why our buildings can't be painted like theirs are, why ours are required to be shades of gray. Color would certainly make us happier. Maybe that's the point. The Council doesn't want Imps to be happy.

The line is shorter at Cashlin's gate. In all my sixty years I have never been through any of these gates — which is rather depressing. Out of the seven Rings of Regalia, I've only been to two. I suppose it's good that I've never been to the Council Ring — for the only reason any Imp would go there is to be put on trial.

My son was tried there, but he'd forbidden any of us to come to the proceedings. After he'd been arrested for preaching in public, he'd been insistent about facing the charges alone lest his crime and punishment attach to us.

The memory of it forces me to take a deep breath and let it out slowly. A Serv in front of me turns and gives me a look. I lower my eyes as quickly as possible. Was breathing not allowed in the Patron Ring?

It's my turn to speak to the guard. At least I'd had practice. "I've been summoned by Patron Cashlin."

With a raised eyebrow he checks the list and lets me through.

I walk into another different world. The street is paved and clean. The stores and pubs are neat and inviting. I pass a pub where laughing people sip drinks and eat outside. The smells make me remember that I haven't had supper. They look at me warily as I pass. I look down and walk on.

I spot a Serv sweeping fallen leaves on the street. "Excuse me?"

She looks up.

"Can you tell me where Patron Cashlin lives?"

Her eyes give me a good once-over and I feel less-than, even though I am an Imp and she is but a Serv.

A Serv working in the Patron Ring. That must have *some* status attached.

"Keep going around the curve. She has the best house in the middle, with a blue door."

"Thank you."

"It's getting dark soon," she says. "They lock the gates at night."

For the first time I noticed a bluish tint to the daylight. "Thanks for telling me."

I might be locked in? I never imagined such a thing. Will I be trapped or will they kick me out? The gate between Servs and Imps is always accessible. Of course, we have nothing to steal.

I hurry past lovely houses built of stone and wood, each standing separate from the other, with so many windows that I lose count. Trees, flowers, and stepping-stone walkways lead to brightly painted front doors. I spot an older woman reading a book in her front garden. She looks at me over her glasses.

"'Evening,' I say.

I feel her disapproving gaze as I walk by.

The homes get larger as I pass. I keep looking for the blue door. And finally, there it is.

I walk through a low ornamental gate and approach the two-story home that could hold at least four Imp families. There is grass on either side of the path. There's no grass in my Ring except in the farming area. To have grass right outside my door? I'd love to lay down in its lush coolness.

My heart beats in my throat. I am going to meet a Patron — Helsa's favorite Patron. I've been sent by the Keeper to meet with her.

I pause before knocking, calling out to him to give me the right words to do the job he's tasked me to do.

Whatever it is.

I knock and the door is opened by a Serv dressed in brown, but not in a simple tunic and pants, but a tailored jacket over a collared tan shirt. He wears a dark brown tie. I realize he is a House Serv, which I have only heard of, but never seen. I can tell by his demeanor he is a cut above the rest — or at least believes himself to be.

"Yes? May I help you?" His eyes skim my dirty gray clothes.

"My name is Solana and I have been invited here by — "

"Yes. Come in. Patron Cashlin is expecting you."

I go inside and am dazzled by the amount of light. There are a dozen lit oil lamps illuminating the entry with its sweeping staircase.

"Wait in here please," the man says.

I enter a room unlike any I have ever seen. There's a blazing fireplace, cushioned chairs, and large furniture where more than one person can sit at a time. The floors are lacquered wood but are covered with large rugs woven into intricate designs. There are small tables everywhere, with more lit lamps, pretty glass statues, and leather boxes set in arrangements to delight the eye. There are paintings on the walls in embellished frames. Freshly cut flowers make me want to drink in their scent.

I see a tray of small sandwiches — bread without the crust. And flat circles of dough with pink and green on top. I didn't have dinner but leave the food alone until it's offered.

I sit near the fire, realizing that my long walk at twilight has left me chilled. I run my hands along the padded arms of the chair and feel velvet. To have chairs cushioned with burgundy velvet seems the ultimate extravagance. I have to sit forward for my feet to touch the floor — one of the downfalls of being short.

"Solana?"

I quickly stand, hoping I won't get in trouble for sitting. "Yes, that's me."

Cashlin enters the room, a tall beauty, her red hair falling over her shoulders in luxurious waves. She wears a caftan of green and gold. She knows her best colors. She is stunning.

She pulls the sliding wood doors of the room closed behind herself and comes to greet me. "Hello, Solana," she says. She doesn't extend her hand to shake, and I'm glad, for I'm not sure about Imp-Patron etiquette—if there even is such a thing.

I nod with a little bow. "Patron Cashlin. Thank you for inviting me."

She indicates we should sit by the fire. I return to my chair.

"Was your travel through the gates without incident?"

"It was. Thank you for arranging it."

We sit in silence. She smooths the fabric of her caftan against her legs. I sit forward in the chair again so my feet aren't dangling. The question that comes to mind should have stayed there, but I hear myself saying it out loud. "Why did the Keeper bring us together?"

I see a flash of relief on her face. "I wondered the same thing. Apparently, meeting each other on the day of the exile was not a coincidence."

"It was not."

"I had never been to an exile before."

I find myself at ease talking with her. "My son was exiled for speaking about the Keeper in public."

Her face clouds. "I'm so sorry. Like the couple?"

"Yes. They were our neighbors."

"Oddly, they seemed . . . at peace."

"They were."

"Why?"

Ah. Her question indicates a lack of knowledge. Perhaps this is one reason we've been called to meet. "The Keeper will always take care of his own."

Cashlin looks skeptical. "The Swirling Desert is hardly 'taking care.'"

She makes a good point.

"Yet your friends didn't die," she says. "The sand parted, and they walked right in without a grain touching them."

"I don't know what you're talking about."

Cashlin's forehead furrows. "You didn't see it?"

"I did not." I don't like that she saw something I didn't. Yet if something happened that allowed Thom and Tamar to enter in safety…

Cashlin looks at the fire. "I saw it and Quan saw it, because he ran into the opening after them."

"So that's why he ran in so suddenly?"

She nods. "And then it closed, and he was swept away."

"I saw that part."

"You really didn't see the sands part?"

I feel left out. "I didn't. But that does put things in context. The parting sands . . . I was told to mention that to you."

"Told by whom?"

Since she lacks basic faith knowledge—and my own knowledge isn't extensive, I'm not sure how much to say—or how to say it. I ask the Keeper to give me the words. "Sometimes the Keeper speaks to me in my dreams," I say. "He gave me your name, spurred me to write a note, and told me to mention parting sands."

Cashlin considers this a moment, then scoots back in her chair. "I saw him," she says. "In my garden."

I stare at her. "Saw him?"

"I touched him. I embraced him." She hesitates a moment, then hurries on with more explanation. "I know there's no reason for you to believe me, but it happened. He was as real as you are."

Her intensity overshadows my disbelief. I have to believe what she says. It's essential.

"Have *you* seen him?" she asks.

"I've only heard him—actually, not really *heard* him, not verbally, just inside." I feel inept in my description. "It's hard to explain." I'm relieved when she doesn't require more details.

"I suppose he needed to do more to get my attention since I know so little about him."

"What did he look like?"

Her features soften and she smiles. "He had longish hair and a beard. Unexceptional really. Except for his eyes." Cashlin sighs. "It was like they saw into my innermost being."

I'm envious. To see the Keeper . . .

"I saw him, and so, I believe."

"But *I* haven't seen him."

"Yet you still believe."

"I do."

"Why?"

Oh my. I sit back and grip the arms of the chair. I've always had faith. My parents and grandparents had faith. Yet here was a grown woman who was starting from the beginning.

"I've put you on the spot," she says.

"You most certainly have, but it's good for me to dig into the whys of my faith. I grew up believing. It was never a question of whether to believe or not believe."

"I grew up with no mention of the Keeper at all."

"Your parents taught you nothing of faith? Of belief in a higher being?"

Cashlin shakes her head and scoffs. "The only higher being they believe in is the Council. Otherwise, our faith is in ourselves and in our own talents and abilities to win the Reveals and influence the Favored."

I want to judge her for her shallowness, but to do so will belittle all of Regalia. "I'm a part of that cycle. My life depends on it."

"See?" She looks relieved. "It's not just me. It's just the way it is. Like the Council says, 'What was was. What is is.'"

I grab onto a new thought. "But what *was* affects what *is*, doesn't it?"

"I suppose . . ."

The thought completes itself in my mind with a clarity that makes me know it's not *my* idea. "The Keeper was *and* is. So, he must be eternal."

"No man is eternal."

I realize it's confusing. "I don't understand how it all works, only that as our Keeper I know he has — and will — take care of us, like a Keeper takes care of his sheep. That's what it says in one of the Relics I've seen."

"Relics? A Serv woman at the exile mentioned Relics. You have one?"

"I do — it belonged to the neighbors who were exiled. It says that he knows his own sheep, and they know him."

"I don't know him," Cashlin says. "Not much anyway."

She knows him better than most. She's *seen* him. "He protects us."

"Like he did when he parted the sands for your friends."

I wish I would've seen that. "Yes. Like that."

Cashlin stands and moves behind her chair, holding its back. "He said I'm supposed to tell people that he offers love and life everlasting. What *is* life everlasting?"

That's a new one. "I don't know."

Cashlin throws her hands in the air. "If you don't know, how am I supposed to find out? And if I don't find out then how can I tell people about it?"

I wish I had an answer for her. "I don't know that either." Her face looks totally dejected. "As a part of him taking care of us I have to believe he'll help you understand so you *can* tell people about it."

Her chest heaves with emotion. "It's so far beyond . . . me."

"And me," I say. "And though I want to help you I'm not sure how I can."

We turn toward the sound of the sliding doors. The butler opens one just enough to speak. "The gates will be locked shortly, miss."

I stand. "I have to go."

Cashlin sighs and nods. "Thank you, Dom."

He steps away.

"I'm sorry that you need to go, Solana."

"Me too. But I need to get home to my granddaughter."

"What's her name?"

"Helsa. It's just us two since her father and mother passed."

"Both gone?"

I nod. I shouldn't have brought it up.

"When can you come again?" she asks.

I'm surprised. "Are you sure you want—?"

"I am. Whatever we need to learn, I guess we'll learn it together. If you want to, that is."

A Patron asking an Imp what they want? But she's right. I *do* want to learn.

"When can you come?" she asks again.

I've been sacked. I *have* the time.

Until I get taken to Debt Camp.

"Tomorrow?" Cashlin suggests. "Same time?"

I'd like to have more time with her tomorrow, but I don't want to be gone when Helsa is home. "Could it be in the morning?"

She cocks her head. "What about your job?"

I wave her question away. "Long story. Tomorrow, first thing?"

She nods, then suddenly notices the sandwiches. "Oh me. I never offered . . ."

"It's all right."

She rushes to the tray. "No, it isn't. You came all this way. Here." She carefully stacks a half-dozen in a napkin. And wraps the pretty circles in another. "Take these with you. Share them with Helsa."

"Thank you, I will. What are the circles called?"

"Cookies. Sugar cookies to be exact. You've never had one?"

"I have not."

She opens that napkin and adds four more. "Tomorrow I will be a proper hostess and serve you refreshments *before* we talk."

I like the sound of that.

She shows me to the door. "Thank you, Solana. I look forward to tomorrow."

"As do I."

**

By the time I get home, Helsa is frantic.

"Where have you been? It's getting dark."

"I'm sorry to worry you." On the way home I'd decided to tell her everything. I don't want to sneak around anymore. "I'll tell you all the details, but first, a treat." I show her what's wrapped in the napkins.

Helsa picks a pink cookie. "So pretty." She takes a bite and her eyes get big. "Oh. My. Goodness. These are delicious. They're sweet!"

"They're called sugar cookies." I take a bite and moan with the taste of it.

We sit at the table and consume every crumb while I tell Helsa about my meeting with her idol.

When I'm done with the telling she sits sideways in her chair, looking away from me. "I'm so jealous."

"Of me meeting Cashlin?"

She pivots to face me. "Yes, for you meeting Cashlin — *my* Cashlin. Plus, you got to see her fancy house and eat her fancy foods."

"I brought the food back to share with you, child. You ate them too."

A small cock of her head tells me she surrenders that portion of her complaint. "But you're going again tomorrow. It's not fair!"

I'm not oblivious. I've worried about what she would think. "Would you like me to tell her no?"

Helsa thinks about it, but only for an instant. "No. Of course not."

"But . . . ?"

She leans on the table. "You talked to her about the Keeper."

"A small bit. We're just starting."

"But you said she'd been visited by him. *That* sounds crazy."

I can't deny it. "I believe her."

"Why? She's a Patron. Surely, she's not one of the Devoted."

I shake my head adamantly. "No, she's not, not at all. She knows far less than we do about him."

"Then why did he appear to *her*?"

I'm taken aback, yet her thought is also my own. "So, you're not only jealous of me meeting Cashlin, but you're also jealous of her meeting the Keeper?"

Helsa lets out a huge sigh and I'm reminded that she's only nineteen. "Sorry, Nana. I don't mean to sound so petty, but . . ."

"What about you?"

"Well, yeah. I want to meet her too. Both of them. I've never even seen her in person. I only know her from the black and white photographs I've seen in the Reveal Revelations. I've read she has auburn hair, and I imagine it's beautiful. Way better than my mousey brown. I've never heard her voice either. What color are her eyes? I can't tell from pictures."

I put a hand on her arm. "I know what I'm doing is hard on you, but it's what I'm supposed to do. I know it."

"Because of a dream?"

I wish I could give her more reasons. "Yes. A dream. That's how the Keeper speaks to me."

"He doesn't speak to me at all."

Oh dear. I stand and pull her into my arms. "If I had control of when and how he speaks — and to whom — I would make sure he speaks to you." I take her head in my hands. "And he will someday. I promise."

"You can't promise that."

Probably not, but I want to give her hope. "What I can promise is that the more you speak to him, the more likely it is that he'll speak to you — in one way or another."

She looks unconvinced.

She gets up from the table. "I need to get to bed. I have a hard day tomorrow."

"Hard day?" I ask.

She gives me a look of impatience. "Did you forget what *I'm* doing tomorrow?"

I look at the air above her head, trying to remember. "I guess I have."

"I'm talking to Bru, trying to get you your job back."

It's amazing how distant my firing seems from this moment. It happened in another time, another world. "You don't have to do that, Helsa." I'm not sure I *want* it back.

She looks confused. "You have to go back, Nana. If you don't, they'll take you to Debt Camp and make me move to a smaller place where I'll live alone. Is that what you want?"

I press my fingers against my forehead. How stupid of me to ignore our very harsh reality. "No, of course not. I'm sorry. I appreciate you doing everything you can for me."

She gives me a look that says she doesn't believe me.

I don't believe me either.

Chapter Seventeen

Cashlin

I'm excited for today's meeting with Solana. I had trouble sleeping, but for once it wasn't because I was nervous about a Reveal. Or my trial. I'm excited to learn more about the Keeper. I feel like a sponge, ready to soak up new knowledge.

It's been a long time since I learned anything new.

I go out to the garden where Dom and Marli are arranging the breakfast I'd ask Irwin to cook for us.

"Very nice," I tell them.

"Thank you, miss," Marli says.

Dom perks up when he hears the bell, and hurries to answer the door. I don't mind that Solana is early. Maybe she's as eager as I am.

My mother bursts into the garden. "Good morning, daughter."

At the sight of her my stomach spins. What is she doing here? I don't want her to see Solana. We air kiss over each cheek.

Mother sees the food and plucks a stem of grapes. "My, my. If you eat like this every morning, you're going to get chubby, Cashlin."

I want to tell her I'm expecting a guest, but since I can't, I get to the point. "Is this a motherly visit, or is there something I can help you with this morning?"

"The latter." She sits at the small table I will use for Solana and me.

I don't sit, so as not to encourage a long conversation. "So?"

"My, my, aren't you brusque. Sit."

I sit on the edge of my chair, trusting Dom to keep Solana separate when she arrives. "I'm sitting."

Mother gives me a long-suffering look. "Barely. But since you've obviously lost your manners, I'll get to the point: why did an Imp visit your house last night?"

I feel my face move into its shocked expression, so I give myself time to recover by picking up a leaf that's fallen near my feet.

I wish there was a way I could deny her words. But there isn't.

"I met the woman on the way to Quan's exile," I say. "She'd sewn the embroidery on the caftan I was wearing."

"So? Imps make everything you wear. We wear. Everything everyone wears."

"I know, but—"

"Why this particular Imp? And why allow her into our Ring? That's highly irregular."

I hear the doorbell ring and nearly panic.

"You're expecting a guest?"

"It's probably a delivery for the cook."

"A delivery using the front door? How odd." She shrugs. "Back to you hosting an Imp . . ."

The truth won't do. But then I remember one of my first impressions of Solana. "She reminds me of Grandmother—your mother. She has kind eyes."

Mother harumphed. "You were the only person my mother was ever kind to."

"That's not true."

She plucks a grape off the cluster and eats it. "It *is* true. My mother never approved of how I handled my Reveals." She shakes her head. "I couldn't please her. Ever."

Like grandmother, like mother?

"I'm sorry you felt that way," I say.

She puts the last grape in her mouth, pushing it into the side of her cheek so she can talk. "My mother is not the subject here. What are you doing, inviting an Imp into your home? You've already dealt with trouble for fraternizing with a Serv, pushing the system by wearing an old outfit, and now you're hosting an Imp?"

Yes? "I did not fraternize with Quan. And in case you don't remember, I was found innocent."

Mother chews the grape she's been saving. "You were given a pass, Cashlin. One pass. Next time the Council won't go so easy on you."

"You're probably right."

"Of course I am." Mother stands and sets the empty grape cluster on the arm of her chair. "I'll leave you to your day as I have a friend arriving soon. We're getting facials together."

"That's nice."

"Yes. Well. Just watch yourself, daughter."

Her exit makes me fear for Solana's discovery. But in the time it takes me to put Mother's grape vine in the rubbish bin, Dom brings Solana into the garden.

"You're here."

"I showed her into the parlor, miss," Dom says. "And shut the doors."

"Thank you, Dom. That was very wise."

He leaves us.

Solana's eyes drink in the garden. "I've never seen anything so beautiful." She touches the petals of a deep pink flower. "It's so perfect it hardly seems real."

"I'm glad you like it. That peony has a luscious fragrance."

She leans down and takes in the scent. "Oh my," she says, smelling it again. "It's intoxicating."

I let her walk the path on her own. I'm happy to share my garden with her but feel bad that she's never seen such flowers. What is a world without flowers and greenery?

I lead her to the breakfast foods. "This time I will be a good host and we will start with the refreshment. Help yourself. Please."

Solana takes a small bit of everything, though I expect most of the food is new to her. I fill my plate too and pour her a beverage.

We sit at the table, and she takes a sip of the juice. Her eyes grow wide. "What fruit is this?"

"Peaches. It's peach nectar."

"Helsa and I occasionally have apples, but never peaches." She takes a bite of bacon, and again I can see she is experiencing something new.

Which makes me curious. "What foods do you generally eat in your Ring?"

"We eat a lot of bread, cheese, apples, and occasionally chicken. Carrots and potatoes too. Beans. I often make soup with whatever I can get from the factory store. It varies."

I glance at the spread of food offerings and feel guilty for its abundance and variety.

Her eyes brighten. "And eggs. Sometimes we get an egg or two."

I know my favorite souffle requires a dozen eggs. A souffle made just for me.

Solana must see my angst for she says, "Don't worry about what we have compared to what you have. I don't. Helsa and I never go hungry."

"You're too noble."

She smiles. "Now *that's* something I've never been called." She takes a bite of a blueberry muffin. "Mmm. I *could* get used to these."

I'm not sure where to start our conversation until I glance at a particular place in the garden. "That's where I saw him," I say, pointing toward the lilies and daisies. "He said he likes gardens."

"You've seen him just the one time?"

I'd thought that was plenty, but now . . . "Yes. Do you think he'll come again?"

Solana puts her hand to her chest. "I don't know one way or the other. I didn't mean to imply it wasn't enough. It's special, even if it is just once."

"It felt special." Yet I don't want to dwell on an experience that was mine alone. "Have you seen any more Relics other than the one?"

"I haven't, but my son saw one. He told me about it."

"What did it say?"

"It was a story. I don't remember it word for word, but I remember the gist of it. It was about a lost sheep."

She looks at me for permission to continue, and I nod. "Do your best to tell me."

Solana sets her muffin down and sits up straighter. "There's a man who has a hundred sheep, but one of them wanders away."

"Don't Keepers always lose a few?"

She shakes her head adamantly. "Not this Keeper. He left the ninety-nine and went off to look for the one."

"That doesn't seem wise. To risk ninety-nine for one?"

"I agree with you, but that's what the story says. The Keeper recovered the one, and that made him happier than the ninety-nine that didn't wander off."

"Why?"

"Because to the Keeper each one is precious."

I cock my head as the connections build. "Each one of *us* are precious?"

"We are. Very good."

I feel proud. I don't have a chance to challenge my mind very often. And yet . . . "The Keeper loves us and cares for us and goes out of his way to bring us to safety. But he also told me I'm supposed to talk about everlasting life. You said you didn't know, so how am *I* ever going to know?"

Solana shakes her head. "Don't assume I'm a wise old woman. I know what my parents and grandparents taught me. And my son. But my knowledge about the Keeper is limited."

"Then why were we brought together?"

"I don't know."

I sigh. "What I really need is for the Keeper to show himself again and explain things."

"That would be nice," Solana says.

"I guess we're going to have to meet many more times for us to figure this—"

"I can't come again."

I'm thrown off course a moment. "Of course. You have your job."

"Actually, I lost my job, and they've sentenced me to Debt Camp. They pick me up tomorrow."

I tried to wrap my head around that. "For what? Why are they sending you there?"

Solana shrugs. "I won't be able to pay rent or taxes without a job. The Debt Camp is another form of exile. There's no coming back."

That does not fit into my plans. "You can't go. I won't let you."

She snickers. "Unfortunately, it's not up to either of us."

My frustration propels me to move. I pace in front of the table. "You and I have work to do. We're just getting started."

"I know. Believe me, going to the Camp is the last place I want to go."

I stop in front of her. "Then *don't* go."

She looks at me as if I'm crazy. "I don't have a choice."

My mind flits through a litany of possibilities.

Solana looks at her plate. "I don't have any debt yet, but I will as bills come due."

"That doesn't seem fair. Maybe they'll give you more time until you *do* have debt."

"I don't think they work that way."

"I . . . I would pay your debt except there's a problem. I have little money, only money for incidentals."

Her eyebrows rise. "*You*, don't have money?"

I return to my seat. "I know it's odd, but as Patrons all our needs are met by the Council. I have this house and clothes and everything I need given to me. Even when I go out to eat, there's no bill."

"I had no idea," she says. "We get paid by the factory, but we have to pay for rent, food, and taxes."

"That's definitely not fair."

Solana sighed. "More and more I'm realizing how unfair Regalia is."

"As am I."

Dom comes out to the garden and checks the food trays. "Are you needing anything, miss?"

"No, thank you." But as soon as he leaves, I'm given an answer to our problem. "You can move in here, Solana. I have extra rooms."

"You want me to hide out?"

Maybe it isn't a good solution. I certainly don't want Enforcers raiding my house. But . . . "Not hide, per se. What if you worked for me?"

Solana looks confused. "But if you don't have money, how can you pay me, so I can pay—?"

"The Council pays for my House Servs."

"Would they approve of one more?"

I have no idea. "I can ask. As the Premier Patron, I don't think they'd deny me."

"But I'm not a Serv. If they've specified money for House *Servs*...."

I hate such details, yet the Council thrives on them. "You're a seamstress."

"I am."

"Then I need to get you assigned here as my personal seamstress."

"I would be happy to help you in any way I can," she says. "But won't such approval take time? They're coming for me tomorrow."

I'm used to dealing with fashion logistics, not life and death ones. "Then come back here tomorrow. I'll put your name on the list at the guard gate—indefinitely. I'll pen a letter to the Council office, requesting funding for your new position. I'll have my assistant bring it there today." Actually, I'll have her bring it to my Enforcer friend, Xian.

Solana looks scared. *I* am scared. The idea of willingly drawing the attention of the Council again is frightening.

She stands. "I'll take the job. It will give you and I more chances to talk about the Keeper—we can start again tomorrow. And if I'm paid, then Helsa and I can remain in our house." She takes a deep breath. "I really appreciate your help, Patron. You're a lifesaver."

That remains to be seen. But one thing is certain: there's no turning back now.

Chapter Eighteen

Helsa

I wish I didn't have to talk to Bru today. Just being in the same air space as Bru creeps me out. But I have no choice but to beg him for Nana's job.

I wish Papa was here because he always took care of the hard things. With him gone, and Mama gone, and Nana virtually gone . . . it isn't fair I'm left to handle this. It isn't fair that I have no choice.

I've gone in early before other workers arrive because it's my only chance to talk to him one on one. It's eerie entering the factory when it's empty. The quiet is unsettling. I walk as silently as I can so as not to disturb the stillness.

I slow down as I approach Bru's office, putting a hand to my stomach. What if he says no?

I assume he will. Bru isn't the sort of man to give favors — though he expects favors in return.

I brace myself to deal with that fact. The idea of being alone with him makes me shudder, but I have to do it.

His door is open, but I knock anyway.

He's lounging with his feet on a table, picking his teeth. He sits upright, clearly startled. But he recovers quickly. "What do ya know? A special early-morning visit?"

I step inside. The whole office smells rank.

He scowls at me. "If you're going to say something, say it, otherwise I have work to do — unlike some people."

"Master Bru, Nana wants her job back. Please."

Bru stands to his full height, towering over me by at least a foot — in all directions. He looks like the brute he is. "Why isn't she here, doing the asking?"

I thought of playing up Nana's age and her grief, but making her sound weak wasn't the way to go. "She knows she was in the wrong and respects your authority too much to beg."

His beady eyes brighten. "Beg? That might be interesting — if you do the begging." He points at the floor in front of me. "Beg."

I take a step backward toward the door. "I will do no such thing."

"Hmm." He starts to stroll toward me.

"So does she get her job back?" My nerves bristle, and my muscles tense, ready to flee.

"Not so fast, girl." He closes the door, then stands inches from me. I clench my fists, getting ready to hit him if I have to.

Bru puts his thick fingers under my chin, forcing me to look up at him. "Maybe you and I can come to some kind of agreement." He cocks his head to the side and smiles a smarmy smile. His teeth are yellowed and rotten. "Your nana's job for a little..." He runs a finger along my jaw.

I want to beat him with my fists but decide on something else. I calmly take Bru's offending hand in mine and stroke it once. "Not if my life depended on it."

I can tell my words surprise him, but unfortunately, he recovers quickly. He jerks his hand free and slaps me, first one way, then the other. My face burns in pain. My nose bleeds onto my hand.

He pushes me backward to the floor. My head hits hard, and he climbs on top of me. I can barely breathe under the weight of him. I try to push him off, but he holds my arms down on either side of my head.

"I'll teach you to act high and mighty with me, you troublemaker. You're nothing, you hear me? You are nothing!"

He kisses me hard, over and over. I flip my head from side to side, trying to get away from his disgusting, slobbering lips. When he lets go of one of my arms and starts to touch my body, I scratch his face.

When he reacts, I push him off. He grabs at my leg, misses, but gets hold of my foot and pulls me toward him. I fall to my knees. He tries to drag me all the way down, but I kick him hard, in the face.

I manage to get free and run out of the office, out of the factory, into the street.

People are walking to work. I start to hide from them, but then think otherwise. I move so they can see me.

My injuries have the desired reactions: *What happened to you, Helsa?* and *Who did that to you?* They share words of horror and concern.

"Bru did this to me," I say, pointing toward the factory. "I went in early to ask for Nana's job back and when I refused to..." I let them fill in the blanks. "He did this."

Someone hands me a handkerchief.

There are more cries of anger.

"You need to report him, Helsa," my friend, Edan, says.

"Who to?" I ask. There are no higher powers-that-be at the factory than the manager.

An Enforcer Serv approaches the small crowd that's gathered around me. "What's going on here?"

I step forward. "I've been attacked by Master Bru." The bloody handkerchief speaks for itself.

People offer their opinions. "You can't let him get away with this."

"She's just a girl!"

"Do something! He's a brute!"

The Enforcer looks nervous, but wisely says, "I'll take care of it."

I'm glad for whatever he can do. My ears are ringing from Bru's slaps. "I need to get home."

"I'll come with you," Edan says.

I begin to shake my head but stop when it hurts. "No, Edan. I don't want you to get sacked too. I'll be fine."

We both see the Enforcer talking to a coworker. "He hurt her before, too," Edan says.

"There are more," I say.

"Maybe they'll all come forward now, add their stories to yours and hers."

"I hope so."

I walk home alone to an empty house. I look in the mirror. My cheeks are red from the slaps, and I can feel a welt on the back of my head. My wrists are sore where he held me, as is my ankle. My knees are red and angry. I wipe the last of the blood off my nose and contaminated lips.

The memories of what he did flash back—along with thoughts of what he *might* have done.

I curl up in bed and cry.

Chapter Nineteen

Helsa

I feel someone nudge my shoulder. I open an eye. "Lieb? What are you doing here?"

"Checking on you. Someone told me Bru hurt you. Everybody is talking about it."

I try to sit up but have to press a hand to my head against the pain. "I don't want to be talked about."

He touches a scratch on my forehead. "Poor Sa-Sa. Everyone's on your side. Everyone hates him—they always have, but they hate him more now." He makes fists and punches the air. "I want to beat him hard!"

"Calm down. I appreciate your anger, but you'd only get yourself hurt."

"I'm strong. I can fight."

Lieb is tall, but there's no violence in his heart. Bru would annihilate him. "Anyone going after Bru will only make him mad—mad-der."

"He's mad all right," Lieb says with a smile. "They arrested him."

I sit fully upright. "For hurting me?"

"Not just you. Three others said so too." He kneels beside the bed and squeezes my forearm. "They say Bru has a lot of demerits. With all this, he's . . . going down."

Those are not Lieb-words. "Meaning exile?"

His forehead furrows. "He needs to go far, far away."

Exile is certainly that.

I pivot and put my feet on the floor. "I need to talk to Nana."

"She's not here. Where is she?"

I don't know how hush-hush her meeting with Cashlin is, but Lieb is like family. "She's meeting with Patron Cashlin. At her house."

"Cashlin. I know Cashlin. I gave her Nana's note."

It's starting to make sense. A little.

"Why is Nana there?" he asks.

That's as much as I want to say. "You'll have to ask her." I put a finger against his chest. "Do *not* tell anyone about their meeting, understand? It's an important secret."

"Secret. Yes." His hand grabs onto air and presses it against his chest. "I'll keep it safe. I promise."

Lieb is the most honest person I know, and yet, by his pure nature, he is also the most gullible, an easy mark. Yet with Nana gone he is the only person I can confide in.

"When will Nana be back?" he asks.

"I don't know." I try to stand but wobble.

Lieb steadies me. "Go back to sleep. There's no reason to get up. Not yet at least."

"What does that mean?"

"I heard you're going to be called to test against Bru."

"Testify?"

"Yes. That word."

I ease down to the bed "I don't want to have anything to do with all that. They'll never believe me—any of us."

"I don't think you're going to have a choice."

I rub my sore wrists. I'm going to have bruises.

Maybe that's a good thing.

**

Lieb tucks me back into bed, then leaves to finish his deliveries.

As if I could sleep.

And yet I do.

I wake up when Nana touches my shoulder. "What are you doing home, child?" But when I turn on my side to face her, her eyes grow wide. "What happened?"

"Bru happened. He assaulted me."

"Because you asked for my job back?"

"Because I wouldn't pay him for it."

Her face turns red with anger. "He can't do that to my granddaughter. I won't let him. I'm going there right now—"

"Stop! He's been arrested."

She's stunned and quickly falls to her knees beside my bed. I tell her everything about the assault, Lieb's news about testifying, and Bru's possible exile.

"All that," she says.

"Exactly. And with both of us out of a job, and them coming to take you to Debt Camp tomorrow . . ."

She shakes her head once. Adamantly. "I'm not going to Debt Camp. I'm going to work for Cashlin as a personal seamstress—for a wage. So, everything will be all right. We can pay the rent and stay here, in this house."

"No, we can't. Because *I* don't have a job now. They'll probably be coming to take *me* to Debt Camp."

Nana moves from her knees to fully sitting on the floor. She pulls her legs toward her chest, making her look like a pensive child. "If they're coming . . . then you can't be here. You have to come with me."

"To Cashlin's?"

She nods. "As a Patron she has influence. She'll have a solution."

This is not the way I ever wanted to meet my idol.

**

We are so lucky to have friends. In the evening, many stop by to check on me—and Nana. To have both of us get sacked within days of each other, *and* to have Bru attack me. . . we are the talk of the Imp Ring for all the wrong reasons.

It seems we are in good company as we hear stories that reinforce our hatred of him. Oddly, it helps to know he wasn't just mean to us.

Some are curious about Nana and the Debt Camp. I can tell she doesn't want to tell them the truth—that she isn't going—but as they press, she gives in.

"Actually, I have a new job," she says.

"At which factory?" my friend Edan asks.

"Not at a factory, as a personal seamstress to a Patron."

Her eyes widen. "Which one?"

Nana hesitates. "Cashlin."

I wish she hadn't said her name. I don't want Cashlin to get in trouble because of Nana. There's something about Nana's new job that doesn't seem quite right.

And it isn't just me who thinks so.

A woman who works as a pattern cutter asks, "Can you do that—work for a Patron?"

Nana glances at me. I hold back a shrug. *Don't look at me.*

"She's a very kind young woman," Nana says.

Which doesn't explain anything—to them, or to me.

As they talk about Cashlin and the other Patrons, I notice a young girl of twelve or thirteen standing by the door, inside, but barely. She squirms as if she's fighting an inner battle.

I leave Nana's conversation and walk over to her. "Hi," I say. "Thanks for coming."

"You're—" She clears her throat and tries again, a bit louder. "You're welcome."

"I don't think we've met. I'm Helsa."

"I'm Falla."

"Do you work at our factory, Falla? I haven't seen you there."

She looks at the floor. "I sweep. After everybody's gone."

As she says the words her forehead furrows and she draws an extra breath.

That's how I know she's been hurt by Bru.

"Do you want to take a walk?" I ask.

"Okay."

We go outside. The sun is nearly set behind the tall walls of our Ring. I want her to tell me about her experience with Bru, but I'm not sure how to go about it.

We walk past the long strip of rowhouses, past small groups of people standing outside, chatting about their day. A few recognize me and give me a nod of support. But when we're finally at a place where no one's around she says, "Bru's hurt me. Lots of times."

I stop walking, appalled that this child . . . "I'm so sorry. He's an evil man."

She nods but doesn't meet my eyes. "He sometimes stays late while I'm sweeping."

I fill in the blanks. "Have you ever told anyone?"

She looks up at me. "I'm telling you."

I feel the weight of responsibility fall upon my shoulders. "Have you talked to any Enforcers?"

She shakes her head. "They won't believe *me*."

"They might not have believed you before, but now . . . there are others who've come forward. You can too."

She looks away. "I need my job. My mama is sick."

"Mine was too." As soon as I say it, I anticipate her next question.

"Is she better now?"

"She died."

"Oh."

I put a hand on her shoulder. "That doesn't mean your mama will die."

She shivers. "I hate Bru."

"I do too."

Falla looks at the sky overhead. "I need to get home. I just wanted to see you."

"Why?"

"Because I want you to get him. Make him pay." She runs down the street, into the shadows of the darkening night.

As I return home, I feel the burden of carrying her pain along with my own.

Chapter Twenty

Solana

"Please come to Cashlin's with me, Helsa."
She shakes her head.
"It's not like you have to go to work."
She eats the last bite of her breakfast. "Thanks for reminding me, Nana."
I look at the clock. I have no idea when the Debt Camp Enforcers will show up to take me away. "I have to leave *now*, child."
Helsa blinks, as if just remembering what staying home holds for me. "Sorry. Yes. You need to go."
I pick up a cloth bag that I'd packed with a few essentials for staying with Cashlin. The thought of Helsa, being here alone, makes me sad.
And scared.
"What are you going to tell the Debt Camp people when they come for me?" I ask.
She cocks her head. "What *should* I say?"
"I suppose you tell them that I have a new job. They'll argue with you, and probably say they have no record of it." I take a fresh breath. "That's why you need to come with me. And the Enforcers who want you to testify against Bru? They might show up too. You can't be here when any of them come."
"I can pretend no one's here. I'll bar the door."
"That won't stop them. Remember your father?"
I see her thinking. She has her father's eyes.
Then she says, "Fine. I'll come with you. For today." She stands and adds, "I do want to meet Cashlin."
Whatever works.

**

As we approach the gate leading to the Favored Ring—and the Creatives and Patron Ring beyond—I grow nervous. Not for myself, for I trust Cashlin has arranged for me to come back to her house, but for my granddaughter. Cashlin knows nothing about her coming with me. Will I be able to convince the guards to let Helsa pass?
The answer becomes clear when the first guard denies her entry.

I pull Helsa aside to let others talk to the guard. "Wait here and I'll get a note from Cashlin to let you in."

She looks uneasy. "Maybe I should just go home. It's obviously not meant to be."

"Yes, it is," I say. But as I watch people stream into the Imp Ring from the Serv Ring I fear my Debt Camp Enforcers will come through at any moment. I doubt they know what I look like, but then there's the Enforcers who may come for Helsa . . . I'm hesitant to linger any longer. "Stay out of sight as much as you can. I'll be right back."

The guard lets me pass and I rush through the next two gates and run to Cashlin's. I am exhausted and sweaty by the time I knock on her door.

Dom greets me and asks me in. He offers me a seat in the parlor.

I shake my head. "I have an emergency. May I see Cashlin right away, please? It's important."

He nods and I wait near the door. He disappears upstairs, and within moments, Cashlin comes hurrying down.

"What's wrong?" she asks.

I give a side glance at the butler, and Cashlin motions him away. "My granddaughter was assaulted yesterday," I tell her. "She's lost her job and there are Enforcers wanting her to testify against the beast."

"Which she should."

"It's not that easy. I don't want her home alone to deal with them, or to deal with those who will be coming to take me to Debt Camp — or even take her to the Debt Camp because she lost her job." I pause. "Have you received confirmation that I can work for you?"

"I have not — as yet." She nods. "Your granddaughter is welcome here too."

"But she can't get through the gates. She has no clearance."

Cashlin nods. "Where is she now?"

"Waiting on the Imp side of the Favored gate. I'm afraid Enforcers will see her there."

"Then let's get her through." She heads toward the door.

I'd expected her to write a note. "You're coming?"

"It's the fastest way to get her to safety."

As we hurry toward the gates, I can't believe someone like Cashlin is willing to go to such pains for me and my family.

We pass through two gates with no trouble, with Cashlin adding Helsa to the list of people who can pass. At the gate leading to the Imp Ring she adds the name, but I balk at re-entering the Imp Ring to collect Helsa.

"What's wrong?" she asks.

"I don't want to be seen and have Enforcers take me."

"Then I'll go."

Her words are strong, but I see a flash of fear in her eyes. I suspect she isn't used to traveling alone, much less passing into a strange Ring without an escort.

Just before she goes through the gate, she asks me, "What does Helsa look like?"

"She's nineteen, light brown hair . . ." I scoff. "She'll be the girl who looks terrified. She'll recognize you."

Cashlin takes a deep breath and passes through. I watch her look to her right, then her left, then see her take steps in that direction. She moves out of sight, but I can imagine Helsa's reaction to seeing her favorite Patron in person.

As I wait for them to get in line, I spot two Enforcer Servs pass through the Serv gate into the Imp Ring. They don't saunter in but are clearly on a mission. They turn right—toward our house.

Hurry, Cashlin! Hurry, Helsa.

Thankfully, they get in line, and by the glance Helsa makes toward our house, I suspect she saw the Enforcers too.

When they get through, they don't pause to greet me, but the three of us pass through the next two gates without incident.

Once in the Patron Ring, Cashlin still walks quickly without speaking. I agree with her actions. Helsa and I walk behind her. I won't feel completely safe until we're inside her house.

Even with our speed, I see Helsa taking in the beauty of the homes as we pass. Despite the seriousness of our situation, I'm excited for her to experience Cashlin's home.

As soon as we enter, Dom appears. "Did everything go smoothly, miss?"

Cashlin leads us into the parlor. "It did. Perhaps we could have tea and breakfast cakes?"

He nods and withdraws.

Cashlin moves to the two chairs near the fireplace. "Please, sit." She draws a third chair close.

I watch as Helsa sits in the chair I enjoyed just a few days previous. She has the same reaction, running her hands over the padded arms, relaxing into its cushions.

"Your house is beautiful," she says.

"Thank you." But Cashlin's face is serious. "Your grandmother mentioned you had a horrible experience with a man at work."

Helsa looks at me as if she's appalled that I'd said anything. How else would I have been able to elicit Cashlin's help in getting her through the gates?

She looks back to Cashlin. "My boss attacked me. And sacked me."

I add to the description of Bru's offenses. "Now other women have come forward against him."

"Has he been arrested?"

"He has. They'll want me to testify." Helsa squirms in her chair. "Going before the authorities scares me."

"It is daunting," Cashlin says. "But justice can be done—it was for me."

Helsa shakes her head. "It wasn't for my father. They exiled him because he spoke about his faith."

Cashlin nods her head many times. "Yes. How awful. Your grandmother told me about that. I'm so sorry."

"We were very close. I miss him every day."

Cashlin's face is pulled with compassion. "Of course you do. And of course you're hesitant about testifying. I was too."

I want Cashlin to understand the changes Helsa and I have been through during the past few months. "Her father—my son—was the foundation of our family. We all depended on him. His wife couldn't handle the loss and died of grief, leaving Helsa and I to carry on."

"And now this," Cashlin says.

"And now this," I say.

"You're both welcome to stay here—you're safe here."

Dom comes in with a tray of food and drink. Cashlin stands. "Come and have refreshment. You've already had a trying morning."

**

After eating the scrumptious cakes and fruit—beyond fullness—Cashlin suggests we walk out to the garden. I'm glad for the suggestion. I want Helsa to see its loveliness and the place where the Keeper appeared.

Helsa's eyes widen as she takes it all in. The color, the lush greenery, the heady fragrance.

"Did Solana tell you about my visit with the Keeper?" Cashlin asks.

"Yeah. She did." Her tone suggests skepticism.

"I know how surreal it sounds, but I assure you, he really came. He really talked to me. Right here." She moves to a place on the path with orange and white flowers growing on either side. "He was as real as you are." She raises her hand as if taking an oath. "I promise I'm telling the truth."

Helsa's expression changes, her doubt gone. "I believe you. Nana gets directions from him too."

"Though I haven't seen him," I say.

"He brought your nana and I together," Cashlin says. "She's already taught me new things about him — because I knew nothing about faith before."

"Nothing?" Helsa asks.

"Nothing."

I want Helsa to know what needs to happen next. "The Keeper asked Cashlin to be like your father and talk about him to others. Influence them."

Helsa immediately shakes her head. "Don't do that. Don't do it. You'll get in trouble."

Cashlin skims her fingers along a blossom as if finding her words. "I know that's a possibility. But I don't think I have a choice."

"Of course you have a choice." Helsa sweeps a hand to take in the garden and house beyond. "Why would you want to mess up your life? You're the top Patron. You worked hard for that."

A flash of doubt passes over Cashlin's face. "I know. But this is more important." She scoffs. "I'm not exactly sure how, but I know deep down I need to do this." She smiles at me. "I'm so thankful that I met your nana so I can learn from her."

"I'm thankful I met you too," I say. "Though I'm not sure how much more I can share. My knowledge is limited too."

Cashlin moves to the chairs, where we sit. "None of the people in my life — not my mother, my brother, not the other Patrons . . . no one has faith."

There, she was wrong. "You've mentioned that your assistant is Devoted."

"Marli, yes. And she said that Dom and my cook Irwin believe too."

"Are they open about it?" Helsa asks.

"I don't think so. They're very careful."

"But you're *not* going to be careful," Helsa says. "Surely the Keeper doesn't want you to put yourself in danger."

"I honestly hope not," Cashlin says. "But yes, it does frighten me a little." She chuckles. "A lot."

I have an idea. "Maybe your House-Servs can help us learn more. Maybe they've seen more Relics."

Cashlin cocks her head. "I'll ask." She leaves the garden.

Helsa immediately jumps on me. "Nana, what are you doing? Are you sure you want to get others involved?"

"I think we need to. I'm here to teach Cashlin, but it's made me realize that all I really know is what your father and our neighbors said about him. Cashlin's got a big job to do and needs more than just me to help her do it."

Cashlin returns with her House Servs. She gives formal introductions. "This is my butler Dom, my cook Irwin, and my assistant Marli—yet she's so much more."

When Marli returns the smile, I know they're friends.

"And this is Solana and her granddaughter, Helsa. They'll be staying with me for a while."

I notice their eyebrows rise.

As does Cashlin. "I've put in a request for a personal seamstress, which will be the position Solana fills. She does the handwork in the Imp Ring. And Helsa? I'll work on getting her a position here too."

I'm beyond grateful.

"And there's more," Cashlin says. "More that I haven't told you three about."

They look slightly nervous—as does Cashlin.

"I want you to change your point-of-view right now. Don't think of us as Regalia has deemed us: as Patron, Servs, and Imps. Right now, I need you to start thinking of us as sisters and brothers of the Devoted. Can you do that?"

"Are you one of the Devoted, miss?" Dom asks her.

"New to it, but yes. I believe I am."

Marli beams. "I'm so glad."

"How long have you been one of us?" Irwin asks.

"Not long." She takes a fresh breath. "Perhaps you'll feel more comfortable after I'm open with you. Let me tell you a story..."

They exchange skeptical—but curious—glances.

"Please sit," Cashlin says. "This might take a while."

They sit shoulder to shoulder on a bench.

Cashlin tells them about everything, from the parting sands, to the visit from the Keeper, to my nudges to contact her, and her knowing that an invitation would be arriving. But most of all, she shares her divine assignment.

The three Servs seem enthralled by her words, yet more than a little confused.

Dom is the first to speak. "We thank you for sharing all that, miss. But... the Keeper was in this garden?"

"He was."

"I would have liked to see that," Irwin says.

"Perhaps he'll come again," Cashlin says.

"What would you like us to do with what you've told us, miss?" Marli asks.

"I want you to share with the three of us, any and all information you have about faith and the Keeper."

"And Relics," I add. "Have you had access to any Relics?"

Their eyes grow large. Obviously, bringing up something so secret has made them wary.

"Sorry," I say. "That was reckless, and not my suggestion to make."

"No, no," Cashlin says. "Your suggestion is mine, Solana." She looks at the Servs. "Do you have any Relics?"

Dom nods. "We don't have any, but we've seen one."

The other two agree.

Cashlin claps her hands together. "Excellent! Tell us what it said."

Marli looks aghast. "Here? Now?"

"Yes," Cashlin says. "Right now." Yet she stands. "Or hold that thought. Let's go to the dining room where we can be more comfortable."

As we return to the house, Helsa whispers to me. "Is this really happening?"

"I certainly hope so. Isn't it wonderful?"

She looks less certain.

**

The six of us sit around the table, yet there are still chairs for six more. Cashlin, myself, and Helsa are on one side, with the Servs on the other.

"Now then," Cashlin says. "Tell us what the Relic said."

Dom presses his hands flat on the table and takes a deep breath. "It's a story about a godless judge and a widow who keeps pestering him."

"Go on."

"She keeps going before him, asking the same thing, even after he sends her away time and time again."

"What is she asking for?"

"She wants justice against an enemy," Marli says.

How timely.

"What happens?" Cashlin asks.

"Eventually the judge admires her persistence, gives in, and says he'll do as she asks."

I see that Helsa has her arms crossed. Is she thinking about the Council and Bru? For I certainly am.

"How does that apply to the Keeper?" Cashlin asks.

Irwin sits forward. "If an ungodly judge will give in to persistent requests for justice, so will the Keeper."

"We're to pray and not give up," Dom adds.

Helsa looks down, shaking her head.

I put a hand on her back. "You'll get justice against Bru, child. I know you will."

"Who's Bru?" Marli asks.

Cashlin quickly explains the situation, keeping it brief so as to not put Helsa through the experience again.

"He's going before the Council?" Dom asks.

"I think so," Helsa says. "They want me to testify."

"Then you have to do it," Marli says.

"And not give up," Irwin says. "Like the widow."

"They're right," I say.

Helsa pushes back from the table. "I have to go home."

"Why?" Cashlin asks.

"I have to be there for the Enforcers to find me, so I can testify and get justice."

It takes me a moment to understand — and accept — her logic. Even though she's right, I don't want her to leave. I take her hand. "Can't you stay here and still do that?"

She shakes her head and peers down at me. "They don't know where I am, Nana. Bru was arrested because of me. There are other victims, and last night I met a girl named Falla who's suffered under Bru more than once." She takes a fresh breath. "I have to do this."

There's a look in her eyes I've never seen before. She's not a dependent child. She's a determined woman.

"Stay here, Nana," she says. "You belong here. You're safe here."

"You can be safe here too," Cashlin says.

But Helsa shakes her head. "As long as I agree to testify, I'm safe at home."

"But what about a rogue Enforcer coming for me there?" I ask.

Helsa shrugs. "I'll say you're not at home because you have a new job." She turns to Cashlin. "Besides, I don't want to bring any of Bru's nastiness to your door."

As Cashlin begins to object Helsa heads to the door. I hurry after her, pulling her into an embrace.

"Be careful, child. And let me know what's going on."

She holds me tight. "I will."

"Your name is at the gates so you can come here at any time," I add.

She nods and pulls back to look me in the eye. "You're doing a good thing here, Nana. I don't understand how it will play out, but…"

"We don't either."

She smiles. "I guess you have to move forward on faith, right?"

"As do you." I sweep a loose hair behind her ear. "I'm glad you got to meet Cashlin."

She shakes her head.

I lower my voice. "You aren't glad you got to meet your idol?"

"Cashlin *was* my idol. Now you are." She kisses my cheek and runs down the street toward home—and whatever will transpire there.

I've never been prouder of her.

"Will she be all right?" Cashlin asks from the dining room.

I close the door. "I hope so."

Dom sits with others nearby. "One thing the Relic implied is that we are to come before the Keeper as relentlessly as the widow went before the judge."

"Meaning we need to pray to him often."

"We do."

And so, we did.

**

I am relieved Cashlin has a Patron gathering to go to in the afternoon because I'm exhausted. She suggests a bath and a nap.

I can't remember the last time I had either.

I'm shown to a guest bedroom. When the door opens to an opulent space as large as our entire house it hits me: I am the guest of Cashlin, the Premier Patron of all Regalia. Me. Solana. An old Imp whose most prized property is an ancient rocker with dinged up arms.

Marli has drawn a bath for me in an adjacent room that has its own tub, sink, and even a privy that flushes. The scent of flowers fills the room, a far cry from the horrible stench of the public privies I'm used to. I get undressed and slip into the warm water, immersing my entire self, letting my long hair float around me.

It's unreal. Almost ethereal. Is this what it feels like to die? To float from one world to another?

My mother told me when we die, we will go to a place called Paradise. Everything is good there. Peaceful. There are no tears or pain. But she's the only one I've ever heard speak of it. I've neither seen nor heard of any Relics that mention it. And so, I expect it was a Paradise of her own making, to ease her own fear of dying. And yet... Cashlin said the Keeper mentioned everlasting life. I long to know more.

My lungs insist I leave this underwater place, so I rise to the top of the water to breathe, proving I'm still alive. I wallow in the warm water a while longer, then step out of the tub and grab an enormous towel that fully wraps around me more than once. I'm glad I brought along clean underclothes and a fresh tunic and pants.

I dress and comb out my hair, pulling it back into its requisite low ponytail. Then I lay on a bed so large that my arms can't touch side to side. The bedspread is a soft brocade, woven in blue and green.

I don't want to go to sleep and miss a moment of this extravagance. It's a world away from how Helsa and I sleep back home. We used to share a room, sleeping in narrow beds. Since Fet's death I've moved into the room she shared with my son, but even that bed is narrow compared to this.

And now, Helsa is there alone, choosing to deal with Enforcers coming to take me away, or Enforcers coming for her testimony. It's frightening. Going back is not a choice I'd make, and I'm still surprised Helsa made it. The old Helsa — the child Helsa — was happily dependent on her father, mother, and me. I'm not sure why she's suddenly become brave.

I mentally take that back. She's often shown spurts of bravery, like the time she stood up to the Comfort Serve at her mother's funeral, demanding he say Fet's name. And running back to the Pile to apologize for her harsh words. Plus, when she met with Bru to ask for my job back.

Which led to her attack.

Which led to her firing.

Which will lead to her testifying before the Council against him.

I shudder at the thought and turn on my side to hug a pillow.

Like father, like daughter. There are two brave souls in my family.

Regrettably, I am not one of them.

Chapter Twenty-One

Helsa

I don't go straight home from Cashlin's. After passing through the Patron gate, my bravado leaves me. I don't want to hurry home to deal with the Enforcers who will surely come. So I hang back.

I am alone in the Creatives Ring for the first time in my life. Seeing the luxury of the Patron Ring ignited my curiosity to see more of Regalia.

Yet I'm not sure it does any good to see how others live better than we do. To see more is to want more. Since there is no way to move up in our world, does seeing and wanting serve any purpose except to make us envy and feel bad—or mad?

I don't let myself think about it much, but walk into the Ring.

My heart pounds. Will someone stop me? I mentally rehearse an excuse, saying I'm on my way to the Imp Ring—and have Patron Cashlin's permission. If they press me more, I'll . . .

I'll deal with it if and when I have to.

For now, I walk with a confidence I don't feel.

I'm immediately astonished by the colors. The long, low buildings that are on one side of the street have painted pictures on them of fanciful birds and clouds, and flowers winding around images of shoes and clothing. The people wear tunics and pants like I do, but they're colorful and inconsistent. One wears a solid red, the other orange, and others blue or green.

Through open doors I see a group sitting around a table inside a building that has stylized jewelry painted on its walls. They discuss drawings laid out between them. It must be a design studio.

Another studio has hats and headdresses painted on its side with colorful people coming and going.

What would it feel like to wear a color—any color besides gray? These people carry themselves differently. They don't look down as they walk, or even look straight ahead. They look around, and I see more than one pause and take out some paper to sketch something they've actually seen or imagined in their minds.

I don't know what it's like to be creative like that, to have talent. I have skills to sew the garments that these people design. That means something, but it's merely a matter of following directions. To pluck an idea from one's mind and run with it, share it, and see it materialize must be heady stuff.

There are only a few Imps walking around, but mostly Servs. We don't make eye contact, as if being invisible is an accepted part of who we are.

I reach a green area with trees, grass, and flowers. There are benches, and children playing. There seems to be no practical use for the area—not like the green areas in my Ring that are farmed or used for raising animals. *They* are not used for play. Or for relaxation.

There is little relaxation in the Imp or Serv Ring. To have this green space with no purpose but pleasure seems the height of extravagance. It lures me in. I follow the short path along the trees, and it makes me think of the path through the woods leading to the Pile. Yet those trees were wild and menacing, while these are manicured and inviting.

But then I do a double take as I see a tall, bald man leaning against a tree, jotting down notes.

He's the man I saw in the scary woods. He'd stared at me then and I'd scurried away, but this time . . . I step behind another tree and watch him. He wears the brown tunic and pants of a Serv and has a large leather bag slung across his chest, reminding me of Lieb's messenger bag. He's intent on his writing, and scribbles something out, then writes it again. He pauses to take a deep breath and looks up as if searching for the right words.

A child cries in the open grass area nearby, and I look in its direction.

So does he.

That's when he sees me.

He immediately stands upright and slides the paper and pencil in his bag as he walks toward me.

I suck in a breath, my nerves on edge. He spooks me. I hurry back, past the studios of the Creatives. I glance behind and see him following me, though with his long legs, his stride requires little effort to match mine. It's a race I'm going to lose unless I run.

So I do just that. I run the rest of the way to the Road. Luckily, the line at the gate is short. I see him stop nearby, but he doesn't follow me into line.

As I stand there, I can feel his eyes staring as he intently watches me until I make it through the gate. What does he want with me? To see him twice, acting suspicious and menacing . . .

Once I'm back in my own Ring, I run toward home, eager to close and bolt the door behind me. But when I get close, I pull up short as two Enforcers nail something to my door.

I duck out of sight until the pounding stops. I hear their voices as they walk past my hiding place. I wait until I don't hear them anymore. Then I rush home, yank the paper off the door, and go inside. I slam the door behind me and drop the plank into its latch.

I pull the street-side curtains shut, then sink onto Nana's rocker to let my heart find its normal rhythm again.

I read the note from the door:

> *Implementor Helsa is ordered to make a statement regarding Master Bru at the Enforcer General's office tomorrow morning at nine.*
> *Failure to comply will result in swift punishment.*

As compared to slow punishment? At least I'm not going before the Council. I've never been to the Enforcer General's office, but it's in the Serv Ring, which somehow makes me feel a little better about it.

I shove away such useless thoughts. As expected, I'm being summoned. I can't lick my wounds and return to a normal life.

Thanks to that awful man everything has changed.

I fold the note in half and lay it on my lap, covering it with my hands. I rock up and back. When was the last time my life was normal?

Papa. It was normal when Papa was alive. Why hadn't I appreciated how good things were back then? Why had I taken everything for granted? I'd been so spoiled.

That attitude is gone now, as dead and gone as Papa and Mama.

And Nana.

For I've lost her too. She has a new job and a new life with Cashlin. In fact, she *can't* come home or risk the Debt Camp.

I should've stayed at Cashlin's to be with her. It was my one chance to escape. All I have here is fear and confrontation and stress.

I never should've told anyone about Bru's attack. I should've run home and dealt with it by myself. *Telling* gave me the kind of attention I don't want. *Telling* made me an enemy.

Bru will never forget that I told on him. What if the Council lets him go? Will I be forced to look over my shoulder the rest of my life?

I close my eyes. I have never felt so tired.

I have never felt so doomed.

**

I'm startled by fierce knocking on the door.
I freeze and hold my breath.
They knock again. "Open up in the name of the law!"

There's no escape. I can't go on fearing their arrival, so I accept defeat. I have no choice but open it.

Two Enforcers stare down at me. "Yes?"

One shoves a piece of paper at me. "This is an order. We've come for Implementor Solana to take her to the Debt Camp."

They're not here for me? "She's not going there."

"Our papers say she is."

I hold up a hand to explain. "She has a new job, which means she can pay the rent and taxes."

The Enforcers exchange a look. "We have no notice of that."

"It just happened."

"We need to speak with her."

"You can't. She's at work." I do *not* want to send these brutes to Cashlin's. Their intrusion might make her change her mind about helping Nana.

"Where's that?"

I have to lie. "I'm not sure exactly. But you should get verification very soon."

"We'll wait."

I panic. "No, no! I mean, there's no reason to do that. Truly, you *will* get notice very soon, but not momentarily. If you don't, you can come back, all right?"

They exchange glances with each other. One of them shrugs.

"This isn't going away," one says, pointing to his order. "Unless we get verification by the end of day tomorrow, we'll come back and take her."

As they walk away, I see Lieb walking toward me, but he wisely puts his head down and veers in the other direction.

I crack the door open, and within a few moments he slips in.

"Who were they?" he asks. "They looked mean."

"They're from the Debt Camp."

"Nana's not here?"

"Have a seat. I have a lot to tell you."

**

Lieb puts a piece of paper in front of me and hands me a pencil. "Write Nana a note about the Enforcer General stuff."

I shove it away. "What good will that do? She can't do anything to stop it."

"She can pray to the Keeper. She can get Cashlin and her House Servs to pray too."

That would be nice.

"Plus," he says, pushing the paper back in front of me. "You need proof she works or else they'll come looking for her."

"I don't want them going to Cashlin's."

"No, no. They shouldn't go there. She's nice." He taps on the paper. "Write the note. Sa-Sa. I'll bring it there tonight. Nana needs to know what's happening." He takes my hand. "You shouldn't face all this by yourself."

I squeeze his hand. "I agree Nana should know, but I have no choice *but* face it by myself. Even if she was here, she couldn't go with me to the General's tomorrow."

He doesn't nod, but he doesn't shake his head either. "Are you scared?"

"Petrified."

"Do you want me to stay here tonight?"

"That's not necessary. Just deliver the note for me."

Lieb taps on the paper. "You have to write it first."

Chapter Twenty-Two

Cashlin

After the drama of the day—between Solana and Helsa and my Devoted House Servs, I don't feel up to the quarterly Patrons celebration. Yet I have to go. I can't accept the perks of my position without jumping through its hoops.

This is the first time I haven't wanted to go. It's always a fun time, with all twenty Patrons, their Creative Directors, and even some of the retirees gathered to celebrate a successful Reveal and vote. It's also a way to pass the time while the top ten outfits are being manufactured, before the stores are stocked for the Favoreds to dive in and pick the stores clean on Shopping Day.

One much-appreciated custom is that the designated attire is casual—or as casual as flashy Patrons allow ourselves to be. I'm wearing a floral caftan, belted at the waist. And flat sandals. The tall heels of the Reveal-wear are styles I avoid when I can. I've done nothing to my hair all day other than brush it. Solana's panicked arrival interrupted my usual routine. My makeup was quickly applied at the last minute, not wanting to miss a moment of the Keeper discussion that continued after Helsa's departure. If anyone at the party doesn't like it? At the moment I don't care.

I usually have no problem doing the meet and greet. It comes naturally—I was raised to do it. But today it feels forced. Does it look forced? I just want to get through the party and go home.

The food is too much—in quantity and presentation—especially since most of us fill our plates with dainty nibbles. I spot Amar and see that his plate is heaped from edge to edge. He's always had a big appetite.

He's talking loudly to a small group, telling a story that makes them laugh. Needing a laugh, I join them.

"The man who was supposed to be putting the heels on Cashlin's shoes, falls asleep on the job. I actually saw him fall off his stool." He makes a *plumph* sound with hand gestures.

"Must've had too much to drink the night before," someone says.

"Or the shoes were so boring they put him to sleep," someone else says.

Me? Have boring shoes? I don't think so. And I don't like their attitude. After meeting Solana and Helsa, I know the Imps work extremely hard. "Maybe he was tired from dealing with a difficult situation at home."

Amar looks at me as if I've said his face is blue. "Way to gloom up a story, Cash."

I can tell the others agree with him, but I continue. "Their lives aren't easy. There's a lot of pressure to get the clothes made, and I know of a young factory worker who was assaulted by her boss."

Amar makes an explosion sound and hand gesture by his ears. "And *poof!* My story is now officially dead."

"What I said is true. She—and other girls—have been attacked."

"That's none of our concern," Amar says.

"Isn't it?"

"We don't have control over what happens in the outer Rings," the number sixteen Patron says.

"We have enough to worry about right here, in our own Ring," number eight says.

I take issue. "What worries do we have here in the Patron Ring—or in the Creatives Ring?"

They look at each other as if my question is ridiculous.

Eight answers. "We worry about winning. You've had the luxury of being the Premier Patron for three Reveals in a row, but—"

"Due to your unorthodox choice to re-show an old outfit—"

"Because your initial Reveal was a loser."

They make me weary. "I thought we were done with all this."

Sixteen puts her hands on her hips. "*This* affected all of us. It's not just about you, Cashlin."

I feel their contempt like a stab to my heart. I am not oblivious to their envy or the consequences of my bold choice. I understand we are all competitors, but . . .

But what? Wouldn't I feel the same if one of them had done what I'd done?

"I'm sorry you feel that way." I turn to walk away, to find a new conversation.

Eight scoffs. "It's too late now, Cashlin. Go back to your Premier house and let the rest of us muddle through your wreckage."

I open my mouth to speak but know there's no changing their minds. They hate me.

I'm not sure how I feel about them.

And so, I keep walking and leave the gathering. I head home where there are lovely people who think lovely thoughts and share lovely ideas about a lovely Keeper that none of these very *un*lovely Patrons know anything about.

So there.

**

I go inside my house and call out, "I'm back!"

I turn toward the parlor where I find my three House Servs and Solana standing together, with Xian standing before them.

"Xian," I say. "How nice to see you."

"You may not think so after I tell you why I'm here."

Dom says, "Come everyone. Let's leave Miss Cashlin alone to—"

"No," I say. "Stay. You can stay. Please sit."

Xian remains standing, so I do the same. "Tell us."

"The Council has *not* approved your request for the addition of a personal seamstress to your household."

I hear Solana gasp. "I can't stay?"

"You can stay," Xian says, "but they will not fund your wages."

I sit beside Solana on the sofa. "You *can* stay," I say. "That's good news."

She shakes her head. "But if I have no wages then I can't help Helsa pay for our home. Since she's without a job *she'll* end up in the Debt Camp."

I look at Xian. "Did they give a reason for their decision?"

"They see no need to create a position that has never been needed before, in all Regalia's history. Something like that."

"I can't blame them." Solana looks at me with sad eyes. "Thank you for the invitation and the hospitality you've already given to me. I will always be thankful." She looks at Marli, Dom, and Irwin. "To all of you."

There has to be a way around this. "The Council pays my bills. I have no income to share—or I would, Solana. I really would." I look at these precious people. "This can't end here. It can't end like this. We're just getting started."

Xian raises a finger. "Started?"

Although I consider him my friend, I realize I haven't spoken with him since our last time together at Quan's exile. So much has happened since then.

"We're learning things. Together," I say weakly.

"About what?"

Dom stands. "If you'll excuse me, I would like to offer a portion of my wage so Solana can stay."

Marli and Irwin exchange a quick glance, nod, and stand with him. "We'll do the same."

I am touched beyond measure. "That's so nice of you. Our work here is important and I—"

But Solana interrupts. "You can't do that for me. I won't let you."

"We're not giving you a choice," Marli says.

"What *work* are you doing?" Xian asks.

I hesitate. It's not that I don't trust him—he's never let me down. But so far all we've shared were logistical challenges, from the exile to my note about Solana. My encounter with the Keeper happened after we'd parted at the Road. He is still an Enforcer—an Enforcer in the Council Ring. And as an Enforcer he will be against the Devoted and the Keeper.

He's waiting for my answer.

I move in front of him. "Can you and I talk about it later? Can you trust me?" Trust me to not break the law, even though I am doing just that.

He studies my face. I try to look sincere—which I am. And honest and trustworthy.

"Yes. I suppose," he says.

"I'll see you out."

We go outside and pause on the edge of my property. "I have a question for you," he asks. "It's none of my business really, but—"

"What question?"

"Why are you allowing your House Servs to sit in the parlor? When I came, they were all gathered there—with Solana, an Imp. It's highly unusual."

"Yes, it is—I know it is. But they've become friends."

"For this 'work' that you won't tell me about?"

"Yes, Xian. For our work. I'm sorry. I *will* tell you. It just can't be right now."

He nods once, but I can see he's hurt. I long to make him feel better. "I do want to thank you for helping me—again. You always go above and beyond your duties for my sake."

"I said I will always be there for you, and I will."

It's my turn to study *his* face. *He* is sincere. And honest and trustworthy. I long to tell him everything.

But not now. Not yet.

For once in my life, I have more than myself to think about.

Chapter Twenty-Three

Cashlin

I enter the dining room for breakfast. The table is set for two and Solana is standing by her chair.

"Good morning," I say.

"Good morning."

I take my place, but Solana remains standing. "Is something wrong?" I ask.

"I'm not sure."

"Please sit and we can talk about it."

"Sitting is part of the problem."

I have no idea where this is going. "All right then. Stand. But please explain yourself."

She puts her hands behind her back, then at her side, then behind her back again. Then she pulls out her chair and sits.

I am somehow relieved. "Tell me what's going on, Solana."

She fingers a fork, then puts her hands in her lap. "My position in your household has become . . . complicated."

"You're my guest."

She cocks her head. "You invited me into your home. You welcomed me here."

"The Keeper brought us together."

"Yes, he did. But in order to keep me here you had to create a position for me—that the Council denied. And then Dom, Marli, and Irwin offered to pay my wages."

"All true. It's amazing how it's all turned out."

"It is."

"But?"

"Am I an employee? Or a guest?"

"A guest. Saying you were an employee was a way to legitimize you being here."

"Because I am an Imp and you are a Patron."

She reminds me of my mother. "Can't we just forget that? We've been brought together to learn about the Keeper. All the rest is just details."

Solana lowers her voice. "I'm staying upstairs in a lovely guest room while the others stay in their quarters."

"Yes . . . that can't be helped. I only have three staff rooms."

"They eat their meals together and I sit in here, eating with you."

Oh my. As much as I want to ignore it, I see the problem. "I don't think the others mind."

"They're too polite and kind to say anything."

She's probably right. "So, what's your solution? I want—I need—to continue our learning."

"I agree." She presses her hands flat on the table. "I need to move home."

"What about the Debt Camp Enforcers?"

"As long as I'm able to pay my debts, they should leave me alone. Depending on what happens to Bru, I might be able to get my old job back."

"That would greatly limit the time we have to meet."

"It would." She lets her gaze take in the beauty of the dining room, the hand-painted floral walls, the hand-carved furniture. "But I also don't like the idea of Helsa being home alone. With all she's going through..."

"How is she?"

"I don't know. I've been here."

Ouch.

There was a knock on the front door and Dom answers it. He enters the dining room carrying a note.

"Thank you, Dom." I hold out my hand.

"It's for Solana, miss."

I pull my hand away. Solana opens the note and reads it. Her forehead tightens.

"I have to go home right now."

"What's happened?"

"Helsa has been called before the Enforcer General to give her testimony about Bru. Today." She stands. "I don't want her facing that alone."

I stand too. "Maybe I can help? I could contact Xian and —"

Solana shakes her head. "This has nothing to do with you, Patron. Bru is someone we've dealt with for years. And it's not just about Helsa but the other victims too." She sighs. "Helsa needs *me*, her nana."

"I understand." I feel panic rise as I see her to the door. "When will I see you again?"

She stands in the open doorway. "I don't know." She reaches out and touches my arm—the first time we've ever touched. "Thank you for all you've done, Patron. Helsa and I will never forget it."

Impulsively, I pull her into an embrace. "Neither will I."

At that moment I see Mother opening my front gate. She stares at us, wide-eyed.

I let go of Solana and she hurries out.

Mother's timing is impeccable.

I pretend nothing is amiss. "Good morning, Mother."

She flips a hand in the direction that Solana has gone. "What was all that?"

"All what?" I close the door and prepare myself for the onslaught.

She gives me a disgusted look. "First you kiss a Serv, now you embrace an Imp? At your home? I hate to think about what's next."

I immediately think of Xian, but go into the dining room, assuming she will follow. "I'm just starting breakfast. Would you like to join me?"

I sit at my place. Mother eyes the other place setting. We both know the truth of it, but I simply say, "Have a seat."

Dom appears and I see the briefest doubletake at the change in the chair's occupant. "Are you ready for me to serve, miss?"

"Yes, thank you."

"What's going on here, daughter? I won't let you pretend I didn't see what I saw."

Unfortunately. I unfurl my napkin in my lap. "Take a breath, Mother. I was thanking a fellow human being. Surely that's allowed — even in Regalia."

"From what I hear, you're causing a great imbalance in Regalia."

"I don't know what you're talking about." And I don't. Not for certain anyway.

"What I'm talking about is the party last night, where you shared some claptrap about Imp and Sev problems. Although I wasn't there, I heard enough to be concerned. You know the people in those Rings don't deserve—"

"Don't deserve compassion?"

"Don't turn this on me, young lady. I'm as compassionate as the next person."

"Which is the problem."

"What's that you say?"

Dom comes in with a tray and serves us. I'm glad for the distraction for it gives me a moment to think.

Unfortunately, Mother is not distracted enough to let it go. "Answer me, Cashlin. Why are you questioning my compassion?"

I decide to make it less personal. "As Patrons we are not the most compassionate people. Our job is to think of ourselves first — which we do very well."

She butters a muffin. "We think of others. We think of the Favored. We constantly try to please them."

True.

She continues. "I find no fault in fulfilling the requirements of our position. And I suggest—for your own sake—that you remember those requirements and stop rocking the boat with your forays into the problems and issues of other Rings. Each to his own, I say."

I understand everything she's saying, and until the Keeper came into my life, I would have agreed with her terms wholeheartedly. But with his arrival, my life changed. My thinking changed. I'm not sure exactly how much—or whether it's for the best—but I'm different now.

He said as much. He told me I'd be different.

It amazes me that he was right.

I hear a ruckus outside. Mother and I go to the window.

"Ah," she says. "Moving day. I always hated moving day."

"Unless you were moving up."

"Very true."

Outside, the street is full of carts moving the personal possessions of Patrons to their new home for the next three months—until the next Reveal and the next vote causes the fruit-basket upset to begin again.

"I'm exhausted just looking at them," Mother says.

I see LaBelle's things being moved out of her house next door. She's moving to the number three house on the other side of mine. Odd rankings on one side of me, even rankings on the other.

And I remain in the Premier home, right in the middle.

I let the curtain fall into place. "Maybe they should change the calendar and only have two reveals a year instead of four."

Mother returns to her seat. "It would never work. The Favored have a 90-day attention span. If they don't get new costumes, they grow antsy."

"They'd get used to it." I sit and take a bite of my lukewarm eggs. "I just wonder if this mad press from Reveal to Shopping Day is necessary. It might benefit the quality of life for all involved if the calendar was more relaxed."

"All involved?" Mother asks. "You mean it would make life easier for the Imps?"

Although I haven't specifically been thinking of them, it's true. "What would it hurt?"

Mother shakes her head. "Laziness does no one any good."

"No one's suggesting anyone be lazy, but—"

"Aren't you? By giving your precious Imps more free time?"

"They are not my precious Imps. Everyone needs free time to rest."

"Free time." She shakes her head, incredulous. "I mean, imagine the chaos of that. There you go, threatening the balance of Regalia again."

From experience I know there's no winning this argument, and so I do what I always do: I deflect by getting mother to talk about herself.

"Your front garden is looking especially beautiful, Mother. What is the red flower called?"

And she's off, talking about plants, leaving me free to finish my breakfast.

**

After Mother leaves, I walk toward the door to my garden.

Dom intercepts me. "Excuse me, miss? May we have a word?" He looks over his shoulder and I see Marli and Irwin standing behind him.

"Of course." I motion them forward. We stand awkwardly by the door. "What's on your mind?"

"Solana, miss. She's left?" Dom asks.

"She has. Her granddaughter has been summoned by the Enforcer General to testify."

"About that horrible Bru-person?" Marli asks.

"There's all kinds of talk about him," Irwin adds. "He's been a bully a long time."

"Then hopefully justice will be done," I say.

"She's a very brave young lady," Dom says. "Will Solana be back when that's over?"

"I don't know." I don't mention the awkwardness of the situation.

A knock on the front door startles us. Dom goes to answer it, and I follow.

Two Enforcers stand at the door. "Is Implementor Solana here?"

My stomach tightens as I step forward. "She is not. What is this about?"

"We're here to take her to Debt Camp. The guards at the gate said she came into this Ring."

"So why do you come here?"

"They said you came and talked to them."

When I went to get Helsa through. If only . . .

"Is she here?" one asks.

"She is not here, but you need to make note: she works for me."

The Enforcers exchange looks. "That's what her granddaughter said."

"Because it's the truth. Since she has a job, you have no reason to look for her. Or take her away."

"But our superiors say she doesn't have a job."

"They are misinformed. I am paying her to work in my household, which means she has the means to pay all future debts. As such, I must ask you to leave my house—and leave her alone." Will they buy it?

Another look is exchanged. One of the Enforcers shrugs. "As you wish, Patron." He bows.

I close the door. My heart pounds in my chest.

Marli rushes toward me. "Are you all right?"

"I'm fine. I hope that gets rid of them for good."

"I'm not sure that's entirely possible," Dom says.

I hope he's wrong.

Chapter Twenty-Four

Solana

Helsa and I sit together at the Enforcer General's office in the Serv Ring. Her left leg bounces up and down.

I touch it to make her stop and take her hand. "It will be all right. You're not the one at fault here. Bru is." I nod at the three other women in the waiting area. "And you're not alone."

"I know. That helps."

The other women are here by themselves. I suppose getting someone to leave work to accompany them is not an easy task. Once again, my lack of a job has given me the freedom I need at just the right time.

"Is he fair?" Helsa asks. "The General?"

I'm not sure what fair is anymore. "I'm pretty sure dealing with him is better than going before the Council."

Her forehead furrows. "Papa went before the Council."

"He did. As did Cashlin, because they broke Council laws."

"Bru broke laws too."

"Against other citizens. That's what the General handles." I cupped her cheek with my hand. "The fact the Enforcers listened to you right away when you condemned Bru, the fact others talked, the fact he was arrested soon after . . . that all points to justice being brought *against* him."

She nods but remains unconvinced. I don't blame her. Though logic says Bru should be punished, the ways of Regalian justice can be fickle.

The exterior door opens, and a young girl walks in warily. She looks as though a loud noise would make her run away.

But Helsa stands to greet her. "Falla. Over here. Wait with us."

She sits on the other side of Helsa, a tiny thing, no more than twelve. "I'm Helsa's Nana," I say.

"I'm Falla."

"Nice to meet you, Falla." I wish my smile could take her fear away but know it doesn't have that power.

"How's your mama?" Helsa asks her.

"Better." Her face loses a layer of worry—which returns when she looks toward the door leading to the General's chambers. "She says I'm supposed to be strong and tell the truth, no matter what."

"That's good advice," I tell her — tell them both. "You're both doing something very important today, very brave. You're helping to bring down an evil man."

"I hope so." She tucks her hands under her legs and leans forward, as if wanting to make herself as small as possible.

The chamber door opens. All talking stops. All bodies tense. A woman comes out. "Helsa?"

Helsa stands. "Here."

"Follow me."

I stand too, but the woman motions me back. "Just her."

Helsa gives me one final look, but also has one for Falla, along with a smile.

That's my girl.

As we wait, I see Falla lower her head. Her lips move, and though I can't hear her words, I can guess what they are.

I call out to the Keeper on behalf of all the women gathered here. It's the only way to make me feel less helpless.

**

In less than fifteen minutes Helsa comes back to the waiting room. Her expression is one of exhaustion, but she gives a thumbs up to the other women. "It's fine," she tells them. "You'll be fine."

Their relief is palpable.

The next name is called. "Falla?"

Helsa quickly pulls her into a hug. "We'll wait for you."

She nods and goes inside. As soon as the door closes, the other women pepper Helsa with questions.

She presses their words down with her hands. "It's not as bad as I thought it would be. Just tell your stories."

"Does he listen?" asks one.

"He seemed to," Helsa says.

The women still look frightened. I hope Helsa is right.

**

Helsa and I stand when Falla comes out of the General's chamber. Her arms are wrapped around herself.

She immediately embraces Helsa, who puts a comforting hand on the back of her head. "Are you okay?"

Falla lets go. "I am. But it was scary. He asked so many questions, the same question over and over."

"He did the same to me."

Falla smiles. "But I did it."

"Yes, you did," I say. "We're proud of you."

She looks at the exit. "I need to get to work."

It's nearly the end of the normal workday—which is when Falla's work begins.

"We'll walk with you," Helsa says.

As we stand in line at the gate to enter the Imp Ring, I think longingly of Cashlin and the short time I spent at her house. Had I been hasty leaving there today? I'm glad to have been with Helsa for her testimony, but now what? Helsa and I are both out of a job. I have a fabricated job at Cashlin's, so I feel beholden to do some work there, especially since Dom, Marli, and Irwin are paying my way. But our financial situation is tenuous.

"You want to go back to Cashlin's, don't you?" says Helsa, noticing my gaze.

"I do."

"Then go," Helsa says.

"Go where?" Falla asks.

I hesitate to tell her. I don't want everyone in the factory to know my business—more than they already do. "I have a friend in another Ring."

Falla's eyes follow the direction of my gaze—which is forward, to the gates beyond our Ring. "A Creative?"

"I can't really say."

Falla nods, receiving my secret as acceptable. I'm not sure it is, but for the moment I'm relieved.

We walk her back to the factory. "Are you going to get your jobs back?" Falla asks. "With Bru gone . . ."

"We probably should," Helsa says. "Could." We pause at the entrance and Helsa turns to me. "Nana, I'm going to ask about that. Do you want to go with me? Having two incomes again would solve a lot of our problems."

I don't like the idea of it. To not have time to see Cashlin and the others? They've become such an important part of my life. "Not yet," I say. "But you go ahead."

Helsa takes a deep breath. "I'm going in." I walk home alone, feeling guilty for *not* trying to get my job back, and proud of Helsa for stepping up. She's shown herself to be immensely strong. Immensely sure-minded.

I am neither.

I consider going to Cashlin's, but I want to be available when Helsa comes home.

I hope she gets the job.

**

"I got it back," she says as she bursts in the door.

"Congratulations. Is the new master nice?"

She shrugs and sits at the table to eat some soup. "It's a mistress. Mistress Toffa. One of the cutters."

"I know of her. She's a good woman. Things have to go better now. What's the mood around the factory?" I ask, cutting bread.

"Hopeful. Everyone was curious about my testimony and they're all excited to see justice done."

May it be so.

Chapter Twenty-Five

Solana

I'm glad Helsa got her job back. Maybe things can get back to normal now—or as normal as our lives can be considering she will be there and I'm going to be at Cashlin's during the day. I purposely wait until after breakfast time so as not to impose.

Dom welcomes me inside. "Glad to have you back, Solana."

"You're so kind." He closes the door behind me. "But, Dom, since I owe my new position to all of you, I do need to work. I'll do anything: dust, wash dishes, sweep . . ."

"There's no need for any of that. But I think Miss Cashlin has sewing for you."

"That's even better."

He points at the stairs. Marli stands on the landing. "Up here, Solana."

I follow her upstairs and into Cashlin's bedroom—which is lavishly decorated with sage green brocades and intricately carved furniture. The underside of the canopy bed is drawn toward a middle ornament of beads and fringe. Extensive draperies with valances frame the large windows looking out front. It's a bedroom fit for a queen.

Cashlin pops her head out of a doorway. "In here, Solana. Marli and I went through my clothes and have found a few items that could use mending or alterations. We need you."

I doubt they do but appreciate the opportunity to feel useful.

As soon as I enter the room I gasp—which makes Cashlin laugh.

"I know, I know. I have far too much." She picks up a purple dress with an embroidered hem.

"I sewed that embroidery," I say as I look around. "And that one, and that one." I'm amazed by how many clothes she has.

Cashlin puts her hand under the hem, then a sleeve. "See where it needs mending? I must have caught it on something."

The embroidery is intact, it's the sleeve and the hem in general that's come loose. "This is an easy fix."

She points at two other garments. "I only have a few repairs, nothing large."

"I have needles and thread," Marli says.

I expect Marli could do the repairs herself, but I appreciate their effort to give me something to do. "I look around the closet. "Where would you like me to work?"

"Right here, if you'd like. Or you choose. My home is yours."

The idea of sitting among all the gorgeous clothes excites me. "Here would be perfect."

"Very good then." She raises her finger. "Forgive me, I should have asked this first: how is Helsa? Did she testify?"

"She did. We're hopeful everything will be resolved soon and Bru will be exiled. Then we can all breathe easy. She also got her job back."

"I'm sure that's a relief. She's a brave girl."

"That, she is."

A clock in the other room chimes and Cashlin takes a step toward the door. "I have Patron business to attend to this morning, but this afternoon, I'd love to spend time with our studies."

"That would be perfect."

"Marli, please bring Solana whatever she needs." With a final smile she says, "I'll leave you to it."

The two women leave, and I stroll through the closet, drinking in the kaleidoscope of colors and textures that seem almost too fantastical to be real. Yet they are real. I helped create many of them.

I reach out to feel a satin sleeve, pull my hand back, then touch it again, realizing I did more than touch these fabrics, I held them in my lap, babied them, fought with them, and finally transformed them from something plain into something exquisite and special. For generations my family honed their skills to create clothes like these . . . this art.

"Did you work on that one?"

Marli stands in the doorway of the closet, a sewing basket in her hand. "I did."

"You're extremely talented."

"Thank you. Helsa embroiders too, and there are dozens of people in the factory who work together to create . . . all this."

"Cashlin is an expert at displaying *all this* to its fullest and finest."

"Helsa is her biggest fan."

She hands me the basket. I sit on the ottoman and begin threading a needle.

"I'm glad she's okay," Marli says. "I can't imagine . . ."

"I'm very proud of her—and all the other women who testified. Plus, Helsa getting her job back means with her income and mine, we can stay in our home. I owe you, Dom, and Irwin so much for your generosity."

"We're glad to do it." She adjusts a few blouses on their hangers. "We've called to the Keeper on your behalf—and hers."

I'm touched. "We felt his protection. Testifying could have gone badly."

"But it didn't?"

"But it didn't. Praise him."

"Indeed."

We hear Dom's voice calling for Marli from elsewhere in the house. "I need to go," Marli says. "Please let me know if you need anything else."

It's strange being left alone in such a place—a place that I never imagined I would see, much less spend time in. A place I didn't know existed. Of course, I knew that the clothes we created ended up somewhere, but to have so many displayed in one room is exciting.

Life is good.

**

As I finish the last bit of sewing Dom appears in the closet.

Is he checking on me? "All done," I say, hanging it up.

"That's nice. That's good."

There's a stitch in his voice. "Is everything all right?" I ask.

"Actually no," he says. "Enforcer Xian is downstairs with a message."

"But Cashlin's not here."

"I told him that, but then he insisted on speaking with you."

I sit on the edge of the ottoman. I don't know this man. What does he want from me? "Am I going to Debt Camp?"

He seems surprised by my words. "No, it's not that. Would you come downstairs please?"

"Of course." Whatever it is, it can't be good.

I walk down the stairs warily. He stands in the foyer waiting for me. He towers over me. "Yes?"

"I have news of Bru."

"What about him?"

"He's been found not guilty."

These impossible words fight against logic. "Five women testified against him."

"I don't know what to say. He's been let go. He's back at work, at the factory."

"No!"

"I'm so sorry. I thought you'd want to know."

Panic takes over. "I need to go. I need to be with Helsa."

I barely hear his condolences as I run out the door.

**

The Imp Ring buzzes with the news. Those who know me, stop me to say how sorry they are, how unfair it is, and to wonder what will happen next.

I wish I knew.

I briefly stop at home, assuming Helsa has been sacked again. But she's not there. Surely Bru won't let her keep her job.

I hurry to the factory. From the outside nothing seems amiss. I stop a few people walking by. "Is Bru in there?"

"That's what we heard."

Bru is in there. As are Helsa and the other three witnesses. Falla isn't due to work yet, but when she arrives . . .

I shiver at the thought of it.

I pace in front of the factory door, wishing someone would come out and tell me details.

Finally, I can't stand it any longer and slip inside. What can Bru do? Sack me?

I notice how quiet it is. No one is talking at all.

Helsa intercepts me and practically shoves me outside. "You can't be here, Nana," she whispers. "He's on a rampage."

"What's he doing?"

"What he always does — times ten. People are scared to death."

"Has he singled you and the others out?"

She nods. "He told us to meet him in his office after work."

"You can't do that."

"We don't have a choice." She takes a deep breath. "Why did they let him off? *How* could they let him go?"

I can only shake my head. "I'll wait for you."

I'm glad she doesn't argue with me.

We hear Bru's booming voice. "I have to go." Helsa disappears inside.

I stare after her. I've never felt so helpless. Helsa is my only family, and I'm supposed to take care of her. But what can I do?

My legs lose all their strength, and I fall to my knees. I let my body finish the motion, and bow to the ground.

People come to my aid, comforting me, telling me everything is going to be all right.

I don't believe them.

**

I snap out of my despair enough to sit at the well. I've made a fool of myself and know the Imp grapevine will make sure everyone knows that Solana lost it and collapsed. I'll be gossiped about, and worst of all, pitied.

I don't want to be pitied. I want to be strong—or thought of as strong.

"Solana."

I look behind me and see a man in a brown, hooded caftan. He has a pointy black beard, and I realize where I've seen him before. He's the Comfort Serv from Fet's funeral. Was his name Teel?

"What are you doing here?" I ask.

"I heard the news and came to help."

I scoff. "How can you help?"

He is honest enough to shrug. But then he says, "Have you considered appealing to the Enforcer General?"

I perk up. "Can I do that?"

"I'm not sure. But since his job is to get testimony for citizen against citizen crimes . . . I feel bad for all your family has gone through. I think it's worth a try to appeal to him. I'll go with you."

"I'd like that very much."

At least I'd be doing *something*.

**

Walking with Teel in the Serv Ring I notice many people subtly touching their chest as he passes. I remember Helsa saying that there were a few Comfort Servs who believe.

"You're respected here," I say.

It takes him a moment to understand my reference. "I try to help."

There's more to it than that. "I've never seen you or your kind in the Imp Ring before."

"You can thank your granddaughter for my presence there."

"How did Helsa—?"

He stops walking and draws me toward a building for privacy. "When she chastised me for not mentioning . . ." He cocks his head, and I know who he's talking about. "She shamed me."

"She apologized."

He lifts a hand, stopping me. "I was in the wrong. And it made me realize that I've been a coward."

Gracious. "And that led you to come to the Imp Ring?"

"More than that." He pulls a small piece of paper from his pocket. "The Devoted among my colleagues have decided to act. We have made hand-written copies of the Relic we have in our possession and today I distributed many of them in your Ring."

"May I have a copy?"

"Of course." He hands it to me, and I immediately slip it into my pocket.

Since he confided in me, I decide to do the same. "I've been speaking with Devoted in the Patron Ring."

"So there *are* Devoted there?"

"Some House Servs . . . and one Patron."

His eyebrow lifts. "Really."

"Her interest is new. But I believe her faith is genuine."

"May I ask who it is?"

I'm not willing to go that far. "You may ask, but I won't answer. She's already in a precarious position."

"I understand."

As we begin to walk again, I take advantage of his presence. "Helsa told me you said, 'So grows the seed'. What does that mean?"

"Every bit of knowledge about *him* is a seed that needs to be nurtured until it reaps a harvest."

"Meaning?"

"Hundreds of Devoted. Not just dozens."

"That's a tall order."

"I believe it's what we've been called to do." He returns the sign to a few more people we pass. "Would you thank Helsa for me — for being hard on me."

"I will." Helsa will be shocked but pleased.

We reach the Enforcer General's building and enter. The waiting room is full of nervous people.

I approach the man sitting at a table near the chamber door. "Excuse me?" I say.

"Name?"

I shake my head. "Solana, but I'm not here for me, but for my granddaughter. Helsa? She testified yesterday."

"Then move along."

"I've come for information regarding the verdict in the case."

"What's the name?"

"Bru."

He blinks. "Citizen Bru was found not guilty."

My stomach tightens. "I wish to appeal the verdict."

The man scoffs. "There *is* no appeal. Move along." He looks down at his papers, dismissing us.

"Please, sir," Teel says. "At least listen — "

He stands. "I said, move along."

182

For him to dismiss me so quickly, without even listening is one thing, but to dismiss a Comfort Serv . . .

Impulsively I sweep a hand across the table, making the papers fly. Then I face the others in the room. "There is no justice in Regalia!" I yell. Remember that, everyone! There is no justice in Regalia!"

Teel physically pushes me out of the office, nearly carrying me. "Be quiet or you'll get arrested too."

"I don't care." I wiggle out of his grip.

"You need to care. Helsa needs you."

Helsa. I came here to help Helsa. The air goes out of me. "I shouldn't have done that."

"No, you shouldn't have. But I understand why you did."

We duck into an alley, and I lean against the building. "I feel so helpless. The authorities don't care about those women."

"You care. I care."

"Little good it does."

He puts a hand on my shoulder and lowers his voice. "*He* cares."

I shake my head. "If he's our protector then why did he allow them to be hurt at all?"

"You'll like the Relic I gave you. It will help."

I become aware that time has passed since I left the factory. "I need to get back."

"And I need to get back to the Pile. Read the Relic tonight. It will help."

I'll have to trust him on that.

Chapter Twenty-Six

Helsa

As my first day back at work ends, I watch for Falla. I don't want the girl to come inside the factory without support.

Then, there she is.

She stands just inside the entrance as if ready to flee. She sees me and I motion her over.

"It's so quiet," she whispers. "I heard the bad news. Is he here, or not?"

"He's here."

As if to prove it, Bru's voice booms from across the factory. "Do it over!"

Those three words are his battle cry. We've all been hunkered down, trying to please him—if that's even possible. At the very least we're trying not to make him notice us at all.

"I've got to get my supplies ready." Falla scurries away. I hope she can stay out of his sight.

No such luck. He sees her.

"Well, well," I hear him bellow. "The last of the whiners is here." He grabs hold of her upper arm and drags her toward me. "I think it's time to gather all the traitors together. Helsa? Come join us—and bring your basket of finished collars."

I eye the door. It beckons me to run. But I don't. I can't leave Falla alone. Plus, me running will only anger him more.

Everyone has stopped work. I stand beside Falla, and thankfully, he lets her go. She takes refuge under my arm.

"Now we need the rest of the traitors: Ana, Meli, Vue! Come join us and bring along your completed work."

They approach warily, each holding a basket of sewing. They line up beside me.

"Follow me."

Bru grabs an oil lamp near the door and leads us outside.

"Dump your baskets there." He points to the ground.

We do as we're told. How can we do otherwise?

Then he tosses the lit lamp onto the pile. The fabric catches fire. We take a step back.

I feel the heat of the flames. The others cower in shock.

"There now," he says, grinning. "Ain't that pretty?"

No one says anything, but we all share anger at the loss of a day's worth of work. It's no accident that he waited until now to do this.

A crowd gathers, and someone brings a bucket of water.

"Put that down! The work of the traitors needs to burn." He turns in a circle to catch every eye. "This is what happens to those who tell lies about me, who threaten my position with their pettiness. When they hurt me they hurt my work, so I hurt them and theirs. I will not be terrorized by such evil-minded, deceitful people." He points at each one of us. "I will not be challenged by anyone. Ever."

I feel Falla shudder under my arm. My shudder joins hers.

"This is *my* factory. I am the master in charge. I make the rules. Do you understand?"

We all nod, but it's not enough. His eyes bulge and he waves a hand at us, waiting for more.

"Do you understand?" he bellows.

"Yes!"

"Yes, what?"

"Yes, Master Bru."

He has one more jab to make. "Remember this: *you* always lose, I always win." He kicks the embers with the toe of his boot. "Falla, clean this up. The rest of you, back to work. You won't leave until you make your quotas."

Which means we are never going home.

We go inside, sending a few brave coworkers scrambling away from the door where they'd been watching. We return to our worktables where I pick up the bodice I'd been working on.

"Are you all right?" Edan asks.

"No. I'm not." I have twenty buttonholes to create and it's nearly closing time.

Bru walks up behind me and puts his grubby hands on my shoulders. "I hope it was worth it, girl."

My skin crawls under his touch. My mind goes blank, and I don't know what to say.

"Though I have to say my cousin was impressed with all the testimonies."

"Cousin?"

He moves in front of me so I can see his face. "The Enforcer General." He cocks his head. "Didn't you know?"

He cackles and walks away.

The whole thing was rigged.

Rage builds and I can barely see clearly enough to thread a needle. Everything we did by testifying was for nothing.

Nothing is ever going to change.

This is how my life is going to play out, day after day after day. I think of a dozen ways I could hurt Bru for what he's done—and is doing.

If only...

**

Everyone in the factory files out at the end of the day—except the five of us who testified against Bru.

When we are alone, he strolls between us, rubbing his hands together like a maniacal villain. If it wasn't so real, I'd laugh.

No one laughs.

"I'd love to stay and enjoy the night with you, but I have better things to do. My cousin and I are going out to celebrate my victory." He laughs. "My gain is definitely your loss." He turns serious and sweeps a pointed finger at all of us. "No one leaves until your work is finished—high quality work or I will burn it all again." He smiles. "I may burn it all anyway, I haven't decided yet. See you tomorrow when we can start this all over again." He gives a mock bow. "Ladies."

As soon as he leaves, I hear crying. I hold up my hand. "Stop. Let's make sure he's not lurking outside. We don't want to give him the satisfaction." I go to the door and peek out. He's down the street talking with someone, then keeps walking out of sight.

Suddenly, Nana rushes to the door and slips inside. She pulls me close. Then Falla. "I'm so sorry. I heard what he did and what he's doing."

The five of us gather near my table. "It's completely unfair," Ana says.

"There's no end to it." Mali says. "You know there isn't."

"I have a family," Vue says. "I can't stay all night."

"I'll help," Nana says. "I'll help all of you meet your quotas."

"Thank—"

The door of the factory opens and Lieb comes in. His face is red with emotion. "He burned your work?"

"He did. And now we have to stay to remake it."

He flings his messenger bag off. "Tell me what to do."

The door opens once more, and four women slip in. "What can we do to help?"

I am touched beyond measure.

**

Injustice brings out the best in people.

While the eight of us sew, others bring in food. Lieb helps Falla clean.

But it's not the work that matters. It's the camaraderie. Someone starts a familiar song, and we sing all the verses. We share stories about our families—turns out we didn't know that much about each other before our shared troubles with Bru.

As the only man present, Lieb repeatedly reminds us that he'll protect us. As if he could. I notice a scrap of Cashlin's purple velvet wrapped around his wrist. I expect it will show up in his vest to earmark the occasion.

As the clock moves after midnight, as our trust grows, Nana bridges an important subject. "I think we need to ask the Keeper to watch over us in the days ahead."

The women exchange glances. We all know the risk of speaking like this. Leave it to Nana . . .

"I will," Ana says.

"He's our protector," a woman adds.

But Vue shakes her head. "I can't do that. I can't add more drama to my life."

"Drama?" I ask.

"It's not easy talking about him. It's a risk. My aunt was exiled for being Devoted."

Ana balks. "Well . . . maybe you're right. I don't want to go before the General again—or worse, the Council. It's not worth it."

The words hang there, potentially scaring everyone off.

"I think it is worth it," Nana says, lighting the way again. "In fact, I was just given a new Relic that speaks of him."

"How did you get it?" I ask.

"From Teel."

"My Teel?" Helsa asks.

She smiles. "The very one. In fact, he says you were instrumental in getting him and the other Devoted Comfort Servs to be more courageous." She looks at the group, who are finishing their last handwork. "They've been copying their Relic and handing it out."

Vue tosses her hands in the air. "I don't want to hear about Relics. That's what got my aunt exiled."

I have a sudden worry that speaking of such things in a mixed crowd is risky.

Nana must have the same thought, for she says, "Vue—and any of you who are not among the Devoted? I won't force my beliefs on you, but in return, I ask that you honor the bond we've made here tonight, and never speak against each other in any way."

Vue sighs deeply, then nods. "Agreed."

"What's the Relic say?" Ana asks.

"Honestly, I haven't looked yet." Nana unfolds it, takes a second to scan it, then smiles. "How appropriate. 'Don't try to get even. Let the Keeper take revenge. He will pay them back.'"

Meli laughs aloud. "How did he know what we needed to hear?"

"Because he's with us," Nana says. "He knows us, and we know him. We hear his voice."

"I don't hear his voice," Falla says.

Nana presses a hand to her chest. "In here you do, if you listen hard enough."

Vue puts her last piece of sewing in her basket. "It sounds good, but I can't deal with him right now. I need to get home."

I look at the clock. "We've reached our quotas. Plus, we have to be back here in four hours."

"To do it all over again," Meli says.

The women move their chairs and their baskets back to their stations and gather by the door. We hug each other, as well as all those who came to help us.

Nana raises her hand. "Dear Keeper, bless our work and keep us safe. We trust you to bring us justice."

As we file out, a few helpers hang back to talk to us. "Thank you for what you said in there, Solana."

"You're welcome."

"We want you to know that there are many Devoted in our Ring — and beyond."

"Many others," the other woman confirms.

Nana squeezes their hands. "I'm so glad. Let's meet again."

Nana and I walk home in the dark. "You started something in there," I say.

"*I* didn't start anything, he did. And now we have to trust him to finish it."

Chapter Twenty-Seven

Cashlin

Solana is late coming to my house — which is not like her.

I'm eager to speak with her about Bru's release, and him being back to work at the factory. I wish I'd been home when Xian brought the news yesterday. Not that I could've helped.

I feel helpless a lot lately.

Unfortunately, I can't wait around for Solana, for today is an important day: Choosing Day.

Dom announces that my carriage has arrived. He helps me in, and I am off to the Creatives Ring, to the quarterly Choosing. It has always seemed odd the Patrons choose their next styles even before their last styles hit the shops in the Favored Ring. We never get time to enjoy the fruit of our labors because Regalia always wants more. Our motto: *Always something new* is not necessarily a good thing. The Cycle of Regalia is never-ending and relentless.

As the carriage passes through the gate, I suffer a different feeling than I've ever felt before: discomfort, nearly embarrassment. I'm used to taking a carriage almost everywhere I go as it's one of the perks of being a Patron, it's expected of me. And up until this outing I never thought about it. It just was.

But today, passing by the non-Patrons who wait their turn at the gate — while I am waved through — I don't enjoy the pretentiousness of it. I am afforded this privilege because I wear pretty clothes and know how to preen and show them off?

It all seems so . . . pointless.

Yet it is an undeniable truth that trends drive our world. The entire structure of Regalia is built on consumerism and fame. The latter drives the former, which circles around to drive the latter again. I always imagine the cycle looking like a clock. The Creatives are at the top of the circle, with us Patrons at three o'clock. The Imps are at the bottom of the circle fabricating the product, which is put before the Favored at the nine mark. When their interest wanes, the cycle returns to the Creatives and starts over again.

I admire the creativity of the designers above my own questionable talents. Without them, there is no need for Imps, Favored, or Patrons, and we'd all fade away into lives heavy with shades of gray.

Which makes me think of Imps. And Helsa. And Bru. And the never late Solana.

My, I am pensive today. I usually approach Choosing Day with anticipation. Why am I suddenly questioning the fabric of my being?

Fabric. Very funny.

My carriage stops in front of the shoe studio, which is the site of the Choosing this quarter. Amar steps forward to open the door.

"Morning, Cashlin," he says. As my Creative Director this is a joint event—his chance to showcase what he's helped direct and create. He holds his palm upward at shoulder level, and I place my hand on his as we walk toward the large shoe studio. "You're late," he whispers.

"You're lucky I'm here at all."

He flashes me a sideways glance. "What—?"

"Nothing. Let's do this."

We enter into a display area that's at the center of the studio that contains sixty workrooms which are located down long hallways to the right and left. Every quarter, each Patron has three Creatives design a complete four-piece outfit to present at the Choosing. Today I will see my three latest options.

There are two chairs for Amar and me. The display area has absolutely no embellishment. It's a white box so as not to distract from the design offerings.

Unlike the Reveal, the Choosing is low-key. There is no dramatic spectacle as the Creatives showcase their wares, in fact there is no talking at all. The real drama is that one element is presented at a time—and added to—building on the look. This quarter, shoes are showcased first.

Amar asks, "Are you ready?"

"I am."

He claps his hands, and three Creatives enter the room. One wears a tunic and pants in a nauseating shade of chartreuse which reminds me of my snake outfit. One wears a pastel yellow that I would never, ever wear. And the third has chosen a uniform of royal blue that complements her black hair.

They place white shoe boxes on three pedestals.

Two quarters ago the Creatives were able to present their offerings in decorated containers or garment bags. As of the last Choosing, all outer containers had to be white. I'd enjoyed the elaborate cases. But the Council had deemed such embellishments "undue influence" so now they require the neutrality of sameness, white for all.

Everyone knows who caused such a stupid rule change by complaining to the Council. Two Choosings ago a Creative named Sylvan had *not* embellished his box while the other Designers had. He lost. It irked me that a rule was changed because of one contender's laziness, lack of talent, and hurt pride. But it wasn't the first time the opinions of a few won precedence over the opinions of many. Those who whined the loudest were indulged so they wouldn't whine louder. It was totally unfair, and I'd wanted to go before the Council myself, but Mother and Amar had talked me out of it. It was a Creatives issue. It had nothing to do with me.

I used to think that way about a lot of things . . .

Amar leans close and whispers. "Number one designed the purple outfit that got you the win."

When she and I make eye contact, she gives me a little nod. I nod back. *Well done.*

The Creative who designed my ill-fated snake shoes is not presenting to me. The rule allows the Creative who won the last Reveal to present to the same Patron again, but the other two are assigned at random.

The Creatives withdraw, allowing us privacy to inspect their designs. Amar and I move to the first pedestal and remove the white box. The first Creative's ankle boots are completely covered in black feathers and studded with chartreuse gems. Gems also cover the four-inch heels. I pick one up and some of the feathers flutter. "This would attract some nice attention," I say.

"I thought so," Amar says.

"But black is ordinary," I say. "I never wear black."

"You could. I thought it could be a change for you, Cash. Something different."

"Perhaps." He knows I avoid black. Bright colors make me feel alive, and the sickly chartreuse doesn't count.

"Let's move on."

We stand before the second offering. Amar removes the box. The short boots are intricately painted with abstract swirls in bright colors. The swirls continue onto the chunky heels.

Not bad.

We move on to the third pedestal. The box is removed to show a pair of white flats. Completely white. Completely unadorned.

"Is this a joke?" Amar asks. He calls out. "Send in Ladi, Creative number three."

The dark-haired woman enters the room and stands nearby. "Yes, Creative Director?"

"This is not what you were working on. It's not the design I approved."

"It is not," Ladi says.

"It's a disgrace."

"I'm sorry you think that, Creative Director."

Amar takes a shoe and throws it across the room. "This is unacceptable! You'll be punished for this."

I'm used to my brother's tirades, so my attention is not on him, but on the Creative. Ladi is completely calm, clasping her hands in front. There is a slight smile on her face.

I take a liking to her immediately. She's got gumption.

But as Amar carries on, I intervene. "Wait, brother." To Ladi I say, "You must have had a reason to change designs. Explain yourself."

She steps toward the pedestal. "May I?"

"Of course," I say.

She picks up the remaining shoe, which is more slipper than shoe. "White is the color of purity, virtue, and goodness. Your qualities, Patron Cashlin."

Hardly. "Thank you, but—"

"These shoes are made of the softest sheepskin. Sheep lovingly cared for by their Keeper." She looks me in the eyes.

I suck in a breath. Is she implying something?

Amar grabs the shoe and shoves it in front of her face. "This is an embarrassment. Get out of our sight!"

She nods and walks out.

He slams the shoe on the pedestal. "I apologize, Cashlin. The shoes she was working on were bright blue and—"

"It's all right, Amar. Truly it is. No harm done."

I return to my chair, hoping he follows me. "Let's continue with the clothing choices."

**

My mind is not in the moment. I go through the motions of looking over the clothing, the head pieces, and the jewelry offerings—all with beautiful gems, feathers, and colors. I'm impressed with many of them.

But none so much as the white slippers.

Amar snaps his fingers in front of my face. "Cashlin? Get with it, sister."

"Sorry."

"What's wrong with you? I could have gotten more reaction from a chair than I've pulled out of you today."

"Sorry."

He tosses his hands in the air. "I don't want to hear 'sorry'. I want you to snap out of it. I've spent countless hours curating these alternatives, it's time for you to make your choice."

Amar and I are alone in the room, which is now populated with all the presented items, set together as three complete ensembles. He carries a metal gold star that I will place on my final choice.

The first outfit is black—though it does have chartreuse embellishments.

He waits for my answer. "It reminds me of LaBelle's outfit at the last Reveal. It's a bit . . . boring."

"But hers was all black. This has color."

"It's beautiful, but it's not for me."

He puts his hands on his hips. "Being your Creative Designer is difficult sometimes, Cash. All you want are bright, garish colors. That's very limiting."

Actually, it's just the opposite. "My fans seem to like color."

He waves a hand toward outfit number two. "Speaking of bright colors, I knew you'd like this."

The jewel tones of the flowers are intense with bold black outlines. The dress design is minimal to show off the pattern of the cloth.

The fabric continues in the wrapped headdress. The jewelry consists of wide, solid-colored bangles that would extend from my wrist to elbow.

I can see myself wearing it.

"Yes?" Amar says.

"Maybe."

The final outfit is a metallic royal blue color, designed to look like pliable armor. "You want me to look like a soldier?"

"It's a choice."

My gaze falls on the white slippers. Amar quickly says, "Ignore those. I'll get the original shoes finished. Obviously, Ladi was on a different path until this shoe fiasco. I guarantee she'll be punished."

"Don't do that," I say.

"Why not? She clearly discounted every direction she was given. I won't have it."

"I'd like to speak with her."

"Why?"

I deflect his question by returning to the jewel tone outfit. "I choose this one."

"Good." He sounds relieved.

"But before I leave . . ." I point a finger at him. "There will be no punishment for Ladi. I will speak with her. Understand?"

"Whatever." He calls out, "Will the Creative for ensemble number two, please come out."

She comes into the room and stands before me while I make my choice official. "I, Patron Cashlin, declare your ensemble as my choice in the next Reveal. Good work and well done." I shake her hand, and she leaves.

I turn toward the exit. "I would like to visit Ladi's studio now."

Amar looks taken aback. "If anything, you should visit the winner and—"

"I told you I wanted to speak with her. Show me the way please."

He stands firmly in place. "No."

"Yes. I insist."

"Nothing good will come of it, Cash. It's not your place to discipline her."

I don't plan on doing any such thing. "Let me go, Amar. I said I'll handle it, and I will."

He shakes his head in disgust but finally says, "Follow me."

We knock on one of the workroom doors. "Ladi. Open up."

The door opens and Ladi blinks, obviously surprised to see us.

She nods. "Yes, Creative Director? Patron Cashlin. How can I help you?"

Amar points a stern finger in her face. "*You* are in trouble, Ladi, and you know it."

I brush between them and enter the room. I turn to my brother. "I'll handle it from here, Amar. Thank you." I gently close the door on him.

Ladi looks fully confused at my presence. She fidgets as if she expects me to scream at her or even hit her.

"I'm sorry to disappoint you, Patron."

"You did nothing of the sort." I look around the small room. "Show me your studio."

She seems surprised by my request but directs me to a worktable that's covered with various leathers, fabrics, and trims. I see royal blue boots in the corner—the boots she was supposed to show.

I spot some familiar white sheepskin and pick it up. It's incredibly subtle and soft.

"Why did you choose to present the slippers made out of this instead of what you were supposed to show?"

I see her composure break the slightest bit as if she's unsure how to answer.

I don't want to worry her. She's safe with me. "You mentioned the Keeper?"

She draws a deep breath. "There's someone I'd like you to meet."

"Of course."

She calls out, "Pinno?"

A woman of my mother's age steps out from behind some shelves. She nods at me, then looks to Ladi. "Patron, this is my assistant, Pinno. Pinno, Patron Cashlin."

She nods again. "Miss."

"Let's have a seat," Ladi says.

We sit around a small table, which Pinno quickly clears of sewing supplies.

"Pinno, tell Patron Cashlin who your son is."

Pinno smiles. "His name is Xian."

I gasp. "You're Xian's mother?"

"I am. Proudly am."

I study her for a moment and see the resemblance in their height and strong jawline. "You have the right to be proud," I say. "He's a good friend. An honorable man."

"That, he is. I'm glad you see it too." She looks at Ladi as if asking permission.

"Go ahead," Ladi says. "Share everything."

Pinno leans forward. "Xian has told me about your experience at the exile."

I'm uncomfortable. "I wish he wouldn't have done that."

She lifts a hand to calm me. "Be assured we share each other's complete trust. He only told me about the parting sands because I mentioned seeing the same thing."

My mouth falls open. "You did?" My heart beats faster. "That means I didn't make it up?"

She laughs slightly. "You did not."

"Which means you also saw Quan run into the parting—"

"The parting sands and get sucked away."

I sigh deeply, enjoying the refreshing air of vindication.

"Since meeting you he's asked me more about the Keeper. Growing up I taught him what I knew, yet as an adult he went his own way. But now he's genuinely curious to learn more. He also told me what an amazing woman you are and how your eyes have been opened to what goes on in the other Rings."

I relish hearing Xian's compliments. "A lot of what I've seen and heard is disturbing."

"Agreed. Which is why change is needed."

I put a hand to my chest. "I'm not sure how to extract such change. As a Patron I'm far removed."

"And yet, you aren't," Ladi says. "We fully believe you can help. That's why I had to do something to get your attention."

"So we could talk to you," Pinno adds.

I look from one woman to the other. They are incredibly brave. And reckless.

"Are there many Devoted in the Creatives Ring?" I ask.

"Not as many as we'd like, but our numbers are growing," Pinno says. "Here, and in my Serv Ring."

"We are well aware of the need to be careful," Ladi says.

Pinno puts a fist to her middle. "But for some reason we both feel a stirring, as if things can't stay the same any longer."

Ladi nods. "As if we're supposed to do something to help."

"Help him?" I ask.

"Yes."

I consider telling them my big truth. If I don't share with women like this, then who? They took a risk to speak with me. I owe them. "I actually saw the Keeper in my garden. I talked to him. I touched him."

Their eyes widen. "How astounding!"

"I can't imagine," Pinno says.

Relief fills me. "You believe me?"

"Why would you lie?"

I laugh softly. "I wouldn't."

"What was it like? What was he like?" Pinno asks.

How can I describe him? "He was the essence of love and peace. When he was there it was like everything was right and good, or could be right and good." I take a cleansing breath. "*I* wanted to be right and good for him. With him. He made me feel like I could do that, with his help."

Pinno sighs. "How wonderful."

"How inspiring," Ladi says. Then she cocks her head. "So how can we make things right and good?"

"That's what I'm trying to figure out."

Pinno absently rubs her hands on the table before putting them in her lap. "In your position there might come a time when you could use your influence to help—"

"He told me to influence people— for him."

"There you go," Ladi says.

There's a quick knock on the door, and Amar opens it. "Are you done in here?"

Not really. But I stand. "We are. For the time being."

Pinno steps into the background again, and he points at Ladi. "After being yelled at by me and Cashlin will you do what you're supposed to do from now on?"

Ladi gives me the quickest glance. "I most certainly will."

"Come now, Cashlin. Your carriage is waiting."

"Goodbye, Ladi," I say. I look at Pinno.

"Goodbye, Patron Cashlin." She touches a finger to her chest.

I do the same.

Our pact is sealed.

Chapter Twenty-Eight

Solana

I awaken with a start. The day is at full light.

I toss the blankets off and jump to my feet. "Helsa? You're going to be late for—"

But Helsa is gone.

She's left a note on the table: *I didn't want to wake you. Sorry, but I took the last of the bread. See you after work.*

I press a hand to my forehead, willing my thoughts to organize themselves. Then it comes back to me: yesterday Bru burned the work of his accusers and forced them to stay all night to meet their quotas. I'd stayed to help. So had Lieb and many others.

The quota remade, Helsa and I had staggered home in the early morning hours and had fallen into bed, immediately asleep. But Helsa—bless her—had let me sleep a few more hours after she went back to work.

How would Bru treat the women today? Would he burn the new work? Was there any end to his cruelty?

My stomach growls. Helsa took the last of the bread, which shames me. I've been so distracted from my normal life that I've forgotten my home responsibilities. I will not have her return home to no dinner. And so, before heading to Cashlin's—where I am already horribly late—I hurriedly get dressed and rush to the factory store.

I greet the proprietor as I always do. We've been friends for years. "Good morning, Tam."

He doesn't smile. "Morning."

I accept the absence of the "good" in his greeting as appropriate for the drama Bru has caused in our Ring.

"I'm afraid I've gotten behind in my shopping. We need bread, potatoes, apples, cabbage, eggs, and ham."

Tam just stands there. He doesn't meet my gaze.

"Tam? If you're out of something, I'll be happy with a substitute."

He shakes his head. "It's not that."

"What is it then?"

He motions me to the side and his wife takes care of the people behind me. The crease between his brows worries me.

"I can't sell to ya. Nothin' at all."

"What do you mean, you can't—"

"Bru has forbidden it. Not just for your family, but for the families of the other four too."

I stop breathing for a moment. "How can he do that? We have the money for it."

"He's Bru. He threatened me and the wife with exile."

"He's the one who should be exiled."

I've raised my voice, and the other customers and Tam's wife look at me.

"He should be," one of the customers says.

"A despicable man," says the other. Then he says, "Here. Take my order."

"Will you get in trouble?" I ask.

He shrugs. "Bru said the stores can't sell to you. I'm not a store, and I'm not selling. Take it." He transfers his food into my basket.

"Thank you so much."

He nods. "We Imps need to stick together."

"Well, what do ya know?" Tam says. "You're far braver than me."

I head home, grateful for the man's generosity, relieved to have food, and angry that Bru put us in this position.

Then I stop in the middle of the street. *We* have food. What about Ana, Meli, Vue, and Falla's families? Will they find some nice neighbor to give them some food?

Maybe. Maybe not.

I know of only one person who might have the power to fix this.

**

I drop off my food and walk to Cashlin's. But as I near the Patron gate I move to the side of the Road to make room for a carriage to pass.

As it comes by, I hear "Solana!"

The carriage stops and Cashlin opens the carriage door. "Hop in," she says.

She scoots over on the seat to make room for me. I have never, ever been in a carriage. It's a good way off the ground for my short legs.

She points at something. "There's a little step there that unfolds. Pull it down."

I find it and step inside. Then I pull the door shut.

"How lucky we ran into each other," she says.

I nod, but my attention is drawn to the interior of the carriage. There are two padded bench seats facing each other. Lovely blue fabric covers the walls and ceiling. A single flower graces a vase on the wall. The carriage begins to move, making me jolt.

"Is everything all right?" she asks. "I expected to see you this morning before I left to go to the Choosing."

"I'm sorry I'm late. It was a hard night at the factory, and I overslept." Her smile fades. "Does it have something to do with Bru?"

"Everything to do with him." I tell her about the burning of the victim's work yesterday and having to stay all night—with help from others. Plus, Bru's latest assault against our food and supplies.

"He's prohibited the stores from selling to you?"

"He has."

Cashlin bangs on the top of the carriage. The driver stops and opens her door. "Turn around and go to the Implementor Ring."

"Miss?" He looks skeptical.

"We're going shopping."

**

"There," I say, pointing out the window. "There's the shop."

Cashlin pounds on the ceiling again and the carriage stops. The driver opens the door and we both get out.

I know I will never forget the looks I get from Imps on the street. I am fairly sure there has never been a carriage in our Ring, much less a Patron's carriage, much less a Patron.

Cashlin strides into the store. "Good day," she says.

Tam, his wife, and three customers freeze.

I follow in behind and make the introductions. "Patron Cashlin, I would like you to meet Tam and . . ." I can't remember her name.

"Dira."

"Tam and Dira, the proprietors of this store. This is Premier Patron Cashlin."

Tam bows, and Dira bobs a curtsy, which seems odd, yet appropriate for the moment. "What can we do for you today, Patron?" Tam asks.

"You can sell Solana—and the families of . . ." She looks to me for the other names.

"Ana, Meli, Vue, and Falla."

"All the food they require," she says.

I expect Tam to nod and agree.

"I'm sorry, miss, but . . . but I can't do that."

Cashlin's eyebrows rise. "Of course you can. I'm ordering you to do it."

"Begging your pardon, miss, but Bru has the backing of the Enforcer General—"

"Who's his cousin," I say.

Her eyebrows rise. "Which in this case is totally unethical."

Tam shrugs. "He's threatened exile if we defy him." He looks at his wife. "We don't want to die, miss." He looks at me. "Sorry, Solana."

"There's nothing to be sorry about," I say. I understand their predicament. It makes me hate Bru all the more.

"You're defying my request?" I ask.

"I have no choice, miss. In this, Bru has the power. I'm truly sorry."

Cashlin looks taken aback. I'm as shocked as she is that Tam didn't give in.

But she quickly recovers, lifting her chin in a defiant manner. "I too am sorry," Cashlin says. "Sorry for you. Good day to you."

On the way out Tam hands Cashlin a loaf of bread. "For you, miss."

She takes it and without a word hands it to me.

We get back in the carriage and Cashlin tells the driver. "Take us to Solana's factory. I want to talk to this Bru."

What? "I don't think that's a good idea, miss," I say.

"Maybe not, but I'm doing it anyway."

Chapter Twenty-Nine

Cashlin

What am I doing?

As the carriage takes Solana and me to her factory I feel an inner panic—and try my hardest not to let it show.

I have no experience dealing with bullies—other than my brother and mother. Yes, I've dealt with the Council, but *I* didn't do anything, my solicitor did. I merely sat back and relied on my status and position to see me through. I'm unnerved that neither held any weight with the shop owners—and I could tell they were nice, respectful people. What makes me think my position will make Bru change from cruel to kind?

"What are you going to say to him?" Solana asks.

"I'd like to appeal to his humanity, but I don't think that will work. Do you?"

She scoffs. "I've never known Bru to say a kind word to anyone. People get their work done out of fear."

"Has he ever destroyed anyone's work before?"

"He'll toss a good piece as he's passing by, but we've all learned to retrieve it from the rubbish bin and carry on."

"Who's *his* boss?"

Solana looks stumped. "Other than the Council, I don't think he has one. I've never seen anyone come to the factory and supervise *him*."

"But surely Bru is beholden to someone for *his* quota."

"I'm sorry, miss. I just don't know who it would be."

I sigh. "Which means there's no higher-up to appeal to."

"Other than the Council."

"I do *not* want to go before them again."

"Nor should you. Bru's offenses are far outside your duties—and your Ring. You've already tried to help us."

"And failed. Tam and Dira won't budge. Not that I blame them."

"You offered me sanctuary when the Enforcers were after me, you gave me a job, saving me from Debt Camp. You're letting your House Servs worship. Above all, you're *trying*. That's more than any Creative, Patron, or Favored has ever done for us Imps."

I appreciate her kind words, but good intentions are a far cry from justice.

Solana points outside. "There's our factory."

I pound on the ceiling and the carriage stops. We take deep breaths together.

Solana touches my arm and looks upward. "Keeper, please give Patron Cashlin the right words. And protect her in her bravery."

The right words would be wonderful, but I don't feel brave.

Solana leads me to the entrance. Passersby pause to gawk. Obviously, seeing a Patron is a rare occurrence. I smile but stay the course. I'm here on important business.

Inside the factory I hear the hum of sewing machines and see nearly a hundred people cutting, sewing, and hand stitching garments.

Not just any garment, my garment. My purple velvet dress.

This might be to my advantage.

As people see me, work stops. I hear a man yelling on the other side of the large room.

I approach a woman at a treadle sewing machine. "Hello. I'm Cashlin. What's your name?"

She's flustered and stops working. Then she says, "Yani."

"Nice to meet you, Yani. That's my dress you're working on."

She runs a hand over the velvet. "I really like it."

"I'm so glad."

"Would you like to see a finished one?" Yani asks.

"I'd love to."

She looks at Solana, who nods. "Show her."

Yani takes me to a rack of purple dresses. She takes a hanger down and lays the dress over her arm. "It's a nice design," she says. "I love the weight of the fabric. It makes the full skirt hang so nicely."

I touch it, loving the rich softness. "It's beautiful. You do good—"

"Yani!"

The woman jumps as a man bellows her name. She quickly hands me the hanger and runs back to her machine.

A hulk of a man approaches. He's extremely tall with shoulders far wider than my own. He's unshaven and his long hair is unkempt. I see food stains on the front of his gray tunic. His stern expression changes as he comes closer. A smile is applied but it's far from genuine, for I see no change of expression in his eyes—which are dark and stone cold.

He looks at me, but then at Solana—who has stepped back.

"What are you doing here?" he asks her. "I sacked you."

"Just visiting," Solana says.

I straighten my stance, trying to show strength. "Solana is with me. I am Patron Cashlin, and you are?"

"Master Bru. I run this factory."

"Then you're the man I need to see." I hold out the dress, forcing him to take it.

He looks ridiculous holding it. He immediately returns it to the rack, where it hangs askew. He doesn't fix it. "Ain't never had a Patron here before."

"I'm glad to be the first."

He blinks too much. I've flustered him.

Good.

He nods toward the rack. "As you see, we're working hard filling the orders. I assure you they'll be ready when—"

"I heard that yesterday you had a setback of sorts."

His smile wavers, his eyebrows dip, and he glances at Solana. "Excuse me?"

My stomach is in knots, but I have to say it. "You destroyed the fine work of four women, burning it, forcing them to stay all night to replace what didn't need to be replaced."

"It's up to me to say what's fine and not fine."

"Actually, it's up to me. There wouldn't be any clothes to make if not for me and the other Patrons."

He hesitates the briefest moment. "What I do in *my* factory is no business of yours, Patron."

I nod toward the dresses. "When it involves *my* dresses, it most certainly is."

"As I said, the shops will get your dresses on time. I guarantee no one will suffer."

"Many women have already suffered because of you."

When his smile leaves him, my stomach flips. I've just declared war.

He glares at me and clenches his fists. "I believe you've overstayed your welcome, Patron."

I can't stop now. "Not only did you abuse them physically and mentally, but now you've told the stores in the Imp Ring not to sell food to them or their families."

"What?" A woman joins us. "I can't buy food? Since when?"

Solana answers. "Since today. Bru ordered them not to sell to us."

"How am I supposed to feed my family?"

Two other women also step forward. "You can't do that to us."

"I most certainly can," Bru says.

The other workers disagree, and the volume of their discussion grows.

Bru starts to breathe heavily. "Enough!" he roars. He waves his hands and strides up and down a row. "Back to work! Or there will be hell to pay!"

When he marches back to me it takes all my courage to stand my ground. "You!" He points a grubby finger in my face. "I don't care who you are, you can't come in here and disrupt my factory. I won't tolerate it." His breath is ragged. "I have friends in high places—higher than you, Patron. I guarantee you'll be sorry you ever came here."

Panic takes hold of my throat, making it hard to talk. But talk I must. "And I won't tolerate you bullying, abusing, and otherwise harming your workers. And *I* guarantee *you'll* be sorry *I* ever came here."

With that I turn on my heel and walk out, with Solana running behind me.

What have I done? What have I done? What have I done?

I get in the carriage, my heart racing. Solana begins to enter too but is distracted by something. She walks over to a little girl, speaks with her for a moment, then invites her into the carriage.

"Miss, this is Falla, the fifth girl who was abused by Bru."

The girl is indeed a girl, slight and gangly. "I'm Cashlin," I say.

Her eyes scan the lush interior of the carriage, then fall on me. "Our factory is making your dress."

The change of subject surprises me, and my panicked thoughts pull up short as I change gears. She's such a sweet little thing. I manage a smile. "Do you like it?"

"I like the big skirt. It's really pretty."

"So are you, Falla. I'm so sorry you've been hurt."

She shrugs as if it's her due then looks at Solana. "Mama tried to buy food, but she can't—Bru says she can't. How are we going to eat?"

I think of my combative words with Bru. Nothing has been resolved, and now that I've riled him even more, there's no chance he'll change his mind.

And the people need to eat.

But then an idea comes to me. "Don't worry about eating. I'll make sure you and your family get the food you need." I look at Solana. "Let's go back to my house and gather food to distribute."

"That would be amazing," she says.

Falla nods vigorously. "Thank you, Patron Cashlin."

"You're very welcome."

Falla runs her hands on the plush upholstery. "It feels like your dress."

"You're right."

She takes a deep breath, looks outside, then seems to remember the time. "I'd better get back to Mama and tell her what's happening."

"We'll bring food to your mother," I say.

"She'll like that." She exits the carriage and waves.

"Falla's a little bit of nothing," I say. "How dare Bru hurt her."

"It doesn't help that she comes late in the day to clean and works all night. She's there alone."

"Except when she's not alone?"

"Exactly," Solana says. "What can be done about Bru?"

"I'm afraid I made things worse."

"I'm glad you said everything you said," Solana says. "I know everybody loved seeing you confront him—because we can't."

Perhaps.

I can't think about him right now. I have to think about Falla. And food.

I tap on the ceiling of the carriage. "Home, please."

**

Irwin stares at me. "You want what?"

"I want you to make up food baskets for five households in the Imp Ring." I look at Solana. "We counted their family members as being fourteen total. Enough for a few days."

"May I ask why?"

I nod at Solana, to answer for me. "Because a very bad man forbid the shops from selling food to us."

His head jerks back. "Why would he do that?"

"As revenge for turning him into authorities."

"If the authorities have him, how can he—?"

"They let him go."

His eyes widen. "That's not good." He looks around the kitchen as if checking supplies. "I'll bake bread and portion out our fruit and vegetables. I have a beef roast cooking right now."

"Could you also make some of your cherry tarts?" I ask.

"Of course. I'll get right on it."

"How long will it take?"

Irwin checks the air above his head. "Two to three hours?"

"What if we help?" Solana asks.

Really? But she's right. "Yes. What if we help?"

He's clearly surprised. "I'll get some aprons."

**

I revel in the aroma of the kitchen: bread, roast, and cherry tarts. It's divine.

Marli has gathered ten baskets, and Dom has lined them with kitchen towels. We put produce in five baskets and fill the other five with the prepared food.

We stand back and look at the bounty. "A job well done," I say.

"I thank both of you for being so generous," Solana says.

"I'm glad to help," Irwin says as he wipes off a worktable.

I think of logistics. "Dom ordered two carriages. Would any of you like to go along to deliver the baskets?"

Dom, Irwin, and Marli exchange looks. "We've never been to the Imp Ring before."

I'm not surprised, yet there seems to be something very wrong about that. "Never until today. Let's go."

**

Earlier in the day the Imp Ring witnessed its first carriage. Now, it's seeing two. Irwin sits beside the driver of the second carriage, with Marli and Dom inside. Solana and I are in the first one with baskets all around. People stand aside and gawk at us. I smile and wave as we slowly drive by.

We have one problem: Solana doesn't know where the four victims live. We are about to stop and ask at one of the shops, when she sticks a hand out the carriage window and yells, "Lieb!" To me she says. "Stop the carriage!"

We pull to a stop.

The young man comes to the window. He's beaming with the face of an innocent who sees wonder in everything. He's been to my house before. I spot the colorful garment beneath his brown tunic.

He's a Messenger Serv. What a good idea!

"Nana, what are you doing?" he asks. He sees me and grins. "Patron Cashlin. I've been to your house."

"Yes, you have. Hello, Lieb. To answer your question, we're delivering food, but we don't know where certain people live."

"I know where everybody lives," he says proudly. "Whose house do you need?"

Solana lists them off.

"I know all of those. Can I sit up with the driver?"

"That's a marvelous idea," I say.

He climbs up and the carriage starts again.

As we ride, I have a question for Solana. "Can you explain the garment Lieb wears under his tunic?"

"It's his memory vest," she says. "He collects bits of this and that and weaves them into a vest. It's totally against the rules to wear color, so he has to cover it up."

"But *I* saw it. Surely authorities see—"

Solana shrugs. "For some reason they leave him alone. Lieb doesn't have any enemies. Everybody likes him because he makes people feel good. He's always been a friend of our family; he's like a grandson to me."

"He's a friend of mine today."

The carriages slow and stop. The driver opens our door. Lieb is right behind him. "This is Falla's house," he says.

I motion for Marli, Dom, and Irwin to exit the other carriage, and then Solana and I bring two baskets to the door and knock. A thirty-something woman answers. One arm is small and crippled. "Yes?" she asks. Then her eyes widen. "I know you from the paper. You're Patron Cashlin!"

"I am." I motion toward Solana. "This is Solana, she works with your daughter. And these are . . . my friends."

"Nice to meet all of you. My name is Isa."

"Is Falla here?" Solana asks.

She shakes her head. "She went to work. She won't get back until morning."

I'm disappointed, but I raise the baskets. "These food baskets are for you."

She takes mine. "Oh my. Thank you so much. I wondered what we were going to do since the stores wouldn't sell to me. Come in. Please."

We all go inside. The home is one room, barely the size of my dining room. It has two cots along the wall. There's a fireplace with a cooking pot set over it, a small table and two chairs, and a shelf with a half a loaf of bread, a carrot, and an apple on it. It reinforces how much the food is needed.

"We'll help you unload the baskets," Solana says. "We need to take them back with us in case . . ."

"We need to do this again," I say.

I enjoy witnessing Isa's reaction to the food. She's skinny—like her daughter. I wonder when they last had meat. And her joy at seeing the cherry tarts makes me smile. Irwin is in his element, telling her about the recipe.

When we are finished, she stares at the food. "I don't even know what to say. *Thank you* hardly seems enough."

"I'm glad we could help."

Suddenly, Isa wraps her arms around me. "May the Keeper bless you and keep you, Patron Cashlin."

My throat tightens. "And you."

We say our goodbyes and find the driver and Lieb chatting happily. I've *never* seen my driver smile.

"Did she like it?" Lieb asks.

"She did," Solana says. "Very much."

"Then let's do it again."

We do *it* three more times before heading to Solana's as our last stop.

"My heart feels like it's going to burst from the joy of it," I tell her in the carriage.

"Mine too," Solana says. "It's a wonderful thing you've done, miss."

"I'm glad to do it. But . . . did you notice how all but one of them mentioned the Keeper? To me. They don't even know me."

"Maybe they assume you believe in him because of your kindness."

"People who don't believe in the Keeper can be kind," I say.

"They can. But what you did is different. Extraordinary. It makes people happy, which makes them want to thank the Keeper. I think there are more Devoted out there than we realize."

Which reminds me of my experience at the Choosing. "I met some of the Devoted in the Creatives Ring. One of them got my attention by creating simple white slippers."

"To go with one of the costumes? Isn't that's unusual?"

"It's unheard of. 'Simple' is simply not done. The winners are usually the shoes that are the most extravagant with feathers and jewels."

"Which made the slippers stand out, I'm sure."

"Exactly. Her outfit didn't win, but I asked to talk to her in private just the same." I shake my head. "My brother did *not* approve."

"But you did it anyway?"

I think of Bru and chuckle. "I'm talking to all sorts of people I shouldn't talk to today."

"How did it go?"

"Very well. I asked her about the slippers because they didn't even go with the rest of the costume. She told me white was the color of purity, virtue, and goodness. The shoes were made of sheepskin, from sheep lovingly cared for by their Keeper. She looked directly into my eyes when she mentioned him."

"Maybe she was simply talking about *a* keeper, not *the* Keeper," Solana says.

I shake my head, discounting her comment. "It gets better. It turns out Xian's mother is the Creative's assistant. Surely, that's not a coincidence."

"I'm beginning not to believe in coincidences."

Me too. "We talked about the Keeper, and they told me we aren't alone. There are many Devoted out there. More than I ever imagined." The carriage slows as the streets fill with people going home from the factories. How many of them believed? "It's so odd that I rarely — if ever — thought about the Keeper or the Devoted, and now I'm thinking about them all the time. Those two women were so encouraging. They made me feel strong."

"From what I've seen you've always been a strong woman."

I have to argue the point. "I was never strong. I was arrogant, selfish, and demanding."

"You are a Patron." She makes a face, obviously realizing her words are a jab.

"I *was* that kind of Patron, but since he came to me in the garden…"

"You are a Patron *for* the Keeper, just like he said you'd be."

It's humbling to think that I've done anything *for* him. "I've only taken a few small steps."

"But small steps matter. Small steps can lead to…?"

"I have no idea." I laugh somberly as reality hits. "And not knowing scares me to death."

Solana runs a hand over the handle of a basket. "Don't be afraid. The Keeper is our protector. He'll protect you as you work for him."

"He didn't protect Bru's victims."

Solana doesn't have an answer to that.

We arrive at her house. "May I come in for a minute?" I ask. "I'd like to ask Helsa how Bru behaved today."

"Of course."

The five of us enter again—with Lieb added. Helsa looks overwhelmed at the company.

"We come bearing gifts," I say, handing her a basket. Marli puts the other one on the table.

"Food?"

Solana begins to unpack the produce. "We took baskets around to all the victims. It was Cashlin's idea."

"That's very nice of you."

"Irwin's the chef," I say. Irwin beams and gives Helsa a nod.

Lieb sits at the table, eying the cherry tarts.

Solana takes over. "Helsa, fill us in on what Bru did at work today after we left. "

"Did he destroy more sewing?" I ask.

"He didn't. But he was more blustery than usual, toppling our stools, throwing things, bumping into people so they'd fall or drop what they were carrying."

"What a lovely man," I say.

"But the worst part was when his cousin, the Enforcer General, came in."

"The man who took your testimony?" I ask.

"The very one. He and Bru sat in his office, cackled like they were celebrating, and drank ale for over an hour."

"That was very in-your-face," Dom says.

"Very. Yet as long as Bru was occupied, he wasn't out on the floor harassing the workers."

"I suppose that's true," I say.
I see Marli stifle a yawn. It's been a long day. It's time to go. "We'll leave you to your meal," I say. "Will I see you tomorrow, Solana?"
She gives me a little bow. "Of course."
I have the carriage to myself on the way home. Only not by myself. For I have the feeling the Keeper is with me.
The joy of it makes me laugh aloud.

Chapter Thirty

Helsa

Just as Nana and I finish dressing for the day there's a knock on our door.

Nana opens it. "Isa. What are you doing here?"

She's frantic. "Falla hasn't come home from work. I went to the factory, but I couldn't find her anywhere. She always comes right home. She never makes me worry like this."

Nana immediately invites her in. "Isa, this is my granddaughter, Helsa. Helsa, this is Falla's mother."

We nod at each other, but immediately get back to the problem. "Did you look inside the factory?" I ask.

"I did. But it was dark, and I was hesitant to light a lamp. I called out to her and walked around, but I didn't see her, and she didn't answer. What if she's hurt?"

"We'll help look," Nana says.

"I'll go to the factory," I say.

"I'll check the surrounding streets," Nana says.

"And I'll check between the factory and home again," Isa says.

We fan out. The sky is cloudy, adding to the anxious mood. Fear spurs me to run. I don't want to give into my suspicions, but there's no denying it. If Falla didn't go home she must be hurt, and if she's hurt there's only one person to blame.

I reach the factory and rush inside. I light an oil lamp near the door since the morning light is still dim. "Falla? Falla? It's Helsa. Are you here?"

I risk going to Bru's office first. What if she's in there with him? My heart pumps madly, and I prepare myself for the idea of bursting through the door to save her.

Thankfully, he isn't in there. But she isn't there either. I turn to leave when I feel something sticky under my shoe. It's wet. It's red.

Is it blood?

No!

I frantically run up and down the rows of worktables, looking behind sewing machines, under cutting tables, in supply closets.

Near the back door I see more droplets of blood.

Did he take her outside?

I burst through the door and look around. There's not much back here except garbage.
Bru treats everyone like garbage.
I run to the heaps of fabric scraps that are ready to burn.
And there, tossed on top like a rag doll, is Falla.
She's got blood coming out of her nose and mouth. Her dress is torn and bloody. I put my head against her chest. I don't hear or feel a heartbeat.
I lift her into my arms, brushing her hair away from her face. "Come on, Falla. It's Helsa. Open your eyes. Please."
She doesn't move.
I call out, "Help! Help! Someone please help!"
A burly man comes around the side of the building. With a single look he takes in the scene and rushes to our side. "What happened?" he asks.
"Bru beat her. I'm afraid she's . . ."
He takes her from my arms and gently sets her on the ground. He looks at the cuts on her head. He puts his face close to her mouth. He pulls back and sighs deeply. "I'm afraid she's gone."
All I can do is shake my head. This can't be happening. We were supposed to protect her. "She can't be gone! She can't."
"I'm so sorry." His expression buckles. "You say Bru did this?"
"It had to be him." My thoughts move from sorrow to anger to revenge. "We have to make him pay!"
The man stands. "Yes, we do." He gently lifts Falla into his arms. "Come with me."
He carries her around the building toward the front of the factory where workers are just arriving.
There are screams, crying, and shouts as people see her.
"Who did this?" is asked over and over.
I am quick with my answer. "Bru killed her. There's blood in his office. He assaulted her, then tossed her on the scrap heap like she wasn't worth anything."
Then I hear a scream I will never forget. A scream of a mother's loss. Isa pushes her way forward. She stands in horror, her face frozen in shock as she stares at her child. Then she lunges toward the man, falling at his feet. "Give her to me."
He gently lowers Falla into her mother's arms. Isa rocks her daughter as though the rhythm will get her heart beating again. Her moans quiet the crowd. Most are crying. Some women kneel beside Isa, trying to offer comfort for the tragedy that can't be comforted.

My heart aches for them, for the loss of their future. Falla was just a little girl who worked hard to provide for her mother. She repeatedly endured Bru's abuse, and finally his brutality. She met evil and lost.

Nana stands beside me. "I can't believe he did this."

"I can. Bullies don't stop until they destroy their prey."

"Bru can't get away with this!" someone yells.

There's shouting and yelling. Fists pump the air. There are layers and layers of people. The crowd is becoming a mob.

"Let's find him!"

"Justice for Falla!"

"Death to Bru!"

"Throw him in the Swirling Desert!"

I like that idea.

"To his house! Let's go!"

The crowd swarms down the street. Nana begins to join them. With a look at Falla and Isa I hesitate.

"Come, Helsa," Nana says. "This is your battle too."

Yes, it is. I join the raging crowd.

**

Bru is not at home.

Wise man.

People debate where he might be, but I have the best idea. "We need to go to his cousin's, to the Enforcer General's. He saved Bru once, Bru will expect to be saved again."

The crowd cheers. "Lead the way, Helsa," someone says.

I hadn't meant to be a leader in this. It was just an idea. But I lead the crowd to the Road, to the gate leading into the Serv Ring.

The guards are surprised by our number and are quickly overwhelmed. They try to hold us back, but there's no stopping us.

The gates are opened, and we stream into the Ring shouting "Justice for Falla!"

Servs back out of the way, and some ask what's going on. The crowd grows larger still.

"This is getting out of control," I say to Nana.

"This isn't the way of the Keeper. We shouldn't be taking justice into our own hands."

"But we can't stop it," I say. "Even if we could, I'm not sure I want to."

Nana nods. "But I'm not sure what we can do if he's at his cousin's. The General is the law."

I've thought of that. But it's too late to look elsewhere now. I certainly don't want to cross the mob.

We reach the General's office and the men up front try to go in, but the door is locked. They pound on the door, demanding entry.

Two Enforcers come around the side of the building, holding their batons, ready to strike. "Back! Back away! Now!"

"We want Bru!"

"Give him to us!"

"He's a murderer!"

I feel sorry for the Enforcers — who look scared, like they'd rather be anywhere else.

The Imp men push past them and break down the door. Nana and I are left outside with the crowd.

We hear yelling and I imagine they've breached the inner door to the General's Chamber.

"They're going to get arrested," Nana says to me.

I see a commotion to the right, and see more men run around the side of the building.

"Is there a back entrance?" Nana asks.

"I would think so. But I don't—"

We hear screams and shouts and yells of victory. "They have him!" someone says.

We rush around in time to see three men lift Bru off the ground while he thrashes and cusses and threatens.

He sees me and for a brief moment our eyes connect. There is no remorse or even fear in his gaze, only seething hate and anger.

For this reason alone, I'm glad they're tossing him into the Swirling Desert. If he stayed in Regalia, I would never be safe.

The mob surges around the men carrying Bru, providing a buffer from any outsider who would dare try to stop them. They march to the Desert Gate and others overcome the guards and pull the heavy gate open.

I have never seen the Swirling Desert and stand frozen at the awful majesty of it. It's an ever-moving barrier as tall as the outer wall of the Serv Ring, the choking sand blows past yet doesn't seem to drop a single grain of sand inside Regalia.

The three men who hold Bru by his arms and legs swing him forward and back. "One, two—"

"Three!"

They toss him into the desert and the sand greedily sucks him away. It isn't just his screams that makes the skin on my arms pucker, it's the sudden silence.

Bru is gone. Bru is dead.

The crowd cheers and hugs each other. Nana and I embrace, but then she pulls away and points at the gate leading to our Ring. Enforcers are streaming in.

"This isn't going to end well," Nana says.

One of Bru's victims overhears. "I think it ended very well. Bru is gone!" Vue says.

Enforcers close the gate to the desert, and others arrest the men who threw Bru to his death. It's chaotic and I feel the danger of the mob now more than ever.

Then an Enforcer takes Nana's arm. She shakes his grip away. "Stop it!"

"Solana. It's me. Xian. You have to get out of here. Get to Cashlin's. Come with me."

"Helsa too," she says, nodding toward me.

Xian holds onto our upper arm as if we are his prisoners, and we hurry through the gates to Cashlin's.

Cashlin will know what to do.

Chapter Thirty-One

Cashlin

Marli comes running into the garden. "Miss. Come quickly."
I follow her into the foyer and am shocked to see Xian, Solana, and Helsa. Their faces are drawn, their eyes scared.
"What's going on?" I ask.
"Falla is dead," Solana says.
"Bru killed her," Helsa adds.
"And then a mob killed Bru," Xian says.
My mind is in a whirl. "Slow down. Let's talk this out." I lead them into the parlor for more details. "Tell me more."
Solana starts by telling me about Falla's mother coming to their house when Falla didn't come home from work. Helsa tells of the search and finding blood in Bru's office, and a bloodied Falla tossed on the scrap heap.
"A man carried her out to the street. Everyone saw." Helsa looks at Solana, who nods. "All the workers."
"Then Isa saw her." She shakes her head. "I will never forget the sound of her wailing."
It's hard to reconcile the mother and daughter I just met yesterday with death and unspeakable sorrow.
"The crowd grew and demanded justice for Falla," Helsa says. "Bru wasn't at his house so I . . ." She looks down.
"You what?" I ask.
"I thought he might have gone to his cousin's—the Enforcer General's."
"And she was right," Solana says.
Xian stands at the fireplace. "In the Council Ring we received word about an uprising and some of us were sent to stop it."
"An uprising? That's not what it was supposed to be." Helsa shakes her head. "But it's true no one could stop it." She looks at Solana. "Nana said it wasn't right to take justice into our own hands, but . . ." She shrugs. "What could we do? The men found him, carried him to the Desert Gate, and threw him out."
"Out, out? As in out into the Swirling Desert?" I ask.
She nods. I remember the exile, seeing Quan getting sucked into the black sands. "There was no mercy for Bru today, not from the mob and not from the Keeper."

"He doesn't deserve mercy!" Helsa says, almost hysterical. "You didn't see Falla, all broken and bloody."

I raise my hand to calm her. "I understand your anger. I feel it too."

"People will be tried for Bru's death," Xian says.

"But Bru killed a little girl!" Helsa says.

"The Council won't condone vigilantes," Xian says.

Helsa's face is red with emotion. "Since they condoned Bru assaulting five women multiple times, they should let it go just like they let *him* go."

A ragged silence falls around us.

Solana speaks first. "Falla is gone. Bru is gone. Good people have been arrested. Unfortunately, there's nothing we can do about any of it."

I shake my head, not wanting to believe it.

"Why are you shaking your head?" Helsa asks me. "Everything Nana says is true. We're helpless."

"No, we're not." Even as I start the sentence, I'm uncertain how I'm going to finish it.

"How so?" Solana asks.

As I stand my thoughts coalesce. "Xian, I want you to go to the Council Ring and find Solicitor Nerwhether. Tell him that I want him to represent the men arrested. I will be responsible. If he needs to speak to me, let me know."

Xian nods. "I'll go right now."

As he heads to the door, Solana grabs his hand. "Thank you for saving us," she tells him. "We're in your debt."

He nods and leaves.

We sit again and my thoughts move to the next task; the next player in the tragedy. "I want to go to Isa's to offer my condolences."

"You shouldn't do that," Solana says. "Since the Council is involved, it may not be wise for you to publicly get involved."

"I'm already involved."

**

The three of us ride in my carriage to Isa's house. There are two dozen people outside. I know I'm making a scene by coming here but shove the thought aside. I just want to help.

If that's possible.

The crowd parts as we walk to the open door, and I knock on the door jamb. "Isa? It's Cashlin. And Solana and Helsa."

People step away from Isa to make room for us to enter. People stand shoulder to shoulder. The air is thick with anger and grief.

I sit in the chair beside her. I want to comfort her with a hug, but I know that would make everyone uncomfortable. "I'm so sorry, Isa. There are no sufficient words to make things better."

"Thank you, Patron," she says. "My girl didn't deserve this."

"No, she didn't," Helsa says.

Isa seems to notice Helsa for the first time. "Thank you for finding her."

Helsa's forehead furrows. "I wish I could've saved her."

Isa wipes a tear away from her cheek. "I heard Bru is dead?"

"He is," Solana says. "He can't bother anyone ever again."

Isa takes a deep breath. "That's something, I guess."

"It's a lot," Helsa says. "Now all of us can go to work knowing that his evil is gone. We are free of him."

She nods. "My Falla was so good. So innocent."

My throat tightens, sharing her pain. I have absolutely no experience with the loss of someone so young. Why would the Keeper allow it? *How* could he allow it? I'd like to ask the questions aloud, but I doubt anyone has an answer.

Isa looks at me. "Falla loved the cherry tarts. Will you tell your cook that?"

"I most certainly will." I think of asking Irwin to make more tarts that I could bring her but have second thoughts. Would tarts intensify Isa's pain? I know so little about grief. Which makes me feel even more helpless.

I stand. "We should go. Please know that I'm here if you need anything, Isa. Just send word and I'll come immediately."

Her eyes light up slightly. "Will you come to the funeral? It's tomorrow. That would mean a lot to me."

I'm shocked by her request but say, "Of course I'll come."

The three of us return to the carriage. "That was nice of you," Solana says.

"Are you sure to want to go to the funeral?" Helsa asks. "The Pile is an awful place."

"I've been there when my grandparents and my father died."

Helsa shakes her head. "You've been to *your* side of the Pile, not ours. It's not the same."

I wonder what I've got myself into.

But as we head to their house, I have an idea. "While we're here I want to visit the stores that wouldn't sell food to you and the others."

"To do what?" Helsa asks.

"To tell them it has to stop. I know I went once — without success — but I need to try again."

218

They lead me to the row of Imp stores. I enter the store I'd visited before.

Dira looks up from the counter, her eyes landing on me, then Helsa and Solana. "Hello again . . . can I help you?"

I reach the counter, pick up an orange, and raise it to my nose to take in its scent. "Do you remember me?"

"Of course. I knows who you are. Whatcha doing here is what I wants to know."

"I'm here to ask you to stop withholding food from *any* customers."

"I was just following instructions."

"From Bru."

"From Bru."

"But now Bru's dead." I add drama to my words. "He was thrown into the Swirling Desert by an angry mob after he killed a young girl."

"Falla," Solana says. "Isa's girl."

Dira gulps. "Yeah. I heard about that too."

"So, I ask that you not repay his evil with more evil. You need to band together and take care of one another."

"Who are you to tell us that?" The husband, Tam, comes out of the back room.

I'm not sure what to say.

But Helsa speaks for me. "She's my friend. She made sure the families of Bru's victims had food — from her own kitchen — when you wouldn't sell to them."

Dira picks at a spot of dried food on the counter. "I heard that too."

"Whatcha want for it?" Tam asks. Then he smiles. "I know. Ya wants applause. That's what yer used to, right?"

I expected resistance but not personal assaults. "Don't you agree it's time to undo the evil Bru perpetrated on the people of your Ring?" I soften my tone. "I truly doubt you wanted to go along with his orders. Did you?"

Dira's jaw tightens. "Of course not. We had to do as he said. If we didn't, he'd hurt —"

I put a hand on the counter, close to — but not touching — her hand. "He *did* hurt you by making you an unwilling participant in his schemes. He hurt everyone he came in contact with. But it's over now."

She nods. "I's glad he's gone." She looks at her husband. "Right, Tam?"

He shrugs but says, "Yeah. He *was* an awful one, he was."

I smile at them. "Then it's time to start fresh. Everyone in the Imp Ring depends on you merchants."

With a nod she says, "Start fresh. Yeah, we can do that."

"Promise?"

She looks at her husband, who shrugs. "We promise."

I turn to leave, then pause to say one more thing, "May the blessings of the Keeper be upon you."

The three of us walk to the next store. Helsa whispers, "You were amazing."

"I can't believe you mentioned the Keeper," Solana says.

Neither can I.

**

"Are you all right, miss?" Marli asks me.

"Maybe."

She folds back the covers of my bed. "Maybe?"

I sit on the side of it, trying to get my thoughts to sync with each other. "On the one hand I am very glad that I went to see Isa."

"I'm sure she appreciated it."

"I think she did." I smooth my nightgown against my legs. "I'm also glad I talked with the food merchants. I don't know if they'll do as I asked but it feels good to try."

"That's more than most people do." She fluffs my pillows.

"Isa invited me to Falla's funeral tomorrow."

"Which shows how much she respects you."

Marli doesn't know about my parting comments to the shopkeepers. "And I mentioned the Keeper in public."

Her eyebrows rise. "Which public?"

"The merchants. As I left I said, 'May the blessings of the Keeper be upon you.'"

"Are they Devoted?"

"I have no idea."

Marli puts a hand to her chest and takes a deep breath. "That's . . . bold."

I begin to pace. "Bold, certainly. Stupid? Probably."

"Will they turn you in?"

"I have no idea." I put a hand to my chest. "Why did mention him to everyone? It's not like me at all."

"Maybe it wasn't you talking. Maybe he . . ."

I stop pacing. "Spurred me to say it? I thought of that. It's not like I got the idea to say something and mulled it over—not even for a second. The words just came out when I left the first store, and I repeated them in the other two." I sit on the bed again. "By speaking of him, and by interfering with the issues of the Imp Ring, I'm afraid I've put all of us in danger."

"Sometimes that happens when we do the right thing."

"I don't *do* danger. Never have."

"Never *have*. But maybe it's time."

"Time to . . .?"

She points at the pillows, urging me to lay down. She pulls the covers over me.

"Time to . . .?" I ask again.

"Don't go by my words, miss. It was just a thought I had."

"Tell me that thought. I insist."

Marli takes a deep breath and smooths the covers. "Maybe it's time to take a stand."

"For?"

"For everything that's right. And for the Keeper."

I felt like waving my hands frantically, fending the notion away. "I don't know about that."

"Don't you? Because from what I've learned, the Keeper *is* everything that's right and good."

I'm struck by her words. Simple words that are more profound than any words I've heard or thought of in a long time.

I reach out and she takes my hand. "Thank you, Marli. You've given me a lot to think about."

She smiles as if I made her day.

She's certainly made mine.

Chapter Thirty-Two

Cashlin

"No, miss," Dom says to me the next day. "You may not walk all the way to the Pile for the funeral."

His words run off me as I slip on a black armband of mourning. "I won't be alone. Helsa and Solana will be with me. I told the girl's mother I'd go. I can't go back on that."

"I'm not suggesting you don't go, merely that you take a carriage. You need some sort of protection."

I see his point, but I think he is wrong. "They've gotten to know me a little in the Imp Ring. I'm not a novelty to them anymore. I'll be fine." Yet the Pile was in the Serv Ring.

"Perhaps Xian could accompany you."

I've thought of that, but decided against it. "It puts him in an awkward position. Bru had the backing of the Enforcer General, who I assume had the backing of the Council. Xian works for the Council. He can't be seen going to an Imp funeral."

"What about your brother?"

I scoff. "I haven't talked to him since Choosing Day. Amar is on my side as long as I do what he wants. Beyond that, he wants little to do with me. I'd rather go without him."

But Dom wasn't through. "Then let me go with you. Or Marli. It's a long walk from the Patron Ring to the Imp Ring where you'll meet the others."

Marli stands nearby. She nods. "I'd be happy to go, miss."

"Very well." I see both her and Dom relax. They just want me to be safe. "Let's be going then."

As we walk toward the Road, Mother comes out of her house. She doesn't smile. "Cashlin. Come here and explain yourself right now."

I don't want to talk to her. "Another time, Mother. I'm meeting some people and can't be late."

She comes to the fence that lines her property. "Who are you meeting?"

A few hundred of my closest friends? "I'm going to the funeral of the little girl who was murdered."

Her neatly formed eyebrows rise. "The Imp girl?"

"Falla. Her name was Falla."

With a glance at Marli, she leans toward me over the fence and lowers her voice. "I've heard talk about what you've done in that Ring. It's reckless. It's none of our business." She grabs one of my wrists and pulls me close enough for me to feel her breath. "And you, speaking of the Keeper? What were you thinking?"

I shake her grip away. "I'm thinking I need to go, or I'll be late. Have a nice day, Mother."

I walk away quickly, eager to put distance between us. Why does she always make me feel . . . wrong?

"Miss? Please slow down."

"Oh. Sorry, Marli." I ease my pace. "My mother will never understand me. Even if *I* don't completely understand what I'm doing, at least I'm doing something."

"Maybe understanding comes later."

"I hope so."

**

After entering the Imp Ring I hear the crowd walking toward the Serv gate before I see them. They're singing a song I don't know, a haunting song about love and fate and sorrow.

"There are so many of them," Marli says. "Hundreds."

"I expected as much." I hope everyone stays calm.

"But the Council only allows four at the grave," Marli says.

I'm surprised by this. I remember the funeral of my father and grandparents. There were dozens in attendance. They shouldn't put a limit on mourners. Or mourning.

Isa walks front and center with Helsa and Solana on either side. I spot Lieb in the crowd. And Dira, the shopkeeper.

I'm impressed how Isa walks with strength. And defiance. I'm so proud of her. Every person wears a black armband in Falla's honor. I'm glad I had one to wear.

Isa sees us and smiles. Marli and I walk toward them, and the crowd stops.

"You came," she says.

"I said I would." I nod at Marli. "This is my friend, Marli."

"I'm so sorry for your loss, ma'am," Marli says.

With a nod, Isa says, "Shall we go?"

This time the guards at the Serv gate open it without comment. They too wear a black band of mourning.

I have not been in the Serv Ring since Quan's exile. I see the Desert Gate straight ahead and make note of where I stood when the Swirling Desert violently took two men, and miraculously parted for the Devoted couple. The Keeper told me he enjoyed making miracles for those devoted to him. How stunning that an instrument of nature could be manipulated to do the Keeper's bidding. It was a strong testament to his power.

From what I've heard, the Desert hadn't been merciful to Bru, which meant the Keeper hadn't been merciful to Bru.

I can't help but feel glad about that.

As we pass the Servs who are going about their daily business, they pause and nod at us in an act of compassion. But I notice many tap their hearts with a finger.

I return the gesture as we pass. People look a little shocked at that. I'm used to shocking people with my Reveals, but this kind of surprise is much more satisfying.

It's a long way to the Pile, and my shoes hurt my feet. But I can't complain. I see old people in the crowd, and some with crutches. If they can make it, so can I.

The buildings end and we come to a dense, dark woods. There is a single path leading into it that is anything but inviting. I imagine slimy things inside, bugs, and stalking animals.

A man wearing a brown, hooded caftan stands at the entrance of the path. He raises a hand to stop the progress of the crowd. "Only four may come to the Pile."

I step forward. "These people have come to pay their respects to Falla. Let them go the rest of the way."

He shakes his head. "Only four."

"But this is obviously a special circumstance." I motion back at the crowd. "Please let us pass."

"I will not. Only four."

"It's all right, Patron." Isa takes the hands of Helsa and Solana, then turns to me. "And you. I want you there."

I'm surprised. And honored. "Of course." I look toward Marli, and she nods. She's fine staying behind with the other Servs.

The Comfort Serv stays where he is—for crowd control?—and waves us toward the path.

"I'll go first," Helsa says. "I've been through these woods before."

The road ahead is so narrow that we have to walk single file. Isa goes second, then me, then Solana.

The canopy around us is dense, blocking out the light. I brush flying insects away from my face. Helsa pulls back an offending branch so we can pass. I don't even think of going off the path, as the undergrowth is menacing, like it could come to life, grab my ankles, and pull me under. The sooner we can get through—

Helsa suddenly stops. "You! There!"

She points to the right at a bald man standing amid the trees a dozen yards deeper in the forest.

He points back at her, then runs deeper still.

"Who's that?" I ask.

"I don't know, but this is the third time I've seen him. He followed me once."

"What does he want?" Solana asks.

"I have no idea."

"Do you think he wants to hurt you?"

"I don't know, but I don't like him."

Isa wraps her arms around herself. "Can we keep going? I don't like it here."

"Of course."

We continue on and share sighs of relief when we reach the other side. Where the forest ends the stark nothingness of the Pile begins.

Piles, plural, for there are mounds of dirt and ash for acre upon acre. This is not what I'd envisioned. After the deaths in our family a Comfort Serv had brought a lovely stone urn and flowers to our home, where he'd said some nice words before taking the urn away. We hadn't been present beyond that. It made me shudder to think that this was where my departed family had ended up.

Another Comfort Serv waits for us near a mound. He has a pointed black beard and holds a stoppered bottle.

A bottle filled with ashes? That tiny thing?

When we reach him Helsa says, "Teel. We meet again."

He nods. "Helsa. Solana." He looks at Isa. "I am sorry for your loss, Isa."

"You know her name," Helsa says.

They share a look. "I make a point of it now."

I don't understand the exchange, but now is not the time for an explanation.

He looks at me and nods. "Patron Cashlin. How good of you to be here."

I simply nod back.

He hands the bottle to Isa. So few ashes for such a small girl.

"You may spread them here," he says, pointing to his right.

I am appalled. We're going to witness it? Actually see the ashes fall?

Isa holds the bottle against her heart. Her breathing becomes haggard, and she begins to sob. "I'm so sorry I failed you, sweet girl. I'm so sorry we all failed you."

I feel my own failure as a heavy weight. What good does it do to have status if I have no power to save a defenseless girl?

I join the ladies as they form a circle around Isa and cry with her. The emotions swirl as the feelings of guilt, pain, anger, and love connect us.

When we step back, Isa approaches the pile, then looks at Teel. "Will you say something?"

"Ashes to ashes, dust to dust."

Helsa shakes her head "Teel . . . really?"

As he stammers, I feel a stirring inside. I step forward and look at the cloudy sky. "Dear Keeper, take care of our precious Falla as you would one of your lost sheep. And protect and comfort *us* as we learn to live without her."

They all stare at me but I know speaking out was the right thing to do, when Teel says, "Let it be so" and the others say it too.

Isa surprises me by wrapping her arms around me. "Thank you, miss. Your words mean a lot to me."

"Of course," I say.

But as we return the way we came, I know there is no "of course" to it.

Who have I become? I don't know this Cashlin.

She frightens me.

**

Marli and I make it home, albeit in a daze. Dom meets us at the door. "Can I get you anything, miss?"

"Nothing. Thank you." I turn to Marli. "And thank you for coming with me. I think I'm going to spend some time in the garden."

They nod and leave me alone. Which is exactly what I need. As a Patron I'm used to being around a lot of people—at designated times during short spurts of interaction. Yet the rest of my time is spent at home in acts of meaningless self-gratification. Alone.

I sit in my garden chair and sigh.

In the past week my world has expanded in ways I never imagined. I've met people in the Imp Ring that have changed my life. They've taken me from a willingly naïve, ignorant Patron into . . .

Whatever I am now.

I speak out loud, "Who am I now?"

I blink as a slice of sky opens and a beam of light shines into my garden. Memories of the last time this happened play in my head.

The last time? Meaning . . .

I stand, my heart racing.

"Keeper?" I whisper.

He steps out of the flowers, as he did before. "I'm here."

I gasp with joy. "You've come back!"

"I've come to answer your question."

For a moment I'm not sure what he's talking about. But then I remember. "I asked 'who am I now?'"

He smiles and nods. "Now, you are Oria."

I suffer a twinge of nerves. "You mentioned that name before."

"I did. The time to take your new name has come. For you have pleased me by your actions."

"I have?" He makes me so happy I want to dance.

"You have shown yourself as one who is humble in spirit and manner—as celebrated in the name Oria."

I love the compliment, but it doesn't sit quite right. "I haven't been humble; I've inserted myself in other people's business all over Regalia. I've greatly overstepped my position in the Imp Ring."

"You've helped them."

"But I've also stirred things up."

"Sometimes that happens when we do the right thing."

I gasp. "Marli said those exact words."

He leans close, confidentially. "Who do you think she got them from?"

I love how he makes me smile, as if moments like these are why smiles were created.

"Being humble doesn't mean being weak," he says. "In fact, there is great strength in humility." He walks to a rose bush, leans down and inhales. "I love the smell of a Peace rose—always a favorite."

"Because of its name?"

He shrugs yet smiles. "Shall we sit?"

After we take our seats, he sighs and looks up at the sky, then back to me. "You, my precious Oria are at a crossroads."

I'm glad he's put a word to my feelings. "I've sensed that. But which way do I turn?"

"The first time I visited I asked you to be an influencer for me. To be a Patron of the Keeper. You did that."

"A little. I've done a little."

"See? You're humble, just like your name. But now it's time for the next step."

"Which is?"

"Being fully mine."

Before I rush in and say, "I accept" I balk. "I'm not sure what that involves. It's not that I'm unwilling, but . . ." I take a fresh breath. "I'm not sure what that involves."

"Surrender."

"We're not in a battle."

"Aren't we?"

Ah. He's talking about larger battles. "Do you mean good versus evil?"

"That's one battle."

"There's more?"

"There are many: pride versus humility, selfishness versus generosity, love versus hate, trust versus doubt..." He sighs. "The list is endless."

"But doesn't surrender come at the end of a battle?"

He cocks his head. "It can, but the most satisfying victories begin with surrender—to me. It's the first choice in order to enter the battle my way."

"With you as the general."

He grins. "I'm quite good at being commanding when given the chance."

"I have no doubt."

"Good."

He takes me literally. "I mean I *do* have doubt, but I also mean I believe your way is the best way."

He considers the sky a moment, then says, "Do you know the best way to overcome doubt?"

"No."

"Have faith. Choose faith. Believe."

"In you?"

He nods once. "To have faith, have faith."

I'm taken aback. "That sounds a bit simplistic."

"Simple, not simplistic. As the Keeper I want everyone to follow me. Why would I make the process complicated or difficult?"

I'm wary.

"You're doubting again," he says.

I know I shouldn't feel that way, but I'm honest. "I don't doubt you; I doubt me. I doubt myself being able to be the person you want me to be, just by having faith."

He points at some ants busy at an anthill on the edge of the path. "Faith makes doubt scurry away like ants fleeing an impending footfall."

"I can't force faith to grow."

He spreads his hands. "To have faith, have faith. It perpetuates itself."

He stands and breaks off two marigold blossoms—one bright orange blossom and one that is shriveled and brown. He holds up the pretty bloom. "How does this grow?"

"I'm no gardener—"

"Oria. How does this flower grow?"

"It grows from seeds."

"Where do seeds comes from?"

My ignorance is embarrassing. "I suppose they come from other flowers."

"Exactly." He hands me the blossom and begins to pull apart the wilted flower. He ends up holding many long brown seeds. "Look here. Waiting inside a plant that is spent and waning is new life. Just as one of these seeds will grow into a beautiful blossom, I tell you this: if you have faith as small as a single seed, and you plant that seed by sharing your faith, it will grow into something beautiful and wondrous beyond measure."

Again, I worry about his confidence in me. "I know my limitations."

"I don't."

"What?"

"You have limitations?"

Surely, he's teasing. "Of course I do." I pause. "Don't I?"

"You do—on your own. But with me by your side you have none." He nods to the flower in his hand. "Do the plants in this garden grow by willing themselves to grow? By sheer determination? By trying hard to make it happen? Of course not. They grow because it's what I have created them to do." He gives me his full attention. "Do what I've created you to do, Oria. Be a woman of great faith and influence."

His confidence in me far overshadows my confidence in myself. "I promise I'll try to do everything you want me to do, but—"

"Yes, you will try. And try again. But again, I tell you to begin with surrender. Invite me along for the journey. As we grow closer, living out your purpose will become as natural as breathing." He takes the marigold and slips it above my ear. "I don't expect perfection, Oria, just a willing heart."

"I . . . I have that."

He spreads his arms. "So there you go. You've already surrendered to me. Thank you."

"You're welcome? That's all it takes?"

He laughs. "Not exactly. Surrender isn't once and done, it's a constant choice, repeated over and over in all circumstances." He cocks his head. "But remember this: I don't keep score."

"I'm glad of that."

His face turns serious. "There is one other thing I'd like to discuss with you."

"Anything." I say the word sincerely.

He smiles and I realize I've just surrendered again. Maybe it isn't that hard after all.

"The mob throwing Bru into the Desert."

"I hear it was awful."

"It was. And it wasn't right. Justice belongs to me."

"Nana said as much, but there were so many people. They couldn't be stopped." I thought of something else. "And honestly..."

"You're glad they took care of him like that."

"I am." I sit forward in the chair. "He was evil. He hurt women at work, he was mean and spiteful, vindictive... and he killed Falla." A question demands asking. "Why did you allow him to kill Falla?"

His face was mournful. "My ways are not your ways."

"I understand that. But she was such an innocent. A sweet girl."

"She was. She is."

"Is?"

"She's with me now."

"With you?"

He stands and walks a few steps away, then turns back to me. "There is more to this life than what you see now. Here."

"Like what?"

"That's knowledge for another time. But be assured there is *so* much more for you to know—for everyone to know. That's why I need your help."

I still feel overwhelmed. "I'm used to flaunting clothes, not faith. I'm not wise. I don't even know that much about you."

"You know more than you think. The Devoted call me the Keeper. What does that say about me?"

I've thought about this. "That you are a protector. A provider."

"What about the widow and the judge story in the Relic? What does that say about me?"

"That you reward determination and persistence."

"I do."

"I understand that."

He spreads his hands as if that's enough.

"Don't I need more training?"

"There is no end to training. All of life is training. That doesn't mean I can't use you right now, where you are, with how much you know."

"How little I know."

His eyebrows rise. "I have visited you twice. We've had some enjoyable discussions, yes?"

"Very much so, yes."

"Then you know more than most."

"Do you appear to people often?"

He smiles as if my question is expected. "You want to know if you're special?"

I want to deny my motive but can't. "Yes—in part. But I'm also curious."

"The answer is, yes. I do appear to people, but not often like this. Actually, I appear to people a lot, but they often don't notice me or choose to ignore me."

"How so?"

He takes a deep, cleansing breath. "I appear to them when they cuddle a baby, play with their dog, share a meal, enjoy a sunset, and laugh with their friends. What do those things have in common?"

I think for a minute. "They involve interaction?"

He nods once. "Even more, they involve moments that lift people beyond themselves. You can't be selfish during those moments. You become self-less." He comes close and puts a hand on my shoulder. "You say you have nothing to offer just because you don't know everything?"

I shrug.

"Then answer this, Oria: when will you know that you know enough?"

I scoff. "That's an unanswerable question because there is no time limit. No test. No definable target."

"There isn't. So, share what you know, from who you are now, and where you are now. I called Cashlin where she was then. I call Oria where she is now."

"And beyond that?"

He smiles again. "The rest will come."

Again, he makes it sound so simple. "But what should I do next? I've had Xian contact my solicitor to defend those men from the mob who were arrested."

"Then you've done a lot."

"But what next?"

He cocks his head and smiles. "You are a list-maker, aren't you?"

I don't consider it a negative. "I like to have a schedule, a plan."

He crosses his hands in front of his body. "So. As Cashlin the Patron, what happens next?"

My minds flips back to my regular life, my Patron life. "It's nearly time for the top ten outfits to be sold."

"Which entails . . . ?"

"Going to the stores in the Favored Ring, wearing our outfits, and then . . ." I shrug.

"There's a shopping frenzy?"

"Something like that. It's called Shopping Day."

"Then that is what you do next."

"But shopping has nothing to do with Oria."

"There, you are wrong." He holds out his arms to me. "Come. I must go."

I relish the perfection of his embrace and know that it's perfect because he invented it. "When will I see you again?"

He holds me at arm's length. "Getting a bit greedy, are we?"

Yes. Absolutely. "It's just that I love seeing you. Talking with you."

He touches my forehead. "Then see me in here." Then he touches my heart. "And talk to be in here. I'm always with you."

With a wave, he steps away and walks among the trees and flowers, leaving me alone.

But not alone.

Never alone.

Chapter Thirty-Three

Solana

The new factory manager stands outside, ready to address the workers.

She begins to speak, but Mistress Toffa is short, so someone yells *wait*, and brings her a crate to stand upon. They hold her hand as she steps onto it.

"There now," she says. "This *is* better. For now, I can see all of you." Her eyes scan the sea of workers. "I've been one of you for over forty years. I know you. And I'm honored to have been assigned to be your new manager."

People in the crowd begin to chant their approval, "Mistress Toffa! Mistress Toffa!"

Her chubby cheeks redden, and she presses the cheers away. "Now, now. Enough of that." She wipes her hands on her gray uniform, which hasn't changed with her promotion. "We've been through hell these past few years, and now we mourn the death of one of our own, dear Falla."

Heads bow and nod, and a few tears are wiped away.

"But today is a new day for all of us. A new day for the Imp Ring!"

Cheers ring out.

"I say it's time to get back to work. Yes?"

"Yes!"

The doors of the factory are opened, and people stream inside. Two men help Toffa off the crate. I hurry to speak to her.

"Mistress?" I ask.

She turns to look at me and scoffs. "Solana. We've known each other for decades. There will be none of that 'mistress' nonsense. How can I help you?"

"I'd like my job back. Bru sacked me and—"

She shakes her head. "You are welcome back. I believe your worktable is still empty."

"Thank you. I won't let you down."

"Of course you won't."

She goes inside and Helsa and I follow. "That was easy," I say.

"I think a lot of things are going to be easier now."

I sit at my old worktable, feeling nostalgic. I'd been sacked for going to our neighbor's exile. I'd been sentenced to Debt Camp. The

Keeper arranged for me to meet Cashlin, who offered me friendship, safety, and fellowship. Because of our meeting the lives of everyone in our factory have improved. Bru is dead. Justice has been served.

Yet as I pick up a hem to stitch, I feel bittersweet. Getting my old job back eliminates the threat of the Debt Camp, and Helsa and I can continue to work and live together. Which are all good things.

But I know I will miss —

"Are you finding it hard to concentrate?" Helsa asks from her worktable.

"I am."

"Are you missing Cashlin?"

"I am. I will never forget the time I had with her."

"Just because you're back at work doesn't mean you — we — can't see her again. She's a part of the Imp Ring now. I can't see her staying away."

"I can't either. But it's different now."

"It is," Helsa says, "It's better." She waves an arm to encompass the room. "Look around. Listen. People are talking to each other, even laughing. This is the way the factory should be."

"Because of Cashlin."

"And you, Nana. You're part of the change too."

I thread a new needle and see Lieb coming in the door. I begin to wave at him, but there's no need as he walks directly toward me.

"Morning, Lieb."

"Morning, Nana. Sa-Sa." He beams as he holds out a note. "This is for you." He grins ear to ear.

"Who's — ?"

"It's from Patron Cashlin," he says. "She called me to her house this morning and said to bring it to you straightaway."

I open it and read silently before sharing what it says. "She says she needs me. She wants me to come immediately." I'm thrilled and confused. Is she all right? Am I in trouble? Is she? "Was she upset?" I ask Lieb.

"Not at all," he says. "She seemed excited, but she did say that sooner is better."

I stand. There's no question I'll go, yet it's awkward as I haven't been at work for even a half hour. I look across the factory for Toffa. Helsa stands and helps me look. "She's over there. I'll get her."

What am I going to say to her?

Helsa brings Toffa to me. "Yes, Solana?"

"I've received a note from Patron Cashlin, requesting my presence immediately."

"Sooner is better," Lieb says.

"I know I just started again, but—"

"For her? Anything. Go. Do whatever she needs."

"Thank you, Toffa." When she leaves, I look at Helsa. "I'm not used to having an accommodating manager. One who's understanding and kind."

"Welcome to our new life."

**

My heart beats wildly as I stand at Cashlin's door. I only have to knock once before Dom opens it.

"Good morning, Solana. Welcome."

"I came as quickly as I could."

"You most certainly did. Mistress Cashlin and Marli are waiting for you upstairs in her room."

I can't believe I'm back here, but thrilled that I am. I hurry up the stairs and Marli comes out to the hall to greet me. "She's waiting for you."

Cashlin is in her closet, wearing her winning outfit, the purple velvet dress.

She turns toward me. "Do I look as ridiculous as I feel?"

It's an unexpected question. "I'm not sure how to answer."

She sighs. "Sorry. I was too blunt."

I circle around her. "I can see why you won. It's flashy and playful, sexy and different."

Cashlin makes a face. It's not the answer she wants to hear. "Are you aware of what happens next in the Cycle of Regalia?"

"Shopping Day, right?"

"Shopping Day. Tomorrow the Patrons of the top ten designs go to the Favored Ring where our outfits are officially sold in the stores. It's utter chaos. A rabid frenzy."

I'm not sure why she wouldn't thrive on such a day. "Isn't it the culmination of the entire process?" I ask. "It should be a happy day for everyone—especially you, as the Premier Patron."

"It is—for everyone else, and in the past, it has been for me too. My entire job is to strut around my admirers in my costume, letting them fawn over me."

"It's what you live for."

"Lived for."

Ah. I guess where she's going. "You've changed."

She nods mournfully.

"Isn't that a good thing?"

"It is. But . . . ." Cashlin retrieves the purple shoes that go with the outfit. They have enormous bows at the back of the heel. "Take these, for instance."

"They're beautiful. Striking."

"They're ludicrous."

"I don't understand."

"Both of you sit. I have to tell you something."

Marli and I exchange looks. She looks as nervous as I feel as we sit on the large ottoman.

"The Keeper came for another visit."

"That's wonderful!" I say.

"Why didn't you tell me?" Marli asks. "When did this happen?"

"Yesterday in the garden. And it was wonderful. He is wonderful. He approves of me getting involved in Imp issues and speaking his name in public."

"You've done a lot of good."

"But he doesn't approve of the mob taking justice into their own hands with Bru."

I understand. "I didn't think he would. I got a Relic from that Comfort-Serv who handled Falla's funeral. It said, 'Don't try to get even. Let the Keeper take revenge. He will pay them back.'"

"You couldn't have stopped them," Marli says.

"I suppose not, but it was still wrong."

"What else did he say?" Marli asks.

Cashlin looks at the air above us, as if replaying the conversation in her mind.

I wish I could've seen him. To actually talk with him? Not once, but twice. I interrupt her thoughts. "He must trust you a lot to come again."

"He does. The work is just beginning."

"What work?" Marli asks.

"Influencing others for him." She presses down on the wide circle skirt, making it bob and gyrate. "That's why all of this seems absurd. Who will ever take me seriously if I'm wearing this getup?"

"What do you want to wear?" I ask.

Cashlin motions for us to scooch apart on the ottoman — which we do — but her skirt is too large for her to sit between us. She remains standing. "When I went to the Choosing for the *next* reveal I was struck by a pair of simple white slippers. No embellishment whatsoever."

"Hardly your usual style," I say.

"And I didn't—couldn't—choose them because they don't fit with who I am and what I'm supposed to sell. I'm not the Council's Patron anymore. I'm his."

"That's a dramatic change of focus," I say.

"Completely," she says. "All of which has led me to the idea of tomorrow . . . wearing something all white."

"A dress like the one you're wearing, but in white?" Marli asks.

"No, not like this at all. I want you to make me something new." She illustrates her idea with hand gestures. "I want a long white dress with a high neckline, a sleek A-line. Maybe a self-belt. I'll wear the white slippers, and no jewelry or makeup."

Marli nods. "And your hair hanging free."

"Yes! Just me. For once in my life, I want to be seen as just me. Unembellished."

"It will certainly get people's attention," I say.

Marli looks troubled. "You got flack for changing from the snake outfit to this one, and now you're going to change from this one to something else?"

Cashlin looks introspective. "I'm conflicted. I've been given success, yet I'm basically walking away from it. Is that crazy?"

Maybe. But I don't want my misgivings to become hers. "Anyone can walk away from a bad situation because they have nothing to lose. It takes real courage to walk away when you're on top."

"When I have everything to lose."

"And everything to gain," Marli says.

"How do I know that for sure?" Cashlin asks.

Doesn't she see? "You don't. You have to trust the Keeper."

"Who I barely know."

"Who you've seen and talked to twice," I say. "Obviously he wants you to know him better."

"That's what he said. He has things for me to do."

"Such as?" Marli asks.

Cashlin sighs. "Being his completely."

It sounds lovely. "How do you do that?" How do I do that?

"I surrender to him. Then follow."

"So you think wearing white is his idea?" I ask.

She hesitates a moment. "Yes, I do. But to move forward, knowing it will get me in trouble again . . ."

"You're a brave woman," Marli says.

"The bravest I've ever met," I add.

She is silent for many breaths in and out, then says, "If I get in trouble, I get in trouble."

Does she mean it? Because trouble *will* certainly come.

She kneels beside us and takes one of our hands in hers. "Here's my plan: I need both of you to make me the dress. ASAP. Can you do it?"

My mind races. "I don't have any fabric. The factory only has the fabrics used for the top ten designs. And I'm used to hand work. I'd really need a sewing machine to work so quickly."

"I thought of that." She stands, drawing us to stand with her. "And so, the three of us are going to the Creatives Ring to talk to the makers of the slippers. The Creatives have access to all sorts of fabrics and machines."

She seems to have thought this through. "All right . . ."

"So, you'll do it?" She looks at Marli too. "And you, Marli?"

"Of course," we both say.

"It will be an honor."

Cashlin shows Marli her back. "Now, please get me out of this thing. We have work to do."

**

I am in awe.

Walking through the Creatives Ring is even more jarring than when I'd first walked to Cashlin's house in the Patrons Ring. That was a matter of going from my Imp world of basic living into a world of extravagance and wealth. The Creatives Ring was like walking from a world of neutral numbness into a world of life-altering color. Like a gray sky suddenly painted blue, pink, and purple by the sunset.

And the people . . . they wear the same tunic and pants that I do, but theirs are blue, red, green, or yellow. How would my life be different if I could wear colors like they do? It seems a silly thought, yet I know my life *would* be different.

"This is amazing," I say, almost reverently.

Cashlin stops walking, letting me stand in awe for a moment. "You've never been here?" she asks.

Is she ignorant or naïve? "There's no reason for an Imp to come here—or at least no reason for this Imp to come here."

"The same applies to me," Marli says. Her face is as awe-struck as my own. "The murals and the colors . . ."

I'm glad I'm not the only newcomer. To think we were literally kept in the dark until now. "It takes my breath away."

Cashlin looks around at the embellished buildings. "I guess it does. Huh. I like seeing it through your eyes. I've obviously taken it for granted. And I always come in a carriage. To walk . . . it's the better way, I think."

We walk past a building with jewelry painted on its side. Cashlin stops to admire the mural. "Someone had a lot of talent to do this, didn't they?"

"They certainly did," Marli says.

I watch Cashlin's face glow with appreciation of someone else's talent and *have* to comment on the change I see in her. "If I may, miss? You'd mentioned you're different now?"

"I am."

"I see it. I see a definite change from the first time I met you."

"A good change, I hope?"

"Of course. An amazing transformation from the star of Regalia to..." I'm not sure of the right word.

"To?" she asks.

"To a hero," I say.

Her forehead crumples with emotion. "Really?"

I'd like to pull her into my arms to assure her I'm right, but it's not proper, especially here. Instead, I briefly touch her arm. "Absolutely."

"I agree," Marli says. "It's marvelous to witness. I'm grateful to be a part of it."

She takes our hands and gives them a quick squeeze. "I couldn't have changed without the two of you."

Suddenly a man rushes toward us. "Cashlin!"

She startles and lets go of our hands. "Amar. Good morning."

Her brother. Her Creative Director. Marli and I step aside to let them talk.

"What are you doing here, sister?" he asks. Demands. "With them." He looks at us as if we are dung on his shoes.

"I'm showing them the Creatives Ring."

"For what purpose?"

"Education."

He shakes his head adamantly. He lowers his voice, but we can still hear him. "You've done enough educating, Cashlin. Too much. It's time for everyone to return to their own Rings so things can settle down."

"Is there anything you need, Amar?"

He looks taken aback. "I need you to do your job and stop this other . . . nonsense."

She nods calmly. "I appreciate your advice."

His eyebrows dip. "Are you ready for Shopping Day tomorrow?"

"I will be."

"Promise?"

She crosses her heart. "Have a good day, Amar."

We receive odd looks from people on the street. Cashlin moves on and we hurry after her. I think it's best not to speak at all, yet inside my mind is screaming. I dislike her brother immensely. He is the opposite of his compassionate sister. And more than that, I sense he's trouble.

As we walk, I admire Cashlin's composure. Occasionally she pauses and points at a building, showing us where the clothing and the headpieces are designed, as if giving a tour. Each building is painted with graphics to suit its purpose.

Finally, she stops and points at a building with illustrations of shoes on it. "There. That is our destination."

"Do they know we're coming?" I ask.

"They do. I sent word with Lieb early this morning. I've been to their shoe studio before, so arranged to meet here."

We enter into an open area that's completely white. "This is the room that was used in the last Choosing where the Creatives presented me three choices for next quarter."

"Do you have the same Creatives each time?" I ask.

"No. They are assigned."

I do the math. "There are twenty patrons with three Creatives for each Choosing . . . so there are sixty of them?"

"There are." She points down two hallways on either side of the main room. I see many doors. "There are sixty studios in each building so the Creatives can concentrate on the part of the costume they're designing: the shoes here, then clothes, headdresses, and jewelry in the other buildings."

As we walk down a hall some doors are open and I see worktables with shoes and raw materials on them. The Creatives look at us curiously. Warily.

Cashlin goes to a specific door and knocks.

The door is opened by a forty-something woman wearing a brown tunic. She smiles immediately. "Patron. Come in, come in!"

A woman in green who is slightly younger, sits at a worktable. She immediately stands to greet Cashlin, who gives her a nod. "Patron Cashlin. We were excited to receive word you were coming."

She glances at me, and Cashlin makes the introductions. "Solana and Marli, I would like you to meet Ladi, a Creative, and her assistant, Pinno. Ladi and Pinno, let me introduce you to Marli and Solana, my friends."

Friends? I bask in the title. We nod a greeting to each other.

"Pinno happens to be Xian's mother."

"He's a wonderful young man," I say. "He's helped me more than once."

Ladi asks us to sit. "How can we help you today?"

Cashlin takes a deep breath, then says, "I need you to do some private work for me."

"Of course," Ladi says. "Anything."

"Clandestine work."

Ladi's blonde eyebrows rise. "Oh?"

"Please show my friends the white slippers."

Pinno retrieves them from a drawer. Cashlin holds them as if they are a precious treasure. "See what I mean?" she asks us.

I need to touch them. "May I?"

Cashlin hands them to me. The ivory leather is the softest I've ever felt, like the skin of a baby. And just like a baby, I want to hold one to my cheek, to fully immerse myself in the experience. "They're . . ."

"Perfect," Marli says, taking a turn. "Absolutely perfect."

"And pure," I add.

"Like the Keeper," Ladi says. She quickly looks to me and Marli, as if only in that moment realizing we might not be Devoted.

"I agree," I say to ease her mind.

Ladi's breath eases. "We're glad you like them so much."

"I want to wear them," Cashlin says.

Marli hands them back to her as Ladi says, "Of course. They're yours."

Cashlin shakes her head. "I want to wear them on Shopping Day tomorrow. In the Favored Ring."

Eyebrows rise again. "But you're supposed to wear your winning costume."

"I know."

"You're welcome to wear the slippers with the purple dress but they—"

"They don't really match." Cashlin continues. "Which means I need a new dress. A white dress. Made by the four of you. For tomorrow."

Ladi and Pinno exchange a look. "What kind of dress?"

Cashlin paces around the room, explaining the details of what she wants. The Creatives are clearly confused.

"I assume you have access to white fabric?" Cashlin asks.

"We do . . ." Pinno says.

"And can you do the work in such a short time frame?"

"We can," Ladi says.

"Without letting anyone else know about it?"

Ladi blinks, but nods. "We're used to working in secret as we're always designing for the next Choosing without letting any of the other Creatives see."

Cashlin waves at me. "Solana and Marli will stay here to work. Solana works at the clothing factory and Marli has sewing skills too."

"Do you have a sewing machine?" I ask. "The time is too short for me to hand stitch it."

Pinno nods. "We can move to our workroom in the Clothing Studio."

"Excellent," Cashlin says. She stands. "I'll leave you to it, then."

Ladi stands too. "We'll need a few additional measurements for length..."

"I have them," Marli says, as she pats her pocket.

I have a sudden question. "Shopping Day is the day the Favored buy the top ten outfits. They won't be able to buy dress we're making for you. They'll be buying your purple outfit."

"They most certainly will," Cashlin says. "I don't need them to buy the white dress. I need them to see the white dress and feel what it represents."

"Which is?" Pinno asks.

"The purity of the Keeper, and the precious hope that comes from believing in him."

Silence falls between us as if everything that needed to be said has been said.

"And there it is." Cashlin turns to leave.

Ladi takes a step toward her. "May I ask why you're doing this?"

Cashlin exhales. "It's time for a change in Regalia."

"It will be a change, all right," Ladi says. "Will you get in trouble?"

Cashlin hesitates only a moment. "Probably."

"Will we get in trouble?" Marli asks.

Cashlin blinks as if she hasn't considered this. "Perhaps." She looks at each one of us. "Forgive me for not thinking of that. If you don't want to be involved—"

"I'm in," I say.

The others nod.

"How will you defend what you're wearing?" Pinno asks.

"I have no idea."

"Then why—?"

"It's what the Keeper wants me to do."

No one can argue with that.

Cashlin looks at each one of us, her face a little less certain than it was just a moment before. "In truth I'm not sure why I'm doing it, or what will happen. It may turn into a disaster. Yet just maybe, a few people might take notice of the joy and freedom of the dress's simplicity—for all the right reasons."

"Are you going to say something to those who see you?"

"Probably."

"Probably?"

She scoffs. "I have no idea." Cashlin takes a deep, cleansing breath. "I guess now you're aware that my plan isn't much of a plan. I have no end game in sight, no step-by-step process. All I know is I have to do it. I've got to have faith that everything will work out as he wants it to."

Her faith inspired me. "Then we'll make it happen," I say. I have never been so proud to be her friend.

She smiles and looks a bit more confident. "I trust all of you." She blinks once as if changing subjects in her mind. "When it's finished, please bring it—and the slippers—to my house. I'll arrange for your passage at the gates. I need everything by nine tomorrow morning."

"You will have it," Ladi says.

Pinno timidly raises her hand. "Patron Cashlin?"

"Yes?"

"I heard from my son, Xian, that you hired a solicitor to defend the men in the mob who . . ." She shrugs.

"So, it's been done? They're working together?"

"They are. I wanted you to know that Xian and I, and everyone in the Serv Ring are very grateful."

"I hope it helps." Cashlin sighs deeply. "Anything else, ladies?"

"That's it," Pinno says.

"We're good to go," Ladi says.

"I want to thank all of you for your skills and for your bravery. May the Keeper bless your work."

As soon as she leaves the four of us look at each other. "She's one amazing woman," Ladi says.

"That, she is," I say. But it's time to work. "Can you show me the fabric?"

And so it begins.

Chapter Thirty-Four

Kiya

It's the evening before Shopping Day. As one of the Favored, I love this party before the party. It's my favorite time of the year. My husband's too.

Speaking of . . . I hear Gull singing as he gets dressed to go out to dinner.

It's painful. If I didn't recognize the words to the song, I wouldn't be able to name it relying on the indecipherable tune.

He comes out of the bathroom and stands in a ta-da position before me. "What do you think?"

He's wearing an outfit from three Reveals ago: pants whose legs are segmented by four horizontal, elasticized puffs. The first puff wraps around his thighs—which frankly are a bit large for the style. And the matching jacket sleeves are adorned with similar puffs in four shades of purple. He wears a beret with green feathers. The costume doesn't do him any favors. Especially at age forty. Maybe he could've pulled it off when we were twenty, but now?

He just looks silly.

Of course, so do I.

"It looks great, hon." I say.

I used to criticize Gull—give him pointers so he could look his best—and he used to listen. But after eighteen years of marriage, he's gotten grumpy and doesn't want to hear it.

So I keep my suggestions to myself.

I glue fake jewels to my cheekbones and move my facial muscles to make sure they don't come off when I talk or eat. I apply a little more pressure to the blue one.

"Hurry it up," he says as he preens in the mirrors that line an entire wall of our bedroom. "I don't want to be late and miss the best appetizers."

Far be it for Gull to ever miss any portion of any meal. Honestly, I'm a bit tired of eating out every evening—and often at lunch too. Sometimes I'd like to just eat an apple, a small salad, or even—gasp—skip a meal.

But that's not allowed in the Favored Ring. As the recipients of extravagant stipends to buy the winning ensembles and the newest makeup and accessories, we are required to live a life of frivolity, fun, and fads.

I'm not complaining but—

I catch my own eyes in the mirror.

I'm complaining. And I hate myself for it.

"Enough, Kiya," I whisper to myself.

I stand and pull on a jewel-encrusted vest that nearly reaches the floor. The jewels catch the light—which is what first drew me to Cashlin's outfit, but it *is* horribly uncomfortable to sit on. Such is the price of fashion and being one of the Favored.

"It's time to party," I say.

**

"A toast!" a friend raises his glass, which means we must raise ours. "To tomorrow's Shopping Day!"

"To Shopping Day!"

I pretend to drink, but merely sip.

I pretend to eat, but only nibble.

I pretend to laugh, but barely manage to smile.

I pretend to listen to this story and that story—all of which I've heard a million times before—but my mind wanders.

I want to be anywhere but here.

But not home, or at the next hot spot. In truth, my feelings have nothing to do with this restaurant or this meal.

I want to be anywhere but the Favored Ring.

Leaving is impossible, of course. And even the thought of leaving is a sacrilege and a violation of numerous Council Commandments—both written and unwritten, for one never really knows when one is breaking a rule. Not until one is caught.

Well, they can't catch me for thinking.

At least I don't think they can.

Four children run by carrying balloons that gyrate wildly. Other children crawl under the table, or whine in their parents' laps. They are little clones in silly clothes with silly looking parents acting silly.

I am annoyed, but not for the reason most people would think. I am annoyed because I'm jealous. I wish we had one or two kiddos. After all, the Council encourages children—though only one or two. And it isn't a requirement.

I don't remember the exact year that Gull and I decided not to have any. In fact, I'm not sure I fully agreed. But I do remember discussing how our lives were so fulfilled and overflowing with giddy happiness that we didn't want any munchkins to distract or detract from it.

But in the past few years, as I see wrinkles sprouting around my bejeweled eyes and find it hard to stay trim enough to fit into all the clothes in my closet—75 Reveals' worth—I wonder if we made the right decision. Right now, I could use distraction from the utter and total insignificance of our lives.

I raise my glass to my own thought. "To insignificant lives!"

"What?" my friend asks from the chair beside me.

"Nothing."

It's a weighty word, *nothing*.

**

People dance. They laugh. They drink. They eat.

And I want no part of it.

My mood isn't new, but in the past few days has become more intense. I have no clue what started it.

In his drunkenness, Gull dances like a madman having a fit, oblivious to how ridiculous he looks. Everyone is oblivious. They all truly and fully believe they are special. After all, their—our—Favored status has been thrust upon us as our birthright. Do they ever stop and think that we've done nothing to deserve it, we do nothing to earn it, and we produce nothing because of it?

I have, and I'm disgusted and more than a little embarrassed. I don't want to get to the end of my life and look back onto the nothingness of my existence.

There's that *nothing* word again.

I leave the restaurant, knowing that no one will notice I'm gone. There are small groupings of people outside, but they are so intent on impressing each other they don't notice me walk past.

My shoes are painful—as they always are—so I take them off and walk barefoot on the cobblestones, enduring a different kind of pain. Somehow a more real kind of pain.

Yet the pain has little to do with skin against pavement. I feel it deep inside. Something has broken in me and I don't know how to fix it.

As I walk, I pass revelers and a few couples kissing in dark corners. Been there. Done that. With Gull and . . . without.

I approach another Favored hot spot and *feel* the beat of music. I hear the noise of the crowds. I keep walking through the rows of Favored homes, needing to get away from . . . all of it.

There's a park up ahead so keep going until I get there. I just need to be alone—which is not an easy task in the Favored Ring.

The streetlamps are sparse as I reach the dark greenness of the park. I walk along the path, past benches that are occupied. People lay on the grass, talking and . . . doing other things.

I am desperate to be away from all of them. I quicken my pace and turn from the path, walking among the trees that line the outer wall of our Ring, pressing my way through branches that scratch and grab at me like dark fingers wanting to take me captive. Out of nowhere I get the notion that something is after me. I walk faster, having to get away. My feet object to the sticks and stones that own the trail I'm blazing.

Suddenly, I trip and fall. But instead of trying to stand, I immediately draw my knees to my chest in a fetal curl, making myself a small target for whatever wants to get me.

I begin to cry.

I never cry, which upsets me even more.

But then my cries turn into wrenching sobs. What's going on?

I wrap my arms around my head. I writhe as my inner pain claws its way out. Logical thoughts that ask what's going on remain unanswered. I have no control over any of it. I'm at the mercy of an undefined *something*.

I hug myself as if trying to find the childhood comfort of my mother's arms. *There, there, Kiya. It will be all right.*

But it's not Mother's voice I hear in my head. It's a man's. The deep tenor of his mellow words calm my tears and I relax my grip on myself.

I roll onto my back, spent. With purpose, I urge my breathing to slow, and my heart to calm.

Somehow, I know it *will* be all right.

I gaze upward through the branches to the dark, cloudy skies. The moon is hidden but offers some wayward definition of soft edges among the shadows. I stare at the clouds, reveling in the peace of the moment.

But suddenly a slice of sky opens up as the clouds part like minions making way for their liege.

I stare in a moment of utter joy as the moon peeks through. It is night's beacon telling me that I am not alone—there is something beyond right here and right now. Something bigger and better and brighter and . . .

"Mine."

My whisper settles softly around me as I lay there, watching the sky, bathing in the moonlight.

And I know one very important, indescribable, unquantifiable truth: everything has changed.

Everything.

The opposite of nothing.

**

Something tickles my cheek. I brush it away and open my eyes. With a start I realize I'm sleeping on the ground. Morning dew makes me shiver.

I sit up. I'm surrounded by trees, and I see wildflowers snake their way up the Ring's wall. I've flattened a group of daisies and brush them with my hand, hoping they'll pop back to life.

I remember what happened and look up at the sky that was the source of my revelation. It's blue and clear. The clouds and moon that changed me have moved on until it's their time to shine again.

With a moan, I stand. I wobble a bit as my muscles complain about what I've put them through. My feet object to the pebbles and twigs beneath them.

But it's okay. It's good. I raise my hands to the sky to stretch, but it turns into something more. A gesture of praise. A thank you. A moment of awe in something I can't define. It's like an inner contract has been signed and sealed without me knowing its details.

Reluctantly, I lower my arms. I take a cleansing breath, trying to transition from an experience of spiritual intimacy into a reality that's forever changed.

I find my shoes and carry them home, enjoying the authentic pain to accompany the genuine excitement that stirs within me.

There aren't many people on the streets. Most are at home, sleeping off the past night's revelry, or getting ready for today.

For it's Shopping Day. *The* day we anticipate each quarter.

I've always enjoyed the day, for it means getting fresh pretties and wallowing in their decadence. I'm excited for all that, yet today promises to offer something new, undiscovered and unexplored. There's an anticipation of another sort stirring within me.

Something amazing is going to happen today.

I just know it.

Chapter Thirty-Five

Cashlin

I stand at my bedroom window as the last traces of night give way to the morning. Surely everyone in the Patron Ring is up and busy, getting ready for Shopping Day.

I haven't slept all night as thoughts race through my brain like a swarm of gnats, intent on annoying me. None of them land for more than a second before buzzing off again in a frenzied pattern of panic.

It comes down to this: what am I doing?

I fall into a nearby chair, mentally exhausted before the day even begins. The ladies who are making my white dress asked good questions about how everything will play out—questions I have no answers to, no matter how many flies buzz around inside my head.

How will people react?

I predict it will be mixed: derision, laughter, shock, and probably anger and resentment that once again Patron Cashlin has changed the rules.

Will I be arrested?

I figure it's a sixty-forty chance—for. I've already had one trial for the kiss, and one very strong chiding for wearing the purple dress. I've tested boundaries by getting involved in the business of the Imp Ring—confronting Bru and distributing food. I've even gone to an Imp funeral. And now, on the day when people are going to buy my number-one outfit?

I wear a white dress devoid of any style.

As a Patron of style and fashion—as the Premier Patron—it's as good as slapping the establishment of Regalia in the face.

Someone will demand an answer, right then and there.

What will I say to them?

I look over my shoulder at the bedroom door, thinking about the garden. Is the Keeper nearby? Can I somehow conjure him up at will?

I shake the thought away as presumptuous and greedy. He told me more than once he trusts me to represent him. I certainly didn't choose today's course of action because it will get me points and applause from my audience. In fact, it will probably get me derision and . . .

Consequences.

My sigh breaks the silence of the room. "How can I defend myself? How can I explain why I'm doing this when I don't really know? How can—?"

I hear commotion downstairs and race to the bedroom door. The ladies are here! They hurry upstairs. Marli carries the dress draped over her arm, covered in a blanket.

"Come in!" I say, stepping aside. "Let me see it!"

Ladi removes the blanket and Marli unfurls a sleek, long-sleeved, collarless dress with tight sleeves, cut in a flattering A-line. It's just as I'd pictured it.

I reach out to touch it and love the feel of the fabric. "It's got a nice weight to it."

"It drapes beautifully and will flow when you walk," Pinno says.

"Let me try it on."

Marli follows me into the closet, and I put it on. She fastens pearl buttons at the back as I knot a fabric belt at my waist. I look in the mirror and just stare.

"Don't you like it?" Marli asks.

It's perfect. I need all of them to hear my praise. "Ladies, come here, please."

They enter tentatively, and I notice Pinno and Ladi's eyes widen at the size and extravagance of the closet.

But their attention is quickly focused on the dress. And me.

"Oh my," Solana says.

"You're stunning," Pinno says.

Ladi's eyes glisten with tears. "It's beautiful."

"Yes, it is," I say. "I'm in awe of your talent and am forever in your debt."

"We were so happy to do it," Ladi says. She points toward the bedroom. "Pinno? Will you get . . . ?"

"Of course." She comes back with a box.

I know what's inside. "The shoes," I whisper.

The box is opened, and Pinno hands them to me.

"They fit," I say.

"They should. We made them especially for you," Ladi says.

"And we made you something else." From the box Solana lifts out an odd-looking fold of fabric. "It's a cowl that turns into a hood," she says.

"Show me."

The ladies place the open hood over my head and adjust its folds around my shoulders.

"You can wear it down like this," Ladi says, "or pull it up like a hood."

I do just that and find myself once again staring at my reflection. My copper hair is a stunning contrast against the white. "It's . . . perfection."

They all nod.

My heart seems to expand to twice its normal size. "I feel something special in this moment. Yet . . . that seems silly. It's just a dress."

Solana shakes her head. "It's not *just* anything."

"It represents your commitment to the Keeper," Ladi says.

My breath catches in my throat as the full weight of my surrender flows through me.

I hold out my arms and the ladies gather round, holding hands. The touch between Patron, Imp, and Serv may be illegal, but to me the human contact feels exactly right, exactly the way it should be.

Solana looks upward. "Dear Keeper. You have led Cashlin to this moment."

"Us to this moment," I say.

"Us to this moment. Please watch over Cashlin today as she steps out in public."

"Protect her from all harm," Pinno says.

Harm? Yet I know that's a possibility.

"Honor her commitment to you in amazing ways," Ladi says.

"And give me just the right words at just the right time," I add.

Solana and Ladi squeeze my hands before we all let go.

We take a breath together, which makes us laugh.

"Well then," I say. "Shall we go?"

"You want us to come along?" Ladi asks.

"Of course. I *need* you to come along."

We will do this together.

**

Dom arranges a carriage for us. Ladi and Pinno are giddy about the new experience, and I enjoy their banter. It's a distraction from the nerves that make me want to tell the driver to go back; I've changed my mind.

But there is no going back. The need to keep going is a stirring, an urgency that originates in a place I've rarely visited.

As we ride along, I grow pensive, and the ladies seem to sense — and honor — my need for it. The panicked thoughts I'd suffered during the long night aren't any more well-defined, but they've mellowed, as if a soft blanket has created a buffer between then and now. I have no clear thoughts about what will happen in the next few hours, but I feel a calm assurance that whatever it is, it will be all right. It will *be* right.

I'm not a woman of great faith. I believe in what I know and see. Yet if that's what defines my faith, then I have to fully believe in the Keeper, because I know him, and I've seen him. He's filled me to overflowing in a way I never imagined, like a bottomless glass of water that is never empty, always ready to restore and refresh.

As we pass through the Creatives Ring and stop at the gate to the Favored Ring, I close my eyes and take slow breaths, willing everything that's supposed to happen to happen in the perfect way that only the Keeper can arrange.

"You're smiling," Solana says softly.

I open my eyes. "I am."

Marli leans forward and squeezes my hand. "He's got you."

I rest in this one great truth.

**

The ladies are a flutter at seeing the throngs of the Favored in their bright outfits. The shops have been decorated with bunting and flags, their doors propped open, welcoming all to come in and buy.

"I didn't realize there were so many of them," Ladi says.

"There's one of your outfits from two quarters ago," Marli points out my side of the carriage.

"It's Kiya!" I say. "I know her." She wears my dress of orange paisley chiffon. It looks good on her. She's arranged the turban in a way beyond my original styling, and I like it.

At that moment she looks in my direction. Our eyes meet. I raise a hand in greeting.

She bobs a little curtsy in recognition.

I enjoy the moment of one-on-one. I get weary of the masses.

In fact . . .

I knock on the ceiling of the carriage. "Stop here!"

Solana's eyes widen. "This is it?"

My stomach tightens. Is it? But then I hear myself saying, "It is."

The driver opens the door, and the ladies exit the carriage first, stepping aside to wait for me.

The driver takes my hand and I step out. He must sense that something unusual is about to occur for he says, "Good luck, Patron."

I shake my head slightly, not liking the word "luck", for luck will have nothing to do with whatever the day will bring.

As the carriage pulls away, I stand alone. The pure whiteness of my dress makes the Favored stop walking. Stop talking. Then they start muttering behind their hands.

The ladies are rattled. They have no idea how to help me—and I'm not sure they even can. Do I need help?

But then Kiya comes close. "Patron Cashlin. You look remarkable."

"Thank you." I appreciate her proximity. Just having one person to talk to eases my nerves—a bit.

"But why—?" she asks.

Others are emboldened by her talking to me and push close. "Why aren't you wearing your purple dress?" they ask.

I ignore their questions and smile. "Are you excited for Shopping Day?"

Some respond, and others keep after me with the same question.

"Leave her alone," Kiya says. "Patron Cashlin can wear whatever she wants."

Unfortunately, her defense of me makes things worse. "No, she can't," a man says. "She already broke the rules by wearing an old entry. Now, she breaks the rules again by wearing this white robe of nothingness?"

A crowd has gathered and they start arguing with each other. Some are for me, some against. Should I say something? Or should I slink away and let them duke it out?

I feel Solana's hand touch my back. I glance over my shoulder. "Say something," she whispers.

Although I have no words in mind, I raise my hands to quiet them. They look at me expectantly.

Keeper? Help me now!

"Good people, Favored people of Regalia. Have no worries. I am but one woman, come to serve you."

"But where's your purple dress?"

"In the shops," I say. "Ready for you to purchase and wear. How many of you voted for my dress?"

Many hands go up.

"I certainly did," Kiya says.

"I appreciate your support more than I can say."

"But why are you wearing white?"

Five words come to me and are spoken before I can hold them back. "Because I have been cleansed."

"What's that mean?"

"I have been changed by the love of the Keeper."

There are gasps.

"Silence!" a man shouts. "You can't say his name!"

"Why not?" I ask. "Why can't I? Why shouldn't I? Why is someone who's pure and good banned? Ostracized from our lives?"

The crowd is restless. People frown and mutter, their words churning like a pot read to boil.

"It's against the Council Commandments!"

"You're breaking the law!"

"You can't do this!"

Although my insides are in turmoil, my mind is clear. I wait for their shouts to dissipate. "Perhaps we should ask ourselves *why* he is banned? As our Keeper, he is our protector and comforter. He poses no threat to the Council, or to any of us. He loves us."

"Arrest her!"

There is a disturbance to my right, and I see three Enforcer Servs talking to the crowd.

They look in my direction.

This is it.

Do I wait for them to reach me? Do I run?

Neither.

I am spurred to walk in the opposite direction, slowly winding my way through the crowds of shoppers as I smile and greet them. Kiya steps beside me, assigning herself as my escort. The ladies walk behind me.

"Thank you for walking with me," I say to her.

"Of course. Whatever you need."

"At the moment, I'm not sure what that is."

She chuckles. "You're certainly getting a lot of attention."

"I figured I would."

"Is that why you wore the white?"

"Not exactly. I wore the white because it's what the Keeper led me to do."

Kiya shakes her head as if his name is acid. "We can't talk about him. It's forbidden."

"I know."

"But you're doing it anyway?"

"I am. I have to."

"Is he making you do it?"

What an interesting question. "I don't think he makes anyone do anything. He opens doors. He invites us to walk through them. He offers us an alternative to . . . to . . ."

"To what?" she asks.

I stop and sweep a hand over the chaos of Shopping Day. "An alternative to all this."

"Shopping Day?"

"There's more to life than pretty clothes." I see a change in her face, as if a light has flipped on in her mind.

"I've been thinking the same thing." Kiya's face is serious. "This all seems so frivolous and meaningless. There has to be more purpose to life than this."

I touch her hand. "There is. There's so much more."

"How do I find it?"

"By opening yourself up to him."

She shakes her head. "I wouldn't know how to do that."

I chuckle. "I didn't know how either. But he came anyway."

"Came?"

I know the Keeper doesn't appear in people's gardens often. I don't want to make a promise he won't deliver. "Call out to him and he *will* answer you—in a very personal way."

"You know that for sure?"

"I do."

"What about using the sky? Could he—?"

I stop walking. "Sky?" Yes, yes!

"Like showing me a slice of sky, and the moon, and—"

We hear a ruckus behind me. I see Enforcers pushing their way through the crowd. "They're coming for me, Kiya. I want you to come to my house tomorrow. Ask for Marli. She'll help you know what to do next."

And then I turn to face the Enforcers. Although my nerves stand at attention, I'm not afraid. Somehow, I know this is the way it's supposed to play out.

I clasp my hands in front of my body and wait for my arrest. I glance back at the ladies and mouth, "Go home."

When the three Enforcers reach me, they seem a bit confused, obviously expecting me to argue or fight. Then one of them speaks. "Patron Cashlin, we place you under arrest for the illegal mention of his name."

"As you must."

They take positions, one in front and two behind. We walk back the way I'd come. But this time instead of shouted questions and complaints, the crowd parts. Men remove their hats and women bow their heads.

It's extraordinary in every way.

I wouldn't expect anything less from the Keeper.

**

I'm led in custody through the streets of the Favored Ring. Somehow, I manage to appear calm. More than that, I feel no fear. I still smile at the people and walk with my head held high. For I am not walking alone. He is with me.

We walk through the gates leading toward the center of Regalia, past the lovely mansions, and into the Council Ring. I'm glad I've been here before during my trial with Quan. Perhaps the Keeper planned that so I wouldn't be frightened.

I'm led into the same entrance as before and led to a room in the Council Tower. For the first time I fully breathe. Obviously, the Keeper wants me here. I have to trust him to see me through whatever happens next.

The door opens and Xian enters. I rush into his arms. I don't care if it's wrong. "I'm so glad to see you!"

He hugs me tight. "Are you all right?" he asks.

"I am."

He lets me go and looks at my clothes. "Did my mother help make this for you?"

"She did."

He shakes his head, yet says, "You look amazing."

In spite of the situation, I blush. "Thank you."

"Solicitor Nerwhether has been notified. He should be here soon."

"I'm not sure how he can help. I'm guilty of everything they say."

"Word has already reached us of what happened. To be so blatant, Patron. Why take the risk?"

"Because it's what the Keeper wants me to do."

His eyebrows nearly touch. "How do you know?"

"He told me. In person. Twice."

Now, his eyebrows rise. "Told you?"

I take his hands in mine. "Trust me, Xian. Trust your mother and her faith. It's real. The time has come for the Keeper to come out in the open."

"The Council will never allow that."

"I'm not sure it's up to them."

"But they have the power."

He's right, and I feel a twinge of fear. Yet . . . "So does he."

At that moment, Nerwhether comes in.

"We meet again, Citizen Cashlin."

"We do."

He notices Xian and does a double take. Does he remember him from my house?

"You may go, Enforcer."

Xian looks at me. "Let me know if you need anything."

He leaves and Nerwhether sits across from me. "That man . . . at your home and now here? He was your cook's friend, but seeing you two together again? Are you and this Enforcer . . . involved?"

"No, sir. That would be against the law."

"Hmm." He gets out a notepad and pen. "So. Three offenses, Citizen Cashlin."

"You can call me Cashlin."

He shrugs. "What are we going to do with you. . . Cashlin?"

I have no idea what to say other than, "I am guilty of what they say."

"Hmm," he says again. "You get in trouble for wearing the purple dress, and today when you're actually supposed to wear the purple dress you wear this . . . this . . . robe?"

"The purple costume is already produced and in stores. Regalia doesn't lose a single sale from me wearing what I'm wearing."

"But again . . . it's the attitude, Cashlin. Despite being the Premier Patron you are not the queen of Regalia. There are rules. There are traditions. There are laws."

"I realize that."

"Do you?"

The tone of his voice scares me. "I meant no harm or disrespect, Solicitor. It's just a . . . robe."

He flips my words away like a pesky fly. "It's not just the robe, it's what you said after a crowd gathered—as you surely knew they would do. Your words are a huge problem, and you know it. The Council Commandment states, 'There shall be no worship of any deity', much less speaking about him in public."

"But—"

He lifts a hand to stop my excuse. "You are not ignorant of that law—no one is."

I simply nod. "So, what happens next?"

"Next, you will be brought before the Council."

"Where you'll defend me?"

He hesitates. "To be brutally honest, there is nothing I can do to save you."

I gasp. "I don't understand. No harm came from either my robe or my words. I didn't speak against the Council; I merely spoke *for* the Keeper."

"Speaking for one means speaking against the other. You have no defense. You chose the robe and the words. End of story. People have been punished for a lot less."

This is going as I expected, but not as I'd hoped. "What will they do to me?"

He takes a deep breath, reaches across the table, and takes my hands in his. "There's a very good chance you will face exile."

I yank my hands away. "They're going to kill me for this?"

"You leave them no choice. You've been involved in three infractions, Cashlin. They don't dare show leniency — Premier Patron or not. By doing so they would set a dangerous precedent."

I shake my head, back and forth, back and forth. I don't know what to do.

"Honestly, Cashlin, there's more — that they may or may not bring up."

"More?"

"Word has gotten around that you interfered in the Bru situation, visited the Imp Ring, handed out food, and attended an Imp funeral. You must have a death wish."

"I have no such thing." I change the subject. "What about the men who were arrested for throwing Bru into the desert? You *are* defending them as I asked, yes?"

He shrugs. "Nothing to defend. The Council is not a lenient bunch. They're being exiled too."

Too. As if my fate is already determined.

I feel defeated. Deflated. Disgusted at the system. I am cornered with no way out. "When is my trial?"

It's a bad sign that he looks at his watch. But then he says, "I'm not sure exactly. Probably in the next few days."

"Can I go home until then?"

He scoffs. "I'm afraid not. You'll stay in a cell, here in the Tower."

A cell. Cold. Dark. Dank. Scary.

"I'm predicting they will move things around to get your trial over with ASAP. They want this behind them, Cashlin. They want you behind them."

As if I'm without merit, an annoyance. And dangerous.

Me? Dangerous?

I pull the sleeves of my dress over my hands. "Will you call witnesses stating that no harm was done, that my words were to encourage, not anger?"

He shakes his head. "There will be no witnesses. No one from the Favored Ring will dare come before the Council and speak about the Keeper — whether they repeat your words or not. People in Regalia go out of their way to prevent *any* encounters with the Council of Worthiness. I guarantee you, the Favored are not going to risk their status for you. Sorry to be so blunt, but it's the truth."

I think of my one Favored friend, Kiya. Yet I don't want to put her in danger.

The fact is, I'm going to die.

Nerwhether stands. "It's time to get you to your cell. Let me get an Enforc—"

"Can Xian do it? Can you get Xian to take me there?"

"There you go, bending the rules again."

I tighten my jaw. "If I'm going to die, what does it matter?"

"Hmm. Touché. I'll see if I can find him."

He leaves me in the room alone. I am numb. If someone ordered me to stand, I'm not sure I'd be able to do it.

How could a dress and a few words go so wrong?

How could a dress and a few words lead me to death?

I hug myself, repeating two words over and over. *Help me. Help me. Help me . . .*

**

I have no idea how long I've been in the room. But finally, the door opens, and Xian enters.

In a sudden burst of energy, I fly into his arms. "I'm going to be exiled."

"No, you're not," he says, holding me tight. "Surely, you're not."

I nod against his chest. "Yes, I am. Nerwhether said as much."

He pushes me back to look at my face. "*He* said that?"

"He did. I've pushed the Council too far. They have no choice."

"Of course they have a choice. You're their Premier Patron. They wouldn't dare do that to you."

I feel a glimmer of hope. "You think so?"

He lifts my chin and smiles. "You're special, Cashlin. Everyone realizes that. Special people aren't exiled."

I love that he called me by name. I take a breath that starts in my toes. "Thank you for making me feel better. I hope you're right."

He glances at the door. "I do need to take you to your cell now."

I physically shudder.

"It'll be okay. The cells aren't that bad. And it's only for a few days."

Until I'm exiled.

He leads me down many corridors, holding my upper arm like I'm in custody—which I am. But I feel the warmth of his hand, which reminds me of the hope we share. I'm extremely thankful Xian's the one who's taking me to my jail cell. The result is the same, but the journey is tempered by his presence.

We finally reach a bank of six cells, three on either side of a wide walkway. They are open to the hall separating them, with floor to ceiling bars allowing no privacy whatsoever.

"Hey, girlie!" a man yells from a middle cell. He makes crude gestures.

Xian slams a hand on his cell door, making the man jump back. "Watch yourself, cretin!" Then he stops in front of the first cell on the opposite side. "This is yours."

I hesitate at the door. There are two beds with a small table in between, a privy, and a sink. There is one high window. I walk inside and sit on a mattress.

"I got you an extra blanket." Xian points at the foot of the bed, which is no wider than a cot.

"Thank you."

"I have to go now, but I'll come back."

I only nod.

"It will be all right, Cashlin."

I'm glad one of us thinks so.

Chapter Thirty-Six

Solana

After seeing Cashlin taken away, Pinno, Ladi, Marli, and I can't get out of the Favored Ring fast enough. If someone as influential and important as Cashlin can get arrested, all bets are off for our own safety. We don't even speak as we make our way back to Cashlin's house to regroup.

But once safely inside we fall into each other's arms and let the tears flow.

Dom comes into the foyer and balks. "What happened? What's going on? Where's Patron Cashlin?"

"They arrested her," Marli says.

"For her dress?"

"Not for her dress," I say. "Or not merely for causing a stir with her dress. For speaking about the Keeper—to everyone."

Dom's eyes grow wide. "Was she planning to do that?"

I look at the other ladies. "I'm not sure."

"I don't think *she* knew what she was going to say," Pinno says.

"Despite it all, she was very brave. Very eloquent," Ladi says.

Dom motions toward the parlor where we all sit. "How did the Favored react?"

"Some yelled at her, some just listened," Pinno says.

"Everyone was shocked."

"One Favored woman had a one-on-one talk with her," I say. "*She* seemed genuinely interested."

"Did anyone object when she was arrested?" Dom asks.

"No one," Marli says.

I feel a wave of shame. "We didn't object either. Maybe we should have."

The women shake their heads. "We were visitors in a strange Ring," Pinno says.

"We got out of there as fast as we could," Marli says.

Dom nods. "That was probably the wisest choice. Is she going on trial?"

"We don't know." I look at Pinno. "Can you send a message to your son and find out what's happening?"

"That's a good idea. Do you have paper?"

Marli leaves to get some just as Irwin comes in from the kitchen. We bring him up to date.

"What can we do to help?" he asks.

It's a good question and no one speaks right away. Then I think of Helsa and the factory and Falla's mother...

"We need to go back to our Rings and spread the news that Cashlin's been arrested for talking about the Keeper. She's done so much for so many people, surely—"

"Surely they'll come to her defense?" Ladi asks. "How exactly do any of us do that? If we rile people up like they were with Bru more people will get arrested."

Dom keeps shaking his head. "I don't think Patron Cashlin wants that to happen."

Marli returns, handing some paper and a pen to Pinno, who writes a short note for Xian. "There," she says. "Do you have a regular messenger you use, Marli?"

"Lieb usually shows up mid-morning. I'll put out the flag so he stops to get it." She goes to the front door and places the mail flag up, then we hear her say, "Lieb! Come here, come here!"

They both come inside. He looks uneasy at seeing all of us gathered in the parlor, but quickly focuses on me. "Nana?"

"It's all right, Lieb," I say. "We have an important message that needs to go to Xian."

He nods. "Xian. I like Xian."

Marli hands him the note. "This is from Xian's mother." She points at Pinno.

"It's important he gets the message quickly."

"I'll run really fast," Lieb says.

"And please wait for a reply," I say.

He puts the message in his messenger bag and pats it once. "I'll be right back. I promise."

"Do what you do best," I tell him.

When he leaves, we're faced with what to do next. "I can't wait here for the answer," I say. "I want to get home and tell Helsa and the others."

"Us too," Ladi says.

Dom stands. "As soon as we read Xian's reply, we'll send Lieb to your house, Solana, and you send it on to Ladi's. Until then, everyone spread the news and unite the Devoted for Patron Cashlin."

It's a plan.

**

I hurry back to the Imp Ring and head to the factory, needing to speak with Helsa. I find her outside at lunch.

"Good," I say, running up to her.

She hands me a slice of apple, but I decline. "How was Shopping Day?" Her voice reveals her mockery. "Did the Favored Ring come to its knees when Cashlin wore the white dress?"

I hate her demeaning tone. "She was arrested."

Helsa stops mid-chew. "It must have been some dress."

"Not for the dress — entirely. She spoke about the Keeper in front of everyone. They took her away."

"Is she in jail?"

"We don't know. We sent a note to Xian, trying to get answers."

"I don't understand her," Helsa says. "Why does she continue to risk her privileged life by wearing what she shouldn't and butting into places she shouldn't. It doesn't make sense to me."

"She's a woman with a big heart. She wants to help people."

"By getting arrested? That doesn't help anybody."

I'm appalled by her attitude. "How can you speak about her like this? Without Cashlin's help Bru would still be working at the factory, harassing you, abusing people."

Helsa sighs. "It's not that I don't appreciate everything she's done, but—"

"It sure sounds like it."

Helsa's eyes flit around as if she's searching for the right words. "It's just that talking about the Keeper — in the Favored Ring, no less — that's not just crazy, it's reckless."

A part of me agrees with her. "I believe she spoke the words the Keeper wanted her to speak."

"He gave her the words?" She looks skeptical.

"I believe so, yes. They were great words, Helsa. Words of encouragement. Words beyond herself."

"But what good did they do if they got her arrested? She can't do anybody any good in jail."

Helsa confuses me. "We can't just abandon her. We have to do something to help."

"What did you have in mind?" When I don't answer right away, she says, "Good plan, Nana." Then she gives me a mocking look of feigned excitement. "I know! Let's storm the Council Tower and break her out!"

"Now, who's talking reckless? I'm not saying that."

"Then what? Cashlin is a Patron. She got herself in trouble and there's nothing any peon like you or me can do to get her out of it."

I hate the logic in her words. "We can tell others how brave Cashlin was to speak of the Keeper."

"And then what?"

"Maybe . . . maybe it will spur people to speak out about him."

"So *they* can get arrested?" She bites into her apple.

I snatch it from her and throw it across the square. "Then go ahead. Just ignore the whole situation. Eat your lunch, go back to work, and forget everything Cashlin has done for you — for all of us. I, for one, am going to tell everyone I see what's happened and urge them to speak out and pray for the Keeper's protection during this scary time."

With that, I storm away. If my own granddaughter doesn't understand what's at stake what hope is there that anyone else will?

Chapter Thirty-Seven

Kiya

I was done with Shopping Day as soon as they arrested Cashlin. To have them snatch her away as we walked . . .

And talked.

I try to remember the words she said to everyone, yet the concepts are new to me, so they're like butterflies fluttering around my head, there, but elusive.

After she was taken, I heard smatterings of talk about her. Mostly derisive chatter—because it's more fun to be negative than positive. But when the shops opened, Cashlin was forgotten as the Favored focused on spending their allowances on the newest pretty bauble and frill.

Gull found me soon after and swept me from store to store, fully in the thick of the frenzy. I bought Cashlin's purple outfit and he bought a ridiculous orange jumpsuit with massively wide bell-bottom pants and triple suspenders that served no purpose whatsoever.

As soon as our purchases were made, I was ready to go home. Gull insisted we stay and eat food cart delicacies, meaning we didn't get home until late afternoon.

Gull falls back on the couch. "I am stuffed to my gull-gills."

"Gulls don't have gills."

He shrugs.

I grab our shopping bags. "I'm putting things away."

"Let it wait." He pats the couch beside him. "Sit with me."

I have no wish—

"Don't tell me you don't have time, because we have nothing else to do the rest of the day until we party tonight."

I have no feasible excuse other than the fact I don't want to talk to him right now.

"Sit," he says again with more force.

I sit a few feet away from him and mentally say, *Now what?*

"I heard something about you today," he says.

"Oh?"

"I heard that you had an intense conversation with crazy Cashlin, walking with her, side by side."

My throat tightens, but I say, "So? She knows me by name. She's an interesting person, with interesting things to say."

"Rebellious things to say. She spoke of the Keeper."

"She did."

"You should've avoided her."

I shake my head. "I am drawn to her—always drawn to her. That's why I introduced myself to her a few quarters back. And it's not just about the clothes." I look past him to a memory. "There's something about her that's special."

"She's got the 'it' factor, that's for sure."

I shake my head again. "That's not what I'm talking about. Today when I saw her in that plain white dress amid all the gaudy clothes around her, I knew she was—"

"Daft?"

"Changed." Even though he's never going to understand I try to explain. "There was an aura around her, a presence, an air of . . . mystery, yet also of blatant truth. I know she and I were supposed to meet today. I know it."

"Says who?"

"I don't know. Says my gut?" I'm weary of explaining myself. "She's a kind woman who has a lot of insights."

He scoffs. "Insights into how to get in trouble with the Council. Or how to get arrested. She does that really well."

I angle to face him. "She has insights about there being more to life than clothes and shopping and parties."

He chuckles. "If there is, I don't want to know about it." He spreads his arms wide across the back of the couch and I see sweat stains under his arms. "We don't want for anything, we have all the free time we can handle, we have friends, have fun, and are paid to wear cool clothes and party. I, for one, am thankful we are who we are, living where we are. We have no responsibilities whatsoever. Isn't that everyone's dream?"

I wasn't so sure. "But what *good* do we do?"

He stretches his arms overhead and yawns so wide I see his tonsils. "Good? As in purpose?"

"Yes. What purpose do we have?"

He lowers his arms with a huff. "*We* are the key to keeping the Cycle of Regalia going. Without us nobody has a job. That's enough of a purpose for me." He looks straight at me. "And it needs to be enough for you too, Kiya."

His tone is slightly threatening.

I'm tempted to walk away, yet I have another important question. "What good is it being one of the Favored if we have no power?"

"What are you talking about? We have *all* the power."

I haven't been clear. "I mean, what good are we if we have no power to do good in Regalia, if we can't make people's lives better?"

He sits up, shaking his head vigorously. "Enough, Kiya. Don't stir up what shouldn't be stirred. Be grateful for what we have and be done with it."

Even though I nod, I know that's impossible.

**

When Gull goes out with friends, I decline. I'm glad to have the house to myself for the evening.

I need time alone.

I decide to straighten our closets as the two overflow with past costumes. It makes no sense to have so many choices. Maybe I can give some of them away to Imps or Servs or—

I dispel that idea as quickly as it comes. They are required to wear their assigned uniform: gray and brown. Everyone in Regalia has a uniform—even us. But what if they *could* wear other things? I'd be happy to clear out most of my closet for them.

I straighten my vast store of shoes. "Do good intentions count?"

I hadn't meant to ask the question out loud but repeat it. "Do good intentions count?"

Unlike my time in the woods, I don't hear any soothing male voice responding. Then I remember Cashlin telling me that I need to open myself up to the Keeper. I'm supposed to call out to him, and he will answer me.

I turn my back on the shoes and look upward, wishing a slice of sky would appear to inspire me.

"Hey, Keeper? It's Kiya."

I feel silly for telling him my name. And yet . . . "Do you already know that? Do you know about me?"

I shiver.

Is that an answer?

I take it as one and enjoy a wave of calm. "I want to know more, okay? Show me more."

I stand there, waiting. Oddly, I'm not antsy about it. And though I don't hear any words I start to feel that everything will be all right.

I do admit I'm a bit disappointed that nothing dramatic happens. No shoes suddenly fall off the shelf, and the Keeper doesn't knock at the door. Yet I feel an inner stir of anticipation that something *is* happening.

Which is enough—for now.

Chapter Thirty-Eight

Cashlin

In my cell I have no idea what time it is. They've brought me two meager meals, so perhaps food will be how I time the day.

How many days will I be here?

At least I've had one visitor. Xian stopped by and told me there was no word about my trial date. Nerwhether hasn't visited me. Is that a bad sign?

I can only see two of the three cells across from me, the middle one houses the crude man, and the other, a Serv woman. I've heard two other men's voices coming from other cells. The place is surprisingly quiet. Everyone is probably in their own heads, trying to sort through what got them here and what their future will be. I'm in that head space too.

How, in the span of three weeks, did I go from Quan's kiss and the trial that followed, to seeing his exile, to twice meeting the Keeper who ignited my faith, to meeting Solana, Helsa, Pinno, and Ladi. And sweet Falla. Her death still haunts me—as does Bru's. Although I wasn't there when the mob threw him into the Swirling Desert, I suspect my involvement in his Ring was a catalyst to his death. Which makes me wonder: if I hadn't gotten involved would Bru and Falla still be alive?

I have a new thought and go to the door of my cell. "Hello? Are any of you here for Bru's death?"

A woman across from me shakes her head.

There is silence for a moment, then three male voices chime in. "Here."

"Me too."

"I'm one of 'em," the crude man says. "Who're you?"

"I'm Cashlin."

"Patron Cashlin?" asks the first voice.

"Yes."

"My wife is Vue, one of the women Bru hurt."

The dots connect and I am overwhelmed by a feeling of compassion and empathy for what he and his family have gone through. "I'm so sorry he made her suffer."

"Yeah, well. I wants to thank you for bringing food when the stores wouldn't sell to us."

"You're welcome."

The second voice speaks. "Falla was my niece."

Oh my. "I'm so sorry for your loss. I only met her once, but she was a sweet girl."

"I hadda kill 'im," the man says.

"Bru's cousin was the Enforcer General," the third man says. "He wasn't gonna do no justice on him."

"I know," I say.

"Hey," man one says, "You got us our solicitor, didn't cha?"

"I did. Has he helped?"

"Not yet."

"He's my solicitor too," I say, hoping it makes them feel more confident. Although *I* am not confident.

The woman stands at the bars. "Why are *you* here?" I ask her.

"I had a few meetings in my house."

"Meetings for the Keeper?"

She looks at me aghast. "Shh!"

"I'm here for that too," I say. In part, anyway.

"Really? You're a Patron. I didn't 'spect there to be Devoted in your Ring."

"There aren't—at least not that I know of. Other than my House Servs."

"Then why did you risk it?"

And there it is. A chance to talk about him. I press a hand against my chest, desperate for him to give me the right words.

"It's a long story," I say.

"Ha!" laughs a man. "All we's got is time."

And so, I begin. "Three weeks back I went to the exile of an Entertainment Serv who got in trouble for kissing me during the last Reveal."

"I remembers hearing 'bout that."

"Was the exile awful to see?" the woman asks.

"I saw four people get sent into the Swirling Desert. For one—a criminal, it was horrible. The sand sucked him away."

"What about your kisser?"

"I'll get to him in a minute. There's more of the story I have to tell first. Because before him it was the turn of a married couple who were Devoted."

"Really?" The woman's voice breaks.

"But then a miracle happened. A miracle from the Keeper."

"This, I gotta hear," says a man.

"Shh!" someone tells him. "Go on, Patron."

"Just as the couple were on the edge of the desert, the sands parted, blowing upward, forming a path—"

"A path going into the desert?" the woman asks.

"Exactly that. They were able to walk into the desert without getting hurt."

"Sure, they were."

"They were," I say. "The sands parted and they just walked in. Others saw it too."

"I never heard nothing about it."

Ah. The sticky part. "Not everyone saw it, but at least three of us did—including my dancer, Quan. He was going to be thrown in next but when he saw the safe pathway, he ran in after the couple. But immediately the sands swept down around him and sucked him in."

"Whoa. That's harsh," says the third man.

"Served him right," says the woman. "The couple's only crime was being Devoted."

"If a little thing like a kiss got 'im exiled, we're doomed," a man says.

I've thought that too. "Quan had been before the Council of Worthiness multiple times," I say. "I think the kiss was the last straw."

"So yer saying because the couple was Devoted, they went . . . easy?"

"Yes. I believe that's the reason."

The woman grips the bars. "Did seeing what you saw get you believing?"

"It certainly was the start of it." I don't want to tell them about the visits of the Keeper, as I don't think that will help right now. But the aftermath of his visits . . . "My eyes were opened to the possibility of *him* and then I met an Imp woman who was a strong believer and—"

"What's 'er name?" a man asks.

"Solana. And her granddaughter, Helsa."

"We knows them. We knew Helsa's ma and pa too."

The first man continues. "They exiled her pa 'cause he talked about the Keeper. A lot. All the time, even at work. I told Devin to hush up, but he wouldn't do it. I don't think he *could* be quiet about it."

The woman sinks to the floor and begins to cry. "They're going to exile me too, aren't they?"

I wish I could hug her. Comfort her. Yet her fear becomes mine.

"Don't cry, lady," a man says. "We three killed a man. Maybe our death'll be enough for 'em."

Another man speaks up. "Hey, maybe the sands will part for us too."

"Yer not Devoted, are ya?"

"I could be."

I remember something the Keeper told me during our first meeting. He said he wanted me to influence others to buy what he was selling: *love and life everlasting.*

I'm not sure if it will help, but I feel a nudge to share. "Even if we die, I believe the Keeper loves us enough to give us something beyond death."

A man scoffs. "Sure he does. Ashes to ashes."

Another man laughs. "There, you're wrong. It's sand to sand."

The men chuckle. But the woman is interested. "What do you mean about *after* death?" she asks.

"I don't understand completely, but I believe that after our bodies die there is a life everlasting."

"Where?" she asks.

I wish I knew more. "I'm not sure. But I expect it's a better place."

"Anyplace is better'n here," a man says.

"I hope they have lots of beer there."

"And bratwurst."

"And me wife's apple cake — as much as I want."

The conversation veers into a discussion of favorite foods until the woman says she's tired and is going to bed.

The five of us wish each other good night. I call out softly, "Keeper, watch over us," and hear grunts of affirmation as we all go to sleep.

Chapter Thirty-Nine

Helsa

After our argument about Cashlin at lunch yesterday, Nana and I haven't talked much. She's on a crusade to free Cashlin and talk openly about the Keeper. And I'm...

Over it?

Confused?

A little of both.

I find Nana at the table, writing frantically. "What are you doing?"

"Copying Relics."

"Why?"

"It's something I have to do."

I don't want to argue again, so let it go. I finish packing two lunches. "Put that aside, Nana. We need to leave for work."

"I'm not going to work."

I don't understand. "Toffa gave you your job back."

She stares past me. "I know. But I can't go back just yet."

I know where she *is* going. "Cashlin's not at home, you know. She's in jail."

"She doesn't deserve to be."

"That's not up to you, Nana."

"She did nothing wrong."

I raise my brows and start counting Cashlin's transgressions on my fingers. "One, she refused to wear her winning costume on Shopping Day and came dressed in some white robe that she forced you to make for her—which could make you an accessory to her crime."

"Don't be ridiculous."

I was far from through. I touched my second finger. "Two, she grabs the attention away from all the other Patrons, and makes people notice her pared-down getup. Then three, she starts preaching about the Keeper to the Favored, who I assume are as far from being Devoted as *any*body in *any* Ring."

"You don't know that."

"Do you know different?"

She hesitates. "No. I don't."

I touch my ring finger and keep going. "And four, let's go back to when she wore the old purple costume instead of her snake getup, then five, when she interfered at the factory, riling Bru even more — which probably made him kill Falla, and —"

"Cashlin is not responsible for Falla's death."

I don't agree. "Six, she goes all holier-than-thou and visits Isa. Seven, she tags along to Falla's funeral. And eight, she brings food to our Ring in a blatant act of self-serving charity, which means she's bribing people to like her." I look at my hands. "I'm almost out of fingers."

"You're not being fair, Helsa."

"I'm being honest, which is what you need to be, Nana." I put my hands on her shoulders. She's inches shorter than me, and suddenly looks very old. "Stay away from her. Showing yourself as her ally will get you in trouble. Actually, you're putting both of us in danger."

Nana's brows dip, and I see the struggle in her eyes. "I don't want to do that," she says.

"Good." I step back. "Now you're talking sense."

"But I still have to do it."

I toss my hands in the air. "*That* doesn't make sense!"

"In many ways it doesn't. But . . . I keep going back to knowing that the Keeper brought Cashlin and I together. We were supposed to meet and get to know each other — and him — together. She's changed me. She's changed the factory, she's changed the Imp Ring in its entirety, all for the better."

"That's a matter of opinion."

"The Keeper appeared to her in person."

"So she claims. She's used to being dramatic, so who's to say she's not embellishing."

Nana shakes her head. "It's not drama, it's the truth. She's changed completely from the woman I first met. She went from a self-centered Patron used to getting her own way, to a selfless woman, giving food to the poor and standing up for what's right."

"Give her a medal and call it good."

"Helsa, enough!"

I've gone too far. I don't know why Cashlin annoys me so much, only that she does.

"You should have seen her in the white dress, Helsa. All of us gasped. The purity of it was symbolic of the change in her. She's gone from someone who people worshiped to someone who worships."

In spite of not wanting to be swayed, Nana's last words impressed me. A little. But not enough to remain silent.

"Little good it did her," I say. "How can she help anyone if she's stuck in jail, or has to go through another trial, or if she's exiled?"

"I don't know. Yet. But I'm sure good will come from it. The Keeper called her to be an influencer for him. He won't abandon her."

"Are you sure about that? She seems pretty abandoned to me." I see the frustration on Nana's face, and I'd like to make it go away, but I also need her to see the truth.

She presses a hand against her forehead. "I don't know how all this is going to turn out, but I do know I can't just wait around and do nothing."

"Even for my sake?"

She hesitates, then touches my hair. "It's for your sake—for the sake of all Regalia—that I do it." She neatly packs up the Relics she's been copying in a shoulder bag. "There's change afoot, Helsa. Good change for all of us. I don't know why the Keeper chose Cashlin to be the impetus for it, but he did. I, for one, am not going to question his choice. I'm going to help her. Help him. And help all of us."

I still think she's being naïve at best and delusional at worst, but I admire her passion. I hug her tightly. "If you have to do this, please be careful. Promise me you won't let Cashlin pull you into anything that will get *you* in trouble. I've already lost Papa and Mama." I squeeze her harder. "I can't lose you too."

Nana hugs me back, then kisses my cheek and heads out the door. Only as the door closes do I realize she didn't promise me a thing.

Chapter Forty

Kiya

I hate lying to my husband, but Gull gives me no choice.

As I leave the house the morning after Shopping Day, he asks where I'm going.

I give him the one answer that assures he won't join me. "I'm going on a very long walk."

He sips his coffee and flips me away. "Go for it."

"I may be gone all morning, but I'll be back for lunch."

He shrugs.

As I begin my trek to Cashlin's house, I realize how much his shrug symbolizes our lives. The word "whatever" comes to mind. There is no excitement anymore—and I don't just mean between him and me. Nothing ignites my emotions. Not clothes, not food, not parties, and not friends.

Only two things consume my thoughts: my amazing conversation with Cashlin, and my experience under the trees. My slice of sky.

It's hard not to run through the streets of the Favored Ring to get to Cashlin's house. I notice no one is wearing her purple outfit. Has everyone shunned her already?

It doesn't matter. I know deep in my gut that *something* is going to happen at her house which is far better than the nothing I feel in the rest of my life.

I have dressed down for the journey, wearing a navy dress, more classic than showy. I don't want to stand out.

I pass through the Creatives Ring without incident—the guard was busy peeling an apple, so merely wrote down my name and waved me through. When I reach the gate to enter the Patron Ring, I ask the guard which house belongs to Cashlin.

"What do you want with her?" he asks.

Too late, I realize being friends with her may not be advantageous. "I want nothing *with* her." I slip a ring off my finger. "I'm simply returning something that was hers as I no longer want it."

He eyes me suspiciously, then grunts. "I guess you can come through. Hers is the biggest house, halfway 'round. Blue door."

I give him my name and thank him. I've never been in the Patron Ring. The only other Ring I've visited is the Creatives Ring, and that was on a lark when a few of my friends decided to go on an outing to see where the clothing was designed. Other than that one time, I've stayed safely—stupidly?—ensconced in the Favored Ring. I'm not sure why. Out of habit? Cowardice?

I know it's not out of contentment.

Yet that's not true. For many years I *was* content there. It's only in the past few months that doubt crept in. And regret about not having children, which led to a reassessment of my life and a realization that I want more. I have every *thing* yet I want more. It's strange, and more than a little unsettling.

I'm putting all my hopes and dreams into finding that *more* today, at Cashlin's.

The homes in this Ring are beautiful, and huge compared to the very nice-but-small homes we Favored live in. Of course, there's space here as there are only twenty Patrons and assorted retired relatives. In my Ring there are a hundreds of homes, along with a lot of clubs, restaurants, and shops.

The entire street is lined with lush trees. In the Favored Ring our houses are connected to each other and are lined up on both sides of the street. Here, there's a lot of breathing room between each house, and large stretches of manicured grass.

I see a blue door. This must be Cashlin's. The house is set back from the street and has a path leading to the door. There are two dormer windows and more rooflines than I can count. I spot an extensive garden in the back with trees and flowers. It's the home of someone with status and power: the Premier Patron. Yet, where is Cashlin's power now? Where is Cashlin?

I take a deep breath for courage and knock.

A middle-aged man opens the door, his left eyebrow lifted in a question. "May I help you?"

"My name is Kiya?" Why do I state it as a question? "I met Patron Cashlin yesterday during Shopping Day and we talked and—"

"Kiya, you say?"

"Yes. She told me to come to her house today."

"Come in." He steps back and I cross the threshold. Overhead, the crystals of a chandelier reflect over every surface like dancing fairies.

"Your name really is Kiya?" he asks again.

"Is there a problem?"

He shakes his head. "No, but as I awakened this morning I thought of that name. And . . . here you are."

I'm pleased with the coincidence. "Here I am."

Two women that I'd seen near Cashlin yesterday are in the parlor.

"It's you," the younger one says.

"You walked with Patron Cashlin yesterday," the older one adds.

"I did."

"You seemed to know each other," the younger one says.

"A little. I introduced myself a few Reveals ago. I'm a big fan of hers."

"So you were there when they arrested her?" the man asks.

"I was." I look to the ladies. "It was horrible, yes?"

The young one puts a hand to her chest. "Awful. I'm still shaken."

"Is Cashlin all right?" I ask. "Have you heard from her?"

They look a bit wary—with good reason. I realize they don't know anything about me. "Cashlin and I had a short but nice discussion about the Keeper, and she told me to come here today. To learn more."

The older woman says, "My name is Solana, this is Marli, and Dom answered the door." She points at another man I hadn't noticed in the parlor. "And this is Irwin."

"Hi," I say awkwardly. "I'm Kiya."

"You're one of the Favored?" Irwin asks.

"I am."

"Are you . . . Devoted?" Solana asks.

That's a tough question. "I'm not—yet. But Cashlin's words to the crowd touched a chord in me, and then our discussion—brief as it was—made me want to learn whatever you can teach me."

Dom looks skeptical. "Forgive me, miss, but toward what purpose?"

"*My* purpose. I know there has to be more to life than clothes and parties. I said that to Cashlin, and she says there *is* more, there's . . . him."

Dom nods, as if my answer is the right one. "Forgive our manners, please have a seat. We were just discussing how to help her."

I sit in a chair near Marli. "So, you *have* heard from her?"

"An Enforcer friend, Xian, came last night to tell us she's being brought to trial."

"For speaking his name?" I ask. "Or wearing the robe?"

"We're not sure yet. But she *was* taken to a cell."

I shudder at the thought. "A cell? As in jail?"

"As in jail," Irwin says. "It's appalling, that's all I can say. She's used to me cooking her favorite foods. I can't imagine the slop she's being forced to eat."

I'm a bit taken aback by his talk of food. That seems the least of her worries. "When is the trial?"

"Xian didn't know yet," Dom says. "She might be in there for days."

The thought makes me cringe. "What can we do?" I ask.

"Beg the Keeper to protect her," Solana says.

"How do we do that?" I see by their expressions that they're shocked by my total ignorance. "I need guidance. I need knowledge. Please teach me about the Keeper so I can help."

And so, they did.

**

My mind is on overload and my heart is full.

While they teach me, we spend an hour copying special Relic pages they want to hand out. I hadn't realized anything was written down about the Keeper, but it excites me because it's tangible. Permanent. Real.

But then I notice the time, and know I have to get back. Gull will be wondering where I've been.

I hug my new friends, knowing — but not caring — that the Council forbids it. "How can I ever thank you?" I ask.

"Talk about him to others," Solana says. "Hand out the Relics."

It's a terrifying thought as both are against the law.

They must see what I'm thinking because Marli asks, "Is your husband open to him?"

I shake my head adamantly. "He is not and will never be."

"Have you sensed discontent among any of your friends?" Dom asks.

"Or interest in him?"

I try to think of someone. Anyone. "Not really. Everyone seems fully immersed in being Favored. I've felt very alone."

Solana touches my arm. "You're not alone now. We are here and so is he."

Happiness tightens my throat. "I knew this was an important day. I knew I would be changed."

"And so you are," Irwin says.

Dom opens the door. "We'll send word when we know more about the trial."

"I'd appreciate that." As I'm about to leave I have a thought. "Can I visit Cashlin in jail?"

Marli exchanges looks with the others. "I don't know. Xian says *we* can't, but maybe as one of the Favored . . ."

"I'll go right now," I say with a determined nod. "I'll let her know we're rooting for her."

I leave with a plan, and more than that, a purpose.

Chapter Forty-One

Cashlin

Before today I'd heard the term "gruel" but had never tasted any. Yuck.

A bowl of gruel, cold coffee, and an apple are my breakfast. I think longingly of Irwin's elaborate food and remember Solana sharing a meal with me. She marveled at the peach nectar, bacon, blueberry muffins—and sugar cookies too. She hadn't even known what a cookie was.

I shake the memories away for they're not helping me accept the meager meal in front of me, or the fact I might go on trial today. If so, who knows when I will eat next. And so, I savor every bite.

When I'm through I stand at the bars. "Morning everyone," I say.

"Yeah, it is," says a man.

The man I can see says, "You gonna talk Keeper bunkum to us again today?"

Oh my.

"Behave yourself, Yert," one says. "Her talkin' don't hurt."

"It don't help neither."

"It could," I say.

I hear a laugh. "Can it open these doors and walk me outta here?"

I'm not sure what to say.

The woman speaks for me. "It could," she says. "He has that kind of power."

"Then why don't he use it?"

She and I look at each other. We don't have an answer. I've never been asked hard questions before.

At our silence Yert says, "Just as I thought. It doesn't sound like believing offers any a us nothing, considering that's why you ladies are here."

Again, the woman and I exchange a look. But this time, I answer. "We may be imprisoned the same as you, but I feel a peace about it because I trust the Keeper. No matter what, he's my protector."

He laughs. "Yeah, I can see that."

I wish I knew what to say to make him understand.

One of the other men says, "Don't let 'im bother you, Patron. I ain't Devoted, but I can see the draw of it."

"I *am* Devoted," says the third man. "I'm aching for some of his protection right now."

Aren't we all.

We hear the main door open and I'm relieved to see Nerwhether. He stops at my cell. "Citizen Cashlin," he says.

His formality doesn't bode well.

"What's the news? When's my trial?"

"Tomorrow, first thing."

"I have to spend another day in here?"

He gives me an ominous look that implies that's the least of my worries.

"Hey, Nerwhether!" a man calls. "What about us?"

He looks toward their cells. "Behave yourselves. I'll be there when I'm through with the Patron."

He looks back at me, sighs, and lowers his voice. "I'm doing all I can, Cashlin, but you need to prepare yourself for the worst."

I step back. "Worst?"

He nods and mouths, *Exile*.

I grip the bars. "No, no, no, no," I say. "They can't do that to *me*."

"Actually, they can," he says. "It's unprecedented, but . . . but so are your actions. They don't want anyone else to feel emboldened. They *have* to punish you this time."

I can't escape the truth of his last two words. "Fine," I say. "Punish me, just don't send me to exile."

The woman overhears. "Exile? For you?"

"That's what he says."

Nerwhether looks nervous. "Cashlin. Please . . ."

I point toward the men's cells. "What about them?"

"Yeah, what about us?"

Nerwhether gives me a nasty look, but he steps toward them, out of my sight. "Gentlemen, your trial is last on the docket today."

"I can hardly wait," one says.

"Can't they just get it over with?" one says. "Exile us already? This waiting is hell."

"Hey, don't speak for me! I don't want exile."

"You were with us, Yert. Where one goes, the others follow."

"I want another solicitor!"

"Normally, I would say that's your right," Nerwhether says calmly, "but it's too late. No one else is available."

The woman speaks up. "What about me, sir? I haven't seen my solicitor in two days."

He strolls to her cell. "Their name?"

"Corton?"

He was Quan's solicitor.

"I'll check with him."

"Thank you, sir."

He looks at me one last time. "Do you need anything?"

"I need freedom. I need out."

"Us too!" the men shout.

He doesn't nod *or* shake his head. He just leaves.

Any hope I had has been dashed.

"Where's yer protector now, Patron?" a man yells.

I have no idea.

**

I hear the door to the jail open again, and rush to the bars. Is Nerwhether back?

It's not him. I'm shocked to see the woman from Shopping Day.

"Kiya?" I say.

She looks nervous. "Patron."

"Why are you here?"

"I . . ." She looks around at the other cells and lowers her voice. "I went to your house this morning."

I'm surprised but pleased. "I'm so glad. Did you meet . . .?"

"I did. They were very helpful. I learned a lot."

"This is such good news."

"Hey!" Yert yells. "Why do you get visitors and we don't?"

The jailed woman answers him, "Because we're not Patrons. Shush. Leave them be."

I nod my thanks to her, then sit on the floor on one side of the bars while Kiya sits on the other. It's far from comfortable, but I want to encourage her to linger as long as possible.

"I want to thank you for speaking out on Shopping Day like you did, Patron. I—"

"Cashlin. Call me Cashlin."

She nods once. "Your words . . . they reinforced something that happened to me the day before."

"Really?"

She lowers her voice even more. "As I told you while we walked, I've felt discontented lately. It's like my eyes finally opened and I realized that our Favored lives are frivolous and pretty pointless."

"I've had similar feelings," I say. "About my life, but also about the whole Cycle of Regalia."

"You have?"

"I have. Tell me what happened to you."

"I was out partying—as I do many nights a week, but this time I just wasn't into it." She looks down, as if ashamed. "Everything annoyed me: the laughter, the music, the drinking, the dancing, as well as the clothes. But it was more than being annoyed." She looks at me eye to eye. "I suddenly saw a gaping hole in our lives."

"Our lives?"

"I have a husband, Gull."

"Do you have children?"

Her face looks sad. "No. And it's a huge regret that added to my mood. Put these things together and I . . . I just couldn't take it anymore. I left the party and walked through the streets of our Ring. At night. Alone. But not alone. There were small groups of people everywhere."

It sounds like something bad happened.

"I ended up in a park—but there were people there too, kissing and...more." She shakes her head. "I was desperate to be fully alone, so I walked through the trees near the wall. It was dark and it felt like the branches were grabbing at me. I panicked, walked too fast, and tripped." She draws her knees to her chest. "I just curled up in a ball and sobbed. And I never cry."

Her eyes glisten now, but no tears fall.

"Then suddenly I heard a man's voice, like it was in here." She put a fist to her chest. "I know it sounds ridiculous, but—"

"Actually, it doesn't. Tell me what he said."

"He said, *There, there, Kiya. It will be all right.*"

I gasp and clasp my hands to my chest. "It was him."

"Him?"

I reach through the bars and touch her hand. "The Keeper."

Her eyes grow big. "How do you know?"

I realize I've taken over her story. "Tell me what happened next."

"I felt better, like everything *would* be all right, and I turned over on my back and looked up at the sky. It was cloudy, but suddenly the clouds seemed to slice open, and the moon peeked through."

"A slice of sky," I say, almost to myself.

"Yes!" She's excited. "That's exactly what it was."

I'm as excited as she is. To meet someone who experienced him . . .

"It *was* him, Kiya. I experienced my own slice of sky."

"I did too," the woman in the other cell says.

We beam at each other in awe, three lucky women with a shared encounter. A Serv, a Patron, and a Favored.

"Praise him," the woman says.

"What's your name?" Kiya asks her.

I feel ashamed for never asking her myself.

"Siem," she says.

"I'm Kiya, and this is Cashlin."

"We're Devoted sisters," she says.

I love that title.

We all look toward the door as it opens again. A guard comes in. "Time to go, Favored."

Kiya scrambles to her feet. She turns to me. "What I learned . . . what do I do with the knowledge?"

"Come on," the guard says. "Now."

I can only think of one thing to say. "Pass it on."

As she's led away, she touches her heart, and Siem and I follow suit.

My heart races and neither of us can stop smiling. "The news of him is spreading," I say to Siem. "Just as he planned."

"Everything's going to be all right," Siem says.

I nod with full confidence. Everything will be all right. No matter what.

**

I'm not accustomed to waiting. All my life, my needs have been met immediately. I wanted for nothing.

Now I want for everything and the wait is excruciating.

Late afternoon they take the three men to trial. As they pass my cell, they look petrified — with good reason.

When they return, they don't even look at me as they pass. Their heads are down, their shoulders slumped.

After the guards leave, I ask, "What happened?"

"We're dead men," one says.

"Exiled, day after tomorrow," says another.

I hear the third softly sobbing.

"So much for your protector," Yert says.

I have no answer for him. Siem withdraws farther into her cell, and I do the same. I curl up on the bed and pull my hood over my head.

Will I be exiled too? Nerwhether mentioned as much, but it didn't fully sink in until the men were condemned.

The past few weeks seem surreal. The kiss and its trial, the parting sands, the Keeper, the purple dress, Bru, the food, a white dress, and bold words that broke the law.

I hear Mother's voice in my head. *Cashlin, what were you thinking?*

That was her response to the kiss. The stupid kiss that started it all. I'm sure she's heard about my arrest and the reasons why. The fact she hasn't lowered herself to visit me speaks volumes about her disapproval. When I'm exiled will she come see me die?

I curl up tighter, tucking the robe around my feet.

My mind flits through the "before" moments of my life. Perhaps it was good that Rowan and I never got to the point of an engagement.

And it's very good I have no children to grieve for me. I'm even glad that my father is no longer alive. Whether Mother and Amar will grieve my passing is questionable. Most likely they'll find solace in each other, as they simmer in anger that I disgraced the family name.

The Keeper mentioned life everlasting, but said he would explain more when I was ready.

I'm ready now.

A tear escapes—the first of many.

Chapter Forty-Two

Solana

I'm desperate for news and decide if anyone knows anything about Cashlin's situation it's probably Xian. I take the chance that he's contacted his mother.

I have no idea if the guard at the gate leading to the Creatives Ring will let me through. My name is not on the list. I make up a reason, by pretending I have supplies in a bag slung over my shoulder — though if he knew what I really carry I'd be arrested.

He looks at me. My heart beats out of my chest.

"Name?" he asks.

"Solana. I have business with Creative Ladi. Supplies."

"Open it."

I've tried to hide my treasure under scraps of fabric and trim. I start closing the bag, but he stops me. "Wait."

He puts his hand in the bag and pulls out a copied Relic.

My heart falls to my toes. I'm going to faint.

He reads it, grunts, then puts it back. "Go through."

Oh. My. Goodness. I want to hug him.

Instead I hurry into the Creatives Ring, thanking the Keeper for protecting me. I don't know which studio Pinno and Ladi will be in today, so I ask at the jewelry studio. A woman thinks they're in the shoe building. I walk with new confidence and enter the studio. Ladi is in the Choosing area, talking to another Creative.

She immediately comes to me. "Solana. How nice to see you."

I pat my bag. "I brought those supplies you asked for."

There's the briefest look of confusion on her face, but then she nods. "I've been waiting for them. Come in."

We enter her studio. Pinno sits at a table and quickly covers a piece of paper with a cut of leather — until she sees it's me.

Ladi closes the door behind us.

I open my bag. "I've been copying Relics to hand out."

Pinno reveals her work. "Me too. Let's share."

She takes half of mine and I take half of hers.

"I'm desperate for word about Cashlin," I say. "Any word?"

Pinno nods. "Xian told me her trial is tomorrow."

"They're really taking her to trial?" I ask.

Ladi pulls out a chair for me and we both sit at the table. "Since they tried her for something as small as a kiss it follows that they'd try her for speaking about the Keeper."

"And wearing the white outfit," Pinno says. "Maybe we shouldn't have made it for her. It certainly didn't do her any good."

Although she's right about the outcome, I disagree about the dress. "She only felt emboldened to speak because she wasn't dressed like Patron Cashlin anymore but as a lamb of the Keeper. The robe and slippers were for her sake, not for anyone else."

"Xian says there's not much he can do for her."

If he can't help, we're of no use whatsoever. "Is she crushed by all this?" I ask.

"No," Pinno says. "He says she's strong—stronger than any of the rest of would be, I'm sure."

"We wish we could do something to help," Ladi says.

I pat my bag. "Handing out Relics is a start."

"I posted one on the side of the food store," Pinno says, "but someone ripped it down."

"Maybe it's better to pass them on to people we know—or at least suspect—might be open to the Keeper? Tell them to copy and share?"

Ladi nods enthusiastically. "Copy and share. Those are good instructions."

I stand. "I'm going to check up on a woman in my Ring who lost her daughter."

"Falla?" Pinno asks. "The girl Bru killed?"

I'm surprised they know. "That's the one."

"Tell her there are people thinking of her in the Creatives Ring and praying for the Keeper to give her peace."

"I'll do that."

On my way back home, I see a folded piece of paper on the ground. I pick it up and see that it's a Relic—one I haven't seen before. I slip it in my bag. I'll copy it tonight.

Funny how new Relics are appearing.

Only I know it's not funny at all.

It's him.

**

When Isa opens the door she looks surprised to see me. She has bags under her eyes.

"Solana."

Not exactly welcoming. "May I come in?"

She blinks but opens the door. Her home smells stale, like dusty grief.

She walks to a rocker and sits. I move some clothes and sit on a chair nearby. I take two apples out of my bag. "For you."

She doesn't take them but says, "Thank you."

I set them on the table and return to my seat. "How have you been?"

She shrugs.

"Do you need anything?"

She scoffs. "Falla. I need Falla."

I regret my question. "Of course you do. But anything else?"

She rocks up and back a few times. "Friends have paid my rent, so at least I don't have to move to the Debt Camp."

"That's good."

She shrugs again.

I pull out one of the Relics. "Maybe this will give you comfort."

She barely reads it and lets it fall onto her lap. "I'd like to turn to the Keeper, but why should I? I don't understand why he allowed Falla to die."

It's a question for the ages. "No one does. But maybe some good came from it. Bru is gone."

"I hope he suffered before he died."

I've had the same thought. "Helsa says working at the factory is enjoyable now. The new manager is a nice woman."

Isa nods. "I've been told people aren't afraid anymore."

"See? Another good thing."

Isa stops rocking. "People have been really nice, making sure I eat, bringing me little presents of this and that."

"I'm glad."

"That food store that wouldn't sell to us? He gives me a big discount now."

"Thanks to Cashlin."

"She did right by us," Isa says.

"Did you know she's been arrested for talking about the Keeper in the Favored Ring?"

Her eyes widen. "She gets arrested for doing good. That's another question for the Keeper."

"But if someone as important as Patron Cashlin is willing to take a risk for him . . ." I point at the Relic in her lap. "Many of us have been copying and handing out Relics as a way to help. Would you be willing?"

She looks skeptical.

"I've got some extra paper here. I can get you as many pieces as you need."

Her eyes flit around the room as if she's weighing the pros and cons. "I suppose I—"

Her door bursts open and a woman rushes in. "Enforcers just arrested three people at the end of the street."

"For what?" I ask.

"Handing out Relics. I have to go." She runs out to spread the bad news.

When Isa crosses her arms over her body, I know I've lost her. "I do *not* want to be arrested."

"Neither do I. But...at least it's doing *something*."

She's rocking again, shaking her head.

"How about this: if you copy the Relics, I'll pick them up and do the distributing."

She stops rocking. "I guess I could do that."

But can I?

**

I'm exhausted from visiting Isa and handing out Relics. I need to sit down and regroup.

When I head back to Cashlin's through the Favored Ring, I see Lieb handing a man a note. This isn't odd, of course, because Lieb is a Messenger Serv, but then I see them both make the sign against their chest.

Is he handing out Relics?

"Lieb!"

He runs toward me, beaming. "Greetings, Nana."

"Greetings to you." I draw him to the side of the Road. "Are you handing out Relics?"

He nods enthusiastically. "I am! Mama's been copying them, and I hand them out."

I don't want to discourage him, but . . . "That's a very good thing you're doing, but you have to be careful."

His young face looks stern. "I am. I do this to people." He touches his chest. "If they do it back, I give them a Relic."

It's not a bad idea.

"Mama says I'm perfect for the job because I'm handing paper to people all the time."

I am surprised his mother is helping—and is being nice to her son. Is her change another miracle from the Keeper?

"You *are* perfect for the job, Lieb. Just be careful."

"Oh, I will. I tried to see Cashlin in jail, but they wouldn't let me in."

"It's nice of you to try."

"Is she going to die?"

I'm shocked by his words. "I certainly hope not. Her trial is tomorrow."

He shakes his head mournfully. "I don't want her to die."

"No one does."

"I want to help more. What can I do?"

I put my hand on his. "Just keep doing what you're doing, and ask the Keeper to protect her."

"I can do that." He hugs me and walks off.

I'm so proud of him. I'm proud of all the people who are stepping up, sharing what they know about the Keeper.

As I approach the Patron gate, I notice a man I've seen before. He's tall and bald, and . . . where have I seen him?

Then I remember. I saw him after Falla's funeral. Helsa said he'd followed her once. There's something odd about a man who hangs out in the forest near the Pile. That alone makes me question his intentions.

And then he walks toward me.

I tense, then slip behind a stack of crates.

A bad move, as he follows me. His massive frame blocks my escape.

"What do you want?" I ask.

"Give me one of your papers."

"What papers?"

He gives me an annoyed look.

"What do you want with it?" I ask.

He looks around, impatient, then taps his fingers to his chest. "You going to give it to me, or not?"

I am completely torn. If I don't do it willingly, I expect he'll take what he wants by force. I do *not* want to draw attention to myself. But he's so menacing. How can a person like him be Devoted? Having no choice, I reach into my bag and pull out a Relic. "Here. Copy it and pass it on."

He reads it, but his face shows no expression. He puts it in his shoulder bag and walks away.

I just stand there. Am I going to get arrested? Is he one of us? I press a hand against my chest, trying to calm my breathing. I come to a conclusion: what happens happens. I can't worry about it.

I step out warily but see that he's gone. I head to Cashlin's, my last stop of the day.

I spot Kiya walking ahead of me. "Kiya!"

She stops and waits for me. "I saw Cashlin," she says.

"How's she doing?"

Kiya shakes her head once. "Let's wait until we're with the others."

Dom lets us in, and Marli and Irwin are summoned. We sit in the parlor to get Kiya's report. She stands in front of the fireplace.

"Cashlin is wonderful," Kiya blurts out.

It's an odd beginning. "*Wonderful* as in she's doing well, or wonderful in character?" I ask.

"Or both," Dom says.

"Wonderful in character," Kiya says. "But I think she's doing all right too."

"What did you talk about?" Marli asks.

There's an air of excitement about her. "I know this will sound presumptuous, and I wouldn't have ever assumed such a thing on my own, being so new to everything but—"

"Just say it," Irwin says.

"Cashlin and I have both had encounters with the Keeper."

I suppress my envy. "Cashlin saw him here, in the garden. Where did—?"

"Saw him?" Kiya asks.

Cashlin didn't mention that to her? "She touched him. Spoke at length with him. Twice."

"I didn't see him. But I heard him. I looked up and saw a slice of sky open up and—"

"Cashlin mentioned a slice of sky," Marli says.

"And there was another jailed woman who said she had a similar sky experience."

Dom shakes his head. "Then I must be doing something wrong, because I have never experienced anything like that."

Kiya looks panicked and waves her hands. "No, no! I'm not telling you to brag, but to tell you what we talked about. I'm sorry if I made you feel bad."

I flash a look at Dom, who shrugs. "Forget I said anything, miss. What else did you talk about?"

"There wasn't time for more because the guard came to shoo me out, but I did manage to ask her what I should do with the knowledge you've taught me."

"And . . . ?" I ask.

"She said, 'pass it on.'"

"How do we do that?" Irwin asks. "I'm no preacher."

"Neither am I," Marli says.

I get out my shoulder bag and remove some of the Relics. "I think this is one way we can do it." I pass them around. "There are people in

290

all the Rings copying Relics and passing them out—being careful, of course."

Irwin hands it back. "I don't see anybody else but food delivery men and my brother, back home."

I'm reminded of Isa's reservations. I look at the Relics—I now have four different ones. I hand each of them one. "Copy your Relic as many times as you can, and hand them out to whomever you can—even if it's just within your own family. You don't have to speak to a crowd. You can reach people one at a time."

"What if we get caught?" Dom asks.

I don't have a good answer for them. "Then you can say hello to Cashlin for us." People don't look enthused. "I just talked to Lieb and he's vetting people by making the Keeper sign. If they make it back, he gives them a copy."

Irwin shrugs. "That *could* make it safer."

Kiya takes a deep breath as if the discussion has taken everything out of her. "I need to get home. My husband will be wondering . . ."

I stand. "I do too. I want to be there when Helsa gets off work."

She and I leave the others in the parlor, staring down at their Relics. I have no idea if they will follow through.

I have no more energy to worry about it.

**

I'm dozing in my rocker when Helsa comes home from work.

"Must be nice to be able to nap," she says.

"I put soup on."

She plops on a chair. "I'm teasing. But I'm worried. You look pale. Wrung out."

"I am."

"How come?"

I stand with a moan and hobble to the fire to stir the soup.

"You can barely walk, Nana," Helsa says, taking over the stirring. "What happened today?" She points at the rocker, and I sit.

"I walked. A lot."

"Where?"

"I went to the Creatives Ring to see Ladi and Pinno, back here to check on Isa, then I ran into Lieb." She blinks. "I also had a run in with our bald man, who trapped me in a corner."

"Did he hurt you?"

"No. He wanted one of my Relics."

"You gave him one?"

"He insisted."

"He could turn you in."

"We'll see."

"We'll see? Nana, you have to stop being so reckless. Cashlin is in jail for merely speaking of him, much less walking around with a bag full of Relics."

I can't let her warnings stop me. "I also met a Favored woman who came to Cashlin's house to learn about the Keeper."

"She was probably a spy."

"No, she wasn't. She knows Cashlin. She was walking with her when Cashlin was arrested."

"So Cashlin reached one person. Big deal."

"One is better than none. Kiya also visited Cashlin in jail."

Helsa taps the spoon on the edge of the pot. "I suppose I should ask: is Cashlin okay?"

I don't like her attitude. "Your genuine concern is touching."

"I *did* ask, Nana. That should count for something."

I let it go. "Cashlin's trial is tomorrow. She could be exiled."

Helsa throws up her hands. "That's it then. Case closed. I forbid you from handing out any more Relics."

"I can't stop now. This is important."

"And I'm not? We're not?"

Normally, I would give her a hug and tell her everything will be all right. But tonight, I can't say it, because it might be a lie.

So I simply get up and say, "I'm really tired. I'm going to bed."

I leave Helsa alone in the room.

I have the awful feeling she'd better get used to it.

Chapter Forty-Three

Kiya

I feel like I'm living on borrowed time.

When I returned home yesterday afternoon after a day learning about the Keeper, visiting Cashlin in jail, and giving a report to my new friends at Cashlin's, Gull was waiting for me.

"Where in the name of Regalia have you been all day?"

Finding a new purpose?

"Time got away from me. How did you spend your day?"

Luckily, Gull is so self-centered that he doesn't ask more, and happily turns the conversation to himself. He told me about organizing an all-day poker event with friends. Gambling makes no sense to me, for isn't the fun of gambling winning something? In the Favored Ring everything is given to us. We don't use money. Everything is free. He explained they were going to win a traveling trophy.

Whatever. At least it keeps him occupied.

Today, I'm scheduled to have lunch with two friends. These get-togethers are usually frivolous fun, but today I have an ulterior motive.

I meet them at the restaurant and do a double kiss-kiss on their cheeks, and they on mine. I take note that neither of them wear Cashlin's purple outfit.

Of course, neither do I.

We indulge in some meaningless chit-chat and order food. While we're waiting . . .

I'm not sure how to bring up Cashlin and my discontent, but Doli does it for me.

"You seem . . . intense today, Kiya. Is something wrong?"

How about everything? But I say, "There's nothing *wrong*, but I *have* been discontented."

They look incredulous. "Why?"

"Our lives are perfect," Uhli says. "We have everything we could ever want—and then some."

I lean forward on the table. "But do we?"

They look at each other as if I'm crazy.

Then Uhli says, "I certainly do. I couldn't want for more."

Doli chuckles. "I could use a new daughter. She's driving me crazy with her attitude."

"She's thirteen," Uhli says. "What do you expect?"

I know I'm asking them to dig beyond the obvious—which is something we Favored aren't ever asked to do. "I'm not talking about material things, fun experiences, or even children, I'm talking about finding a higher purpose."

Doli scoffs. "The only thing higher than us is the Council, and I'm quite content to let them run things."

"So we don't have to," Uhli adds.

They don't get it. Maybe if I add the Keeper to the mix . . . "What do you think of the Cashlin situation?" I ask.

"She's over-the-top whacko," Doli says. "First pushing boundaries with the kiss and wearing that old dress, but then on Shopping Day she completely lost it."

Is she talking about the white robe or her words? "Why do you say that?"

Doli flips a hand. "What sane Patron wears a plain white robe to Shopping Day? That's not the way to influence any of us to vote her number one again, that's for sure."

"Yet we always vote for her," I say.

She blushes. "She offers great clothes. I'm not denying that."

I digress, but I'm interested. "Would you have voted for her snake costume?"

They both make faces. "Never."

"So, she was wise to resurrect the purple outfit?"

They shrug. "I suppose. Cashlin *is* all about winning. How many has she won in a row? Four?"

"Three," Uhli says.

"I believe that's a record," I say.

"No one can deny she's good at her job," Uhli says. "Which makes me question why she would cause a stir wearing something so horribly blah. I mean, no one is going to buy that robe. Ever."

I'm not surprised they've focused on Cashlin's clothes. Now, to the other subject. "What did you think of her words—what she said to the crowd?"

"I wasn't there," Doli says, "but from what I heard, her ramblings about you-know-who prove she's *not* all there."

"I *was* there," Uhli says, "and I was completely shocked. Talk like that does *not* belong in our Ring."

"Why not?" I ask.

"Because it goes against the core of Regalia." Uhli leans forward confidentially. "We worship what's important—fashion."

I've never heard anyone state it so plainly. It's utterly offensive. "Don't you think it's arrogant to say such a thing? Fashion is just frou-frou frippery."

Their eyes widen.

"Fashion gives us our lives, Kiya," Doli says. "If we didn't focus on fashion, what would we do all day?"

"Which speaks to my point," I say. "Surely there's more important things than fashion."

"Like what?"

"Like helping other people?" My answer sounds lame.

"We're helping plenty of people by increasing the demand for the goods they supply. If we didn't do that, they wouldn't have a job."

"They could do something else," I say.

"Then it wouldn't be Regalia." Doli shakes her head adamantly. "I don't like this discussion, Kiya. Rocking the boat never ends well."

Is that a threat?

"I like things as they are," Uhli says. "I see no need for change of any kind."

I struggle with the urge to leave. Yet somehow, I stay. I have to finish this. "Back to Cashlin's words . . . it doesn't make sense that having a belief in a higher power is against the law. What harm does it do?"

"The Council is *the* higher power."

"But are they? They're just people."

"Don't let them hear you say that," Doli says.

Uhli is suddenly quiet.

"What do *you* think?" I ask her.

She stirs another sugar into her coffee. "I guess I'm open to the *notion* of a higher power."

"Uhli!" Doli says.

"It makes sense, doesn't it? I mean life comes from somewhere. It's too intricate to have simply popped into being."

A door has opened. "That's what I think. And just because I think that way doesn't mean I want to overthrow the Council or disrupt the economy."

"Are you sure?" Doli asks. "Talking about some greater purpose than fashion sounds like that's exactly what you want to do."

"If I gave that impression, I apologize. I merely think it would be nice to do something to better Regalia *beyond* fashion."

"Actually . . . I'd be open to that," Uhli says. "I do get kind of bored sometimes."

Ha!

Doli dabs her mouth with a napkin even though she hasn't eaten anything yet. "You two go on your quest for meaning but leave me out of it. I will *not* encourage people like Cashlin who have lost their sense of duty to their assigned Ring. I hope she gets exiled."

"That's awful," I say.

"It's what she deserves. Every society needs boundaries, and she's pushed ours to the breaking point. There must be consequences."

The first course of our meal comes, and Doli changes the subject to a party she's having this weekend. "Everyone who's anyone is coming."

Except me.

**

My friends and I leave the restaurant and do the goodbye kiss-kiss. Doli walks to the right. I head to the left.

"I'll see you this weekend, if not before," Uhli says to me. But she's not walking, and her eyebrows are nearly touching.

"Is something wrong?" I ask her.

"Not wrong, no," she says too quickly. "But . . ." She sighs deeply. "I didn't want to say more in front of Doli, but my husband and I *are* kind of interested in . . . him."

My hope sparks to life. "That's fantastic."

"We don't make a big deal of it. But we do talk about it in private."

"Good for you."

"So, what I heard Cashlin saying on Shopping Day? Her saying *he* is our protector and comforter? That he loves us?" She takes a new breath. "I'd like some of that. I need some of that."

I touch her hand. "We all do — whether we admit it or not. Do you know if there are others who believe?"

"My husband says there are."

"That's exciting." I look up and down the street. For the moment we are alone. "There's something important going on in all the Rings right now."

"How so?"

"People are more open about becoming part of the Devoted."

She shakes her head. "We're not Devoted by any means. We like the *idea* of the Keeper, but we don't know much about him."

If that isn't an invitation . . . "Have you ever heard of the Relics?"

"Once or twice. But I've never seen any."

I reach into my purse and pull out two different pages. I slip them into Uhli's purse. "Now you have two."

She pulls her purse against her chest protectively. "Oh dear. If I get caught with them . . . "

I ignore her fear — though I share it. "In all the Rings people are copying whatever Relics they have and passing them around."

"That's a good way to get arrested."

"You have to be discerning and discreet. But if you think someone is open to him, give them a Relic and ask them to copy it and pass it on."

Her breathing is heavy, yet she smiles. "I'm eager to read them."

"They'll change your life." I think of something to add. "This is the sign the Devoted give each other. It might come in handy." I touch two fingers to my heart.

Uhli does the same. Then she pulls me into a full hug. "I don't know how to thank you, Kiya."

"Thank him. And learn about him."

If I was thirty years younger, I would skip home. As it is, I'm flying high.

Chapter Forty-Four

Cashlin

I'm dozing when I hear a ruckus. I rush to the bars and see guards bring in a group of prisoners. Some wear brown, some gray, and one wears the orange tunic of a Creative.

There are not enough cells, so the Creative is put in with me. The three men who are convicted of killing Bru complain. Siem gets a fellow Serv, and the empty cell gets two Imps.

As soon as the guards leave, I introduce myself to my cellmate. "I'm Cashlin."

"Zee." She's my mother's age, with pretty blue eyes. "Sorry, but I need to sit."

I point to her bed and sit across from her. "What happened?"

"I was handing out . . ." She whispers the next word. "Relics."

"You can speak freely here. And good for you. I'm glad no one else in your Ring was arrested."

"When I saw them coming for me everyone else scattered."

"I don't think I've met you during the Choosing."

"Not yet." She scoffs. "I guess not ever now."

"If it's your first offense you may go free."

She looks around the cell mournfully. "I've never been in a situation like this."

"None of us have." I thought of my friends. "Do you know Pinno and Ladi?"

Her smile transforms her face as she nods slightly. "We've been meeting."

I sit forward. "How many Devoted are in the Creatives Ring?"

"About a third of us now."

I'm shocked. "That's way beyond what I expected."

"I remember when it was just me and my helper Serv."

I look out to the corridor. "What are the crimes of the others who were brought in?"

"I'm not sure. We weren't allowed to talk." She goes to the bars. "Hey. New prisoners. What are your crimes?"

They call out crimes that involve being Devoted, from handing out Relics to calling out to the Keeper in public.

Yert hangs his arms out his cell door. "Like I says the other day. Why would I want to believe in something that gets me nothing but trouble?"

People ignore him.

Siem says, "Isn't this amazing? It means word is spreading."

"But they're also cracking down," says a man I can't see.

"You're all very brave," I say.

"I heard you were in here for the same," a woman says.

"Partly at least."

"That's brave of you," one says. "You're the first Patron I know who's acknowledged him."

Hopefully, not the last.

Suddenly one of the new men begins to sing in a deep baritone voice. "'My Keeper, you supply my need, most holy is your name; in pastures fresh you make me feed, beside the living stream . . .'"

Others join in, and the cells are filled with beautiful music.

I'm in awe. I have never heard people spontaneously sing together. And for them to sing about the Keeper?

My throat tightens, and I feel . . . complete.

Zee puts her arm around my shoulders and sings.

I am sure—I know—the Keeper is pleased.

**

My heart is full.

The Devoted sang songs until the guards came in and told them to shut up. Then they talked about their lives, and I learned that Siem has a husband and two children. Zee has a grown daughter and a new granddaughter. They all have much to lose, yet they still chose to stand up and share their faith.

I am humbled.

After we lay down for the night Zee asks me, "Are you sleeping?"

"I'm not sure I can. My trial is tomorrow."

"Are you scared?"

"Very. My solicitor told me to prepare myself."

"For?"

"Exile."

She sits up in bed. "I would've thought you . . . being a Patron and all . . ."

"Apparently I angered the Council too many times."

"Don't give up hope," she says. "One Relic I memorized is easy to remember. It said, 'Fear not for I am with you always.'"

I sit upright and pull my blanket around my shoulders. "That's exactly what I need to hear."

"Glad I could help."

"The thing is... if I'm going to die... do you know anything about life everlasting?"

She shakes her head "I've only heard *of* it, not *about* it."

I'm beyond disappointed.

"I like the sounds of it," she adds. "I do believe there's something beyond death. Something glorious. With him."

"I hope so."

She comes over to my bed, and I make room for her to sit beside me. Then she begins to softly sing another verse of the Keeper song. "'When through the shades of death I walk, your presence is my stay; one word of your supporting breath drives all my fears away. Your hand in sight of all my foes, does still my table spread; my cup with blessings overflows, your oil anoints my head.'"

"Amen," Siem says from her cell.

"Do you want to learn the entire hymn?" Zee asks. "So you can sing it anytime you want?"

"I'd like that."

And so, she teaches it to me. I drink in the words of comfort like a hungry baby needing nourishment.

When I finally sing it back to her, she says, "Well done. Now you'll have those words of reassurance whenever you need them."

"Thank you for that. I won't forget them."

"But now... you need to sleep," Zee says. "You have a long day tomorrow."

A long day. My last day.

Chapter Forty-Five

Cashlin

Before I've eaten my breakfast, a guard appears at the door of my cell.

"Citizen Cashlin. Come with me."

This is it. It's time for my trial.

But I act ignorant. "May I ask where?"

"Your solicitor is waiting for you."

Zee embraces me and whispers in my ear. "Fear not. He is with you always."

I'm counting on it.

**

Nerwhether is in a waiting room. He looks up when I enter.

"Are you ready, Citizen Cashlin?"

I sit across from him. "More importantly, are you?"

He bobs his head—which does not give me confidence. "Actually, I am mildly—very mildly—optimistic."

I sit up straighter. "Why?"

"I found two people to stand up for you."

Bless them! "Who?"

"Xian and your assistant, Marli. They're very brave."

Which means *they* have something to fear. "What will happen to them for speaking on my behalf?"

"Nothing good."

Oh.

"Will their testimony improve my chances?"

He considers this a moment. "Probably not."

I sit back, deflated. A man I care about and a loyal friend are willing to risk everything. For me.

I shake my head without realizing I'm doing it.

"Why are you shaking your head?" he asks.

"I can't let them testify."

Nerwhether tosses his hands in the air. "You asked me if I had any witnesses. I come up with two—which was no easy feat—and you say no?"

Had I said no?

The realization sinks in.

I'd said no.

The bile of panic rises.

"If you don't let them testify, it's over," he says. "You're done. You'll be found guilty of any and all charges, and you'll be exiled."

My heart beats in my throat. It's hard to swallow.

"Cashlin, I'm afraid I—"

"I'm not."

My words have come unbidden.

He cocks his head. "You should be."

My heartbeat feels even now, no longer out of control. "The Keeper told us to 'Fear not, for I am with you always.' So, I refuse to be afraid."

Another idea comes to me in a flash, as I remember the Keeper's wondrous smile of approval. It takes me a moment to put the bits together, but then it's as clear as if it's written out before me.

I lean forward, pressing my hands on the table. "Here's what I want you to do for me, solicitor. I want a deal. I will plead guilty—which will save the Council's time and let them write me off as one bad apple—if they give me two things."

"What two things?"

"I want to be able to make a statement—on the record. And I want them to release all the Devoted who are in jail, removing the charges against them."

"They'll never agree to that."

"Which?"

"Probably both, but for sure they won't set the Devoted free."

I put my hands in my lap. "Then we go to trial—without Xian and Marli's testimony."

"Which means you'll be found guilty."

I shrug. "If I die, I die." I touch his hand. "Give me this, solicitor. Do this for me."

"You're sacrificing yourself for those two witnesses?"

"I'm sacrificing myself for all the Devoted. I'm guilty as charged. Let me take my punishment with honor."

He pushes back from the table and stands. "I'll talk to the prosecutor, but don't get your hopes up."

He leaves me alone.

But I'm not alone. Never alone.

**

I try to push aside any doubts about what I asked Nerwhether to do, but am only partially successful. Yet each time I feel the spark of panic, I repeat Zee's last words to me: 'Fear not, for I am with you always.' Like a balm they soothe and calm me. The Keeper is with me now, but he'll also be with me when I'm exiled.

When I die.

The thought produces a lump in my throat.

I don't want to die.

But then I think about life everlasting. And Zee's verse of the song.

I sing it now. "'When through the shades of death I walk, your presence is my stay; one word of your supporting breath drives all my fears away.'"

The fears remain, so I sing it again.

And again.

I'm interrupted by Nerwhether's return. He sits across from me and takes a deep breath. "So."

"So?"

"They will agree if—"

I clap my hands together.

"Wait. They have a few conditions of their own. They will agree if you itemize your crimes, be repentant, accept your fate gracefully and without incident, and show the Council their due respect as the law of the land."

"I can do that. But I can also make a statement?"

"In keeping with their terms, yes. A short one."

"And the Devoted will be set free?"

"One."

"One?"

"One will be set free. Your choice."

I thought of Siem. But now I also know Zee. "Make it two and it's a deal."

"I think they'll agree to that."

"Yes!"

He stares at me, shaking his head. "I don't understand you, Cashlin. You had the full power of Regalia at your beck and call, yet you threw it all away."

"I set it aside for something better. More fulfilling. Him."

He looks skeptical. "Him, an invisible being who obviously allows his people to suffer."

"He also offers life everlasting."

"What's that?"

I can't say I don't know, yet I can't lie. I lean my arms on the table. "Don't you ever have a feeling that there *has* to be more to life than what we can see, touch, and hear?"

He fidgets.

"Be honest," I say.

"I guess so."

"The Keeper fills me up in a way that makes me feel more satisfied and more full of purpose than winning any Reveal ever did."

"Winning the Reveals earns you status and the best house in the Patron Ring."

"It does."

"You have everything. What does being Devoted get you?"

I *knew* what to say. "Peace."

He crosses his arms. "A lofty, indefinable, and unquantifiable answer."

"But it's not lofty. It's real." I press my hand against my heart. "But yes, it is indefinable because it's immeasurable. It's limitless. It's eternal. *I'm* eternal because he is eternal."

Nerwhether reaches across the table and takes my hands in his. "You, Cashlin, are unlike anyone I have ever met. I don't understand what you're doing, but I respect your passion for doing it."

I squeeze his hands. "Thank you."

There is a knock on the door and a guard says, "They're ready for you."

I stand before Nerwhether does. "And I am ready for them."

I stride out of the room and follow the guard to my destiny.

**

I remember the chamber of the Council of Worthiness—I hate that I have cause to remember it, but I do. I sit in the same chair I sat in for my first trial and suffer a bit of déjà vu.

After that trial I was set free. This trial is destined to be different.

I try not to think about it and will myself to withdraw just a smidge from this reality so I can cruise through it with a little less panic and pain, being separate, yet still here. I know I should be thinking about what I'm going to say, yet that pragmatic thought enters my mind and quickly exits as if it's of little worth. I feel with solid certainty that words will come to me when needed. Good words. His words.

Nerwhether and the prosecutor stand before the Council Judge, no doubt speaking about my deal. I take a moment to look at the ten other members of the Council. Five women and five men. They are all older—as befits a Council who is supposedly wise and experienced—but I wonder if any of them have ever considered the possibility that the Keeper is real and doesn't need to be feared. Regalia would be a better place if only they—

"Let's proceed."

The prosecutor and Nerwhether return to their tables. I search his face for . . . *something*.

He gives me a small nod.

All right then. This is happening. Now.

The judge looks directly at me. "Citizen Cashlin, a plea has been presented to the Council and meets our approval. Are you entering into this plea of your own free will?"

"I am, your honor."

"Very well. Please come forward and make your statement."

As I push back from the table, I see that my beautiful white robe is dirty from my walk in the Favored Ring *and* the time in my jail cell. I run my hands down the soft fabric, wanting to brush the dirt away. But it can't be helped.

I am directed to stand in front of the two solicitor tables, facing the Council.

"You may begin."

My nerves are on full alert, but I don't feel the panic I thought I'd feel—though I'm not calm either. Every cell in my body is active, as if I've been given an important job to do and am prepared to do it—prepared by the Keeper to do it.

I stand tall before them. "Esteemed Council, I come before you a guilty woman. Repeatedly I have willfully overstepped the boundaries of my position for my own gain. In doing so I have disrupted the Cycle of Regalia."

I look at each face. They don't seem angry, but they don't look approving either.

"Yet when I spoke of the Keeper on Shopping Day? I caused no harm. I only spoke words of encouragement." I take a deep breath. "Why do you fear the Devoted? We are not a government trying to overthrow your authority. We are a way of life *within* the dictates of our lives here in Regalia. We simply believe there's something above all of us, a being who created us, loves us, protects us, and wants what's best for us. Believing in the Keeper doesn't affect us going to work nor does it upset the Cycle of Regalia. It enhances both because we the Devoted are happier and more content within ourselves, which makes us happier and more content outside ourselves."

They're looking at me intently. They're listening.

"As far as my meager offerings to help some victims of the factory manager Bru? My actions did not upset the balance of Regalia but made it better. I saw people in need of relief from his tyranny. How can anyone with a heart of compassion not help?"

Most of their faces are stern, yet I see one or two who seem pensive.

"I've come to realize there's more to life than pretty clothes and winning Reveals, there's the opportunity to support each other, and show compassion and kindness as a way to encourage all the Rings to live together in peace. Instead of having a law that makes the mention of the Keeper a punishable offense, I ask you to encourage such discourse as a way to bring harmony and satisfaction to your citizens."

I glance back at Nerwhether. His face shows *his* interest. If I only reach this one man . . .

I turn back to the Council. "I know my offenses go beyond the offenses of being Devoted. I was selfish and upset your laws by doing things my own way. For that, I should be punished. But consider changing the policy of Unlawful Piety. Do not punish the Devoted for having faith, as that very same faith leads to good works and kindness that benefit everyone in Regalia. You don't need to believe as we do, but don't condemn us for believing in something and someone who makes us feel better about our lives, and who makes us better people. Isn't it time we worshiped something other than ourselves? Isn't it time we change the declaration that's always repeated at the vote from 'May the glory be yours' to 'May the glory be his?'"

With that, I know I'm done.

"Thank you for listening."

When I return to my seat Nerwhether gives me a nod. Did he approve?

He stands. "I appeal to the Council to be lenient, to bear in mind the long-standing status of Patron Cashlin and her family, as well as her honest assessment of her culpability, her deeply rooted convictions, innocent intentions, and good works. Thank you."

"Please leave us as we deliberate the sentencing," the judge says.

Once again Nerwhether and I withdraw to the corridor to wait. Last time I was found innocent. This time I've admitted my guilt. Will they be merciful?

When Marli and Xian rush toward me Nerwhether steps away. "Are we next?" Marli asks.

"No," I say. "It's over. You won't have to testify."

"Why not?" Xian asks.

"I'm willing," Marli says. "I'd do anything for you, miss."

I touch her arm. "I know you would—you both would. But my solicitor said you would be punished for speaking up for me."

"I could accept that," Xian says.

"Me too."

I'm moved by their loyalty. "I appreciate that, but Nerwhether didn't think your testimony would change the outcome, so . . ."

"That's not fair," Xian says. "We would have liked to say our piece."

"I know. But something good came out of my plea deal. I asked them to release all the Devoted who are jailed. They only agreed to release two, but still . . ."

"That's something," Xian says.

"How many are jailed?" Marli asks.

I count everyone in my head. "At least twelve." I know my time is short. "How is everyone at home?" I ask. "And Solana and Helsa?"

"We're all fine but worried about you. We've been copying and handing out Relics as fast as we can. And Solana has been a whirlwind, checking in with everyone, with us, with Falla's mother, even going to the Creatives Ring."

"Good for her."

Xian moves a hand forward, as if to touch me, but pulls it back. "My mother and I are also making copies," he says.

"So, you believe?"

"I do." He looks down. "Thanks to you."

I choke up. This is such a victory. "No matter what happens, I'm grateful that some good has come from all my . . . indiscretions." It's a generous word for all I've done.

The doors of the Council chamber open. "They're ready for you," says a guard.

My heart jumps into my throat and I squeeze the hands of Xian and Marli. "This is it."

"May the Keeper protect you," Marli says.

We return to our places in the chamber, but don't sit.

The judge speaks. "We, the Council of Worthiness, accept Citizen Cashlin's guilty plea and will abide by the arrangement made between Solicitor Nerwhether and the prosecution."

"Thank you, your honor," Nerwhether says.

"And though we have been moved by the sincere and eloquent discourse of the defendant, and though she presented some interesting points regarding certain subjects, we have no choice but to deliver her sentence based on the laws that are currently in place."

My heart skips a beat. I am doomed.

"Patron Cashlin, you are sentenced to exile . . ."

I don't hear the rest of his words. Only one word matters.

Exile.

Meaning death.

I fall into my chair and cry.

**

I walk without feeling. I hear without thinking.

"I'm so sorry, Cashlin," Nerwhether says. "It's what I expected, but certainly not what I hoped for."

"When?" I ask.

"Two days."

I see people in the corridor, yet only two register. Xian and Marli stand nearby, their faces reflecting the truth that must show in my face. I don't encourage them to come forward. I can't right now. I just can't.

I take a step in the direction of the jail, but Nerwhether says, "No, Cashlin. Didn't you hear what the judge said? You are exiled, but you can return home until then."

I stand there, blinking at him. "Home?"

"You did not commit a violent crime," he says. "And after all, where can you run to? The Desert?"

Very funny.

He is the one to beckon Marli forward. "Take her home. Enforcers will come to get her at nine in the morning, two days from now."

"Make me one of those Enforcers," Xian says.

"I'll see what I can do."

It's not easy for me to turn in the opposite direction of the jail but my friends give me the support I need.

Before I leave Nerwhether, I say, "When will Siem and Zee be freed?"

"Immediately," he says.

"You'll see to it?"

"I will." He extends a hand for me to shake. "I'm truly sorry I couldn't do better for you, Cashlin, but I think you are the bravest, most honest woman I know."

I shake his hand. "Thank you, Solicitor. That means a lot to me."

And so, I go home.

**

Word spreads fast in Regalia.

As I walk home with Xian and Marli, everyone knows my fate. They stop what they're doing and stare. I'm relieved they don't yell obscenities at me. Maybe they're too shocked that a Patron is being exiled.

I certainly am.

Would I have done what I'd done, if I'd ever believed they would do such a thing?

I don't know. The fact that my recklessness has harsh consequences can't be changed. Ignorance is *not* bliss. Ignorance is dangerous.

What does the Council say all the time? "What was was, what is is?" As inane as it sounds, it *is* the truth. I can't change what was, nor what is—or will be in two days' time.

As we walk toward home around the Patron Ring, I take it all in: the lovely homes, the tree-lined street, the lush lawns. I took all of it for granted, accepting my privileged life as my due. I realize I will not "go home" again, and the next time I leave my house? It will be for good.

Forever?

When we reach home Dom and Irwin greet me at the door, giving their condolences, expressing their shock.

I nod and say, "I need some time in the garden."

They let me go, and for once, Dom doesn't ask if I want any refreshment.

I do want refreshment, but not of a flavorful kind. I go to the garden to seek the refreshment of the Keeper. Surely, he will come to me now in my time of greatest need.

Although I'm exhausted, I don't sit. I stroll along the paths, seeking him. Yearning for him. "Please come to me, Keeper."

I look up, hoping to see a slice of sky. But the sky is blue and cloudless. It's a lovely day.

Yet how can it be a lovely day when I've been sentenced to death?

I close my eyes, willing the Keeper to come.

I hear the buzzing of bees and open my eyes. The insects are busy with the sky-blue flowers in front of me. A butterfly sweeps past my shoulder and lands on a bloom.

And then, I realize the name of the flower that's aroused all their attention. They are Forget-me-nots.

I laugh out loud.

There is no way I can be sure the Keeper arranged this little scene, or that he chose the Forget-me-nots as a reminder that he hasn't forgotten about me, but I embrace the thought because it gives me comfort.

I pluck a cluster of blooms and hold it to my chest. "Fear not, for I am with you always."

I know—that he knows—I'm counting on it.

**

When I leave the garden, Dom insists I have something to eat in the dining room. I agree to bread and cheese.

"If you don't mind me saying so, miss," he says. "You seem . . . happy. How can you possibly be happy?"

Marli brings in a tray of fruit. "I've noticed that too." She sets it in front of me. "Out in the garden . . . did he come again?"

I'm pleased they see the influence of his presence in me. "Not like before. But I felt him with me. Inside me. He calmed me—calms me still."

After eating, Marli suggests a long bath before bed—and clean clothes. I agree but have a request. "Would you please wash my white dress and see if the slippers can be cleaned? I'd like to wear them tomorrow on my last day—and I also want to wear them for my exile."

She nods, but her face is troubled. "You say it so easily."

"Fear not," I say. "For he is with us always."

"Is that from him?"

"It is. A woman in jail shared that Relic with me. It's already helped me repeatedly."

"I can see why. It's so . . . timely."

"And eternal," I say.

Later, in bed, I have trouble getting to sleep because sleep seems like such a waste of time when I'll be experiencing eternal sleep soon.

Maybe.

Or will "everlasting life" be different from what my meager mind can fathom?

I turn on my side and smile. "Fear not, for I am with you always."

And then, I sleep.

Chapter Forty-Six

Solana

There's a knock on the door. Helsa and I look at each other. No one comes calling this early in the morning — not with good news.

I answer it. "Cashlin!" We embrace and I invite her in. "We're so glad to see you." Surprised too.

"But what are you doing here? *How* are you here?" Helsa asks.

"Helsa. Where are your manners?"

I invite Cashlin to sit in our small sitting area. "This is my last day of life," she says simply.

I want to object because I hate her words, but obviously I can't. "I'm so sorry."

"I didn't come here for sympathy. When I awakened this morning, I realized I could spend the day at home worrying about tomorrow, or I could get out and do something productive. I chose the latter."

Helsa stands. "Sorry but I have to get to work."

I flash her a dirty look. What's wrong with that girl?

She sees my disapproval. "Well, I do, Nana." She gathers up her lunch.

"You don't like me very much, do you?" Cashlin says.

Her statement takes both of us by surprise.

"I like you well enough," Helsa says. "I admired you. I followed you."

"But now you don't."

She shines an apple against her tunic. "It's just that I don't understand you. You had everything: a great life, status, wealth, and all the applause a person could ever want, yet you threw it away." She shakes her head. "I don't get it."

"The Keeper showed me something better."

"Exile and death?"

"But he promises everlasting life."

"Which means?"

"I don't know exactly. But I trust him."

"Why?"

Cashlin makes a fist at her gut. "Because he makes me feel different inside. Before him, my mind and heart were closed off. He opened a door that allows me to think and feel and understand and imagine and dream and —"

"I'm Devoted and I don't feel any of that." Helsa sits on the edge of a chair. "He hasn't come to visit *me*."

I pity Cashlin's predicament. This is a delicate conversation.

"He hasn't visited you visually, but I know you've felt his direction. You've felt the extraordinary courage he gave you when you needed it. He was with you then and he's with you now."

Helsa begins a shrug, but stops it. "He let Falla die."

There's no getting around that.

"He did," Cashlin says. "And we'll never understand why. But we've all become bolder in our faith since her death. Have you considered that it might be time for you to be courageous and step out on faith with us?"

"I am not courageous."

"Of course you are! You stood up to Bru, you endured his abuse, you confronted the Enforcer General, and you became a champion for others who were abused."

There's a slight change in Helsa's expression, a softening, yet also a strength.

I think of another way the Keeper helped Helsa. "The Keeper also helped you stand up to Teel at your mother's funeral. Your words awakened something in him, letting him know everyone deserves a funeral of respect. He did more for Falla's funeral and probably countless others since."

"I guess so."

"The Keeper also brought Cashlin and I together in amazing ways," I say.

"He most certainly did," Cashlin says. "The faith I have now is because of meeting your nana."

"You give me too much credit."

"I give you the credit you deserve." She sits forward. "I would not have met any of you if not for the Keeper arranging it. I would not have been given any of the opportunities to help in the Imp Ring — I had never even *been* to the Imp Ring."

I step in to continue Cashlin's list for her. "Would you have had the courage to wear the white outfit you wear now, or speak his name in the Favored Ring?"

"Never. And I never would have met Ladi and Pinno and Isa and Siem and Zee . . ."

"Who are the last two?"

"Devoted women I met in jail." She smiles. "Devoted sisters. As part of my plea agreement, they're being set free."

"That's a very good thing," I say.

"So you see, Helsa, what I gave up is far less important than what I've gained."

She springs to her feet. "But you're going to die tomorrow!"

Cashlin sighs. "I am. It's hard to wrap my mind around it, but somehow, I know it's part of his plan for me. Here, there, or wherever he takes me, I'll be all right, because I'm his."

We watch Helsa breathe deeply as she stares into nothingness. Then she says, "I wish I felt the way you feel."

"You will," I say. "Just keep believing and give it time."

"Give him time," Cashlin adds.

With a shake of her head, Helsa says, "I have to go. Do you have anything you want me to do . . . after . . .?"

"Keep on copying the Relics and handing them out," Cashlin says.

"Yeah. I can do that."

"And one more favor . . ."

"What?"

"Will you be there tomorrow when I go?"

I have no idea what Helsa will say. Her father was exiled. She wasn't there to actually see it, but will she want to be a witness to Cashlin's fate?

"Yes. I can do that too. I'll be there," Helsa says.

I'm relieved—and proud. My granddaughter has been petulant, but so was I at her age. She's had to handle a lot with the death of her parents. And Bru. And now . . . this.

She starts toward the door, but Cashlin stands and holds out her arms. "In case I don't get the chance tomorrow."

Helsa tentatively walks into Cashlin's arms and then relaxes. Seeing the two of them embrace . . . a Patron and an Imp. A month ago, it would not have been possible. Cashlin has been the impetus to important change in Regalia. But will the change last without her?

With one final look Helsa walks out the door to go to work.

As soon as she leaves, I sit. "Thank you for encouraging her."

"Of course. Everyone accepts him in their own time…speaking of…I've invited some people to come to your home here, this morning."

"Who?"

"Pinno, Ladi, and Kiya."

My eyebrows rise and I look around our meager home. The floor needs washing. "Why here?"

"It's safe here. We have privacy. Ladi and Pinno work in a studio that's near the spaces of other Creatives. And Kiya? It's not safe for us to visit her Ring."

As if hearing their names, there's a knock on the door. Kiya enters. Again, she's dressed down, but she still looks nervous. "Hello. Is Cashlin here?"

Cashlin steps forward. "Come in."

Pinno and Ladi are right behind. I pull out chairs from the table. "Would anyone like coffee?" I ask — though I'm not sure I have enough cups.

Everyone declines. I'm grateful when Cashlin takes over the gathering.

"I've called you here to thank you for your support during all my challenges."

"Of course, Ladi says. "How are you doing?"

"Better than I ever could have imagined."

Kiya shakes her head. "I'd be a wreck. I mean, I'm a wreck just trying to find other people who are Devoted in my Ring, much less face . . . what you're going to face."

"Finding more Devoted is a worthy quest," Cashlin says. "And that's what I want to talk to you about. I don't want my death to be in vain. I need all of you to carry on after I'm gone. Share everything you know about the Keeper, while continuing to learn from others."

"But we'll be arrested," Kiya says.

Cashlin hesitates. "Perhaps. But I think change is coming."

"Why do you think that?" Pinno asks.

"When I was allowed to speak before the Council, I emphasized that we Devoted and our belief in the Keeper is not a threat to Regalia. Our faith might even make us better citizens because we'll be happier."

"What a bold thing to tell them," I say.

"It was my only chance."

"If they *allow* us to worship, everything *will* be better," Pinno says.

"That's my hope."

Despite her strong façade, Cashlin looks weary and her forehead is furrowed.

"Is there anything we can do for you tomorrow?" Ladi asks.

"Come to the exile. Be my witnesses."

I have a sudden thought. "Do you expect the sands to part since you're one of the Devoted?"

"What are you talking about?" Kiya asks.

Cashlin explains what happened during the exile of my neighbors.

"They walked in?" Pinno asks.

"They did."

"So, *is* that what you expect to happen?" I ask again.

She sighs. "I expect nothing but hope for everything."

With that, she stands. "I should be going. I just wanted to bring all of you together to get to know each other. There is power and safety in numbers." She pulls papers from her pockets. "This is a song one of the Devoted women in jail taught me. Use it in your gatherings. It speaks straight to the heart."

She holds out her hands and we form a circle. Then she sings a verse: "'Your sure provisions gracious God, attend me all my days; oh, may your house be my abode, and all my work be praise. Here would I find a settled rest, while others go and come; no more a stranger, nor a guest, but like a child at home."

We are truly blessed.

Chapter Forty-Seven

Cashlin

I wander the Rings of Regalia.

Many in the Imp Ring recognize me, wave and say nice things. Many say they'll pray for me.

I enter the Serv Ring. I don't know as many people here, but they seem to know me. They don't approach, but nod and many touch their heart.

"Patron Cashlin!"

I see Lieb running toward me and wait for him. He stops short, his usually happy face clouded. "I'm really sorry about tomorrow."

"I am too."

"But don't worry," he says.

"Why not?"

"Because the Keeper is on the other side."

I embrace the image. "I hope you're right."

He lifts up the hem of his brown tunic and points at a weaving of white fabric. "This is from your white dress," he says. "Pinno gave it to me."

I've always been curious about his vest that I've only seen glimpses of. "Can I ask . . . what spurred you to make your vest?"

He cocks his head. "Helsa and Nana know I like color, so they gave me scraps from the factory. I wove them together." He pointed to purple velvet. "See? Here's your purple dress." He points to an orange paisley piece toward the back. "This is from your first win."

"I'm honored."

His face is serious. "No, *I'm* honored. It's the weave of the world. My world."

Weave of the world . . . what a lovely saying.

He pulls his tunic down. "I'm coming to see you off tomorrow."

"I'd like that."

He smiles again, which makes me smile. He is such a pure soul. Regalia could use more like him.

He pats his messenger pouch. "I have to go now. Do you have any messages for anybody?"

I can only think of one. "If you see Xian, will you ask him to be there tomorrow?"

"I'll tell him."

The Keeper has certainly provided for me. At least I won't face death alone.

**

I wander for hours, taking in everything. How tragic that I was ignorant—and arrogant—for nearly all of my twenty-two years. If only my eyes had been opened sooner, I wouldn't have wasted so much time.

I can't think about that now. The Keeper got my attention. I have to believe he had a reason for his timing.

But now I'm done wandering. Now, it's time for two final goodbyes.

I head to the Creatives' Ring, needing to see my brother. I have no idea how he will receive me because my disgrace trickles down to him. What will he do when I'm gone? He's not due to marry yet. Perhaps the Council will make an exception and match him with a Patron bride early.

I walk to the residential area of the Ring. As a Creative Director his house is nice—but not as nice as mine, which *has* been a bone of contention with him. It all seems so silly now.

I knock and wait. I knock again and wait.

I see the curtains to the right of the door flutter. He's in there.

"Amar? Please open the door."

It suddenly opens wide. "What do you want?"

Oh dear. "I came to say goodbye."

He rolls his eyes and lets me in. I'm surprised to see Mother sitting in his parlor.

Two for one. How efficient.

"How are you, Mother?" I ask.

"How do you think I am? After you humiliate yourself in front of the Council and all Regalia, throwing everything your father and I—"

"And me," Amar adds.

"And Amar . . . throwing everything in our faces, as if nothing we've done for you means a whit."

I sit on a chair as far away from her as I can get and feel my energy seeping out of me. I'm not up for an argument. "I'm sorry you feel that way. I did what I did because it was the right thing to do. I wouldn't change any of it."

Amar scoffs. "No remorse. That's just great."

"I do feel remorse—for the pain it's caused you two, but what I did was for a greater cause."

Mother wrinkles her nose as if smelling something nasty. "You choose to follow an invisible being versus following the carefully thought-out commands of the Council of Worthiness?"

When she puts it that way . . . "Yes."

She tosses her hands in the air. "I have no clue where we went wrong with you."

"You didn't go wrong with me," I say. "You've been a good mother—" I look at Amar. "And brother. I'm thankful for my upbringing, *and* for my time with you as my Creative Director, Amar."

He slumps down in his chair, shaking his head constantly. "You have an odd way of showing it."

I see one of his paintings on an easel. He's always had a flair with paint. And then I suddenly know how to explain it to them. I walk to the landscape painting, which at the moment consists of fuzzy-lined dashes of color representing the flowers, trees, and sky. "See all this?" I say, sweeping a hand over the canvas.

"It's not finished."

"I know that. But this," I sweep my hand over it again. "This is what my life was like before the Keeper." I move to a finished painting hanging on the wall. "This is how I feel now. See the shadows you added, the outlines, the detail? Everything was a colorful mishmash before, but now I see things clearly. And it's beautiful." I look at each of their faces. "My greatest wish is that you'll see your life changed as he has changed mine."

"Hmph," Amar says. "Sorry, no. Personally, I don't want to die."

"You will die," I say. "Someday."

"Not at the hands of the Council, I won't."

Mother stands, waving her hands as if all our words are pesky flies. "Enough talk of death. I want you to march yourself back to the Council and tell them you're sorry, you repent, you'll renounce everything you've said and done, and then—"

"I won't do that," I say calmly.

Her jaw tightens. "Then you're a fool." She sits back down. "I have no time for fools."

"Neither do I." Amar stands. "You need to leave."

This was not the way I'd hoped it would go. I extend my arms toward him. "Please?"

He shakes his head and takes a step back. I move in front of Mother. "Mother? Please?"

She also shakes her head and looks away.

All my life I've wanted to please them. It seems like such folly now. Have they ever truly loved me?

I turn and walk away.
My heart is broken.

**

I just want to be home. As I walk through the gate, the guard says, "Best to you, Patron."

"Thank you."

But what "best" is there?

Then I hear my name, "Cashlin!"

Siem and Zee walk through the gate coming from the inner Rings. They run to me and give me the embraces I longed for from my family.

"Thank you for getting them to set us free," Zee says.

"We were both surprised," Siem says.

"I tried to get them to let everyone go, but they only let me choose two."

Zee nods. "We won't waste this second chance you've given us."

"We promise we'll keep spreading the news," Siem says.

"That's all I can ask."

"And we'll be there tomorrow for you," Zee says. "To see you… off."

"I'd appreciate that."

Siem looks back toward the inner Rings "The three men in jail for Bru? They're being exiled at the same time as you."

It's oddly appropriate. I chuckle. "At least I won't be alone."

"One of them started asking questions about the Keeper."

"That's great news."

"He wanted to know if he'd be saved somehow, but I didn't have an answer for him."

"It's hard to have faith when you're not sure exactly what it means."

"To have faith, have faith," Siem says.

I laugh. She's right. As the Keeper said, it's just that simple.

I look at their faces, needing to remember them as they are right now. But it's time to part. "I want to thank both of you for being there for me in jail, for sharing the *Fear Not* Relic, and the song. They helped me immensely and I've shared them with others."

"We're glad," Siem says for both of them.

People stop to stare at us. I don't want Siem and Zee to get into trouble because of me before they get safely home. "I need to go. I'll see you tomorrow."

As I walk to my house, I see a few Patrons on the street. Some look away, and a few nod. Do any of them believe?

I don't have the energy to find out as I stagger the last few steps to my door.

I stumble into Dom's arms. He starts to help me to a sofa but I say, "My room, please."

He helps me negotiate the stairs. Marli gets me in bed. They both fuss over me. "I'll be all right," I say. "I just need to rest."

They leave me to a fitful night of sleep.

Chapter Forty-Eight

Helsa

Other than seeing Bru thrown through the Desert Gate I've never been to a real Exile. Not even Papa's.

I don't want to go today, but Nana insists. Actually, Toffa gave everyone the day off to attend. If the Council expected Cashlin to go quietly, they were in for a surprise.

There is a flood of people trying to get through the Serv gate—so many that the guards let everyone through. Inside the Ring it's much the same. There are already crowds gathered near the Desert Gate. But among the sea of brown and gray there are dozens dressed in the bright colors of the Creatives Ring, and even a few in more elaborate dress. Are they the Favored? I've never seen any of them in person. They don't look any different from the rest of us except for their clothes. Actually, one man was rather dumpy, and two women were unremarkable. I feel stupid for thinking they'd look special, but I've lived my life being told they were the reason we exist.

Nana would tell me that the Keeper is the reason, but I'm not there yet. I want to be all-in like she and Cashlin are, but . . . maybe I'm still mad that he didn't save Papa and Mama. And of course, Falla. That whole Protector thing seems bogus.

I spot Teel. There are a dozen other Comfort Servs around him—up from the three he'd told me about. Good for him.

Nana sees the House Servs from Cashlin's house and we push our way through the crowd to stand beside them. They are right up front, near the gate. I'm not sure I like being so close to it. What if the Swirling Desert sucks us in by mistake?

"You're here," Marli says to us.

"As are hundreds of others," Nana says. "I had no idea Cashlin touched so many people."

"In a very short time." Dom clears his throat. "It's been an honor serving her."

"Knowing her," Nana adds.

When Nana looks at me, I simply nod.

Looking over the crowd I see lots of people touching their heart. If the gesture was once a secret, it certainly isn't any more. There are also a lot of Enforcers around, but none look menacing. Maybe there *is* safety in numbers. I'm sure they don't want another riot like the one that killed Bru.

But then I spot the bald man. Unlike the others in the crowd who are talking and moving, he's standing a head above the rest, staring. At me. Us.

I nudge Nana, "Over there. That man from the woods. He's staring at us." I nod in his direction.

"I'm glad he's here. I wonder if the Relic I gave him moved him in any way."

"Don't count on it. He's up to no good. I just know it."

Nana glances at him again. "I think he looks meaner than he is."

"You have no proof of that," I say. "I don't like how he keeps turning up. I hate how he stares."

"There must be a reason," Nana says. "But we won't know it today. Today is Cashlin's day."

Her death day.

I spot Lieb running toward us, and we make room. We link arms and I give him — what I hope is — a reassuring smile. I don't want him to get upset at what's going to happen. But how can he not?

We hear a change in the noise level and look toward the Imp gate. The crowd parts. Three men walk through, accompanied by Enforcers.

"Those are the men who killed Bru," I whisper.

"They're being exiled with our Cashlin?" Dom asks. "I don't like that at all. Their law breaking was violent, Cashlin's was peaceful."

But then the crowd silences completely when Cashlin is led in. Her Enforcer friend, Xian accompanies her. I'm glad he's there for her.

The two groups walk past us and are lined up in front of the Desert Gate.

Someone in the crowd yells, "Fear not, Cashlin! Fear not!" which makes people begin to chant, "Fear not, fear not, fear not . . ." We join in. I hate to admit it, but it feels good to be united. Fists are pumped in the air.

A gaggle of Enforcers paces along the edge of the crowd. Do they expect us to swarm toward Cashlin and pluck her away? Where would she hide? No one could help her without putting themselves in danger.

But then something amazing happens. Cashlin raises her hands and presses her palms downward, calming us.

And miraculously, we are calmed. Everyone looks at her expectantly.

An Enforcer points at one of the three men. "You who are condemned to die may speak."

He stands defiantly. "I'd do it again. Bru deserved to die."

The Enforcer shrugs and says the same to the next one.

He shifts his weight from one foot to the other. "I . . . I didn't like Bru either, but I's sorry."

The third one says, "Me too. And we want to stand with her." He points at Cashlin. "The way she's calm about all this? That's got to mean something. I want what she has."

"Fear not!" the second man says—to cheers.

They both move to stand behind Cashlin. The Enforcers start to rush after them, but again, Cashlin presses her hands down. "Let them come with me."

The Enforcers look back at their leader, and he flips a 'whatever' hand at her. Then he grabs the arm of the first man and leads him to the gate where he glares at his disloyal friends and waits for the gate to open.

When it does, he takes a step back as the violent winds blow the dark sand horizontally.

It's horrifying. I grab Nana's arm. Its power is terrifying, its darkness is an omen of the death that will come in mere seconds.

I look at Cashlin. She looks straight ahead at the crowd. Although I see the rapid rise and fall of her chest, her expression is steady. Almost serene. Lieb waves at her. She smiles and waves back.

How can she be so calm? She only has moments to live.

The Enforcer yells at the first man. "Step in!"

In a final gesture of defiance, he raises fists in the air and takes a step toward the sand. The whole crowd gasps as the dark wind sucks him away.

I press a hand to my chest and Nana puts an arm around my waist. My stomach churns and I think I'm going to be sick. I can't stand the thought of Papa being swept away like that. I only hope death came quickly.

The Enforcer steps toward the other three. "Who wants to go next?"

"I will," Cashlin says.

"Say your peace then."

She takes a step forward to separate herself from the men. For the first time she looks nervous. I know I'd be a wreck.

"Good people of Regalia. I urge you to stop worshiping yourselves and your material possessions. Worship the only one who deserves your love, loyalty, and faith—our Keeper. Let your faith in him enrich your lives and lead you to works of compassion and mercy toward each other—throughout all the Rings. The Keeper doesn't want you to upset the Cycle of Regalia, but to enhance it. This is my greatest prayer. Fear not, for he is with you always."

With a nod she steps toward the gate. Her pure white dress stands out against the dark winds of the desert.

But then . . .

The roaring eases and the winds shift. The sands part, blowing upward on either side of a path.

"Do you see that?" I ask.

Nana laughs. "Praise the Keeper!" She turns to me. "She'll be all right, Helsa. She won't die! The Keeper has other plans for her."

Cashlin pauses to turn back and wave at the people. Do they all see what we see?

She looks at Xian and blows him a kiss.

Then she walks onto the path until we can't see her anymore.

"I want that too!" the second man says. He runs after her, and the third man follows.

Suddenly, Nana says, "I'm going too, Helsa! Come on!"

Is she crazy?

She tries to pull me forward, but I resist. But then, she lets go of my hand and runs toward the path. What is she doing? She's the only family I have!

Then Lieb takes my hand and says, "Come on, Helsa. Let's go!"

His grip is strong, and in total shock I let him pull me along, horrified at what we're doing, yet not strong enough to stop it.

We reach the edge of the path with the sands sweeping upward around us. It's petrifying.

Yet we don't turn back. Actually, I can't. I have to do this. I feel a foreign urgency that pushes me forward.

We walk onto the path and find it solid and true. But what if the sands blowing upward on either side of us change direction and swallow us up? Lieb still holds my hand. He looks back at me and says, "Run!" We run. It feels like death nips at our heels.

But then the path ends and we reach a clearing.

A clearing where there is no swirling sand. Just a calm desert.

"Helsa!"

I spot Nana, Cashlin and the men. I run into Nana's arms.

We startle when there's a horrific moan of wind. We look back and watch the sands swoop down upon the path, erasing where it had been, becoming a part of the sweeping sea of wind that surrounds Regalia.

Then it hits me.

We're alive!

Chapter Forty-Nine

Kiya

"What just happened?" I ask the two other Favored who'd come to Cashlin's exile.

They stand with their mouths open, gawking at the parted sands that are swirling again.

The man shakes his head. "The path just appeared, and now it's gone?"

The woman grins. "That was so cool."

I see Marli and her friends staring at the sight. I go over to them. "Did you see that?"

"We did," she says.

"It's a miracle," Dom says.

An Enforcer who'd brought Cashlin in approaches. "Shh," I say as Irwin starts to say something.

"No, it's all right," Marli says. "Xian's a friend."

His expression is one of awe. "She told me this might happen, but...did you see it too?"

We all nod.

"I can't believe Solana, Helsa, and Lieb ran after her," Marli says.

"I wish I'd thought of that," Xian says.

His words surprise me. As an Enforcer he's more entrenched in the business of the Council than any of us. Yet I had noticed the glances they'd exchanged, and Cashlin's final wave to him. Did he and Cashlin have a relationship?

What does it matter now?

I study the crowd. Some are walking away but there are many small groups engaged in intense discussions. "I think others saw it too."

Marli walks over to a woman with a crippled arm. "Isa, did you see the sands part?"

"I did." She sweeps her hand over her group of friends. "We all did. Does this mean they weren't killed?"

"That's what we assume," Marli says. "What we hope."

Isa beams. "That means we don't have to be afraid of exile anymore."

She's absolutely right. "We can speak about him and not be afraid."

The man from my Ring isn't so sure. "They still might be dead. It's still a desert out there."

The Favored woman slaps his arm. "Stop it. If the Keeper wanted them dead, he'd have let the sands suck them away. They're alive, I say. I have to believe that." She looks to me for support. "Right, Kiya?"

"Yes," I say. "I think you're right." I *want* to believe it.

"They have to be okay," Dom says. "They *have* to be okay."

A woman in a brown tunic and another wearing green join us. The Serv woman links her arm with the Enforcer. "Xian, did you see it?"

"I did, Mama." He looks at us. "All of us did."

"Wasn't it spectacular?" the Creative says.

A big question looms large. "So, what do we do now without Cashlin here to guide us?" I ask.

"We carry on," Marli says. "We copy the Relics and hand them out to as many people as possible."

A group of Imps walk past and touch fingers to their hearts. Everyone in our group reciprocates the gesture. I feel emboldened. "I'll copy some Relics. I'll hand them out." I look to the other two from my Ring. "Right? The three of us can do that."

"I know there are others in our Ring who are really close to believing," the man says.

I think of my friend, Uhli. I should have asked her to come with me. "We need to tell them what happened to Cashlin. Tell them they don't need to fear exile anymore. Tell them to talk about him."

Xian puts his hand in the middle of our group. His mother puts hers on top of his. Everyone stacks their hands in the middle.

I hesitate a moment—as do the other Favored. But then I put my hand in the center and they do the same. It's the most courageous thing I've ever done.

"To the Keeper," Xian says.

"To the Keeper," we say.

I am excited and emboldened.

And scared.

This moment signifies how much I've changed, how the core of my life as one of the Favored has changed.

And more than that, I have the feeling that all of Regalia is about to change.

To the Keeper indeed!

Chapter Fifty

Cashlin

I'm alive!

And I'm not alone!

I'm overwhelmed with thanksgiving.

I embrace everyone who followed me here: Solana, Helsa, and Lieb—who still has his messenger bag strapped across his body. I touch the arms of the two men from jail. I understand why *they* ran in behind me. The fact they weren't swept away like Quan speaks to their faith.

The fact the others followed me in is hard to comprehend.

"I can't believe you're all here."

"Yeah. Me either," Helsa says under her breath.

I'm surprised by her tone, as if she didn't come voluntarily. "I didn't expect any of you to follow me in. I *had* to go, but you . . ."

One of the men speaks up. "We had nothin' to lose." He looks at the desert surrounding us. "Not the best place to end up, but—"

"Better'n the alternative," the other man says.

"Were you planning on coming with me?" I ask Solana.

She presses a hand to her chest as if she's as shocked as I am that she's here. "I'd heard about the parting sands, so I knew it could happen. I had the thought that I *might* be able to go with you, but . . ."

Helsa tosses her arms in the air. "So, you *planned* on leaving me alone, Nana?"

"I didn't say that."

"You considered it." Her face is red. "I lost Papa and Mama. You're my only family, yet you'd leave me?"

"I'm family too," Lieb says.

Helsa touches his back. "I know. If it weren't for you grabbing my hand, I would never have gone. But Nana . . . you chose Cashlin over me."

Nana takes my face in her hands. "I chose him."

She shakes her head and pushes her grandmother's hands away. I have a fleeting thought that I wish she *hadn't* come along. She is such a petulant person.

"Staying behind alone would have been *your* decision," Nana says.

"That's not—"

I raise my hands, stopping their argument. "We're here now. Your family is intact."

"So now what?" asks one of the men.

I don't know their names. "Can you introduce yourselves?"

"I'm Suel, Vue's husband. We've always believed. Kind of."

"I'm Pali. I'm the one who didn't believe, but now . . ."

The other three introduce themselves to the men.

Then Pali waves in the direction from which we'd come. "The sands parting for you like that? Was that because of him?"

"It was," I say.

"Did you know it was going to happen?"

I share a look with Solana. "I saw it happen before for a Devoted couple."

Helsa crosses her arms. "If it's happened before, why isn't it common knowledge? Other than you, I've never heard anybody talk about it, not even as a rumor."

"I don't know," Solana says.

"Quan saw it," I say. "He was the man who was convicted for kissing me—among other offenses. He tried to run in after your neighbors, but the sands fell in on him and blew him away."

"So, the Keeper only allows a few people see it?" Suel asks.

"Apparently."

"I guess he's worth knowing then," Pali says.

So aptly said. "Yes, he is."

"So now what?" Helsa turns in a full circle. "There's no swirling sand here but there's not much else either." She reaches out and touches an odd tree-like plant with upraised arms. "Ouch! Those are prickles!" She picks them out of her fingers.

We stroll around and notice that the only plants growing in the rocky sand have spikes and needles.

"Not exactly inviting," Pali says.

Solana points. "Look over there. That animal looks like it has leather on its back." It scurries away.

Lieb squats down, inspecting insects. "There are lots of crawlies." Joy.

Lieb stands. "There's no grass. No trees to sit under. And it's hot." He looks behind us longingly. "What about my mama? Will she come here too?"

Solana answers. "No, Lieb. She isn't coming."

His eyebrows dip for a moment, then he nods once. "She can't come because she has to copy Relics and hand them out."

"That's right," she says. "That's what all our Devoted friends will do. They need to stay in Regalia and spread the word about the Keeper."

"We've planted seeds in all the Rings," I say.

"Except the Council Ring," Helsa says.

"The Council Ring too. Think of Xian." I think of Xian now. How I wish he'd come with us.

"Xian lives in the Serv Ring," Helsa says.

A technicality.

"But he works in the Council Ring," Solana says. "And he believes. Don't discount—"

I hate bickering. "It's not just Xian. When I made my plea deal, the solicitor seemed genuinely interested in why I didn't fight."

"Why didn't you?" Suel asks.

"Because Xian and Marli were set to testify for me, and they would've been punished for it."

Pali bites his lip. "Were you the reason those two women got out?"

"It was part of the deal I made with the prosecution."

"I woulda liked to be set free," Suel says.

"I know. I'm sorry I couldn't do more." I turn the conversation back to those left behind. "We planted a lot of seeds in Regalia. Seeds that will grow."

"So grows the seed," Helsa says.

"What?"

"At the Pile, a Comfort Serv said that to me. I didn't know what he meant, but maybe now . . ."

"Maybe now we do," Solana says.

Helsa walks away a few steps, then turns back to us. "I have a question."

Only one? "Yes?"

"What are we supposed to eat here? And drink? And where are we supposed to sleep? I'm not sleeping on the ground with all these critters crawling around."

I look in all directions. The flatness of the desert is interrupted by low dunes created by wind. Yet to the right, in the far distance, I see hills. I can't tell if they're made of sand but I think they might be our best hope toward finding provisions. Yet I could be wrong. "None of us know which way to go, Helsa."

She huffs. "Ask the Keeper to show you. After all, he's your bud."

I hate that she diminishes his divinity. And I don't like them looking to me for direction. I'm as clueless as they are.

"Stop being rude, Helsa," Solana says.

Suel points in the opposite direction. "See that waviness right at the horizon over there. It looks like water."

We all look but I'm not sure what we're seeing. It seems too . . . variable. "I think it's a trick of the eye."

"I'm going toward it," he says. "Pali? You comin' with me?"

Pali doesn't look enthused, but nods.

"Maybe it's good we split up," Solana says. "We can come find each other if our way turns out to be the right way."

I'm not sure about finding anyone. The distances will soon be far between us.

Suel looks at the sky. The sun is high and there aren't any clouds. "All I know is I'm not finding water or food standing here. See ya later." The two men walk off.

I agree that standing here won't help us. "Should we walk toward the hills?" I ask.

"Only because you sound so confident?" Helsa says sarcastically. "Come on, Lieb." They walk off.

Solana and I follow.

**

It's hot. There's no breeze. There's no shade. No water. No food. We've been walking for hours and the hills still seem far away.

"Up here!" Helsa calls out.

Solana and I hurry forward. She points at bones. Human bones.

"Somebody died," Lieb says.

"They most certainly did."

Helsa squats beside the partial skeleton—I hate the word 'partial' because it implies that animals have taken bones elsewhere.

"Is this what happens to the people who get swept away?" Lieb asks.

"They're tossed here?" Solana says. "If so, how sad."

"Or maybe this is what happens to stupid people who are in a desert without any food or water," Helsa says.

Solana shakes her head. "Enough, child. You're not helping."

Helsa throws her hands in the air. "Nobody's helping! Don't you see? The Keeper saved us. I get that. But there's nothing here but death. It seems like the laugh's on us."

Lieb looks ready to cry.

"We're alive," I say. "That's worth something."

"We won't be for long," Helsa says, gesturing to the pile of bones.

Lieb falls to his knees and clasps his hands together. "Keeper, help us!"

He's got the right idea. I kneel beside him, and Solana follows suit. Helsa does so too—reluctantly.

Solana prays aloud for all of us.

I hope the Keeper hears her.

**

I don't think the Keeper was listening.

As the sun goes down, we aren't walking anymore, we're staggering. We've had no food or water. The only blessing is that the night will give us relief from the sun.

Helsa sits on a large rock. "I'm done. I can't go another step."

Solana sits beside her. Her face is red from the sun. "I agree."

Even the always positive Lieb is done. He sits on the sand, his hands dangling from his knees, his head hung low.

I don't know what to do.

Helsa wipes her face with her sleeve. "You going to just stand there gawking at us, Cashlin? Do you have a better idea?"

I'm panicked. I'm exhausted. I'm hot, hungry, and thirsty. I turn full circle to see our options.

"Over there is just as bad as here," Helsa says. "Which is probably just as bad as anywhere. There's no way out of this place."

I've had enough of her attitude. "What do you want me to do? I didn't ask you to come with me."

"And I didn't ask to come either. But now we're here. And you know what? I would've rather died outright than suffer like this."

"Helsa, stop," Solana says.

"No, she's right," I say. My anger makes me pace. "When the sands parted, and I knew that I could go into the desert without it sweeping me away. I thought I was saved. But saved for what?" I sweep my arms around me. "*This* is not what I had in mind either."

"Where did you think the path would lead us?" Solana asks.

"To safety. To someplace better. To . . . life." Tears threaten and I have the sudden thought that I better not cry because my body needs the moisture. I will them away.

Solana's voice is calm. "We have to believe that he'll lead us to all those things."

Helsa stands and brushes sand off her legs. "Why do we have to believe that? If the Keeper really cared about us, we wouldn't be suffering like this. I mean, what's the point of saving us from being swept away by the Swirling Desert only to leave us to die?"

"Tomorrow will be better, Sa-Sa," Lieb says.

Helsa pounces. "Are you sure about that? What spark of hope have you seen that the rest of us haven't?" She looks at the darkening sky. "I don't see any rain clouds that could give us relief and something to drink." She sweeps her hand around us. "I don't see an apple tree, or a basket of bread appearing out of the dust."

Lieb hangs his head again. I feel so bad for him. "I agree with Lieb," I say—even though I don't. "Tomorrow will be better, because the Keeper wouldn't save us only to let us die."

Solana nods. "And suffering *is* a part of life."

"Wow. That's profound, Nana," Helsa says.

Solana points a finger at her. "Watch yourself, child."

Helsa takes a few steps away, and sighs deeply. "Sorry."

"What I said about suffering is true," Solana says. "And in my six decades of life I've noticed that something good usually comes from something bad—maybe it's not clear right away, but it *does* come."

"Soon would be good," Helsa says.

We're getting nowhere. I look at the horizon. We only have a few minutes of light left. "Tonight, we sleep here." I toss some stones to the side to try to smooth an area in the sand where we can lie. I notice my beautiful white slippers are dirty with sand.

"Ooh, it looks so comfy," Helsa says.

I glare at her. "You can either help clear a spot or go sleep on one of those prickly plants."

She helps, and we're soon lying beside each other. I'm on one end and Lieb is on the other. "Good night," I say.

I'm relieved when Helsa doesn't laugh at the 'good' part.

I pull my hood up and turn on my side. I see Lieb giving Helsa his messenger bag to use as a pillow. He's such a sweet young man.

Solana faces me. She smiles a wistful smile, then says, "Keeper, thank you for saving us. Please keep us safe through the night."

I say amen as I hear the howling of animals in the distance.

**

I hear growling. My eyes shoot open. I see moonlight reflect in the eyes of a wolf-like animal standing not twenty feet from me.

I bolt to standing. "Get up! Up!"

The others scramble to their feet and see where I'm pointing.

Lieb runs toward the animal, waving his hands, shouting.

It runs away.

"Thank you, Lieb," I say.

He picks up a rock and walks in a wide circle around us, looking around to see if there are any more.

"That was close," Solana says.

Helsa also picks up a rock. "So much for sleep."

I jump when a slithery something runs between us.

Solana points toward the vaguest beginnings of a sunrise. "It'll be fully light soon."

"I am not lying on the ground again," Helsa says. She sits on the rock.

All of us sit, our backs touching as we watch and wait for the morning.

**

Sitting on the rock, I've pulled my knees to my chest. Somehow, I've dozed. I shiver with cold. How many nights will we need to do this? How many nights can we survive doing this? In our weakened state, the animals may get bolder. There aren't trees, so there aren't fallen branches to use as weapons to fend them off.

I stand and groan. All my muscles ache as I stretch. The others slip off the boulder and do the same.

"I'd say good morning, but it's not," Helsa says.

She's such a joy to have around.

"I'm thirsty," Lieb says.

"I know," Solana says. "Me too."

"So which way, fearless leader?" Helsa asks.

I point in the opposite direction as the sunrise. "We keep going that way."

"Why?"

"Because nothing has happened to make us go another way," I say. My tone is as rude as hers. "Sorry, but that's the truth of it."

Lieb fills his messenger bag with stones. "To fend off animals," he says when he sees me watching.

"I think they mostly come out at night," Solana says. "It's going to be heavy to carry that all day . . ."

He cocks his head, then drops them to the ground. A piece of paper is pulled out with a stone. Messages that will never be delivered.

"What do you have in there?" Solana asks.

"Relics I copied."

For some reason I laugh. "Read one. We need to hear it."

Lieb opens the Relic which is folded into fourths. He holds it close to his eyes and reads haltingly. "'He is your protector, there at your right side to shade you from the sun. You won't be harmed by the sun during the day or by the moon at night.'" He looks up and grins. That's us!"

It most certainly is.

Helsa snatches the Relic away. She reads it and cocks her head. "Well, I'll be. That *is* what it says."

"I told you," Lieb says.

Solana draws a deep breath. "I, for one, feel reenergized. It's not a coincidence that Lieb was carrying that particular Relic."

Lieb looks confused. "No coincidence. A man with a pointy beard gave it to me to copy."

"A *black* pointy beard? Wearing a long brown caftan?" Helsa asks.

"Tee!" Solana says.

"What are you talking about?" I ask.

"He oversaw Mama's funeral," Helsa says, but she shakes my question away. "Was that the man, Lieb?"

"Uh-huh." Suddenly, he wants the Relic back. He looks at it again. "No, that's not right. He gave it to me, and said it's a Relic, but he said I was supposed to give it to you, Helsa. It wasn't one I copied. It's a message from him especially to you." He turns the paper over. "See? Here's your name on the message."

Helsa shivers.

"It's as if he knew you were going to be somewhere like this," Solana says.

"But he couldn't have known that," Helsa says. "*I* didn't know that. *I* didn't go willingly, Lieb dragged me in."

I am overcome and clap my hands together. "This is marvelous!"

"This is creepy," Helsa says.

"Not at all. Don't you see? This is the Keeper's doing. Just like Lieb said, he knew exactly the words we needed to hear, exactly when we needed to hear them. And he made it happen."

"We are not alone," Solana says reverently. "The Keeper *is* our protector. He's with us, even here."

"Even here," I say. I'm newly strengthened. "Let's keep moving knowing that he'll be with us every step. He's already been with us. Today's a new day."

"With the sun and the moon," Lieb says.

"With the sun and the moon."

**

After walking for hours, I admit—only to myself—that I'm disappointed we've found no water or food, though the skies did cloud over, giving us shade. It takes everything that's in me not to dive into doubt. I keep coming back to what I said this morning: surely the Keeper didn't save us to let us die here.

I refuse to be defeatist. To keep negative thoughts away I sing the song Zee taught me. "'My Keeper, you supply my need, most holy is your name; in pastures fresh you make me feed, beside the living stream. You bring—'"

Up ahead I see Helsa and Lieb suddenly start running away from us.

"Do they see something?" Solana asks.

Something good? Or something bad?

We quicken our pace, especially when Lieb runs toward us, gesturing for us to hurry. "Come on!" he calls.

I feel a surge of energy, *knowing* it's something good. Lieb comes all the way back and takes Solana's hand, urging her on. "You won't believe it. It's beautiful!"

Beautiful?

And then we see it. A grove of trees—lush, leafy trees! And there's grass and flowers too. Hope and gratitude fill my heart.

"Thank you, Keeper," Solana says.

A thousand thank yous!

Helsa is already there, peeling an orange. "There's food and water. Plenty of it."

We pounce eagerly on the fruit, bread, cheese, and ham. We dip ladles into a bucket of water, drinking deeply. We fill some empty flasks nearby, then sink onto the cool grass and bask in the feast.

When Helsa finishes the meal, she lays back, cradling her head with her arms. "This is more like it."

"It's definitely what we need," I say.

"It's definitely what he provided," Solana says.

"An answer to prayer," I say.

Lieb eats his second orange. "How did he know I like oranges best?"

I chuckle. "He just does." I point toward the sunset. "Look at that." It's a show of pink, purple, and orange.

"The sunsets . . . I've never seen anything like them," Solana says. "In Regalia all we see are walls."

"That's one advantage to being here," I say.

Lieb looks in the direction of the hills—which finally *do* seem closer. "What do we do when we get to those hills?" he asks.

"Yeah," Helsa says. "What's your great plan?"

I sigh deeply. "Please don't look to me for guidance. I don't know what to do any more than you do."

"Great pep talk," Helsa says.

She makes me mad. "I never asked you to join me here. That was your decision."

"Not really." Helsa looks at Lieb and Nana.

"*I* wanted to come," Solana says. "It was *my* choice."

I ask the question that's been on my mind. "Why?"

"Because I believe you have important work to do for the Keeper, and I want to be a part of it."

I appreciate her answer, yet, "Right now, I'm confused. The Keeper wants me to be an influencer for him, but then he let me be exiled from Regalia and . . . there aren't any people here to influence."

"Exactly," Solana says. "Which means there have to be people somewhere who need to hear what you have to say."

"What we have to say," I add. I take another sip of water. "What I'm having trouble wrapping my mind around is that in Regalia I had standing in society, a platform; a presence and even celebrity-status. In a new place no one will know me. Who will listen to a stranger in a dirty white dress?"

Solana swipes sand from her pants. "All of us are starting over."

Helsa breaks off another hunk of bread. "I'm good with starting over. I never wanted to work in a factory. That was my lot. In Regalia there was no way to move up."

Lieb jumps to his feet. "I can be whoever I want to be!" He takes off his message bag, then his brown tunic and colorful vest, and puts the tunic *under* the vest. "This is who I want to be now. Colorful!"

He is truly delightful. "Bravo, Lieb!"

When we clap, he bows.

"I'm going exploring. Is that okay?" he says.

The garden seems to be about three times the size of my garden at home, so I don't worry. Somehow, in this place, worry is unnecessary. "Let us know what you find," I say.

We start cleaning up the leftover food and orange peels.

Suddenly Lieb comes running back, his arms overflowing with blankets. "Look what I found!" He gives one to each of us. "There's more too if we need them."

"Thank you, Keeper," Solana says.

"Just in time for nightfall," I say.

"We could use some good sleep," Solana says.

I look around the area. "Let's sleep in a circle with our heads near each other. I think it's safest that way."

"Safe from what?" Lieb asks.

"Animals?"

Lieb looks around. "I haven't seen any here."

Helsa points to the edge of the refuge. "But the desert is right *there*. There's nothing to say they can't come in."

I have an exceptionally clear thought. "Except if they can't."

They look at me as if I'm crazy.

"What's preventing them?" Helsa asks.

"Him. He provided for us and now he will protect us."

"Just like he protects his sheep," Solana adds. "And with that, I'm lying down." She stretches out, being the first spoke in our four-spoke wheel.

Helsa lies next, then Lieb, then me. We all lay on our backs as the dark descends around us. Until the stars come out.

"Wow," I say. "That's quite a show up there."

"I've never seen the stars so bright," Solana says.

"Is the Keeper up there?" Lieb asks.

"I think he's everywhere," Solana says.

We startle when we hear animals howling in the distance.

"Do I need to get more rocks?" Lieb asks.

The only clear answer I have comes out as, "Fear not, for he is with us always."

"Good," Lieb says. "Good night."

I certainly hope it's just that.

Chapter Fifty-One

Helsa

I'm the first one up—which is fine by me. I've had enough people lately.

I wander through the garden. How can a place this beautiful be smack dab in the middle of an awful desert? Yet I know we wouldn't be alive if it wasn't.

I pluck an orange from a tree, sit on the grass, and lean against it. The smell of citrus makes me drink in its aroma even before peeling it. I think Lieb's right: oranges are my new favorite.

I section the orange and eat. It's so peaceful here. I could use a little peace—a lot of peace. I know we can't stay, but I don't look forward to another day traipsing through the desert toward who-knows-where. I'd like to rebel and stay behind, but Nana and Lieb wouldn't hear of it.

I wipe orange juice from my chin with the sleeve of my dirty tunic. What I wouldn't do with a clean one. It's so stupid we followed Cashlin here. It's all her fault.

I feel a stitch in my gut. I know my attitude has been horrible, but I can't seem to stop myself.

It's because I'm scared. I had no time to make the decision on my own. I was dragged in. And though I wasn't happy working at the factory, at least it was *known*. None of this is known. We're assuming there are people somewhere, a town somewhere. Life somewhere.

Everyone else has faith in the Keeper. I believe in him, but I don't understand what we're doing here. And copying more Relics and handing them out? That's not how I *ever* envisioned my life.

There has to be more to it than that. And this.

I hear someone walking behind me and look to see who it is.

Great.

"Morning, Cashlin."

"Morning." She takes a deep breath, drinking in the place. "We needed this."

"We can stay a few more days. There's food enough."

"It's tempting, but—"

"We know this place. We know nothing about what's out...there."

"I understand how scary it is."

At least she admits it. "Did you ever think there was any place other than Regalia?"

"I never thought about it," Cashlin says.

"So, we're heading to a place that might not even exist."

She sighs. "As I said yesterday, I know that this isn't where we're supposed to end up because there aren't any people here."

I point in the direction of the supplies. "But there *were* people here. Somebody put the food and blankets here. They didn't just appear by themselves."

"Maybe they did."

I don't accept her magical faith nonsense. We prayed for the Keeper to provide for us, and he did — by sending someone to leave supplies for us. *That*, I accept.

The others join us. So much for having time alone.

"Are you ready to move on?" Nana asks.

"If we have to." Lieb offers me a hand and helps me up, plucking an orange for himself.

Back at our camp, I put food in the middle of a blanket to carry with us. "Will you get the rest, Lieb?"

He starts to do just that, but Cashlin intervenes. "We need to leave some for the next person."

Is she crazy? "We have no idea how many days we're going to be out here. We have no idea if there *is* anything out there."

Cashlin looks at the food, probably thinking of ways to keep it from us. Then she says, "Since he provided this garden for us, he'll provide us with another."

"And you know this how?" I ask.

Nana takes food out of her blanket. "Because we have faith. You might try it, Helsa." When Lieb removes three oranges from his blanket I know I'm outnumbered.

I sling my blanket-bag over my shoulder and walk into the desert. "Come on, Lieb."

He walks with me. I assume the rest of them follow. I'm not giving them any satisfaction by looking back.

**

We finally come to the hills, which aren't any different than the rest of the desert except it's harder walking.

"I'm tired." Lieb sits down in the sand.

I sit beside him. The other two are fifty yards back. I feel for Nana. If this makes Lieb and me tired, I can't imagine —

I see them stop. They point at something in front of us. I stand to see.

"Lieb, get up. It's a man!"

He's coming down the hill in our direction. The others hurry toward us. But what if he's unfriendly? What if he means to hurt us? Lieb and I each pick up a rock.

When they reach us, Cashlin motions for Lieb and me to stand with Nana. "You going to do something?" I ask her.

"I am."

I'm shocked when she walks toward the man.

He's dressed in a white caftan with a belt tied around his waist. There are two black studs on either shoulder. He carries a bag slung across his chest. He doesn't look dangerous.

"Halt," Cashlin says.

He stops a dozen feet from us. "Halt?"

"Stop. Who are you?"

He swats a bug away from his face. "I ask you the same thing."

"You first," Cashlin says.

He sighs as if the entire conversation is a huge inconvenience. "My name is Jass. Your turn."

"Cashlin. Where did you come from?"

"Legalis."

"What's that?"

The man's eyebrows rise, and his tone implies we're stupid. "A city."

Cashlin glances back at us. "There are people there?"

Jass scoffs. "A city usually has people."

Nana walks toward them. Lieb and I have no choice but to follow.

"How far is it?" she asks.

Jass points behind himself. "It's a few hills over. You can see it from the top there."

I start to run, but Nana yells, "Wait, Helsa!" To Jass she says, "Do we have to go through the Swirling Desert to get there?"

He chuckles.

"Is there a Swirling Desert that forms a wall around it?"

He opens his arms to encompass our surroundings. "Isn't this enough desert for you?"

"So, we can just walk in?" Cashlin says.

"There's protocol involved. We don't allow strangers free access." He shakes his head. "Where are you from?"

"Regalia."

"I figured as much with the whole Swirling Desert comment. I've met a few people from there."

"Really?" Nana asks.

"Are people in Legalis friendly?" Cashlin asks. "Will we be safe there?"

"If you follow the rules, sure." He adjusts his bag. "I need to get moving. Have a good visit."

He walks past us into the desert.

"Now, can I go?" I ask Nana.

"Wait for us at the top."

Lieb and I run up the hill. When we reach the top we *have* to stop. The sight of Legalis is overwhelming: multi-storied white buildings run from one end to the other. There are no walls. And as the man said, there are no swirling sands. We can walk right up to it.

"Hurry!" I yell at the others.

They join us.

"Notice how there aren't any walls, any Rings," I say.

"And it's all white," Nana says. "It looks so bright and clean."

"Why didn't we know it existed?" Cashlin asks. "Surely the Council knew."

"Why would they keep it from us?" I ask.

"I think they liked us to be contained in our Rings," Cashlin says.

Nana shields her eyes against the sun. "If we were told about this place people in Regalia might leave."

"But maybe it's not a good place inside," Lieb says. "We only met the one man."

"And he was leaving," Nana says.

Cashlin gasps. "If he was going to Regalia he would have said so. So where *was* he going? There has to be another place besides Legalis and Regalia." She looks back the way he'd gone. "Why didn't I ask him that?"

"Yeah," I say. "Why didn't you?"

Nana flashes me a look. "We can ask the people inside."

"More people in more places means more people we have a chance to reach," Cashlin says.

She has a one-track mind. "I'm not thinking of reaching anyone right now," I say. "The people in Legalis will help us survive. The guy said they accept visitors."

"Do they have more oranges there?" Lieb asks.

"Let's find out." I start to walk down the hill.

"Helsa, stop," Nana says. "We need to approach the city together. There's safety in numbers."

I shake my head. "We're clearly no threat to them: three women — one of them old — "

"Excuse me?" Nana says.

"Aren't you old?" I ask.

She sighs. "Comparatively."

I continue. "Three women and one boy."

"Hey," Lieb says. "I am not a boy. I'm a man. I have a rock."

I raise my hands in surrender and laugh aloud. "Gracious, people. Does everyone have to take offense? The point is, we can't—we aren't—going to hurt them."

"Which doesn't mean they won't hurt us," Nana says.

This is ridiculous. I plop down on the sand. "Tell me when the three of you make up your minds."

Cashlin looks at Nana. Nana looks at Cashlin. They don't even say anything to each other.

"I say let's go," Lieb says. "I'm hungry."

Cashlin nods. "I agree."

Lieb helps me up and the two of us lead the way. My stomach churns. I'm not sure whether I'm scared or excited.

I figure it's a little bit of both.

Chapter Fifty-Two

Cashlin

We are quiet as we approach Legalis, each in our own thoughts. I'm thankful there *is* a city to go to, as there's no way we can ever return to Regalia—at least no way that we know of. But I'm angry that we never knew Legalis existed. Never knew anyone existed beyond our walls.

Lieb faces Legalis, as if studying it. "It doesn't have a solid wall like Regalia, but the buildings are all connected."

They look just as impenetrable.

"They're pretty," Solana says. "All different heights. Windows looking out on the desert."

He shakes his head. "But I don't see any doors."

"You're right," Helsa says. "I don't see a way in."

"The man got out somehow," Solana says, looking left and right down the expanse of buildings in front of us. "But the city seems to go on forever, in a massive circle."

"Great," Helsa says. "More Rings."

They're being negative again, which makes *me* feel negative. And impatient. "We'll walk the perimeter until we find an entrance."

"That's a long way," Lieb says. "I'm tired of walking."

So am I. I'd hate to lead them left when the entrance is to the right. I sigh deeply and look at the cloudy sky. "Keeper? You're our provider. Provide us with directions. Which way is the entrance to Legalis?"

"Are you expecting a map to fall from the sky?" Helsa asks.

And then I see it. The clouds part. A slice of sky opens up. A beam of sunlight shines down upon the right edge of the city. I laugh aloud and point. "There! There's his map for us. There, we'll find the entrance."

Lieb takes Helsa's hand. "Come on, Sa-Sa, let's go!"

She shakes his hand away and glares at me. "Prove to me that's a sign from the Keeper."

I feel sorry for Helsa. Being so pessimistic has got to be exhausting. Has she always been like this, or have I inadvertently done something to make her defensive?

I think of a good comeback. "Prove to me it isn't him, Helsa."

So there.

**

Up close, the stucco buildings are taller than I expected, at least five stories high. All the windows are situated three stories or above. In some places, sand is swept nearly to their level.

There is no well-traveled path around the city, which implies two things: those who live there stay there, and Legalis doesn't have many visitors. It makes me wonder what business the man was on to be leaving the city so casually.

He'd said Legalis had protocol regarding strangers. And rules. I've had enough of rules. And councils. And Enforcers. And trials and exile. It would be nice to find a place where people could live side by side, have friends from all walks of life, and use their gifts to live lives of fulfillment and purpose, doing good for one another. Plus, a place where everyone could freely talk about the Keeper.

Is Legalis such a place?

I hope we find a way in soon. We already ate our food, and I don't want to sleep outside when we're so close.

Finally, as we follow the curve of the buildings, I see a tall opening. Lieb and Helsa see it too and run ahead.

"This is it," Solana says.

"Whatever *it* is."

"*It* is anything that gets us out of this desert. Hopefully, *it* is water, food, and a soft bed."

I agree on all counts.

I see that Helsa and Lieb stand a good twenty feet back from the entrance. Something has made them stop short.

We catch up and I see why they stopped. There's a large metal gate, at least ten feet tall. A massive man wearing silver armor stands in front, his arms crossed. He holds a sword.

"Some protocol," I say.

"Not exactly welcoming," Solana whispers.

"He looks mean," Lieb says.

"He's obviously supposed to look that way," Helsa says. "He's guarding the entire city. But he's just one man." She looks at me. "Go on. Do your stuff, Cashlin."

"My stuff?"

"This is your exile. Get us inside."

Keeper, help us. I put on a smile and approach the man. His arm muscles twitch.

"Hello," I say.

He doesn't respond.

"We are visitors. May we enter Legalis?" I'm glad I know its name.

He looks us over. "Weapons?"

"None," I say. I hold out my hands and the others do the same. I hope Lieb doesn't have any rocks in his bag.

The guard must be satisfied because he opens the door.

"Thank you," I say.

I expect to see a bustling city street inside, but instead we enter a room where a man sits at a desk. He wears all white like the man in the desert, but he has only one stud on each shoulder.

He sits up as we enter and wipes crumbs from his chin. He sets a sandwich down. "State your business in Legalis," he says.

"Sanctuary," I say.

"We've come a long way," Solana adds.

"We're hungry and thirsty," Lieb says.

For once, Helsa remains silent.

"We appreciate you allowing us inside your fine city," I add.

He seems unmoved by my flattery. "Where are you from?" he asks.

"Regalia."

He snickers. "That's too bad."

"Too bad?" Solana asks.

He shakes her question away. "How long are you planning to stay?"

"We don't know. We know nothing about Legalis." Or why we're here.

He points to his left. "Go through that door for indoctrination."

It's not a welcoming word.

We enter another room where a woman sits. She gives us a quick once over, then turns to a stack of shelves that are filled with folded white fabric. She hands each of us what looks to be a robe. "Here. Put these on." She eyes my robe. "You from here?"

"No."

"You look like it."

She also hands us a white cloth bag. "Put your old clothes and shoes in here. Then find sandals that fit." She points to other shelves stacked with identical leather sandals.

"We're just visiting," Helsa says. "I'm fine with the clothes I have on."

The woman shakes her head adamantly. "You must wear the uniform of Legalis. Change."

"Here?" Solana asks.

"Here."

We all turn away from each other and undress. The robe has a slit at the neck and long wide sleeves. There is no shape whatsoever. I fold my dress and put it in the bag, along with my sand-tan slippers. When

I turn around I see that Lieb has put his vest under the robe. The robe covers it, but I see a smidge of it at the neckline. I point at my own neck and he pulls the robe over it.

Solana's robe puddles on the floor around her. "Do you have one that's shorter?"

The woman picks up a pair of scissors, sits on the floor by Solana, and proceeds to cut eight inches off the bottom. The cut is not straight — which I suspect bothers a seamstress like Solana as much as it does me.

We find sandals that fit and stand in a row, ready for whatever comes next.

She points to a door. "You're done here. Go outside to number twelve, to your right."

"What's at number twelve?" I ask.

"Your cell."

Cell? I've had enough cells.

"Go on," she says. "Or leave the way you came."

We do as she says. We walk onto a street teaming with people, carts, and horses. The noise assails us, as do the smells of roasted meat and nuts being sold in pushcarts.

"Everyone wears the same thing," Solana says.

"We leave a land of fashion and come to a land of conformity," I say.

Though the buildings are of different heights, they are unadorned white boxes with windows poked in them. The street is also white.

What do they have against color?

We walk to the right, and get a few curious looks, but far fewer than we would have gotten if we'd worn our own clothes.

But then . . .

"Helsa!"

Helsa turns toward a man's voice. She gasps, then runs to him. "Papa!"

Papa?

Solana and Lieb squeal and run to him too. There are hugs, kisses, and tears.

"I can't believe you're alive, Papa!"

Her exiled father lived through his exile as we lived? Thank you, dear Keeper.

Solana motions for me to join them. "Devin, I'd like you to meet a very special friend, Cashlin—"

Suddenly, I feel an inner nudge that propels me to say, "Oria."

My friends look at me, confused.

"Since when?" Helsa asks.

"Since now." We don't need to have this discussion at the moment.

I hold out my hand, but he shakes his head. "No handshakes allowed. But it's nice to meet you."

"And you."

Helsa puts her arm around his waist, but he suddenly looks nervous and removes it. "No touching."

No touching? But they'd hugged each other.

Devin looks upward at a huge clock. In fact, I see clocks on most of the buildings.

"Where are you supposed to go?" he asks.

"Number twelve," I say.

"You need to get there quickly. It's nearly time for the Hourly Count."

"Count of what?" Solana asks.

He urges us forward. "Hurry."

"Are we under arrest?" I ask.

"Not yet."

Have I traded one prison for another?

THE END

Dear Reader:

I have never, ever written a book like this one. I've written biographical novels, historicals, contemporaries, time travel books, and books with magical realism. All those books had one common denominator: reality. They all were grounded in our world.

I was thinking about reality when I got the idea for the Last Call series. In December 2022 my husband and I were driving through New Mexico. If you've never been, you should go. The landscape is stunning with huge expanses of earth and rock, pushed upward by the passage of millennia.

I was thinking about the condition of the world and was disgusted by the contentious division. Everyone was after their own interests—I'd say best interests, but in truth I could see it was just the opposite. Every man for himself is destructive. It made me very sad.

I suddenly thought about a place where there were societies that were totally separated from each other. No interaction. In fact, they wouldn't even know each other existed.

My mind exploded with ideas. But also doubt. This would be different from anything I'd ever written. It was a scary fact. Maybe I shouldn't try it. Maybe I should just write what I always—

But then I saw a vivid rainbow. I could even see where it hit the ground to my right. Which is how I knew it was a sign from God, telling me that this idea was a good one. It was an idea I had to run with.

And so I did.

Creating Regalia was a daunting task—I was used to dealing with a world that I knew. But it also opened a new part of my imagination, constantly surprising me. A world of Rings? A Council of Worthiness?

Deep in the process I realized I needed a map of Regalia. Being a part-time, mediocre artist myself I tried to draw what was in my head. Big fail. Big, big fail. I *had* to find someone who could draw it for me.

I happened upon a video on You Tube (look for Mountainstar) showing someone drawing a Medieval city. It was exactly the style I wanted! I contacted the artist, Alan Bellis, and asked if he would be interested in drawing a map of Regalia. He said yes! It was a wonderful experience seeing my ideas come to life. To make matters interesting, Alan lives in Wales! He loves wild-camping, backpacking, and castles. I'll take the castles.

Once again, thanks to my talented daughter, Laurel, for her editing skills. Both with content and details, she sees what I don't see. Can't see.

By the way, the hymn that Cashlin learns is a real hymn from 1719 by Issac Watts: "My Shepherd, You Supply My Need"—only I changed *Shepherd* to *Keeper*. Also, the Relics contain paraphrases of real verses. See if you can figure out which ones.

For now, that's where I'll leave it. I'm heavily into writing Book 2: *A Rule of Time*. See you in the next world!

Nancy Moser

About the Author

NANCY MOSER is the best-selling author of 46 novels, novellas, and children's books that focus on discovering your unique purpose. Her titles include the Christy Award winner *Time Lottery* and Christy finalist *Washington's Lady*. She's written nineteen historical books including *Mozart's Sister, Love of the Summerfields, Masquerade, Where Time Will Take Me,* and *Just Jane. An Unlikely Suitor* was named to Booklist's "Top 100 Romance Novels of the Decade." *The Pattern Artist* was a finalist in the Romantic Times Reviewers Choice award. Some of her contemporary novels are *A Slice of Sky, If Not for This, An Undiscovered Life, The Invitation, A Steadfast Surrender, The Good Nearby, Crossroads, The Seat Beside Me,* and the Sister Circle series. *Eyes of Our Heart* was a finalist in the Faith, Hope, and Love Readers' Choice Award. Nancy has been married nearly fifty years — to the same man. She and her husband have three grown children, eight grandchildren, and live in the Midwest. She's been blessed with a varied life. She's earned a degree in architecture, run a business with her husband, traveled extensively in Europe, and has performed in various theaters, symphonies, and choirs. She knits voraciously, kills all her houseplants, and can wire an electrical fixture without getting shocked. She is a fan of anything antique — humans included.

Website: www.nancymoser.com
Blogs: Author blog: www.authornancymoser.blogspot.com History blog: www.footnotesfromhistory.blogspot.com
Facebook: www.facebook.com/nancymoser.author
Bookbub: www.bookbub.com/authors/nancy-moser?list=author_books
Goodreads:
www.goodreads.com/author/show/117288.Nancy_Moser
Pinterest: www.pinterest.com/nancymoser1/boards/
Twitter: www.twitter.com/MoserNancy
Instagram: www.instagram.com/nmoser33/

Coming in 2025: *A Rule of Time*
Book 2 of the Last Call Series

Watch for the rest of the Last Call Series

Excerpt from *The Invitation*
Book 1 of the Mustard Seed series

JULIA CARSON STARED out the window of the bus and smiled at the children waiting for her.

"Stop here, Murray," she told the driver of the Book Bus.

Murray stopped the vehicle in front of the Minneapolis Magnet summer school. Two dozen children ages six through fourteen waved at their ex-governor.

"Is it always like this?" Murray asked. He was new on the job.

"Word is definitely getting around." Julia waved at the children through the window. "Some of these kids have never owned a book, so getting a free one every time I come makes it feel like Christmas—for all of us."

"Ho, ho, ho," Murray said.

Julia put a hand on his shoulder. "Hey, I'll take one happy kid over a dozen grumpy politicians any day."

Murray opened the door, and Julia stepped out amid cheers and hugs. She found the open adulation satisfying but also embarrassing. All this gratitude for a few books, for something that was a basic need in every child's development. She vowed as long as she and Edward had money to fund the Book Bus, it would continue.

"Mrs. Carson, Mrs. Carson, I read my last book two times already," said a little boy whose oversized T-shirt skimmed his knees.

She put a hand on top of his head. "I'm proud of you, David. Are you ready for another one?" He nodded, looking up at her with dark eyes. She leaned close and whispered. "Do you want to go first?"

He smiled like he'd won the lottery.

"Me, too!" said ten-year-old Telisha. "I finished *Little House in the Big Woods* all by myself."

Julia tugged her hair affectionately. "Then you shall be second."

David and Telisha's good fortune spurred the other children to all talk at once as they vied for Julia's approval. She was relieved when the director of the summer school clapped her hands, quieting them.

"Get in line, kids. You know the rules. Six at a time. No dawdling when it's your turn. Mrs. Carson will help if you have questions."

The children got in line with a minimum of commotion. There was another cheer as Murray exited the bus carrying a crate of juice boxes and three packages of cookies.

Julia eased her way past the children and entered the bus. She stood in the door. "David, Telisha, come on in. And then you, Sarah? Is that your name? You and Gaylord and Grant, and we'll end the first group with the handsome young man with the gorgeous smile...yes, that's you, kiddo. Come, children."

The children scrambled in, shoulders bumping shoulders as they jockeyed for position near their favorite bookshelf. Julia loved this part. She delighted in helping each child pick out a special book they could take home forever. Books had been such an important part of her childhood. One of her most precious memories was her family's evening ritual: after the dinner dishes were cleared, her father had read to them around the walnut dining table with the tatted lace tablecloth. It was there that Julia had been introduced to Oliver Twist, D'Artagnan, and Anna Karenina.

If only she could do the same for all the children who searched the limited shelves of the Book Bus. With a hot meal warming their stomachs, she'd gather them close and safe and read aloud to them. She'd marvel as their faces glowed while they absorbed the ageless stories.

Julia's attention was brought back to the crowded bus by the sound of a book falling to the floor. "Don't grab, Sarah. There are plenty of books for all of you." She retrieved the book. "*Christy*," Julia said, reading the title as she handed it to the girl. "A very good choice." Sarah beamed and held the book to her chest as she headed for the door.

Julia watched the little girl step out of the way so a middle-aged woman could enter the bus. *Probably someone's mother or grandmother*, she thought. The woman's clothes were rumpled, and a wisp of black hair pointed left when it should have pointed right. Her eyes studied the titles of some young-adult books. She seemed to be looking for something.

"May I help you, ma'am?" Julia asked.

When the woman turned to look at her, Julia felt an odd jolt pass through her. She had the kindest eyes. They were the eyes of an old friend, yet Julia was certain they'd never met.

"Do you know anything about Haven?"

The woman's question pulled Julia out of her thoughts. "Haven? I don't think I've heard of it. I'm afraid we don't have adult books." She looked around at the children, trying to match one of them with the woman. Then she thought of something, "Haven? Perhaps you mean *The Raven*? The poem by Edgar Allan Poe?"

The woman smiled. "No, Julia. I mean Haven." She held out a creamy white envelope.

Julia took it, then looked at the woman. "What's this?"

"You've been chosen, Julia. You have things to do." With that she moved toward the door.

Julia frowned, confused. "Things to do? What are you talking about?"

As the woman stepped onto the pavement, she turned back and pointed to the envelope, then gave Julia a wink.

"Mrs. Carson? Mrs. Carson?" A child tugged at Julia's skirt. "David took *The Dawn Treader* and I wanted that one. Do you have another copy?"

Julia watched the woman walk away from the Book Bus.

"Mrs. Carson? Do you?"

Julia let her attention return to the immediate needs of the little girl. "I'll bring a copy for you next time, Telisha. I'll even put your name on it. Why don't you pick another book for today."

Telisha nodded and wove her way down the aisle to find another book.

Julia looked down at the envelope in her hand. Her name was written in an elegant cursive across the front. She slid a finger under the flap, breaking the seal. She removed an ivory card. Along the side was a botanical drawing of a broad-leafed plant bearing a cluster of small flowers.

"Mrs. Carson, can you help me find a book about spaceships?"

Julia held up a hand, her eyes scanning the contents of the card. "I'll be right with..." She trailed off.

> *Julia Eugenia Carson is invited to Haven, Nebraska.*
> *Please arrive August 1.*
> *"If you have faith as small as a mustard seed,*
> *you can say to this mountain,*
> *'Move from here to there' and it will move.*
> *Nothing will be impossible for you."*

"Haven?" Julia mumbled.

"What'd you say, Mrs. Carson?" asked the boy.

Julia shook her head, trying to clear it. She walked to the door of the bus and called to Murray and the school director. "Do either of you know who that woman was? The grandmotherly type who came in the bus?"

They looked at each other over the heads of the last few children in line. "I don't remember seeing anyone, Julia."

"Me, neither," Murray said. "But we were busy with the juice."

"Mrs. Carson, the spaceships?" asked the boy again.

Julia shrugged. She didn't have time to worry about the odd woman. Or the invitation. She stuffed the card into the pocket of her skirt and turned to help the boy.

Buy on Amazon!

Check out all my books at www.nancymoser.com

Milton Keynes UK
Ingram Content Group UK Ltd.
UKHW022145111124
451073UK00007B/203